Sweet Erianna

Enjoy!

Let me know what you think.

Pat Taby

pattab77@yahoo.com

Sweet Erianna

Patricia Tabeling

Sweet Erianna

Cover Art by EDK Visuals

Printed in the United States of America

Luminare Press
442 Charnelton St.
Eugene, OR 97401
www.luminarepress.com

LCCN: 2022920237
ISBN: 979-8-88679-122-8

Chapter 1

By the time she saw the barrier it was too late. She had no choice but to duck under it and hope that she didn't wipe out on her skateboard.

Her son, Ned, had challenged her to a race on this beautiful Friday evening of the Memorial Day weekend. The first one to ride from her parents' front walk down Crestwood Drive, across the flats, down the short, steeply-graded lower hill, around the dead-end circle and back would be the winner. Her parents' house sat about halfway between the top of the moderately inclined upper hill and the beginning of the level, dead-end section called Crestwood Circle.

"May the best man win," Ned stated. They shook hands and the race was on.

Ned rode the mountain bike that he brought from home and he started the race in the lead. But Erianna, who was on a skateboard that she had rummaged from her old bedroom in her parents' basement, hoped that she could overtake him on the brutal uphill climb and beat him across the finish line. She'd grown up on this quiet, small-town street in Prestwick, Ohio, located due east of Cincinnati. She knew from experience how to maintain a brisk pace on the uphill climb, while Ned would probably be forced to get off his bike and push it up the steeply graded lower hill.

Erianna was not one to *let* her children win. There was no glory in a hollow victory. He was in for a battle, but Ned was up for the challenge. He had learned from his mother how to be a humble winner as well as a gracious loser.

It was unusual, She thought to herself as she sped along, for so many cars to be parked on the 'flats', so called because this section of Crestwood Circle, which was about the length of a football field and was the only level stretch of her hometown street. Cars normally parked only on the right, but today they were parked on both sides, leaving little room for vehicles to pass.

The houses around the dead-end circle at the bottom of the steep lower hill were grand and sprawling, with spectacular views of the Ohio River. The flat grassy center island was used as a playground area where a swing set, slide and teeter-totter, along with a scattering of picnic tables, were set under several large pine trees that shaded the mini-park.

Just as they reached the top of the steep drop-off a Chevy Traverse pulled out of a driveway and started up the hill. Ned had ample time to move onto the sidewalk to his right, but his mother had no time to react and no place where she could bail out safely. So she moved as far to her left as possible in order to avoid the oncoming car. She tried her best to maintain her balance in the extremely narrow space between the parked cars and the SUV.

She didn't see the long A-frame road barricade, which had been set up to temporarily prevent cars from driving into the circle, until the slow-moving Chevy finally passed. By then it was too late to avoid the wide, wooden obstacle. Erianna ducked down and prayed. When, at breakneck speed, her back brushed against the bottom of the crossbar she lost her balance and, try as she might, she could not regain her equilibrium. With arms flailing wildly, she tried desperately to slow down and turn the skateboard, but it was all for naught. The curbed edge of the center island was upon her and there was no hope of avoiding the imminent collision.

Erianna kicked the board behind her as hard as she could, hoping to keep it from careening into the crowd of partygoers in the mini-park and injuring someone. Her feet hit the ground running, but she could not stop her forward momentum and she ran headlong into a man standing between two others near the edge of the curb.

"Ooof—" his breath left him in a rush as they collided. He tipped backward from the force of her impact, and suddenly they were both falling toward the ground.

The men on either side of their companion grabbed him by his upper arms, trying to check his descent and lessen the blow as they fell. It was like moving in slow motion, thanks to their quick thinking.

Erianna landed in a heap with the hapless bystander. Her helmet became dislodged and it fell forward over her eyes, blocking her vision. Lying in a tangle of arms and legs on top of a total stranger, Erianna was mortified. She quickly scrambled to her feet, pushing at her helmet as she tried to set it back in place over the loose, messy bun in her hair.

"Are you all right?" she asked the man. But she was overcome by the sudden urge to laugh, and a giggle escaped before she could squelch it. This was no laughing matter. She pushed at her cockeyed helmet once again.

"What the hell!" the stranger swore.

"I'm so sorry," she said. But she couldn't help herself. The entire situation struck her as hilariously funny, and she began to laugh.

The two men helped the now irate bystander to his feet as she tried her level best to sober up. She unbuckled her helmet and pulled it off as she searched for her son, who was bringing down the kickstand of his bike on the sidewalk to her right. Someone had scooped up the errant skateboard and was walking over to return it to her.

Turning back to the unfortunate guy she had run into, Erianna tried once again to offer an apology in a more sober tone.

"I'm very sorry—" With a sudden intake of breath she gasped. "You!"

"Well, well, well, what have we here? If it isn't Erin Pruitt. Hello, Airhead," the man wisecracked.

Erianna immediately lowered her gaze to the ground. She hunched her shoulders and took a step back. "Hello, Derrick."

Derrick Jansen had been her childhood tormentor. They attended school together, and he had taken immense pleasure in bullying her. Erianna Pruitt, the janitor's daughter, was an easy mark and he spent years harassing and demeaning her at every opportunity.

Just under six feet tall and skinny, the greasy-haired bully stood before her with a thin-lipped smirk on his face. "Look everybody," he raised his voice. "Our airheaded class prude is here. Who the hell let you into the party?" he sneered.

"My mom's not an airhead," Ned shot out from his mother's side. He had run over to see if she was okay and overheard the belittling remark.

Erianna shoved the boy behind her back with a shushing sound.

"And she's not a prude," he popped out from behind her to confront the man.

"And who might this be," Derrick turned on Ned. "Junior Airhead?"

"Why you—" Ned's retort was cut short when Erianna turned to her son, blocking him from Derrick's view. She bent down and said something that only he could hear. He stopped his protests, but looked mutinously at his mother.

"But he—"

She interrupted him once again. Erianna went down on one knee so that she was eye level with her son and quickly explained. "It's alright, Ned. I went to school with Derrick. He's just teasing, it's no big deal."

Ned did not think someone calling his mother names was a joke and he frowned, but did not speak.

"I want you to get your bike and go back to Grandma's house. I'll be along in a few minutes." She got up and gave him a gentle push toward his bicycle. "Go on now."

But nine-year old Ned stood tall, with his arms crossed in defiance as he glared at his mother. She knew he was only trying to defend her, but she needed to get the boy away from the line of fire as quickly as possible. Erianna Fowler did not want her son to witness the unavoidable scene that was about to play out.

"What's the matter little boy, don't want to listen to your airheaded mother?"

"Her name is Erin Fowler, you greaseball!" Ned snapped back.

Erianna gasped. "Nathan Edward," she admonished in a low, hushed tone. She stood to her full height and spoke in a firm, but quiet tone. "Obey me."

Ned looked at his mother, nodded, and turned to leave. But he kept his eyes on the 'greaseball' as he walked over to retrieve his bike. Ned knew that when his mom said those words he was not to question her or protest in any way. She used the phrase 'obey me' only rarely, and only when she wanted her directives to be followed without hesitation. His mother would explain everything to him later when they could talk in private. She always answered his questions honestly, and he had a lot of questions about what had just happened.

Erianna kept her focus on the young boy until he jerked the kickstand back and began to push his mountain bike up the hill. Then she turned back to face Derrick and two other classmates, Josh Dearing and Adam Tremaine.

"Hello Josh, Adam." She spoke softly, with her head bowed in a submissive posture. "Thanks for helping break our fall. I hope you're not hurt, Derrick."

He brushed in annoyance at his shirtsleeves. "No, I'm not hurt," he replied testily. "That was fucking stupid of you, crashing in here like that."

Matthew Prestwick witnessed the collision and went to retrieve the skateboard for the unfortunate lady who had crossed paths with his classmate. He stood inconspicuously nearby as the woman dealt with both her son and Derrick. When Matthew heard Derrick address Erianna by name he moved closer. He had not seen her for many years. Not since their last date in early August the summer before he left for college.

"Hello, Derrick," Matthew interrupted as he closed the remaining distance to the small group.

"Matt," Derrick replied with a sideways nod.

"Here's your board, Erin."

"Thank you," she acknowledged without looking up. "I'll just be going now."

She had hoped to make a smooth getaway, but those hopes were dashed when Chip Neading and his wife, Nancy, suddenly appeared and she was forced to stay and say hello to the couple.

Charles Neading, Jr. was the 2001 Prestwick High School Senior Class President. He grew up in one of the homes around this dead-end circle. Erianna surmised that he and his wife were hosting the party. Nancy loved to entertain.

Nancy Landrew was Chip's childhood sweetheart, and they grew up together here, just four doors away from each other. It was understood by everyone in their class that Nancy was Chip's girl. The couple never dated anyone else, and after they graduated from college Chip married his 'girl next door'.

"Erin, I'm so glad you made it," Nancy said with a happy lilt in her voice.

Made it? What does she mean made it? Erianna scanned the crowd and realized that most of the guests in attendance were from her graduating class.

"Wow!" Chip exclaimed. "That was quite an entrance." He laughed cheerily, the sound more like a girlish giggle than that of a grown man.

"Yes, well, it was unintentional."

Chip moved forward to give her a hug, but Erianna clutched the skateboard defensively against her chest and took a step back. He wasn't fazed by that ploy. He pulled her against his side and wrapped his arm around her, smiling down in his ever-friendly way.

As quickly as possible, Erianna extricated herself from his clutches. Somewhere along the way Chip had decided that they were good friends, but Erianna had no such illusions. There wasn't a single person in attendance who she would consider a friend.

Nancy deliberately situated herself between Erianna and Derrick Jansen. A petite brunette with a heart-shaped face, Nancy wasn't tall enough to be an effective screen between them. Nevertheless, her intent was clear.

She smiled brightly and chirped, "Welcome to our fifteen-year class reunion."

"Class reunion? Ohhh."

Nancy tilted her head to one side. "Didn't your mother tell you?"

"No, she didn't."

"We saw her at mass last month and I asked her to relay the message to you. I even gave her one of the invitations to pass along."

So that's why Mom invited us for the weekend. Erianna was not at all surprised by her mother's underhanded tactic. Colleen Pruitt knew that her daughter would never willingly attend such a gathering, thus explaining the unusual invitation to come for an overnight visit.

"We didn't have an up-to-date address for you," Chip said. "But we're glad to see you, even if it is a surprise."

"Thank you. It's nice to see you, too, but I really can't stay."

She directed her next comment to Nancy. "My kids are at my mother's house and I need to get back." Erianna was absolutely not going to participate in a class reunion, but that decree was left unspoken.

"There's no need to rush off," Chip said. "Let's get you something to drink and we can catch up. It's been way too long since we've seen you."

Erianna put her helmet on and made ready to leave. "No thanks. I'm not dressed for a party." She adjusted the helmet to secure it in place. "It was nice seeing you again—"

Nancy put a stop to her attempted retreat by reaching out and snatching the helmet from Erianna's head before she could secure the chin strap. "Come on, Erin. We're not all boorish idiots." She looked behind her, but Derrick and his buddies had already moved off into the crowd. "Stay for a little bit. I'd love to catch up. I'm sure your son will be fine with his grandmother watching him."

Erianna was not so sure.

"Were you two racing?" Chip asked. "I'm afraid the boy was beating you," he teased.

When he tried to take Erianna's hand she quickly moved back another step, pushing at the riotous mass of honey blonde hair that she was sure looked like a rat's nest on top of her head. Wearing old cut-off jeans and a paint-stained tee shirt, she was clearly not dressed for a party. She looked at Nancy's dress jeans and starched white linen shirt, and with a shake of her head she took another step back toward the hill.

Chip noted her distress. "You look just fine," he assured her. "But if you'd like to freshen up I'm sure Nancy has something you could wear. Or you could go change at your mom's, that is if you brought a change of clothes."

Erianna was not surprised by his suggestion. He was always studying her body language and trying to read her thoughts. Chip Neading noticed everything, and today was no exception. He was trying to wheedle his way in where she did not want him to go. Shy and reserved by nature, she preferred to fade into the background.

"No, Chip."

"No what? No change of clothes?" he asked, placing his hand on her back to prevent her from leaving.

"I brought a change of clothes, but I don't want to leave my children alone with their grandparents." She raised her eyes to his. "I'm sure you understand why."

Chip nodded. "Are your sisters at home? I'd be happy to walk up with you and we can ask them to look after your children for an hour or two."

He reached for the safety helmet that his wife was holding and she handed it off with an approving smile. Nancy knew that her husband was most likely the only person who could convince Erianna to join the party.

Chip looked at Erianna, tilting his head to the side the same way he always did, and she sighed heavily in defeat, knowing the battle was lost.

"Well, good, then it's all settled." They turned toward the hill. "I'll walk up with you and say hello to your father while you change."

Chip guided her along beside him, keeping up a running commentary on current events around town as they started up the hill. "How is Clyde doing? Is he feeling any better after his last back surgery?"

"He's more mobile now, but he'll always need the walker," Erianna responded dutifully.

"I'm guessing his temperament hasn't improved much with all that he's been through,"

"No, not much."

Clyde Pruitt, Erianna's father, was on permanent disability and received a pension from the City of Prestwick Parochial School System. Clyde, a school custodian, had been trying to patch the roof of St. Michael's Grade School just after a heavy rain when the ladder slipped and he fell two stories to the ground. He had been compensated for his outstanding medical bills and awarded a large cash settlement for his injuries from the Prestwick Foundation.

Matthew, who had silently observed the conversation between Erianna and the Neadings, fell into step alongside them. "I'll tag along, too, if you don't mind. I'd like to check in and see how Clyde is doing."

Erianna was now being escorted, not only by the red-headed Chip Neading, but by the class valedictorian as well. A direct descendant of the city founder and heir apparent to the Prestwick fortune, Matthew was tall, dark, and handsome. She wondered what she had done to deserve this dubious honor. She felt like a teenager being hauled home by the cops after getting caught out past curfew.

As they reached the crest of the hill and moved onto the flats, Erianna set her board down with every intention of paddling away from her classmates. She turned to Chip.

"It'll be faster if I just ride home alone and change. You're the host, there's no need for you to leave your duties on my account. I won't be long."

But he reached out and grabbed her elbow, stopping her forward progress. "You have no intention of coming back, do you?" He gave her a knowing look.

"No, I really don't."

"Why not? Be honest with me, Erin."

She hunched her shoulders and lowered her head. Long, heavy bangs hid her beautiful hazel-colored eyes from view. She looked at her board and shrugged. "Why are you pressing this, Chip? You know why. I shouldn't have to spell it out for you."

She was right, he did know. "Look," the illustrious class president began his flowery appeal. "Regardless of what you think, you *are* a treasured member of our class. You should come and visit with your classmates, renew old friendships."

When she raised her head to reply to that statement he guessed what she was about to say and held up his hand. "Yes, Erin, you do have friends here."

"Ucch, some friends." She made a sour face.

Chip offered up a friendly smile. "C'mon. It'll be fun."

"Fun for whom? Derrick Jansen?"

"That was an unfortunate incident," Matthew said as he picked up her skateboard and they began walking again. "Nothing like that will happen again, I promise you."

"It's been fifteen years." Chip continued, pressing hard. "Why don't you step out of your comfort zone and join us for a couple of hours? Fifteen years is a long time, Erin. People grow and circumstances change. We're not kids anymore. Many of us are married and have children of our own. You know I'm not going to give up until you agree, so why don't you just stop balking and come hang out with us for a while."

They had reached the far side of the flats and passed Hillview Terrace on their right. A bus was pulling up to the intersection, which joined Crestwood Drive in a T, and class members and their guests were disembarking.

"The decision *is* yours," Matthew assured her. "Chip shouldn't be pushing you so hard. But whether or not you decide to come back with us, I'd still like to check in with your father. I hope you don't mind."

"Of course not. He'll be glad of the company, I'm sure," she lied.

Matthew wasn't so sure. He wasn't sure at all. Clyde Pruitt harbored a serious case of hatred for the Prestwick family and he wasn't shy about voicing his opinions. Clyde's disdain for Matthew was the sole reason why he and Erianna had been forced to date on the sly after graduation. If Clyde had learned that Matthew was seeing his daughter he would have put a stop to it then and there.

When they turned onto her parents' front walk Erianna took the skateboard and helmet from her companions, jumped the three lower steps, and broke into a jog. "I won't be long," she said.

"Mom!" Ned launched himself out of the porch chair when he saw her. He frowned and put his hands on his hips to show his displeasure at the two men coming up behind her.

"They aren't the bad guys," she smiled at the boy and winked as she passed by on her way into the house.

Ned stomped to the middle of the wide porch steps and took up an aggressive stance. With his legs spread and his fists clenched at his sides, the green-eyed, brown-haired little boy tried his best to strike a domineering pose. But there was nothing even remotely intimidating about Erianna's son.

Nevertheless, he watched the men with a menacing glare. They stopped when they reached the bottom porch step. The red-headed man set his foot on the second concrete step and rested his forearm across his thigh, hoping the boy would see that his pose was casual and decide that they were not a threat.

"Hello. My name is Chip Neading," he introduced himself. "Your mother and I went to school together. I grew up down the street." He pointed in the direction of the circle.

Ned stood proprietarily on the porch, but did not respond.

"I'm guessing that you must be Erin's son." Ned stood motionless and puffed out his chest.

Chip tried again, this time directing his questions to the girl who was sitting in a lounge chair reading a book. "This is Matthew Prestwick. He also went to school with—" Chip paused, "your mom, is it?"

Grace nodded.

"We thought we'd walk up with your mom and visit while she changes her clothes. Do you mind if we steal her away for a little bit so she can attend our class reunion?"

"That's up to her," Ned spoke up boldly. "We don't tell our mother what to do," he stated in a matter-of-fact tone.

"Shut the fuck up and do as you're told!" The shouting could clearly be heard from inside the house. "Don't you disrespect your mother. I'll clip you upside your head if you say one more word to her."

Grace and Ned exchanged knowing looks and Ned ran to the front screen door, disappearing into the house.

"I'm Grace Fowler, Erin's daughter," she said as she closed her book and got up from her chair. "It's nice to meet you," she stated politely, hoping that she could drown out any further outbursts that might be heard from inside the house.

Grace and her brother both knew that Grandpa wouldn't talk that way if Ned was in the room. But in the meantime, Grace did her best to diffuse the uncomfortable situation. "That was my brother, Ned. He's almost ten, but he hasn't quite learned to mind his manners yet."

"I'm happy to meet you, Grace," Matthew replied.

"Ned told me that someone was—" she searched for the right word, "disrespectful to my mother at the party."

"That's true," Chip nodded. "Your brother isn't very happy with us at the moment. There always seems to be one rotten apple in every barrel, you know? And I'm afraid one of our classmates, our bad apple, was rude to your mom. But I can assure you it won't happen again. I'll make sure that she enjoys herself for the rest of the evening."

Ned poked his head out the front screen door, seeming more like a little boy now than an adult. "Grandpa is coming," he said to his sister. "I told him we had visitors."

Grace sighed with relief as she heard the thud, thud, thud of her grandfather's walker on the hardwood floors grow louder as he neared. She quickly sat down on the top porch step, leaned back casually against the square brick pillar and opened her book again. With hair coloring similar to her brother's and the same green eyes, she struck a casual pose as her grandfather neared.

When he reached the front door, Ned opened it and Clyde Pruitt shuffled onto the porch. Both Chip and Matthew stood to their full height as he glared down at them.

"Good evening, Clyde. It's nice to see you up and moving again," Chip offered by way of greeting.

"Harrumph," Clyde responded grumpily. "What are *you* doing here, Prestwick?" he turned his ire toward Matthew. "Come to cheat me out of my rightful due?" he challenged the younger man. "Come to gloat?"

Matthew didn't bother to reply.

Chip picked up the conversation again, trying to re-engage the crotchety old bastard. "My parents told me they ran into you and Mrs. Pruitt not long ago and that you all had a nice chat. I understand your daughter Joanna will be starting college at Ohio State in the fall. You must be very proud, but I'm sure your wife will miss her."

"Yeah, after all these years we'll finally be empty nesters, thank God. I've been overrun by females for all this long time, and it'll be nice to be able to shave in the morning without cleaning long hair out of the sink first."

Clyde lumbered over to a sturdy porch chair and settled himself heavily onto the seat, moving his walker off to the side. "What's all this about a class reunion?"

"Yes. It's been fifteen years, if you can believe that. It seems like only yesterday to me." Chip chatted amiably as they waited for Erianna. Ned disappeared back into the house and Grace sat pretending to read her book.

Finally, Erianna appeared at the doorway. She had changed into boot-cut jeans and a short-sleeved cotton polo with a three-button placket, which was the color of spring lilacs.

Matthew swallowed visibly when he looked at Erianna's face. A thick foundation and garish blush caked her flawless peaches and cream complexion. Dark eye shadow had been liberally applied, and her lashes were in clumps from the application of too much mascara.

Erianna's blonde hair was pulled into a severe knot at the crown of her head and her long bangs had been combed back and sprayed heavily to keep them off her forehead. The severity of the style was unflattering to say the least.

"That explains the commotion earlier," Matthew murmured as an aside to Chip, who nodded in agreement.

Erianna tried to adopt an easy, casual air as she breezed across the porch and started down the steps. She paused momentarily and looked over at her daughter. Some unspoken communication passed between them as Grace lifted her chin ever so slightly and then looked over to her grandfather. Erianna smiled and skipped nonchalantly down the steps.

"I'm all ready," she said.

Chip offered Clyde a wave goodbye and the men fell in step beside her.

When they reached the bottom landing Erianna heard Ned call out to her. She turned as he came running and launched himself into her arms. Whispering near her ear he said, "I'm sorry, Mom. If I hadn't challenged you to a race you wouldn't have to go back there looking like this."

She patted him on his backside and set him down on the step. "None of this is your fault," she whispered back. With a reassuring smile she added, "Mind your sister. I won't be long."

"I will. Don't worry about us, we know what to do."

"Is there a theme for this get-together?" she asked Chip as she turned to face her fate. "I know how you and Nancy love to throw a good theme party."

Chip chuckled good-naturedly. "Actually, we're having a square dance. Nancy picked the theme and planned everything. I just did as I was told."

Erianna stopped walking and looked at him. "A square dance?"

"Yep." He looked at his phone. "The band should be starting in the next fifteen minutes or so."

"Hold on a minute," she turned back toward her parents' house. "Ned," she called out to her son, who was still hovering around the bottom walkway. "Do me a favor and bring me the truck keys, please."

They all waited for Ned to deliver the keys and then Erianna turned back to rejoin the men. She stopped two houses down, where her White Ford F-150 pickup truck was parked. Reaching into the bed, she unlocked the heavy-duty aluminum crossbed tool box, which lifted from each side on a center hinge, and pulled out a pair of western-style boots. Leaning against her truck, Erianna quickly swapped her gym shoes for the well-worn brown leather boots, pulling her pant legs down over them and dropping the gym shoes in the tool box.

"Okay, gentlemen," she pronounced, "I'm ready for a square dance. Shall we join the party?"

They walked down the hill and across the flats in companionable silence. School busses were pulling up from Hillview Terrace and couples were disembarking. There were quite a few people making their way across the flats and down to the circle for the party as the daylight softened.

Erianna tried desperately to assume a casual air as she walked along. She matched her escorts' long-legged strides with ease. Though not the tallest of her female classmates, Erianna was slightly taller than average with a slender build.

She hated that there would be no hope of hiding her hazel-colored eyes from view. Her mother had seen to that. Erianna resented what she had done, but when she objected her father had intervened and put a stop to any further protestations. And so now she had to face her classmates in clown-face makeup with hair that looked and felt like straw.

I won't be surprised if people ask me if I ran away and joined the circus after graduation. Oh, well. She accepted her fate. After all, it wasn't as if the outcome of this encounter with her so called 'friends' would end any differently, even if she had been able to get ready on her own.

Chip and Matthew exchanged several hesitant glances as she walked along between them. Both men wished that something could be done about her appearance. Neither wanted her to spend the evening looking this way.

Chip pulled out his phone and texted his wife, hoping that she could offer a solution to their dilemma. Nancy replied immediately, and he nodded as he scanned his screen.

"Erin," he began. "Nancy wants me to check on the kids at my parents' house. Mom is babysitting for us tonight. Would you like to stop in with me and say hello?"

Erianna shook her head. "Maybe some other time."

"Well, I was thinking that while we're there you might want to—freshen up. I'm sure we won't miss more than the first few dances."

The first few dances my eye. She doubted that she would be asked to dance at all. And that would be just fine with her. Erianna Pruitt Fowler was an exceptional wallflower.

Chapter 2

Erianna stopped abruptly. She had reached the top of the steep lower hill, and looking down onto the scene below she couldn't seem to make her legs work. Her feet were stuck in place and she found herself unable to take another step.

The men stopped and turned back. Matthew took one look at Erianna and his heart sank. She was like a deer caught in the headlights. Her beautiful eyes were big, and round, and fearful. She stood unmoving, as if poised and ready to turn tail and run.

"Erin Pruitt, is that you?" a voice called out.

She turned toward the sound and found Mrs. Beyers sitting on her front porch. "Yes, ma'am, it is," Erianna replied.

She had a sudden thought, and she quickly explained to the men. "I'm going to say hello to Mrs. Beyers. I *promise* I'll be along in a few minutes. You two go ahead without me."

With that she was running up the Beyers' front walk and bounding up the porch steps three at a time.

Matthew shook his head and chuckled. "Just like old times. Wherever she was going, she was always running there."

Chip sighed heavily. "Should we believe her?"

"You go ahead. I'll stay and take care of this. I'll find a way to get her to your mom's and let her clean up before we join the party," he told Chip, who nodded in agreement and set off again, greatly relieved to be freed.

Turning back toward the Beyer house, Matthew noted that they had gone inside, but he was clueless as to why. So he went to investigate.

The half porch of the Beyers' home had a side-entry door that did not face the street. Matthew opened the screen door and let himself into a sunroom / entryway that spilled into a large living room. He could hear the women's voices coming from the back of the house and he turned to follow the sound.

"Why did you let her do this to you?" he heard Mrs. Beyers ask. "Never mind. That was a stupid question."

Matthew followed the sound of running water and stopped at the open doorway of the Beyers' first floor master bedroom. Standing at the sink in the master bath, Erianna scrubbed at her face with soap and a washcloth.

"What are you going to do about that hair?" Mrs. Beyers asked. "It's going to take a jackhammer to get out all that product."

"If you don't mind, I'll just hang over the side of the tub and shampoo it out under the faucet."

"That's fine with me. Just slip out of your top and I'll lay out a clean towel for you. You should probably rinse and repeat several times," she said as she reached up to touch Erianna's straw-like clumps. "Frankie left a hairdryer here. It's upstairs. I'll go get it for you."

"Thank you, Mrs.—"

"Call me Peggy."

"Oh, no ma'am, I couldn't do that," Erianna objected as she scrubbed furiously at the muck on her face.

"Don't worry, dear. It's just the two of us here and I won't tell anyone." Peggy turned to leave, closing the bathroom door behind her.

Matthew retreated to the front porch. He sat down on the top step and breathed a sigh of relief.

As he recalled, Peggy and her husband, Jack, had several daughters. Matthew wasn't sure how many. Jack Beyers desperately wanted sons, but instead he had fathered at least five girls before his youngest, and only son was born. To Matthew's recollection, all of the girls were given boys' nicknames. Frankie, the owner of the hair dryer Erianna was about to use, had been christened Francine. And he knew that the oldest girl's nickname was Jackie, so she had to be Jacqueline, or something of that nature. As he sat trying to recall the other girls' names Peggy came strolling onto the porch.

"Oh, Matt, I thought you went on ahead," she said in surprise as she settled herself in a chair, leaving Erianna to her own devices.

While they waited, each commented on Erianna's appearance.

"Honestly! I don't know how she survived her childhood with those sorry excuses for—" Peggy caught herself. "Can you imagine sending your own child out in public looking like that?"

Several minutes later Erianna emerged looking much more herself than when she went in. Her face was washed clean and her natural, peaches and cream complexion shone through. Apparently her mother had used waterproof mascara and there was some residual mascara on her lashes. But, at least the thick black clumps were gone and the hideous wide stripe of black eyeliner had been removed.

While her hair was still very wet in places, Erianna's long bangs were completely dry and fell softly over her forehead. She had pulled the hair above her temples back and secured it with a hair band. Thick and heavy, her golden locks were in various stages of dampness. Most of the hair in the ponytail was still quite wet, while other sections were almost dry, and the various hues, from light to dark, streamed down her back to her shoulder blades.

Matthew stood and smiled at her in approval. She was the most beautiful creature he'd ever laid eyes on.

He watched her all evening. It was hard to tear his eyes away, but Matthew was careful not to be obvious about his observations.

Unlike most women, who habitually tossed and played with their long hair in overtly-animated flirtations, Erianna's movements were subtle and restrained. She had a calm and composed demeanor and did not call undue attention to herself. She seemed comfortable in her own skin and felt no need to touch and flip her hair or readjust her clothing, although she did keep her eyes averted for most of the evening.

Matthew, Chip and Nancy had made a pact. Each would take a turn escorting Erianna around the party so that she wouldn't be alone. Nancy stole her away from Matthew as soon as they arrived at the refreshment table. The women visited with many of Nancy's girlfriends, most of whom both she and Erianna had known for all twelve years of school.

Chip put on his Presidential cap and went off to schmooze with his classmates in a manner befitting a well-seasoned politician. He was sociable and down to earth with everyone, and with his strawberry colored hair and a sprinkling of freckles, he was impossible to dislike.

When the square dancing began Chip brought over one of the single men at the reunion to partner with Erianna. Matthew immediately grabbed a classmate and joined her square. Erianna was obviously an experienced square dancer. She knew what all the calls meant and she helped the group with their footwork and eased them into the rhythm of the set. Matthew was encouraged by her seemingly comfortable and relaxed manner.

After the first set ended Erianna wandered over to the refreshment table. Chip appeared and handed her a longneck beer, and she sipped at it occasionally as they chatted with couples nearby.

"Where's Jansen?" Matthew asked Nancy as she came up beside him a short time later.

"Over by the cornhole area."

"Good. Keep an eye out, will you?"

She nodded.

When the square dance caller, a man named Eustace MacAvoy, beckoned the partygoers to join him for a line dance, Matthew grabbed Erianna's hand and whisked her to the dance area. She quickly introduced Matthew and Eustace. Apparently she had attended other dances where he and his band played and they had become acquainted.

The band struck up a rendition of the classic "Boot Scootin Boogie" by Brooks and Dunn, and Eustace took up a position in the front row center. Those who knew the steps scattered themselves at various spots along the three lines that had formed, with Erianna one row back from Eustace and several places to the right.

On cue they began the dance, sliding and stepping out to the song. The lines of dancers followed the steps as the band played the lively tune. Feet stomped and hands clapped as they snaked their way back and forth across the pavement. There was shouting and frivolity as some picked up the dance moves quickly while others stepped on their own two feet.

Matthew stood directly behind Erianna and tried to follow her exact steps, but he was one of the slower people to master the moves. When the lines turned to their left he looked sideways as he continued to mimic Erianna's steps. Then he looked up at her, smiled unabashedly and shrugged his shoulders as if to say 'yeah, I really suck at this'. Erianna rolled her eyes and looked skyward. As their eyes came together again they both burst into laughter.

Matthew hadn't changed much. He was still a handsome man. Erianna remembered the twinkle in his chocolate-brown eyes and the hint of a dimple in his left cheek. Tall and dark haired with strong, well-defined lips, he had an easygoing smile.

After the line dance debacle Matthew invited Erianna to join him for the last reel of the night. Squares formed and they danced together for the first time that evening. It felt so good to have her in his arms as they dosey-doed around the circle. She actually laughed out loud again when he allemande right instead of left and they became entangled with Chip and Nancy, who were dancing in the same square.

Light and laughter. That was the gift that Erianna brought to the world. Everywhere she went, every smile she bestowed brightened someone's day. Endearing and appealing, Matthew yearned to be with her again. It had been the same way for him when they dated so very briefly that long-ago summer after high school. He wanted that again. But she was a married woman now with two children, and he knew that it could never be.

He couldn't remember the last time he had had so much fun. When the reel ended he thanked Nancy for coming up with the great party theme. As he looked around, it appeared that most of the crowd had thoroughly enjoyed themselves.

By city ordinance, loud music was prohibited after eleven o'clock, so an after-party had been arranged at Matthew's family home on the other side of town.

The Prestwick estate was nestled along the Ohio River on the southeast side of the city. The area, which harbored no more than half a dozen homes, was restricted to only the wealthiest residents. Sprawling mansions dotted the landscape. Most were spread out over many acres of both woodlands and widespread grassy areas, and several of the estates included horse stables and riding paths.

Groups of partygoers began making their way up the hill toward buses waiting to transport them to the after-party venue. The milling crowd quieted as more and more people slowly moved off. Matthew and the Neadings stayed for a few minutes to thank the band and make sure that the service hired to break down and clean up the site had arrived and begun their work before heading for the buses.

Erianna had intended to fade into the background and make her way back to her parents' house unobserved after the party. She was a master at ducking out of school-sponsored events and she seriously doubted that anyone would take note of her absence. Most of her classmates were walking along the darkened street in small groups, but Erianna kept to the sidewalk and she slowly strolled along, essentially unnoticed, her movements obscured by the line of parked cars.

She had nearly reached the bottom of her parents' hill and was preparing to make the dash for home when Matthew, Chip and Nancy caught up to her.

"You can sit with me on the bus," Nancy told her as she linked their arms, sighing happily. "This brings back fond memories."

Riding a bus would bring back no fond memories for Erianna. She'd stopped riding the bus in the second grade. Being required to leave early and help her father open the grade school building, she either rode her bike or ran to and from school.

"I haven't been on a school bus in such a long time," Nancy continued wistfully.

Chip chuckled and grinned at her. "Yeah, thirteen years to be exact." Nancy laughed at his sarcastic barb and tried to elbow him in the ribs, but he easily evaded her.

Erianna had no intention of getting on the bus. Her night was ending here. Now. But somehow she was jostled and shuffled along, all the while protesting that she did not want to go. Before she knew it she was sitting on the bus with Chip parked in the aisle seat beside her. Nancy and Matthew settled into the next seat back. And suddenly, the doors closed.

She was trapped.

Buses were making loops from Crestwood Drive down Hillview Terrace and past the Prestwick Country Club to the east side. As they rode along Nancy picked up the conversation.

"Maybe next time you can bring your husband along so that we can all meet him."

Erianna nodded, but did not reply.

"It's a shame he had to miss this," Chip added. "Did he have to work this weekend?"

Erianna frowned and finally admitted, "Actually, I'm a widow."

"Oh, I'm so sorry," Nancy offered her sincere apology. "Was it sudden?"

Erianna nodded, but offered no further explanation. Clearly, she did not want to talk about the loss of her husband. Chip quickly changed the subject so as to not cause any further discomfort to his benchmate.

After offloading the majority of the passengers, the buses made their way to the high school where most of the attendees had parked, and then back to Crestwood Drive. They would continue to make the triangular loop throughout the night until the last guests had reached their destinations.

Erianna stepped off the bus and was guided along a well-lit pathway to the back of the house. As she walked she considered her options. It should be easy enough, she supposed, to excuse herself in order to freshen up and then sneak onto one of the buses without being detected. If she timed it right. And she was determined to duck and run as soon as possible.

Surprisingly, it seemed to her that the vast majority of her graduating class had chosen to stay for the late-night party. She also suspected that several couples had opted to forego the square dance and just attend the soiree at the Prestwick estate. The large crowd would bode well for her in making her escape unnoticed.

"It turned out just the way you pictured it," Matthew complimented Nancy as they took in the picturesque scenery.

It certainly did. Nancy had been insistent that Japanese lanterns be strung around the entire area, from the patio, where groupings of tables and chairs were set near a well-stocked bar, to the lake on the far side of the property. A wiffleball game was in progress on the expansive, well-manicured lawn, and more tables and chairs were scattered among the mature trees and around the pool deck. Several couples were swimming, and boisterous revelers were swinging out over the pond and somersaulting into the water on a rope suspended from a massive oak tree, while others sat on the small pier to watch the spectacle.

Erianna stopped at the bar and asked for a longneck beer. She took a sip and wandered away to take in the view. It really was a nice party, with a wide variety of activities to join. Everyone seemed to be enjoying themselves. To her left the tennis court lights were on and a foursome was engaged in a battle. The men still hadn't outgrown their schoolyard competitiveness, with neither team willing to go down in defeat.

Erianna set off to mingle without an escort. She ambled along around the perimeter of the grounds, stopping now and then to chat with a small group of classmates and their spouses for a few minutes. She watched surreptitiously as Matthew, Chip and Nancy slowly let down their guards and became distracted. Left unobserved, at last Erianna was on her own.

She made a small loop, skirting the far side of the pool as she walked along, enjoying the atmosphere as music played softly in the background. Stopping now and again to take a sip of her beer, she blended into the crowd.

She was nearly home-free. All she had to do was cross the grassy area between the pool and the patio and she could sneak out to a waiting bus. She did her best not to pick up her pace and call attention to herself as she headed toward the pathway that led to the front of the house where buses were waiting.

Suddenly a hand snaked out from her left and grabbed her elbow. She looked over and came face to face with Derrick Jansen.

"Fucking bitch!" he spat. "You don't belong here."

In that moment Erianna's hopes for an unobserved getaway were dashed. She turned and looked squarely at Derrick as he sneered at her. She had had enough, and she refused to back down or break eye contact with him. When he finally let go of his death grip on her arm she let it fall to her side as if to suggest that he had not caused her any pain.

With a casual air, she lifted her beer to her lips and took a sip without looking away. Derrick watched her as she drank, then licked his lips and proceeded to down the rest of his beer, taking several long pulls from the bottle. She half expected him to swipe his drooling lips across his shirt sleeve, and she resisted the urge to smirk.

"The cleaning crew doesn't usually come 'til *after* the party," he challenged in a booming voice. "You're early."

He shoved his empty bottle at her. "Here—make yourself useful and throw this in the trash, you fucking low-life. I bet you know exactly where it is. Don't you—"

Erianna stood her ground. When Derrick's hand shot out toward her she did not flinch or step back. She maintained an air of amusement, but did not reach for the bottle. Instead she stated, "You're drunk."

"And you're a fucking nobody!"

Erianna tilted her head slightly. "It's a shame you don't have a better grasp of the English language. You should try to improve your verbal skills and expand your vocabulary a little. You might benefit from learning something other than the F word."

Derrick slammed his bottle to the ground. "You worthless little piece of shit. You owe me an apology—"

"Apology," she cut him off with an easy laugh. "For what? Can you even *spell* the word apology?"

"Fuck you, you airheaded birdbrain."

"Tell me, Derrick, where exactly did you finish in the class rankings? Last?" She took a beat. "Nearly last? You are the dregs at the bottom of the barrel, Mr. Jansen. Maybe you should pick up a dictionary once in a while instead of a beer. You're drunk and you need to go sleep it off." With that last remark she turned and walked away.

Erianna had taken several relief-filled steps when she heard the unmistakable sound of a football lineman's roar at the snap of the ball.

"Arrghh," Derrick growled as he launched himself toward her in an attempt to tackle her to the ground.

Erianna pivoted sharply and quickly jumped out of the way, managing to evade his grasp as Derrick fell to his knees in the grass. She knew instinctively that this was not the end of their confrontation.

"This is pathetic," she muttered as she retreated onto the concrete pad that surrounded the pool.

Matthew had been talking with the three-year varsity football quarterback when the incident began.

"Uh oh," Brad Carter said. "I think there's trouble brewing."

Matthew turned immediately to scan the crowd. Derrick Jansen had Erianna by the elbow, and Matthew could clearly see both their profiles as they faced off. There was very little space between them and Matthew watched as Derrick released her arm and took a step back. *Good for her,* he thought as he began to make his way slowly through the crowd, hoping that he would not have to intercede on her behalf.

Erianna appeared to be unperturbed, despite the vicious rant Derrick was delivering. But when the drunken slob escalated to physical intimidation by hurling his empty bottle at her feet, Matthew picked up his pace. He could see that people were beginning to turn their full attention toward the couple, but he didn't want to charge into the fray and embarrass Erianna further unless it was absolutely necessary. He wasn't keen on the idea of escalating the already public scene. Nevertheless, he continued to make his way steadily toward her.

Derrick Jansen sat back on his haunches and swiped his dirty palms across his pant legs. "You fucking piece of slime! You've crossed over from the wrong side of the tracks, you fucking bitch," he screamed. "Go back to the gutter where you belong."

His foul insinuations hung in the crisp night air and the now silent crowd. Eyes glazed, he became maniacal as his rage increased, and he took aim at Erianna for a second time.

Erianna tossed her glass bottle aside and it landed harmlessly in the grass to her left as she backed away from him until there was nowhere for her to escape. Perched at the edge of the pool, she was trapped.

Using his hands for balance, Derrick worked to regain his footing. From a crouching position he charged again, but in his inebriated state he caught the toe of his shoe on the edge of the cement pad and tripped, losing what little balance he had managed to regain.

Derrick was stumbling straight at her and she had no doubt that she was headed for a dunk in the pool. She felt a moment of panic, followed by a rush of humiliation.

With his feet tripping over one another Derrick lunged at Erianna, aiming for her midsection as he tried to drive her backward into the pool. At the last possible moment she bent her knees and sprang up and to the side, kicking furiously to free her legs from his flailing arms.

She heard an awful scream and wondered briefly if it had come from her. Landing awkwardly on the deck, she teetered perilously at the edge of the pool. One booted foot hung out over open water and the other held a precarious foothold on the curved ledge. She was going in, and it wouldn't be pretty.

Erianna Fowler, a widowed mother of two, was about to land butt first in the Prestwick swimming pool. She just couldn't believe this was happening.

Somehow, someone managed to reach out, grab her arm and pull her back from the brink. Erianna was crushed against a muscular chest and she looked up into the somber face of her rescuer, Brad Carter.

Having launched himself at 'the bitch', Derrick had once again missed. The ground came up to meet him and he did a face plant on the edge of the pool. Hearing the terrible screaming and wailing, Erianna turned in Brad's arms to find Derrick rocking back and forth on his haunches, clutching his bloodied face in his hands.

His nose had hit the raised lip of the curved pool ledge and the loud, sickening crack of it breaking was clearly heard by all above the soft background music. He had split his lip and several teeth were either broken or missing. With his mouth filled with blood, he spit teeth into his bloody hands as he rocked, crying out in agony. Several of her classmates moved forward to offer first aid to the broken man. People dashed in with towels, ice packs and other medical supplies as they came to his aid.

Erianna offered Brad a nod of thanks as she disengaged herself from his arms. Standing silently on the perimeter, she watched the scene play out.

* * *

When Matthew realized what was about to happen he broke into a run, as did Brad Carter, who was also moving swiftly through the crowd. But Matthew hadn't managed to get to Derrick in time to stop his attack. And for that he was secretly pleased. That idiot Jansen deserved everything he got and then some.

How Erianna managed to escape was puzzling. Not once, but two times she eluded him, somehow managing to deflect and divert both physical attacks. Matthew found it quite ironic that Derrick had come out on the losing end of the battle. Matthew watched Erianna, but was unable to read her thoughts as, standing opposite her on the pool deck, he studied her intently.

Erianna pitied Derrick Jansen, but she could not bring herself to feel sorry for her classmate. Derrick's lack of character and hair-trigger temper had caused his self-inflicted injuries, and she felt no responsibility for his current condition. She turned to leave.

When she saw the large gathering of classmates staring at her, she stopped. Standing tall with her head erect, she scanned the crowd. Several women whispered to each other behind hand-covered mouths. A couple of men were pointing in her direction and filling in the juicy details to latecomers on the scene.

"What I just did was wrong," she addressed the crowd in a clear, confident tone. "It was so easy to goad him and I succumbed to the temptation. I should never have let it come to this. I deliberately provoked Derrick, knowing full well what would happen. And to what end?" She paused momentarily and glanced back at him before continuing.

"Nothing has changed, except that now a pitiful excuse for a man has a broken nose and is missing some teeth." Again she paused. "And this woman has lost some of her self-esteem in front of you all tonight."

She turned and addressed her final statement directly to Matthew Prestwick. "Please offer my sincere apology to your mother and tell her that I will pay for the damage to the pool deck. I'll send her a note of apology next week."

With that she turned and walked off through the parting crowd.

Matthew watched her disappear with a hint of a smile on his face. He was so proud of what she had just done. It was a long time coming, and truth be told Derrick's injuries *were* self-inflicted. He was drunk and as obnoxious as ever. And he was about as stupid as they came. Matthew doubted that Derrick would learn anything from the encounter. He would only sink further into the bottle. She was right, Derrick Jansen was pitiful.

Chip appeared at Matthew's side just as Erianna walked away. He stood with his hands in his pockets, trying not to burst into laughter.

"We have to get him out of here," Matthew pointed out.

Chip nodded. "He needs to go to the E.R. I'll find someone to give him a ride. Have you seen his wife?"

"I didn't know he had one."

"That was something to see. I didn't know she had it in her."

"I did. I've seen it before."

With a nod, Matthew set off to find Erianna as Chip took over the management of Derrick's transportation to the local hospital. He caught up with her just as the line began to move forward to board an arriving bus. He stepped up next to her as she shuffled along at the back of the line.

"Why don't I give you a lift home?" he offered.

"No thank you. I'll take the bus."

"C'mon," he smiled softly. "I could use a bit of fresh air and some good company."

"No, Matthew. I'm not in the mood to be 'good company,'" she told him point blank.

He reached over and enclosed her hand in his. "Please, Erin. It'll be just like old times."

He eased her out of the line and began to steer her in the direction of the multi-bayed garage. But Erianna had been manhandled enough for one night and she dug in her heels, refusing to move. Matthew would not release her hand so that she could board the bus, and Erianna refused to take one more step toward the garage. They were at an impasse.

The matter was resolved when the bus left without her. Erianna was furious, but he ignored her indignation as he tugged her along in the dark.

"*Let go of me*." She pulled against him with all her might. "Matthew Prestwick, you let go of me this instant." His lips twitched as he imagined her using just that same tone with her children.

He stopped, but kept her hand in his. They stood there for a few minutes. He had a suspicion that she was stalling in hopes that another bus would come along. It didn't.

Breaking the silence, he asked her, "Do you remember my old car? My Mustang Cobra?"

"No."

"I still have it. Why don't we go for a drive? It'll be just like old times."

"No."

"We can go up to the point. I'll put the top down."

"No, Matt," she declared in exasperation. "You volunteered to take me home. So take me home already."

"It's a nice clear moonless night. You can point out the stars and constellations for me, just the way you used to."

Erianna was confused. None of what Matthew was describing made any sense. She expelled a deep breath with an audible '*poof*' and surrendered. She was mentally and physically exhausted. All she wanted to do was close her eyes and try to calm down.

They were moving again. Erianna shook her head to try to clear some of the cobwebs, but before she knew it they were inside the garage. Matthew turned on one specific light, and a pristine silver muscle car with a rear spoiler and special rims appeared out of the darkness. The display reminded her of TV commercials where a new car for the next model year was unveiled for the first time.

"Look familiar now?"

"No. Why should it?" *What is it with men and their cars?*

Matthew frowned. "It's the same car I drove when we went out." He opened the passenger-side door and let her slide in.

Erianna snorted derisively. "We never went out, Matthew."

"Of course we did. We dated the summer after graduation."

He closed her door before she could respond. Erianna was weary, and as Matthew climbed into the driver seat next to her she let the matter drop. She just wanted to go home and put this terrible night behind her.

Chapter 3

Instead of taking her back to her parents' house, Matthew turned down a service road on the Prestwick property just below the main house. He stopped where the road ended at the overlook onto a bend in the Ohio River. He turned off the engine and sat back, stretching his left arm along his doorframe and the other across her seatback.

"Beautiful view," he murmured.

They sat in silence as the lazy river flowed slowly by. Erianna sighed heavily and relaxed against her seat. The cool night breezes washed over her and soothed her jumbled nerves. She closed her eyes and took several deep, cleansing breaths in an effort to ease the dull ache in her head. Erianna sensed that she was out of danger now and the rush of adrenaline that had overtaken her during the attack slowly subsided.

"I remember the last time we parked here," Matthew said after a time. "I think it was our last date."

Erianna shook her head vehemently. "I don't know what you're talking about. I've never been here before. *Obviously* you've confused me with one of your other lady friends." She crossed her arms defensively and sulked.

Matthew frowned and shifted in his seat so that he could look directly at her. Something wasn't right. How could she not remember dating him? Granted, it was fifteen years ago, but Matthew remembered it like it was yesterday.

He sat quietly with her for a while, looking beyond her and off into the distance. She was a widow. He was truly sorry for her loss, but he felt more than just sympathy. He felt attraction. Erianna was magical, and as he sat beside her he thought not just about their past relationship, but of a future one.

"How did your husband die?" he whispered softly.

Erianna waved a hand as if swatting away a fly.

"Was it an accident?"

"Yes. A car accident."

"I'm sorry—"

"Listen, if you don't want to take me home I'll just walk. It's not that far." She straightened in her seat and turned to open her door.

Matthew reached across and grabbed the door handle to stop her. "No, honey, please don't walk back. I'll take you home in a bit. I just figured you'd like a little time to regroup first."

What was with the odd 'honey' talk? Erianna was becoming apprehensive again. She turned to look at him, and sensing her discomfort Matthew withdrew his arm from her door handle. They were alone out here, and she didn't want to be. A blush crept into her cheeks as she observed him through the veil of her long bangs.

"You're safe with me," he told her with a reassuring smile. "Just sit back and relax for a few minutes. Then I'll take you home. Okay?"

Erianna wondered how he had managed to read her thoughts so accurately. After a few minutes more he withdrew his arm from the back of her seat, pausing to touch a lock of her golden hair, rubbing it softly between his fingertips. Then he restarted the car, turned around and headed toward her parents' house.

Matthew stopped at the top of Hillview Terrace and looked to his right. There were no parking places on the street that he could see, so he turned left onto Crestwood Circle and pulled to the curb, blocking a residential driveway.

"Thank you for giving me a lift."

"My pleasure," he returned the standard reply.

Shutting off the engine, he moved to open his door. But Erianna stopped him, placing a staying hand on his right forearm. "Don't get out. There's no need for that."

He brought his left hand over hers and gave it a warm, gentle squeeze. Then he got out and came around to open the passenger door for her.

"It was nice seeing you again," she fibbed.

Matthew reached out and brushed aside her bangs. "You're a terrible liar."

She lowered her gaze. "Yes, well—goodbye."

Erianna was moving away from him, walking along the sidewalk toward her childhood home, but Matthew was unwilling to let her leave just yet. He started after her.

"Erin?" he called out.

She stopped and turned.

"It was nice seeing you, too."

He pulled her gently into his arms. And then he kissed her—a soft, light brush across her full, pink lips that morphed into a deeper kiss. He indulged in a momentary taste of her sweet mouth before he softened the contact between them and raised his lips from hers.

He stepped away slowly, letting his hands linger until he was sure she had her balance.

"Goodnight, Erianna." As soft as velvet, he whispered her name. His liquid-brown eyes, shining with tenderness, drew her in as she struggled to look away.

"Goodnight," she finally managed.

He could see the puzzlement in her expression. *Does she remember now*? He took another step back, and finally she turned and walked away. Matthew watched her leave. When she reached the bottom of the hill and began to run he smiled brightly.

He returned to his car, but instead of getting in, he leaned against it and shoved his hands into his pockets. Looking off into the darkness, he thought back to days gone by.

Matthew couldn't recall much about Erianna before the Senior Night Dance at the Prestwick Country Club. She kept to herself and didn't hang out with anyone at school or eat lunch with her classmates. Instead, she went to the boiler room to eat with her father. Matthew knew that she worked alongside him at St. Michael's Grade School in exchange for free tuition. But, other than that he really didn't know much about her.

Until that night.

In an effort to stave off excessive partying, the parents and school faculty had come up with the brilliant idea of rounding up all the seniors and confining their activities to just one venue after a car accident had claimed the lives of three students who, several years prior, were out celebrating the night before graduation when they lost their lives. And so the "Senior Night Dance" idea was implemented, and it was a huge success.

Unaware of the subterfuge, the students loved the casual dress and relaxed atmosphere, unlike that of Prom Night, which was a formal affair. Thus the Senior Night Dance had become a new tradition, and it was held each year at the Prestwick Country Club.

The Country Club was located between the east and west side of town, nestled up against the banks of the Ohio River. The highly-rated golf course attracted top players and the Club Pro was well-known in the golfing community.

Matthew played eighteen holes early that day, and at four o'clock he left the club for commencement rehearsal. During that time the parents of senior students descended on the venue and set up an outdoor stage in the open grassy area next to the clubhouse. They set up tables and chairs and decorated the softly-lit area.

This would be the first visit to the member-only country club for many of the graduates. For others, it would be a great party at a familiar haunt. Quite a few parents volunteered to chaperone just to get a chance to see the golf club, and there was never a lack of parental presence at the dance.

Everyone came, even Erianna Pruitt, who was a regular at the club, albeit as a paid summer lifeguard. She kept mostly to herself, but she did stop to speak with several of the parents chaperoning that night.

"How are you this evening, Erin?" Mrs. Prestwick asked her.

"Just fine, ma'am. It's a wonderful party."

Helen Prestwick was standing with her younger sister, Agnes, and Chip's mother, Abigail Neading. Agnes and Gail graduated in the same class as Erianna's mother, the very same school from which their children would matriculate in a matter of hours.

"It's a shame your mother couldn't come tonight," Chip's mother said.

Erianna nodded. "Yes ma'am."

"It would have been just like old times," Gail sighed.

Erianna moved off unobtrusively as the women waxed nostalgic.

Matthew was having a great time. The music from the live band was great. Someone had smuggled in a flask, and he and Chip got in on that action. Chip was his usual smooth-talking self, and Matthew laughed as Chip regaled his classmates with stories as they congregated near their table to the right of the stage.

Nancy and several of her effervescent, bubble-headed girlfriends sat gossiping at the table. Occasionally, one or more of the girls would tear up when they reminisced about old times.

It was the last day of their childhood and the start of a journey into the next phase of their lives.

Gail Neading wandered through the throng of young people, keeping a watchful eye on the horny teenagers on the dance floor. As she moved along she caught site of her son. He and Nancy had cornered Erianna Pruitt against the clubhouse wall and were talking intently to her. Gail wondered what that was all about, and considered the possibility that they were pressuring Erianna to get onstage and sing. That precious little girl had been singing in Gail's backyard from the time she was old enough to be out on her own.

The Neading's property was pie shaped, terraced and yawning. Erianna would escape into the wooded gully behind her childhood home and make her way along the creek to the dead-end circle. The gully ended at the Neading's backyard where it fell into a culvert which drained into the Ohio River.

Erianna would often come to the sanctuary of Gail's lower terrace to read or just relax and take in the view. And sometimes she would settle down on the rock wall and sing to herself: and to the birds, and the trees, and the sun and sky. And any other being that she had conjured up in her imagination. She would dance lightly along the far rock wall as she sang a tune from Mary Poppins, or pretend that she was a pop star as she belted out the kids favorite hits from Debbie Gibson and Bryan Adams.

"You have to try." Nancy was pressuring Erianna, who shook her head in response as the band announced that they were taking a short break.

"It's too late to back out now, Erin. I already gave the band your name and the song tape," Chip announced with finality. "You've sung this one a million times. I've heard you and so has Nancy."

Erianna shook her head more vigorously, but they ignored her as they ushered her backstage.

Just before the last set of the evening, the band had planned an open-mic session for anyone who wanted to come on stage and sing. One of the first volunteers was a guy named Todd Davison. The band's lead singer introduced him and Todd gave a fair rendition of the Garth Brooks hit *Friends in Low Places.*

Meanwhile, Nancy, who had left Erianna in Chip's capable hands, was racing through the crowd trying to find Matthew.

"Come with me," she tugged at his arm when she finally found him talking to his mother.

"Where are we going?"

"Never mind," she hollered over the music. "Just *come on.* You'll see in a minute." Nancy dragged Matthew to the middle of the dance floor. "This is for you," she told him.

Erianna was due to be introduced next. Chip had stayed backstage with her when Nancy left, preventing her from turning tail and running. She looked lovely in a soft, supple lightweight denim shirt dress. The medium-wash fabric was interlaced with a palm tree design in a subtle, slightly darker shade of blue. The bodice had princess seaming, and the A-line skirt fell in soft waves to her knees.

Chip wasn't sure that she would actually go on and he was forced to escort Erianna to the microphone when her name was announced.

Chip, an old pro at public speaking, stepped up to the mic. "Okay, everybody. If you'll all just take it down an octave or two." The crowd laughed and quieted a little. "Erin is just a little bit nervous, but she's going to sing for us now if you'll just settle down a little."

He smiled at her, gave her a 'go get 'em, tiger' look and jumped down from the stage. Erianna began ringing her hands and Chip quickly slapped his hand on the wood floor of the temporary stage to get her attention.

"Look at me, Erin. Just look at me when you sing." He pointed two fingers to his eyes as the intro music began. He retreated several steps onto the dance floor while maintaining eye contact with her.

"*Moon River*," she began softly, "*wider than a mile. I'm crossing you in style, someday*."

Rich, clear and soothing, her mellow mid-tone pitch sounded like that of a professional singer. She held the long notes with an expert vibrato flutter in her voice. The effect added an expressive quality to the old standard made famous by Audrey Hepburn in the movie *Breakfast at Tiffany's*.

Matthew stood transfixed. Who was this woman, standing so poised and dignified in the spotlight? She was beautiful, delicate and willowy as she closed her eyes and continued the song.

"*...Oh, dream maker, you heart breaker. Wherever you're going, I'm going your way*."

Nancy moved through the group of couples who were slow-dancing and made her way to Chip's side. She hugged him and smiled brightly at Erianna. Chip took Nancy in his arms and they moved slowly, dancing cheek-to-cheek as they circled the floor.

Erianna had finished the first verse and the taped music played an interlude. Matthew came forward and stopped at the spot that Chip had occupied. As she started the second verse they made eye contact. The words were basically the same as the first verse, but this time Erianna's voice seemed to strengthen and echo among the nearby trees. She seemed mature far beyond her years.

The music reached its crescendo as the song drew to an end.

"*...We're after that same rainbow's end, waiting, round the bend. My lover and my friend, Moon River, and me.*"

Matthew's eyes widened. Whereas in the first verse she sang the words 'My Huckleberry Friend', as she ended this time she'd changed the words. Erianna Pruitt had looked into his eyes and changed the words to 'my lover and my friend'.

He was mesmerized.

She had just finished her song dedicated to Matthew Prestwick. She had been in love with him since the first day of school as she took the seat behind him when desks were assigned in alphabetical order. She would always take that same spot in class at the beginning of each school year until the teachers had memorized everyone's name and seating assignments were changed.

She loved the beginning of the school year and always looked forward to it for just that reason. She could watch Matthew unobtrusively and dream about the day they would get married and she could move out of her parents' house.

Unfortunately, Matthew Prestwick had no idea that she even existed. *Oh, well.* It was all for the best. Dreams only came true if you worked hard to make them happen. And for Erianna, the truth was that it was only a pipe dream, a childhood fantasy, and no amount of wishing could ever make such a fantasy come true.

Some people clapped, but as she stood onstage the catcalls began.

"You're making a fool of yourself up there."

"Get off the stage!"

"Why don't you go drown in the river!"

Someone launched a small paper plate filled with a large piece of sheet cake and it hit near the top of the low front wall of the stage, splattering everywhere. Erianna turned and ran, and kept on running until she reached the safety of the trees beyond the venue and almost to the far parking lot.

Matthew turned and scanned the crowd, trying to locate the guy who, if Matthew caught up with him, was about to take a royal beating. He didn't care if he was banned from graduation ceremonies the next day. Someone was going to pay.

Chip and Nancy took off after Erianna. Chip barreled over people, trying to catch up and stop her from leaving. Nancy did her best to keep up, and they finally caught her as she reached the safety of the trees.

"Are you okay?" Nancy asked breathlessly.

"*Just leave me alone!*

She was humiliated. No amount of reassurances from them would lessen her embarrassment. They stayed with her until the last, shortened set ended. Then Erianna walked by herself to the student parking area.

Classmates were heading in groups along the path to the lot. Erianna was supposed to get a lift home with Jessica and two other girls who lived in her neighborhood. But as she waited near Jessica's car she overheard the girls talking about her as they approached. Erianna's humiliation grew as she listened.

"Can you believe that?"

"What gall."

"And did you see what she was wearing? I'll bet you five bucks she made that dress herself."

"Homespun." Jessica wrinkled her nose.

"Oh," Jessica frowned when she noticed Erianna standing by her car. "I thought you left already."

"No, not yet," she murmured.

"We thought you left, so we asked Katie if she wanted a lift."

They all snickered.

"Sorry," Katie said. "There's no room for you."

"That's okay," Erianna demurred. "I just came over to let you know that Heather offered me a ride. Thanks anyway."

The petty teenage girls climbed into Jessica's car as Erianna walked away, pretending to head for Heather's car. She lingered in the lot until Jessica drove off. Then she faded into the semi-darkness and waited until most of the cars had disappeared.

Matthew searched everywhere for Erianna, but couldn't find her.

"Where's Erin?" he asked Chip when he caught up with them along the path to the gravel lot.

"She said she was getting a lift with Jessica Hunt and she headed that way a few minutes ago," Nancy turned and pointed.

Matthew took off at a fast jog and got to the parking lot just in time to overhear the conversation between Erianna and the other girls. He watched her wander off toward the back of the lot, and he stood unobserved by her as she moved into the shadows.

Erianna hadn't been offered another ride and he knew it. She hovered near the back of the parking lot as one car after another pulled out, blending into scenery as the lot slowly cleared. Then she began making her way toward the front drive.

Several cars were still parked in rows near the front of the large gravel area, where a group of students were milling around their cars and talking quietly as they smoked their cigarettes. They were parked across the way from Matthew's Cobra, and when Erianna walked past his car he stepped out of the shadows and walked lazily toward his car with his hands in his pockets.

"Do you need a lift? I'd be happy to give you a ride home," he offered in a casual tone.

"No thanks," she said as she pointed to the group across the way. "I have a ride."

Erianna picked up her pace and pretended to wave to someone as she walked directly toward them. Matthew followed. When she got to the group she scooted between the last two cars. Skirting the front of the remaining parked cars, she made her way out to the street. Matthew met her there. She glanced at him through the veil of her long bangs.

"I just want to make sure that you get home safely," he said.

Dashing across the road, she ignored him as she continued to jog along the far side, heading due west toward Hillview Terrace. Matthew followed her, and when space allowed on the sidewalk he came up beside her.

Erianna suddenly turned to her right and slowed her pace slightly. "I can get home from here by myself." And with that she was off in a lope up a dead-end street, heading due north.

There weren't many houses on this street, and she ran to the far end and started up a small concrete walking path to a mountain of steps that led to a small city park at the top. Matthew picked up his pace and followed her. He had no idea the steps were even there. He looked up. *You've got to be kidding me.*

There were easily two hundred steps to the top of the steep hill into which the stairway was cut. As he started the climb just behind Erianna he glanced up again. Seemingly endless clusters of steps loomed above him. Grouped into sections of between eight and twenty steps, they were separated by inclined pathways.

She set her pace and climbed steadily, taking the steps two at a time. It was obvious that she had taken this route before. He tried to match her pace, but about two-thirds of the way up he was forced to slow down and finish at a walk.

She was lying in the grass just below the top of the upper hill when he finally reached the last step. He wandered over and collapsed on the ground by her side as he tried to catch his breath.

She was looking up at the stars on this cool, clear night. When he asked, she pointed out the constellations visible in the night sky.

Neither mentioned what had transpired earlier. They lay quietly, side-by-side in the grass, and then he walked her home. He stopped several houses away and watched her make the rest of her journey alone.

She's always alone. He hadn't realized until just that night how isolated she was, and his heart lurched a little at the thought.

Erianna Pruitt missed her graduation. Her parents caught wind of what had happened the night before and grounded her.

"This is the last time you will ever humiliate me, you sorry excuse for a daughter," her father screamed as he slapped her across the face. "The whole town's talking about you. Do you know how ashamed I am that people believe you sprang from my loins?"

He slapped her again. "If you *ever* embarrass your mother and me like this again I'm going to beat you within an inch of your life."

She spent most of the day in her dingy basement bedroom until her parents left at two o'clock for an impromptu overnight trip to Cincinnati. After all, there was no reason for them to stay in town now that she was grounded from her own graduation ceremony. Leaving the two younger girls at home, they left them in Erianna's charge.

Matthew missed her. He sat in the first row with Charles Neading Jr. As Class Valedictorian and Senior Class President respectively, both he and Chip delivered commencement addresses to their fellow students. Erianna should have been sitting in the front row with them, but she was absent.

She had finished fifth in a class of a little more than one hundred and twenty-five students, and as such she should have taken her seat in the first row alongside the other top-ranked graduates. But she did not come, and Matthew wondered why.

The following week he caught up with her at the pool. She was finishing her early shift when he stopped by to say hello, but she offered no explanation for her absence from the commencement when he asked.

"Would you like to come and get a bite to eat with me?"

"I can't. I'm on my way to help my father at St. Michaels."

Nevertheless, Matthew persisted, and after several more rejections she finally accepted an invitation for dinner. They began to meet at neutral locations whenever she could slip away. He never picked her up or dropped her off at her house. Instead they would meet at some out-of-the-way place and go for a long drive or head into the Queen City for a night out.

He took it slow with her. He'd seen her bruises and knew that Clyde Pruitt was the guilty party. Matthew didn't want to be the cause of any corporal punishment handed down by her father. And so he was very careful not to let anyone in town find out about their dates, and he never picked her up at the same location twice.

The first time he kissed her goodnight he didn't sleep, he couldn't stop thinking about kissing her again. But he was respectful of Erianna's lack of experience and took it slow with her, never pushing when she was unwilling. As the summer progressed, so did their relationship.

Matthew took her to Cincinnati several times. There was little chance of their being found out there. He held her hand as they walked along the Ohio River at Sawyer Point Park one sunny day. Another time they went to an afternoon Reds baseball game and took in the sites of downtown Cincinnati. They visited the butterfly exhibit at the Krohn Conservatory in Eden Park and spent a day at the Coney Island Sunlight Pool.

He kissed her often. Matthew just couldn't get enough of her sweet, luscious lips. And when she was ready, he took their relationship to the next level, with occasional petting and caressing at the end of the night.

Matthew ferreted out places that had Karaoke nights that wouldn't card them, as Erianna was still seventeen, and he took her there to sing. He even joined in once in a while. They sang together, and laughed together, and enjoyed each other's company as their relationship blossomed.

June and July passed, and Erianna's birthday was right around the corner. Matthew made plans to take her out that first Friday in August, the night before her eighteenth birthday. They went to Cincinnati for an open-mic night at a downtown club. She was on the schedule to perform a set of four songs.

She wore the same sleeveless denim shirtdress that she had worn to the Senior Night Dance. Matthew still remembered that dress, all these years later. And he could still picture how beautiful she looked standing on stage that night.

She started with a big hit that year, *I Try*. Lowering her timbre and adopting a deep rasp to her voice, Erianna sounded just like Macy Gray. When she sang the lyric '*my world crumbles when you are not there*' she spread her arms out toward him.

Matthew was enchanted.

She followed that with a classic by the Eagles, *Life in the Fast Lane*. Then she went country with Faith Hill's *The Way You Love Me*. Her beautifully clear voice held him in her spell. He felt as though she was singing just to him. And he knew in that moment that he was in love with her.

With her last selection Erianna had the crowd roaring. One would swear that Aretha Franklin was on stage admonishing everyone to *Think About What You're Trying to Do to Me*. The boisterous Friday night crowd cheered in appreciation.

Erianna had a rare gift. She was not a one-note singer. Her vocal range and flexibility were amazing.

Matthew drove to the overlook on the Prestwick Estate before taking her home that August night. Little did he know that when he dropped Erianna Pruitt off not far from her home that it would be the last time he would ever see her.

As he stood ruminating about the past, a bus pulled up and several people disembarked. Brad Carter and a couple of others walked by toward their parked cars as Matthew was lost in his musings.

"How's Erin?" Brad paused on his way by to ask.

"She's just fine, thanks to you."

Brad chuckled as he ambled off. "Too bad Derrick isn't."

Nancy was in Matthew's office in downtown Cincinnati first thing Tuesday morning. She did not wait for his assistant to announce her. She just barged right in and shut the door firmly behind her.

"There's something wrong."

He sat back in his chair and linked his fingers behind his head. "Do tell."

She gave him a look. "I'm serious, Matt." She walked over and plopped down in a chair opposite his desk.

"Okay," he sat forward and rested his forearms on his desk. "I'm listening, what's going on?"

"It's Erin Pruitt—Erin Fowler. Something isn't right, but I just can't put my finger on it. Did you talk to her?"

"A little bit, yeah."

"Did you notice anything—" Nancy searched for the right word, "off about her? You know, anything peculiar?"

He wasn't sure where Nancy was going with this. But he knew enough about women to realize that he shouldn't volunteer an opinion until she had given hers.

"I'm not sure." That was always a safe answer.

Nancy got up from her chair. "I really think that Erin has some kind of memory loss," she finally stated.

Matthew sat up a little straighter in his seat. She had his full attention now. "What do you mean, memory loss?"

"Well, she didn't seem to remember anything about our senior year. When we were chatting with some of my friends I noticed that she couldn't recall much of anything that happened during that year. She didn't even remember Senior Night Dance or graduation the next day."

"She wasn't at graduation."

Nancy sat down again. "Are you sure?"

Matthew wasn't surprised that she didn't know about Erianna's absence from the graduation ceremony. Nancy Neading, or Nancy Landrew as she was known then, was seated in alphabetical order somewhere near the middle of the auditorium that evening. From her vantage point she probably couldn't see the people in the first row.

"I'm positive. Her parents grounded her when they found out what you and your illustrious husband put her up to the night before." Matthew didn't mention the bruises he'd seen from the beating she took.

"They what?" Nancy was flabbergasted. "From her own graduation?"

"Yep."

She was on her feet again. "That's despicable!"

He shrugged.

"Well, be that as it may, she definitely didn't remember singing at the Senior Night Dance.

"Maybe her father beat that memory out of her," Matthew mumbled.

"What?"

"Nothing."

"And there's another thing. Did she tell you that she has a fourteen year-old daughter?"

"Yeah, so what?"

"The girl will be starting high school in the fall."

"So?" When he didn't immediately catch on, Nancy let out a cry of exasperation and plunked herself back down in the chair.

"Grace—was that her name?" She waved her hand. "I can't remember. Anyway, Erin's daughter was born in February of 2002."

"Okay." He still didn't understand.

"Jesus, you're dense. Do the math, Matt." She sat back in her chair and crossed her arms in frustration.

When he didn't speak she said, "You must be the father of that child."

"Whoa." He held out both hands as if to push away that notion.

"She must have gotten pregnant just around the time we graduated."

Suddenly, Matthew was out of his chair. "Now just hold on a minute. Back up the bus. I—am *not* the father of that girl."

But Nancy was just warming up, and it was obvious that she'd put a lot of thought into this. "There's no other explanation. It's the only possibility. Everybody knew you two were hot and heavy that summer."

"I am *not* Grace's father," he declared vehemently.

That got Nancy's attention.

"Look," Matthew let out a long-suffering sigh and moderated his tone. "I'm sure about this. Okay? Read between the lines, Nancy. Erin Pruitt *did not* give birth to my child." He shoved his hands into his pockets and shook his head in denial. Then he walked over and looked out the window.

Nancy sat quietly for a time before saying, "Then someone else must have had sex with her. Maybe she was raped. Probably the night of the senior dance."

He pivoted sharply toward her with narrowed eyes. When he spoke, his tone was menacing as he threatened her. "No one raped Erianna that night, or any night after that. I don't want to find out that you repeated that gossip to anyone else, Nancy. Not ever."

But she was not intimidated. "How do you know? It is possible."

"It's not possible." He ran his fingers through his hair. "I was with her that night, but not in the biblical sense."

"Oh." She sat back. "I'm sorry, Matt. I didn't know."

Matthew returned to his desk and sat down. With a dismissive tone he said, "I'm done talking about this."

Chapter 4

When Matthew got home from work that night he poured himself a stiff drink. He couldn't get the conversation with Nancy out of his head. One thing he knew for sure. Erianna was definitely not pregnant while they dated that summer.

That left two options. Either she married a man who already had a daughter or she had adopted Grace. And that thought led to more questions. Why did Erianna disappear on her birthday without saying goodbye to him, where did she go, and when did she marry?

There were a lot of unanswered questions. He went to bed, but try as he might to put her out of his mind, sleep eluded him. He just couldn't stop thinking about her.

The only person Matthew could think of confiding in was his mother. So on Thursday morning he decided to drive to Prestwick and talk with her.

Helen Prestwick was in the kitchen when he came in.

"Hello, Matthew. I wasn't expecting you."

"Hey, Mom. Something sure smells good."

"I'm baking a red velvet cake. It should be coming out of the oven any minute now."

"Mmm."

Helen loved to bake. The Prestwick's employed a full-time, live-in housekeeper / cook, but Helen was usually found in the kitchen testing a recipe for a new confection she'd dreamed up, and she had an extensive collection of her own recipes.

The heavenly scent of the red velvet cake took Matthew back to his childhood, of coming home from school to the inviting smells of an apple pie or a peach cobbler, or some other homemade treat.

"Why aren't you at work?" his mother asked.

"I just thought I'd drop by for a chat."

She looked at him. He obviously had something serious on his mind. Helen was grateful that, after all these years, he still brought his problems home to his mother. She was still his sounding board in times of trouble.

"Okay. Chat about what?"

"I was wondering about Erin Pruitt."

"Yes, I meant to ask you about that. I received a letter of apology from her."

Matthew brushed his fingers through his dark hair. "Yeah, she said she was going to send you a note."

What exactly happened here Friday night?"

Helen and her mother-in-law, the dowager Lucinda Prestwick, now eighty-nine years old, had spent Memorial Day weekend in New York City with Helen's older brother. They were out of town when the reunion after-party took place.

"And what's all this about damage to the pool deck? I went outside and looked around, but I didn't see any damage."

"Some drunken idiot fell and broke his nose and bled all over the deck, but I bleached it and lifted out the stain."

"What does that have to do with Erin?"

Matthew settled down on a barstool and recounted the events that night as his mother pulled the cakes from the oven and put them on wire racks to cool.

When he finished, his mother said, "That doesn't sound like Erin."

He chuckled. "It was something to see. She really put Derrick in his place."

"Mmm. Were there any other incidents that I should know about?"

"No." His mouth quirked. He wasn't about to tell her about the rest of his evening. That was private, between Erianna and him.

"Could I take a look at the note?"

Helen looked across the counter at her son. "Why?"

"I was just wondering what she said and if she left a return address where you could bill her."

Helen was suddenly on full mother alert. "The note was addressed to me, Matt. Not you."

But he would not be put off so easily. "Did she give you her address?"

"No," she replied honestly. Erin had provided Helen with an e-mail address, but she was not about to let her son know that.

"Did she include a check with the note? That would have her current address on it."

His mother studied him carefully as she replied. "I know you had strong feelings for the girl, but that was a long time ago. It's all in the past, and you need to let it go."

"That's just the thing, Mom. It's not in the past."

Helen nodded. "Seeing her again must have brought back all those happy memories you had with her. But you're an adult now, and you need to let go and move on."

He sat back and rubbed his fingers across the back of his neck. "I can't, Mom."

"She's a married woman, Matt. You have no right to interfere."

"She's a widow."

Helen was surprised to hear that, but not wanting to prolong the conversation, she made no further comments about that bit of news. Instead, she walked around the kitchen island and began to rub Matthew's back, the same way she did when he was young.

"Don't pursue this, son. Leave well enough alone. She's settled into a new life far away from here. Please don't take this any further."

He looked devastated.

"You still love her, don't you?"

He nodded. "I need to find her, Mom."

"I don't believe she wants to be found. She's safe and happy where she is. I won't help you, Matt."

She hugged him tightly and would have said more, but

Lucinda came into the kitchen just then and they let the matter drop.

On the drive home to Cincinnati, Matthew thought about what his mother said. Apparently his secret date nights with Erianna were not as secret as they thought. Both his mother and Nancy had known all along. It was also clear that his mom knew about the abusive home life Erianna had endured. She was right, he should let sleeping dogs lie. But he couldn't. All Matthew could think about was a future with Erianna.

When he got back to the office Matthew started an internet search for Erianna Fowler. She didn't have a Facebook page. And he couldn't find an Instagram or Twitter account in her name. He finally dug up an old obituary in the Cleveland Plain Dealer for an Edward Fowler of Hudson, Ohio which listed her as his widow. From there he searched real estate records and found that she had sold her house in Hudson not long after her husband's death.

And then the trail went cold. It was as though she had won the lottery and hired a lawyer to help her hide behind a wall of anonymity. Matthew was at a loss and briefly tossed around the idea of hiring a private investigator to locate her, but quickly rejected that notion.

After another sleepless night, Matthew had all but decided to take another run at his mother. Maybe he could snoop around her office and find the note. But then he came up with a better idea. Maybe his sister, Doro, could wheedle the information out of their mother.

So on Saturday morning he took a drive down to Berrington to visit her.

Dorothy Prestwick Donovan lived with her husband, Robert, and their three boys in the quaint Village of Berrington, Kentucky. Nestled along the south fork of the Licking River in the heart of Bluegrass Country, it was a picturesque representation of country living at its best and a throwback to the nineteen-fifties.

In the village square the two-story, red brick Courthouse and Post Office buildings faced each other across a large, park-like grassy area with shade trees and benches. As he drove by, the town square was humming with activity on this sunny early June day.

The Village streets were lined with angled parking spaces for people who wanted to shop in the vicinity. Locals were pulling into the bank and the post office to collect their mail, which was typical of the rural farmers scattered throughout the county, and traffic was stop and go on Main Street.

The ice cream shop had yet to open, but the bakery across the way was buzzing with customers, as were the summer outdoor fruit and veggie stands. A scattering of tourists, who had no doubt exited I-75 in Corinth and headed east just as Matthew had, were pulling up in front of quilt shops, one-of-a-kind jewelry and antique stores, and a handful of other locally-owned businesses.

The tree-lined sidewalks attracted Village residents who were taking their Saturday morning walks, and as he waited for a light to change he saw a couple of boys ride by on their bicycles.

On his way out to his sister's house on the far side of town, Matthew passed his brother-in-law's veterinary clinic on his right. Between the clinic and the turnoff to Berrington Farm he passed Boone High School. The two village grade schools, one on each side of the Licking River, consisted of students from first to eighth grade. The junior high students were housed in separate buildings on each campus. They, as well as the Immaculate Heart of Mary parochial grade school kids, all spilled into this one high school.

As he drove by, Matthew noted that several Little League games were underway at the ball fields.

The Village of Berrington was becoming a mecca for equestrian enthusiasts. A mini-Lexington, it was just as welcoming. Over the past several years the secret of Berrington's excellent boarding stables, coupled with its easy accessibility from Georgetown and Lexington, had begun to attract horse owners to the

Village. Boarding fees were much more affordable here, and some couples were coming into the area to build in subdivisions popping up on the west side of the river near the business district.

Berrington was building a reputation as a place where horse lovers could find first-rate facilities at a reasonable price, and a few professional trainers had recently settled in the area. Although not a thoroughbred racing community, many of the new residents were horse show enthusiasts and three-day eventers.

Matthew cruised along the tree-lined road east of town. Creosote fencing dotted the landscape and sections of antebellum rock walls framed the roadway here and there. He turned left and passed through two tall stone pillars with the sign 'Berrington Farm' on display.

His older sister lived down this private, aptly named Donovan Lane, one of several boarding stables in the Village. The land had been owned by the Donovan family for more than three generations until just recently when it had been sold to a new owner.

Doro, five years his senior, and her husband, Bob, were raising their brood of boys here. Bob owned a veterinary clinic and Doro ran a catering business from their home. She had inherited a love of cooking and baking from her mother, and she brought in extra revenue with her catering jobs.

Matthew pulled into her driveway after an idyllic ride along fence-lined pastureland where he spotted several horses grazing in the late morning sun. But when he knocked on Doro's door no one answered. Matthew jogged around to the back screened-in porch and tried the kitchen door. It was locked.

He stood on the porch weighing his options, then pulled out his cell phone to call his sister, but decided to walk next door first to see if she was at Pap's place.

Patrick "Pap" Donovan was Dorothy's father-in-law. He and his younger brother, Gus, grew up in the old farmhouse at the end of the lane. Gus and Pap co-owned the property until

Pap was injured in a hunting accident about five years earlier. He had lost his footing and fallen down a steep mountain trail in the Appalachians while on a deer hunt. A tree had broken his fall, and also his back, and he was now paralyzed from the waist down.

Pap had incurred extensive medical bills and needed money to pay them, so he sold his share of the land to his brother Gus. And when Pap was well enough he and his wife, Ginny, moved into Doro and Bob's newly renovated two-story home on Donovan Lane. An addition to the house now included a mother-in-law suite. Pap and Ginny shared a common wall with the main house in their two-bedroom unit.

Matthew was aware that when the current owners moved onto the property Doro and Bob built a new house next door. But he had yet to meet the current owners of the renamed Berrington Farm.

He took a shot and walked along the paved path to Pap's side door. "Hello," he called out through the screen door after ringing the bell. "Pap, are you home? It's Matt Prestwick, Doro's brother."

"Matthew, my boy, come in, come in," the response came over an intercom.

He let himself in and made his way past the bedrooms on his right to the combination living room / kitchen that could have been called a Great Room if not for the standard-height ceilings.

Pap was sitting in his hospital bed, which was positioned between the south-facing living room and the kitchen at the back of the suite. The kitchen was U-shaped and boasted a large garden window over the sink. With room to maneuver comfortably and a long marble-topped kitchen counter that looked outward into the living room, it was an efficient and workable space. A row of three low bar stools sat under the overhang of the countertop for added seating.

Pap's hospital bed was pushed up against the common wall between the two units of the house. He faced inward into his suite, with the kitchen to his right. A wide walkway, where the doorway to the other residence was located, allowed for traffic flow between his bed and the counter. The solid, soundproofed door could be shut for privacy, but was standing open at the moment, as it was during most busy summer days such as this.

Bob had installed a round, wall-mounted convex mirror with a one-hundred-and-sixty degree angle of sight on the upper wall opposite Pap's bed, and he had an unobstructed view from his suite to the end of the long hallway that ran the entire length of the other house. It reminded Matthew of those used in hospital corridors.

"Hi, Pap, how are you doing today?"

"Fair to middling." It was his go-to response. "Have a seat, my boy."

Matthew took a seat on a bar stool and rested an elbow on the countertop behind him.

"What brings you by?"

"I thought I'd take a drive this morning and I ended up here. I was wondering if you know where Doro is."

"She and Ginny went to the supermarket to restock their pantries."

Pap quickly shot off a text from his computer keyboard. It dinged a response almost immediately.

"They'll be back in about half an hour. You're welcome to stay and visit until they get home if you like."

"Thanks. I should have called first, but I decided at the last minute to come by for a long overdue visit. I figured if she wasn't home at least I had a nice drive."

Pap chuckled. "You took a real chance. These days the boys are so busy that our schedules are packed. I'm constantly updating the calendar to figure out who needs to be where at what time and with which kid. And I also keep all the schedules for riding lessons and group trail rides."

"I don't know how you manage it all."

He tapped lovingly on the laptop resting on top of an attached swing stand with an elbow swivel arm that was pulled across his bed. "This is a well-oiled machine, my friend," he quoted from one of Ginny's favorite movies.

Matthew leaned forward to get a better look. "What can you do on that thing?"

"It's got all the bells and whistles," Pap stated proudly. "I'm consistently upgrading for the quickest connectivity available."

"That must be some sweet system," Matthew nodded at the screen." What kind of software are you running?"

The men talked about his computer and its software for several minutes. "I can pull up whatever I need on my twenty-four inch touchscreen." With a tap of his finger, Pap pulled up the live feed from a closed-circuit monitoring system that ran from the front gate to the stables. "I'll just leave this on so we'll know when the girls pull up."

Through a wireless network connection and Bluetooth technology, Pap could tap the screen and start a face-to-face computer link next door. Thus, he was able to be involved in his grandchildren's daily lives from his central command here in the suite.

"I take calls and I like to talk-to-text from my computer, and I can watch TV from here as well."

Pap's system was state of the art, and in a loud stage whisper he poked at his chest and boasted, "I am the heart of this operation."

"Well, you're really in the loop here," Matthew agreed.

"Yep. I know when the boys are messing around instead of doing their chores and I'd know right away if any of them tried to sneak out of the house at night."

Matt snickered. "I bet they don't like that much."

Pap laughed, a hearty sound filled with merriment. "You've got that right, my friend."

"What kind of—" Matthew stopped short when he heard a voice call out from the other side of the house.

"Pap, I'm running to Beulah's and then to the boys' games. Do you need anything before I go?"

"Nope, I'm fine."

Matthew heard the sound of a wooden screen door closing.

He knew that voice. "Who was that?"

"Just my neighbor. The lady who lives next door."

"Your neighbor—who's your neighbor?" he asked as he stood up and began moving toward the door separating the two units.

Pap frowned. "Why?"

Matthew took off through the doorway.

"What are you doing? You shouldn't go over there."

But he didn't listen. He ran down the hallway and out to the garage, but was too late to see who was pulling out and heading up the lane. And he couldn't make out the driver as he stood in the driveway watching the mid-toned metallic blue Subaru Outback pull away.

Not Erianna's car, he thought to himself.

Matthew rubbed the back of his neck in irritation. He could have sworn that he heard Erianna's voice, but it couldn't be. What would she be doing here of all places? He must be losing his mind. Turning back the way he had come, he stopped short. There, parked in the garage of his sister's former home, was a white Ford F-150. Erianna's truck.

Ginny and Doro passed Erianna just as she made the right-hand turn from Berrington Farm's front gate onto the main road into the Village. They beeped a friendly greeting in passing. Erianna was on her way to B's Textile Emporium. Most visitors to the area assumed the B was a moniker for Berrington Textile Emporium, but it was actually the first letter of its owner, Beulah Hutchins, and the locals commonly referred to the store as Beulah's.

A family-run purveyor of fabrics, yarns and notions, B's was a big draw for quilters and home sewers throughout the county. Beulah often carried the same quality fabrics that some high-end stores did, but she stocked her shelves with an emphasis on the local home sewing market. She carried very few fabrics such as satin, silk and velvet. They did not sell well. She had developed a keen eye toward her customers' preferences and had learned to stock her emporium with that in mind.

The basement floor carried an extensive assortment of quilting fabrics, but Erianna did not have any interest in quilting. She wandered downstairs anyway to check out the wide assortment of yarns, both natural and acrylic, displayed by shade in cubbyholes. Erianna had an electric knitting machine in the corner of her basement rec room and could finish a sweater in a day or two, depending on the intricacy of her design.

In her former life, Erianna Fowler of Hudson, Ohio worked from home doing alterations from her converted garage. She was only open during school hours, and she worked at her leisure. Erianna liked to sew, learning first by necessity, and then continuing for pleasure. She also knew how to crochet, embroider and cross-stitch, and was very good at tatting.

After perusing the yarn display she headed back to the main floor and browsed through the bolts of fabric for any new inspiration. She spent about twenty minutes looking around before she headed out to the boys' baseball games that were due to begin soon.

Doro and Bob had three boys, ranging in age from fifteen to nine. Ryan was their oldest. The two younger Donovan boys, James, or Jamie as he was called, and Theo, a shortened version of Theodore, were very close in age. Along with Ned, they were often referred to as the three musketeers as it seemed they were almost always together. Jamie was one year older than Ned, who would be turning ten in a few weeks, and Theo was nine.

The youngsters all had games this morning. Jamie played third base for the Blue Jays, made up of eleven and twelve year olds. His game started before the two younger boys' team, the Tigers, played.

After the games ended, with both teams winning, Erianna gathered up the crew and headed home. She was surprised that

Doro hadn't shown up to watch them play. But she had seen a car in Doro's driveway as she drove past. Someone must have stopped by for a catering consultation and she had been waylaid. It wasn't unusual, as their schedules were in a constant state of flux, and everyone was used to readjusting when needed.

Erianna was right. Doro did have company, namely her younger brother.

When Ginny came breezing through the door with an armful of groceries a couple of minutes after Erianna left, Matthew helped carry in the rest of her bags. Then he went to help his sister with her much larger haul, and when everything was unpacked and put away Matthew sat down to talk with his sister.

"Why didn't you tell me Erianna Pruitt was living next door?"

"Erianna Pruitt—" she frowned.

"Erin Fowler," he supplied.

"Oh. Why would I? Do you know her?"

"Yes. I know her from school. Don't you remember her?"

"No, I don't," she said. "Erin is from Hudson, not Prestwick."

Matthew ran his fingers through his dark, wavy hair. "Are you telling me that she never once mentioned that she grew up in Prestwick?"

"That's what I'm telling you. I had no idea. What does it matter anyway?"

Doro settled in at the dinette table with a cup of coffee as Matthew brought her up to speed. As he talked he paced back and forth across her large kitchen. When he finished, Matthew sat down across from her.

"What do you think?"

"I think Mom's right. If Erin wanted me to know she would have told me about it. But she didn't, and I'm not about to question why. And I don't think you should come down here and rock the boat."

"Jesus Christ," he swore.

Doro scowled at him.

"Sorry. But honestly, Doro, I can't believe you're taking Mom's side." He got up and began to pace again.

"Well, you asked for my opinion and that's my opinion. I can't stop you if you're hell-bent on having your own way. But keep in mind that she obviously never mentioned growing up in Prestwick for a very good reason. She didn't want me to know."

Pap called over on the intercom just then. "The boys are home."

"Okay, thanks Pap. Who won?"

"Both teams did," he supplied.

Matthew started for the front door.

"Don't go out there, Matt. Leave her alone," Doro commanded.

Once again, Matthew did not listen.

Erianna pulled to a stop beside Doro's driveway to drop off Jamie and Theo. Someone was walking toward her SUV.

"Uncle Matt," Theo cried out as he jumped out of the car and ran toward his uncle.

"Hey there, guys. I heard that you won your games," he said as Theo launched himself into Matthew's arms.

"Yep," Jamie replied. "Did you just get here?"

"Yeah. Sorry, if I had known you were playing I would have stopped to watch."

Ned recognized the man from the week before in Prestwick. "What's he doing here?" he asked his mother as Jamie and Theo stood by the car visiting with their uncle.

"I don't know," she murmured quietly.

The boys gathered up their gear and headed up the driveway, but instead of joining them Matthew turned and closed the short distance to her car.

"Hello, again," he greeted Erianna with a friendly smile.

"Hello."

"Hello, Ned."

Matthew wasn't surprised when he got no response from the boy. Ned wasn't happy about seeing him again and he made that very clear as he sat sulking in the passenger seat.

"What a surprise, running into you here," he continued. "A happy accident."

"Yes, an accident all right," Erianna quipped. She put a halt to any further chit-chat when she said, "I have to get going. I have work to do."

With that she continued down the lane and pulled into her garage, disappearing from view.

Matthew couldn't be happier. He'd found her by chance, right in his sister's backyard. She'd been hiding in plain sight and he couldn't believe his luck. Erianna Fowler was the new owner of the former Donovan Farm.

He felt like skipping up the driveway, but refrained as he headed inside to visit with his nephews until they left to go to the stables to help saddle horses for the next group riding lesson.

Realizing that his sister was not going to volunteer any more information about Erianna, he headed out with the boys when they left to do their chores, walking along with them toward the stables. Then he ducked back to Pap and Ginny's place.

He wasn't the least bit sorry about tricking them into giving up more information about Erianna as he visited with the couple. He kept the conversation casual, every once in a while asking about their neighbor and wondering how things were working out.

It was Ginny who gave him the juicy tidbit that Erianna enjoyed country-western dancing, and that she and Gus went to a local dance club in the Village a couple of Saturdays each month. It was just the tip he needed.

As he drove home that afternoon, Matthew wondered if it was possible to learn how to dance in just one week, because he fully intended to "bump" into Erianna at that very same club if she was there the following Saturday night.

Matthew arrived at his office bright and early on Monday morning.

"Allison, would you come in here, please?" His Executive Assistant gathered up her notebook and pen and followed him into his office.

He dispensed with his usual pleasantries. "I need you to call around and find me private dance lessons," he began. "Country-western dance lessons to be exact. I need to learn at least one couples' dance and one line dance by the end of the week."

He pushed a piece of paper at her. "This is the name and number of a club in Berrington, Kentucky. Have the dance instructor find out what line dances are the most popular there. I need to learn one of those. And one couples' dance that goes something like long step, long step, short, short, short. You know?"

Allison smiled. "Okay, I'll tell them that."

He frowned. "Very funny."

"I think you want to learn a two-step. That's probably the most common country-western dance."

He ran his fingers through his hair. "Whatever," he sighed. "I need lessons this week, starting today if possible. And re-arrange my schedule around any openings the instructor has. I'm going to need a lot of help, so the more lessons the better."

Matthew knew that Erianna had enjoyed herself at the square dance and he hoped to recreate that experience when he dropped by The Hoot 'n Holler on Saturday night. But, like most men his age, had learned nothing more than how to rock back and forth, shifting his weight from one foot to the other when slow-dancing with a woman. This was new territory for him and he hoped he wouldn't fall flat on his face.

He'd do anything to rebuild a relationship with Erianna, and if that included learning how to dance, then so be it. Now that he had found her he would stop at nothing to win her back.

And so on Monday afternoon he went to his first country-western dance lesson.

The instructor, a woman named Sharon Zimmer, offered dance lessons at The Silver Spur, a country-western dance club across the river in Northern Kentucky. Sharon offered lessons there in the afternoons before the place opened for business. Matthew walked in at three o'clock.

"Hello, Dr. Prestwick. It's nice to meet you. I understand that you're interested in country-western dance lessons?"

"Yes." He explained that he needed to learn the basics and that he hoped to be competent enough so that he would not embarrass himself when he went to The Hoot 'n Holler on Saturday night.

"I've never been to a country-western dance club. My friend loves to dance, but—" he shrugged.

It was obvious to Sharon that he wanted to learn because he wanted to impress a lady friend. He wasn't the first man to use this ploy.

"I've been there several times," she told him. "It's a very nice place. Most of the regulars are middle-aged and very good dancers.

"I'm really not sure if I'll be able to catch on or if I have two left feet, but I'm willing to give it a try."

"Okay," Sharon said. "I think we should start with a two-step. It's easy to learn, and I can teach you the basics quickly. We can spend the rest of the week graduating to a few more advanced moves and you should be able to make a fair showing for yourself."

She began by helping Matthew find the beat. "Okay now, tap your foot once."

Matthew dutifully tapped the toe of his right boot on the dance floor.

"Next, tap it two times, like this," she showed him.

He followed along and they were tapping their feet in rhythm to her established beat.

"When your foot falls, I'll say 'one' and when it rises I'll say 'and'.

Matthew looked lost.

"Watch me." She lifted her toe and began to tap to the rhythm of the music she had just put on. "One-and-two-and-three-and—do you see? I'm counting to the beat."

He nodded.

"Now try it with me." Sharon was relieved to see that he had a good sense of rhythm. She now stood a decent chance of teaching him the basics in the short span of one week.

"The two-step follows a quick, quick, slow, slow pattern."

She explained how to find the downbeat and they moved together, side by side to the quick, quick, slow, slow movements. Once he had mastered that, she turned into his arms and showed him how to establish a frame.

"Put your right hand on my shoulder blade, and I'm going to rest my left hand at the top of your arm, here." Sharon placed her thumb along the inside edge of his upper right arm where it met his torso, resting her fingers on his arm. "This way I'll be able to feel your movement as you lead me and you won't have to push me along."

He nodded in understanding and did as she instructed.

"Now take my right hand in your left, like this." She showed him how to make an L with his thumb outstretched and she settled her fingers lightly in his hand.

"You will lead your partner and she will dance backwards in your arms. We're going to progress in a circle around the floor. Start with your left foot, and follow the beat. I'll count it off for you."

They began moving in unison to the music she put on and he took his first stab at two-stepping.

"Very good. Okay, now bend your knees a little for me. It'll help you create a proper dance posture."

He tried, and immediately lost track of everything else. They started again, and within a relatively short time Matthew caught on to the basics of the two-step. She spent the rest of the first lesson taking him through the moves while she played several country songs that had the right beat. By the end of the first lesson Sharon was relatively comfortable with his progress.

In the following lessons she taught him how to spin his partner and bring her back into frame without losing count, as well as a wrap frame maneuver that brought his partner to his side in a two-hand hold.

She explained to him that learning to dance was like learning your Internet password. "After a while your fingers just go there automatically. It's the same with dancing, with regular practice it'll come naturally to you."

He tried his best, but Matthew was still having trouble keeping his eyes off Sharon's feet.

"Stop looking down," she admonished him. "When you do that your posture suffers and you lose your good frame with your partner."

On Friday night he met her at the Silver Spur where he took a stab at the Barnyard Mixer, a couple's pattern dance he had also learned. And he practiced his two-step with Sharon and a couple of other women in attendance. When he finally got home that night, Matthew felt fairly confident in his dancing prowess, but only time would tell if he could pull this off.

Chapter 5

Matthew arrived at the Hoot 'n Holler in the Village of Berrington on Saturday night. He waited in his car for a while to see if the men were wearing western hats into the club. Noting that the majority were, he got out and put on his black Stetson as he headed inside.

Pausing just inside the door, he surveyed the room to get the lay of the land and spotted Erianna and Gus in the crowd. They were sitting at a table for six on the far side of the large room beyond the dance floor.

Their meal was just being served, so he decided not to approach them while they were eating. Instead, he went over to the bar, located to the left of the front door, and ordered a beer. There were several tall, circular standing tables occupying the space from the far end of the bar to the back wall, and he made his way to that area.

Matthew saw two middle-aged women standing by themselves at one of the tables, so he approached them asking, "Do you ladies mind if I join you?"

"Not at all."

"Thanks." He set down his beer and offered his hand. "I'm Matt. I'm pleased to meet you."

"I'm Bernice," the gray haired woman said as she shook his hand. "Is this your first time here?"

"Yes," he chuckled. "Does it show?"

Both Bernice and her friend, who were regulars, laughed.

"I think we'd remember seeing a handsome young man like you here," the other woman said. "I'm Sally."

Matthew stood and chatted with the ladies while he watched the dancers on the polished wood floor. A variety of songs were played and different country-western dances were performed, but Matthew didn't recognize most of them.

When a two-step song came up Bernice asked him, "Do you know how to dance?"

"I know this one," he admitted. "But I'm just a beginner. Would you like to take a chance and try it with me?"

"I'd be happy to."

Matthew escorted her to the dance floor and brought her into frame. She helped him find the downbeat and they began their quick, quick, slow, slow pattern. Matthew looked beyond her left shoulder and kept his movement light as he eased into the dance.

Bernice smiled up at him and said, "You're doing fine."

Matthew smiled back, but didn't say anything. He was too busy counting. After a while she asked him, "Would you like to try a spin?"

He nodded.

"Okay, count out loud—"

"Three, four, five, six—" Matthew and Bernice, in rhythm, executed an incident-free spin and she came back into frame without either of them losing a step. She was a good dancer, nimble and light on her feet, and he relaxed a little.

As his confidence grew, Matthew led her through several more spins and into a couple of wrap holds. Dancing at her side, he finally spoke up.

"How am I doing?"

"Really well for a beginner."

When the song ended, Matthew escorted Bernice back to their table.

"You really do have nice movement to your dance," she told him as he thanked her for her bravery. "And you didn't stomp on my feet, not even once," she teased.

Matthew excused himself and headed back to the bar. As he sipped his second longneck he kept an eye on Erianna. After she and Gus danced a couple of times, he went off to ask a lady friend for a spin. Erianna danced with another man from their table, who Matthew assumed must be a friend of Gus's.

There was no live band tonight. A D.J. was spinning crowd favorites and the dance floor was full, but not overcrowded. Matthew made his way to the D.J.'s booth and slipped him a note, along with twenty bucks. The note requested that the guy play a two-step song immediately after the next Barnyard Mixer line dance. Then he headed back to the table where Bernice and Sally were standing and bided his time, waiting for the D.J. to call for a Barnyard mixer.

It was now or never, this was his chance. He turned to Bernice and said, "I actually know this one. May I?" he held out his hand.

Sally was also asked to dance, and the women were escorted to the dance floor alongside each other. Everyone took positions in two circles, the men on the inner circle and the ladies outside. The music for *Wild, Wild West* by The Escape Club began.

Matthew waited until the guy next to him took a step. With Bernice's help, he found the beat and they began. The men moved with their partners to the left. Step together, step touch. *So far, so good.*

They moved back to the right: step together, step touch. Then he spun Bernice out. At the downbeat Matthew joined his free hand in hers, which was resting across her midsection. He spun her back to his right side in a two-hand wrap hold and then, hip to hip, they step hitched four times. He silently counted it off. *Step, hitch. Step, hitch. Step, hitch. Step and roll.*

With the final hitch he rolled his partner out, then spun her back and handed her off to the man on his right. Sally was next. Once again, Matthew had no difficulty with the set, and as he handed her off Sally smiled and said, "Good job."

As the music played the snaking lines moved to the beat. By the time the third lady was passed off to the next gentleman Matthew had settled comfortably into the pattern. He was very lucky. Sharon told him that this was the most basic Barnyard Mixer pattern.

"Other clubs use a more advanced floor pattern," she had informed him.

He actually began to enjoy himself as one lady after another was met, taken through the pattern and handed off as the mixer progressed.

It was worth all the trouble when Erianna came into his arms for the first time.

"Hello," he said.

Matthew wanted to make sure that he didn't lose the beat while he danced with her, so he smiled, showing a bit of dimple, but said nothing else as they step hitched, rolled out, and she was spun on to the next partner without incident.

He breathed a sigh of relief.

What is he doing here? Erianna was shocked, but she tried not to let it show as she moved along the line from one partner to the next. She felt exposed and all alone in the crowd of dancers, as though she was enduring a home invasion and the room was full of bystanders witnessing the event, but doing nothing to help her.

Erianna passed Matthew for a second time, but he didn't speak to her again. When he brought her into the corner wrap against his side she couldn't breathe. They step hitched and he rolled her out, Erianna felt dizzy. The room seemed to be spinning out of control. At last she was with a new partner, and she drew a deep breath and regrouped.

When the song ended Erianna was three partners to Matthew's left. He quickly thanked the woman in front of him and walked over to Erianna as the music for a two-step began.

"May I have this dance?"

She had no time to react before he grabbed her hand and brought into frame and began the quick, quick, slow, slow rhythm of the two-step. She was mortified. Matthew had a firm hold on her, and unless she was willing to make a public scene, she could not seem to extricate herself from his grasp.

Matthew didn't speak. He just led her through the steps to the George Strait song *I Just Want to Dance with You*.

Erianna lowered her head and hid her eyes behind her long bangs and he noticed that her chin was quivering a little. He knew she was upset, but he hoped that she would settle down as the dance progressed. No matter how unhappy she was at the moment, he knew in his heart that over time he could reignite that long-lost spark between them.

Erianna's embarrassment gave way to resentment as the dance wore on. Matthew Prestwick had invaded her personal space. This was her world and he was not welcome in it. She wanted no part of this. It was time to put a stop to this charade.

"What are you doing here?" she demanded.

Looking up, she was not surprised to see the tender smile he offered her. But she was not amused. Those puppy-dog eyes and that little bit of dimple were not going to work on her. Not here. Not now. Not ever.

Erianna was gathering up a head of steam and Matthew knew that at any moment she could unleash it on him.

"What am I doing here?" he finally repeated her question. "What am I doing here? Well, at the moment I'm trying to come up with an answer that won't result in you ripping me to shreds right here in front of everyone."

Erianna scowled and looked away in annoyance. It took a lot of effort to control her emotions and she took several deep breaths as he led her around the dance floor. She prayed that this torture would come to an end, but the song seemed to have been looped and she felt trapped in a cage, on full display at a traveling carnival. After what seemed like an eternity the music finally ended and Erianna broke frame and made a beeline for the ladies' room.

Her world had just become a little less safe.

Matthew returned to his table and bid his farewell to Bernice and Sally. His plan had not gone as he had hoped. All he had accomplished was to alienate himself even more in Erianna's eyes. She had not accepted his presence at the club and made it crystal clear that he was not welcome here.

As he drove down the long row of parked cars toward the exit onto the main highway, Matthew wondered how he might set things right. *If only*—If only what? He had no idea what to do. *I'm not giving up. Not yet.* His happiness depended on it. And hers, too, for that matter. *But who am I to assume that she isn't happy?* Was it arrogant of him to believe that her life was unfulfilled? That his love for her would somehow make her life complete?

They had been so in love once. How could she reject him now? What had changed? All he knew for certain was that having Erianna in his life would bring him full circle. She had reawakened the joy that he had known for such a short time all those years ago. Until she had, by sheer luck, magically reappeared at the class reunion, he'd been unaware that there was a hole in his life. And now, having seen her again, he was powerless to control his desires.

Just before he reached the main highway he noticed a woman walking along the side of the asphalt-paved drive. He chuckled at the sudden feeling of déja vu. Erianna was obviously so determined to get away from him that she intended to walk home rather than endure his company at the club. It was clear, even after all these years, that she was still prone to running from uncomfortable situations.

He slowed to a stop and rolled down the passenger-side window. "Would you like a lift?"

"Go away, Matthew!"

"Come on. What are you going to do, walk home? You can't walk that far."

"I called an Uber."

He knew very well that she hadn't and he snorted. "You're a terrible liar, Erín. Let me drive you home."

"No!"

"Please—" he tried a different tack. "I'm sorry."

She stopped and crossed her arms in defiance, but wouldn't look his way. Matthew waited as she deliberated. If getting away from him was her goal, she had but two options. She could either continue walking or return to the club.

"Please don't try to walk all that way," he reiterated. "If you want, I'll take you back to the club. I won't go back in with you. I promise. Only *please* don't try to walk home alone."

Erianna had no intention of returning to the club. She had been humiliated in front of her friends and neighbors. At least that was how she saw it. The women in the ladies' room had pounced on her with questions about him the moment she went through the door.

She couldn't think of anything more dreadful than getting back in a car and being driven home by him for a second time in as many weeks. But she finally opened the door and climbed in beside him.

They rode home in silence, and when he turned onto Donovan Lane and passed through the gate she asked him to stop. Without another word she got out.

"Erin—"

"Go home!"

She began to jog down the lane.

Matthew sat in his car and rubbed the back of his neck. Then he turned off his headlights, but left the running lights on as he slowly followed her down the lane.

She stopped suddenly and pivoted. "Get off my land, Matthew. Get off my land and don't ever come back here again."

With that she took off to his left, climbed through a pasture fence, and headed toward the back of the equipment barn where he lost sight of her.

Matthew weighed his options carefully. He didn't want to leave things like this. Not like this. Should he run after her? That was a fool's errand. He didn't know the terrain and he'd never be able to catch up with her on foot in the dark.

Why was this perplexing woman always running? He pondered that question as he continued down the lane and pulled into Erianna's driveway. Shutting off his engine, he climbed out of the car.

He was fairly certain that he had arrived here before her, so he went around to the back of the garage, figuring that she would come in this way when she spotted his car parked out front.

The first quarter moon had already set in the west and the yard was in deep shadow, making it hard for him to see very far. He waited patiently, but she never appeared out of the darkness. He'd all but decided to call it a night when he noticed the faint smell of marijuana and he turned, slowly scanning his surroundings until the red glow of the joint tip caught his eye.

Someone was sitting under the oak tree that grew between Erianna's house and the stables on the long gradual downslope of the hill. He headed that way to investigate, and as he closed the distance he recognized Erianna sitting there. He approached her slowly, walking around the far side of the tree and settling himself to her right on a circular wrought-iron bench.

Erianna loved this grand old Chestnut Oak. Whenever she needed time to herself she would come here and sit under its enormous canopy. The Chestnut Oak was indigenous to the Appalachian area. The bark of the mature tree was dark brown and deeply furrowed. She had installed the scrolled, circular bench around it not long after she moved here. This was her quiet place, a place for introspection and contemplation.

She sat forward with her forearms resting on her thighs. After a time she sat up, staring off into the darkness.

Matthew broke the silence. "Do you know a woman named Bernice?" he asked. "I danced with her several times tonight. She thought I was a decent enough partner, considering I'm a newbie." He paused. "What did you think?"

Erianna sat back and sighed. "You were fine." The effects of the pot were beginning to take hold and her anger dissipated somewhat.

He sat beside her for several more minutes until she finally spoke.

"I remember the first time I came out here to this tree," she murmured as she put the rest of the unsmoked joint into an Altoids tin and slipped it into her boot.

It was right after Grace had a severe allergic reaction to the horse dander, but she didn't tell him that.

"My husband was an occasional pot smoker. I found his stash after he died, and for some reason, I don't know why, I held on to it."

"Did he pass after you bought the property and moved in?"

"No, he died before we moved here. And we didn't purchase the land. Hasn't Doro told you this story?"

"No," Matthew admitted. "Why don't you tell me?"

Erianna sighed heavily as the effects of the pot took hold. "My husband traveled for business," she began. "Ed was a wonderful man and a good provider. But he had one vice—he was a gambler."

Matthew turned to look at her as she continued.

"He was making sales calls in Cincinnati, and he went across the river to Newport and sat in on a private, high-stakes poker game. Gus Donovan was there that night." She pointed in the direction of the barn. "He's Pap's brother. He lives in an apartment in the stables now."

"Gus lost this land in a poker game?"

She nodded. Settling back, she turned slightly toward her house, lifting one leg onto the circular iron bench.

"All the legal paperwork had been filed with the court and the deed was transferred into Ed's name, but he didn't tell me about his windfall. I think he was probably planning on selling the property and I would never have known about it. But I found the deed in his safe deposit box when I closed it not long after he died.

"He was on his way home from another sales trip late one night when he died in an automobile accident on I-77, just north of Marietta, Ohio. A trucker fell asleep at the wheel, lost control of his semi, and it jackknifed across the road right in front of my husband's car. The trailer swung around and pushed Ed off the road. His car rolled several times, and he didn't survive."

"I'm sorry," Matthew said as he turned and eased her back against his shoulder. Without objection, she leaned against him.

"I came down here as soon as I could with every intention of returning this land to its rightful owner. But Gus would have none of it. When that didn't work I went to Pap and urged him to see reason and transfer the deed back into the Donovan name.

"We had several meetings, and somehow I was finally persuaded to settle here with my kids."

"Those Donovan's are a stubborn lot," he murmured near her ear.

"They surely are," she agreed. "And now we're just one happy, multi-generational family. My children are thriving and it all seems to have worked itself out somehow."

They sat in silence for a time, and Erianna allowed Matthew to bring her more fully into his arms. She sighed. The pot was working its magic and she felt boneless as she rested in his arms.

He cuddled her as they sat quietly in the dark, and after a time he began to sing. He had a decent enough voice and could deliver a fair rendition of the George Straight song *I Just Want to Dance With You* that they had danced to a short time ago at the club.

Erianna turned to look up at him as he sang. The words were so personal, so intimate.

And then he kissed her. Matthew lowered his tantalizing mouth to hers and kissed her. Longingly. Lusciously. Lovingly.

Erianna was captivated. When he ended the kiss she studied his mouth. All she could think of was that she wanted more. She wanted his lips on hers again. She couldn't stop herself. She initiated another kiss.

He brought her more fully against his chest and wrapped her in his arms. She couldn't get enough. She was tingling all over and her heart began to race. No one had ever made her feel like this, not even her husband during their nearly thirteen-year marriage. She was on fire, and deep down an ache began to grow.

Matthew came to his senses and ended the searing embrace before things got out of hand. "Easy now," he whispered huskily near her ear as he slowly disengaged her arms from around his neck. He brushed his lips across her jawline as he drew away from her slightly, putting a little distance between them as she regained her wits.

When he ended the kiss Erianna fought against the sudden loss of contact. But when he whispered to her she became aware of her surroundings. The color rose in her cheeks and she looked around to see if anyone was watching.

She moved away and rose to her feet. *Stupid pot*, she thought to herself. It had lowered her inhibitions and sent her to a place she never should have gone. She stood silently in the darkness with her hands on her hips.

"You need to leave," she said without looking at him. "It's late."

With that clipped comment she began walking up the hill toward the safety of her home.

Erianna stood by the outside entrance door to the garage and waited as Matthew walked to his car. She couldn't shake off the humming of her nerve endings, and try as she might to fight it the taste of him haunted her. She reached up unconsciously and ran her fingertips lightly across her lips. The tingling sensations persisted. She'd been dreaming about kissing him again every night since the class reunion. But she never could have imagined it would be like this.

Matthew turned to say goodnight—and froze in his tracks. She was so beautiful, with her golden hair shining in the soft glow of the overhead entrance light. When she brought her fingers to her lips he was instantly hard. He knew that her small gesture was not a tease, that she was feeling the same way he was.

He couldn't stop himself. Closing the distance between them, he grabbed her up into his arms, crushing her against his chest. He cupped the back of her head and kissed her senseless once again. There was no doubt about his intentions as he ravished her mouth.

Erianna melted into him in surrender. She wanted more. She was on fire, the heat was excruciating, unbearable, and she wanted him to make love to her.

Somehow she found herself inside the garage, pressed up against her truck. "Mmm," she moaned as he kissed and petted her.

"Erianna—" he rasped, his voice deep and husky with desire.

In the next instant he was dragging her by the hand inside the house.

Matthew knew from the times he had visited his sister that the first room on the right was an office. He hurried her through the door and pushed her inside the semi-darkened room.

"Erin," Pap called out. "Is that you?"

"Yes, Pap," Matthew answered in haste. "And Matt. I brought Erin home from the dance." With that he ducked into the room and quickly closed the door behind them.

Grabbing Erianna, he pinned her against the wall and brought her hands above her head, holding them loosely with one of his. He kissed her and fondled her with his free hand, exploring the luscious contours of her womanly curves.

Releasing her just long enough to tear off his shirt, Matthew picked her up and backed his way toward a tufted leather couch that sat against the wall to the left of the door. Easing them down onto it, he laid back with her in his arms.

She wriggled suggestively against him as their passion grew. Oh, how she wanted this. She was strung as tight as a violin string and she longed for more. So much more. As he explored her jawline, running his lips to a sensitive spot just under her ear, she tensed and her breathing became labored.

When his hands glided over her backside she gasped in pleasure and arched her back. He nipped and nibbled her earlobe and she let out a low, sexy moan.

Working to free the buttons of her blouse, he pulled the shirttails from her jeans and moved his hands lightly across her ribcage and around to her back. He was surprised when he could find no hooks on her bra and surmised that it must have a front closure. Changing gears, his deft fingers sought and released the front clasp of her bra and he moved the material to the side. The thrill of her naked skin against his nearly sent him over the edge.

Matthew gave her bottom lip a light nip and tingling waves of desire coursed through her. Everywhere his lips brushed seemed to set her skin on fire. When he pulled her higher on his torso and began to suckle her nipple she cried out.

In the next instant she was crouched on the floor in a tight ball. She panted heavily, trying to catch her breath as, with shaking hands, she fumbled clumsily to cover her nakedness.

Matthew started to rise, but that small movement startled her and Erianna leaped up, running to the attached half-bath and closing the door behind her.

He sank down and covered his face with his hands. *What have I done? How could I have done this again? I've chased her away.*

The click of the bathroom door lock felt like an explosion in his ears. Matthew got up quickly and brought his hand down to his throbbing erection, trying to relieve some of the pressure as he moved to the door.

"Are you okay?"

He heard her muffled cry of distress. The torturous sound was like having a bucket of ice water thrown on him.

Matthew knocked softly. "Erianna, please unlock the door. I'm so sorry."

He held his breath and listened. The sound of another door opening had him running across the room for the office door. He realized that she was leaving the half bath through the hallway door and he made a mad dash to catch up with her. But she had a good head start and was nearing the step that led from the hallway to the sunken living room by the time he rounded the corner into the hall.

"Erin—wait."

But she didn't. Matthew took off after her, passing the formal dining room on his left. To reach the stairs, one had to take a step down into the living room before reaching the stairs on his left. Matthew forgot that, and in the gloom he missed the step and went down on one knee. He moaned in frustration, regained his footing and raced up the stairs after her.

She took the steps three at a time and reached the safety of her bedroom before he could catch her. Once again he heard the lock fall into place just as he grabbed for the doorknob.

"Erin?" He listened for a response. "Honey, *please* let me in," he whispered. "I'm begging you. Don't shut me out. Please Erin, just open the door so we can talk. Just talk."

He kept his voice low, knowing full well that her children were asleep right down the hall.

Erianna stood inside her sitting room door and leaned heavily against it for support. The long, narrow room ran the length of the house, from the front window to the back. To the right, a recliner and an old sofa faced a small, ancient television on a stand near the front corner of the room. And in the smaller delineated space to her left she had set up a dedicated sewing nook.

She listened as Matthew made his plea. Her eyes began to tear up, and she covered her mouth with her hand to stifle the sob threatening to escape. She could bear no more. Moving silently across the narrow room she went into her bedroom, closing the door quietly behind her and turning the lock. Only then did she let go of her pain as she lay down on the bed and rocked herself to sleep.

Matthew sat with his back against the door and hung his head in shame. He felt like banging against the portal, but he knew that the noise might wake her kids. So he picked himself up and headed slowly down the stairs.

He stopped on the upper landing and looked out the front window into the darkness. Then he turned back to look toward Erianna's door. He'd made a real mess of things. Running his fingers through his hair, he sighed and wondered if this was the fatal blow from which he could never recover.

"I'm sorry," he murmured. And then he went downstairs, turned at the bottom landing and negotiated the three bottom steps into her formal living room.

He paused there and looked around the darkened room, lit only by the light from a lamp in the family room. The furnishings were grouped strategically, creating good traffic flow in the finely appointed room. She had pulled together a clean, tailored look that was both classic and timeless, and he noted that she had a flair for decorating. Accent pieces and wall hangings were kept to a minimum, but without the feeling of minimalistic sparseness. It was a beautiful room. A room he doubted that he would ever be invited into again.

He turned and made his way to the center hall, taking in the view of the family room and kitchen. He remembered the stone hearth that sat against the wall separating the family room and the half-bath down the hall. She had furnished this room with slightly oversized pieces that seemed to invite a person to come in, kick off his shoes, put up his feet and relax.

The long, overstuffed couch faced the fireplace and a recliner had been positioned in an L at the near end, with a square, glass and wood corner table anchoring the pieces in the open concept space. A rectangular dinette table was backed up against the couch. Four chairs were set around it, two on the long side and one on each end. A glass slider led to a three-season porch at the back of the family room,

Once again, Erianna had considered traffic flow when positioning the family room furnishings. He crossed the hall, moving along the designated pathway between the dinette and the kitchen, which shared the common wall between the two units.

He went to the kitchen and opened a couple of cabinets, looking for a glass. Filling it with water from the sink, he looked out through the back window, but with the task light over the sink on, all he saw was his own reflection. He nearly smashed the glass with his bare hands when he saw the man staring back at him. It took all his willpower to lessen his death grip and drink the water.

He turned and looked across the large, low countertop into the family room, noticing a floor pillow wedged against the couch and a laptop computer on the oval coffee table. He imagined Erianna's young son sitting there with his legs crossed, resting his back against the large pillow while he played on his computer and visited with his mother right here in this spot.

His heart sank, knowing that he would likely never be welcomed into the inner sanctum of the happy life she had described to him. Warm, homey, happy; those were all words he would use to describe her life here.

Inviting, welcoming, and comfortable —and off limits to him.

Chapter 6

Matthew felt defeated. He walked back to the center hallway and started for the garage door, but hesitated and looked up the stairs one last time to where Erianna was barricaded in her room.

"Matt, would you step in here for a moment?"

He'd been summoned, and went through to the door to obey Pap's order.

"What's going on?" Pap demanded in a clipped tone.

All the air went out of him and Matthew sat down heavily on a stool. He told Pap everything, from the very beginning. When he finished Pap remained silent for a while.

"That's quite a lot to take in," he finally said. "But, for right now I think you should go lock up next door and move your car out of Erin's driveway. Park it up beyond Doro's house and then come back here. We'll talk some more and see if we can hash this out."

Matthew nodded and did as he was told. When he came back in through the breezeway entrance Pap offered him a stiff drink, which Matthew gladly accepted. He settled into a recliner in the living room with a bottle of whiskey and a glass tumbler filled with ice, swiveling around to face Pap, who lowered his hospital bed to Matthew's level.

They talked for several hours and Pap, just like all the others, suggested that Matthew should back off and let Erianna live in peace.

"That's the same advice that everyone else is giving me. But I just can't do it. I know deep down that we're meant to be together. We're soul mates, Pap. I'm surer of this than I've ever been of anything. I'm not willing to give her up. I love her with all my heart and I know that I can make her happy, if only she'll let me."

They talked about Erianna's apparent memory loss and Pap was as perplexed about that as Matthew. Pap talked a little about her controlling parents and how they had railed at her when she moved to the Village of Berrington.

"I don't think those people want her to succeed or to be happy," Pap said. "They'd have rather seen her peddling burgers in Cleveland for minimum wage than living comfortably here with us. And they've never even bothered to come for a visit. It seems like they're out to destroy her."

"They're a miserable couple," Matthew agreed. "Erin mentioned that you were the one who talked her into moving here."

"Actually," Pap corrected him, "this living arrangement was Doro and Grace's idea. Doro was keeping an eye on Grace and Ned while the rest of us were in some meeting or other and the girls got to talking. They came up with this very workable solution and presented their proposal to us at one of the meetings."

Dorothy Donovan was a successful caterer in and around the Village of Berrington. When Doro met Bob, who was interning at the time with a veterinarian in Prestwick, they fell in love. They married and moved to Donovan Farm, as it was known then. Bob started his veterinary clinic and Doro began a small catering business.

"When Grace found out that Doro always wanted to build a house with a well-equipped restaurant-style kitchen so that she could grow her business, she asked Doro if she had considered building a new house next door. Doro pointed out that yes, she had always wanted to build her dream home, but that they needed to stay under the same roof with us, and we were already settled comfortably here.

"A little while later Grace mentioned that her mom needed help to survive financially. Without a college degree, Erin stood little chance of getting a decent paying job to support her family. The girls put two and two together, and here we are. Erin helps us with our needs, and Ginny and I are here to help

Erin with the kids so she can run the stables and earn a decent living. And with Bob just next door, it's working really well."

Matthew slept in the recliner and awoke to the smell of fresh coffee brewing.

"Good morning," Ginny greeted him as he stood up and stretched.

"Morning," he mumbled. His mouth was dry and it felt like his tongue was stuck to the roof of his mouth.

He had a bit of a hangover. It was his own fault for thinking that alcohol would deaden the guilt he felt. He asked for Ginny's permission to use the bathroom to freshen up and she pointed him in the direction of the guest bath.

By the time he came back Ginny had left for early mass with Bob, Doro and the boys. Matthew served breakfast to Pap, pouring two mugs of coffee and giving Pap a plate with a cinnamon roll that he suspected was homemade by his sister. With his queasy stomach, Matthew declined the sweet confection, opting instead to just sip his coffee.

He sat on the stool closest to the closed pass-thru door, and with his back leaning against the wall he dozed off. And then, like a fresh morning breeze, Erianna opened the door and walked in. She had a hairbrush handle in her mouth and a pair of brown loafers tucked under her arm. Her hair was a riot of gold and she worked to tuck her blouse into a knee-length skirt as she hurried past him.

She dropped her shoes on the floor beside Pap's bed. "Good morning," she greeted him in a sing-song voice as she bent from the waist and began to vigorously brush her hair. "I'm running a little late this morning. Are the kids up yet?"

It was obvious that in her haste she hadn't noticed Matthew sitting just inside the doorway, and he had a bird's eye view of her perfectly rounded backside and long, lean legs.

Pap tapped his computer screen. "Two-minute warning," he relayed over the intercom.

Matthew heard a loud thud. One of the kids must have jumped out of bed.

"Do you need anything before I go?" she asked.

"Nope, I've had my breakfast and I'm all set here."

Erianna pulled her hair into a loose bunch at the back of her head and she straightened up, tying it in place with the hairband on her wrist. With a few twists and loops she fashioned a knot, holding it with one hand while she reached into her skirt pocket to pull out several large hair pins. With a few more twists and the insertion of some additional pins her hair was secure.

Matthew watched in amazement. Without the aid of a mirror Erianna had created a lovely, casual updo. His Adam's apple bobbed as he swallowed. When he saw her swipe her fingers across her bangs his mouth began to water.

She dropped the brush onto the bed beside Pap and slipped into her loafers, tucking the last of the cream-colored blouse tails into an abstract, multi-shaded brown skirt. Then she leaned over and gave Pap a quick peck on his cheek.

"I'm stopping at the grocery after mass. Does Ginny have anything on her list?"

Ginny kept her list posted on the refrigerator and Erianna turned to go see if there was anything written there. On a sharply indrawn breath she jumped back against the side rail of Pap's hospital bed.

There, sitting on a barstool in Pap's kitchen, was Matthew Prestwick.

She sidled along the edge of the bed and then escaped through the door without uttering a single word. She kept moving toward the garage, grabbing her purse from a hook just inside the first floor laundry room opposite the office as she sped by.

"Your mom's on the move, you better come quick," Pap relayed through the intercom.

Grace appeared first. "That wasn't two minutes," she called out.

Ned was not far behind his sister.

Matthew walked to Pap's living room window and gritted his teeth as he watched Erianna back out of her driveway and tear up the lane.

"Well, that was painful to watch," Pap murmured.

Matthew rubbed at the back of his neck. He shoved his hands into his pockets and his shoulders slumped. "Oh, God." He began to pace.

"One thing's for certain. You can't come back here until she welcomes you back. I can't stop you from going to Doro's, but I don't want you here again without Erin's invitation."

"I know," Matthew solemnly acknowledged.

He paced in silence for a time.

"When am I ever going to see her again? If I try to call she's never going to talk to me. I don't know what to do."

Pap sat back, ruminating as Matthew continued to pace. He felt sorry for the guy.

"There is one thing I can think of." Pap paused for several beats and then asked, "Do you own a horse?"

Erianna was distracted, reflecting on recent events as the mass progressed. She was mortified by her behavior the night before and couldn't understand how she had let her base desires override her common sense.

After the death of her husband she had settled into a new life here in Berrington. Things were rocky at first, but as time went on she grew accustomed to her role as breadwinner and sole provider for her children, who were happy and thriving in their new environment.

Erianna had never been a social person, preferring to keep mostly to herself. Running the stables, while necessitating some interactions with others, afforded her the privacy she craved. And, in fact, other than her occasional nights out with Gus, she continued her solitary ways in her new surroundings, keeping her thoughts to herself and confiding in no one.

The sudden appearance of her high school classmate was unwelcome. As she reflected, she thought about some of the remarks he had made to her. Matthew was under the misguided impression that they had dated back in the day. And it was clear that he wanted to rekindle that relationship again. But nothing could be further from the truth. She would have remembered going out with him in high school. That was something a girl didn't forget.

And besides, what would a man like Matthew Prestwick, one of the most popular guys in her class, want to do with her? No, Erianna was certain that no relationship between them had ever taken place. But there was something, she wasn't sure what, but something about him that was familiar. Something that drew her to him. She could only surmise that it had to be her childhood fantasies that explained these feelings.

What happened the night before was, to say the least, distressing. How could she have let such a thing happen? Why would she go so far with a man she barely knew? The truth was that she wanted and had welcomed his advances. But that didn't negate the fact that she never should have indulged in or encouraged him to go so far.

She never felt such desire. Certainly not with her husband. Theirs was not a passionate relationship. He was nearly twelve years older than she, and Erianna had never been so aroused by Ed's sexual overtures.

Try as she might, she could not deny her attraction to Matthew. Even so, such goings on could *never* happen again. She led a well-ordered life. Her routine was settled and she did not want to encourage Matthew to continue his pursuit of a relationship with her. Under no circumstances would she allow him, or any man, to disrupt the status quo.

There will be no more interactions with my new nemesis. Period. End of discussion.

* * *

Erianna was mowing the lawns from the equipment shed to the stables on Thursday afternoon when a pickup truck hauling a double-horse trailer drove by. She noted that a horse was standing on the left side of the trailer.

That's odd, she thought as she turned her riding mower toward the Chestnut Oak. She didn't remember anything about boarding an additional horse. Cutting the engine, she strode down the hill toward the stables. Maybe the driver was lost and looking for another nearby boarding facility, so she went to investigate.

Gus was waiting outside when the truck pulled up. He waved hello as he walked toward the back of the trailer.

"Hello, Gus," Matthew called out as he climbed down from the cab.

"Hey. You're right on time."

Erianna stopped. *What in the world is going on?* She glanced at her watch. It was one o'clock sharp. She stood unmoving and listened as the two men met at the back of the trailer.

"How did he fare?" Gus asked.

"Just fine. No problems at all. He's used to being trailered and the traffic was light."

"That always helps," Gus agreed.

Erianna couldn't believe the casual camaraderie between these two men. She moved forward to break up the love fest.

"What are *you* doing here?"

Gus was surprised by her tone. "He's boarding his horse," he answered succinctly. "What does it look like he's doing?"

She glared at Gus in disgust. "I was unaware of this, Mr. Donovan," she hissed. "He's not welcome here."

Gus shrugged. The formality of her address didn't faze him. "His money spends just like anybody else's. And you can't afford to be turning away new business, so quit your bellyaching."

"Bellyaching!" she sputtered. "I want to speak to you in private, Gus—right now."

The stables were laid out in a modified T, with a wide central aisle intersecting a much longer row of south-facing stalls. A covered breezeway ran the entire south side of the stables, and windows interspersed along the outer wall could be opened for air circulation or closed to protect the horses from the elements, but still allow the horses a view of the pastures beyond.

They walked through the open doors on the west end of the barn and she moved toward the center T. "What do you think you're doing?" she spat when she was sure that they were out of Matthew's earshot.

"I'm bringing in a new paying customer."

"Well, I don't want his business." She shot her arm out in the direction of the parking area. "Go out there and tell him we're *not* going to board his horse."

"I ain't gonna tell him any such thing."

"Do you know who he is?" She was practically shouting in anger.

"Yeah, he's Doro's brother. So what?"

"So, I don't like him and I'm not boarding his horse."

"I don't care if you like him or not. All the paperwork is signed and he's paying double your usual fee. Plus he paid three months in advance."

"I didn't send him any contracts to sign."

"I know. I did. I'm perfectly capable of signing a new customer." Gus's voice was also starting to rise. "Now let's go out there and help the man unload his horse, goddammit."

"Watch your language," she declared.

He snorted, turned and walked away.

Erianna was furious, and she stood with her fists clenched as he walked back the way he had come and disappeared outside.

After taking several beats to collect herself, she followed Gus outside to the horse trailer, noting that they were talking as if they were old pals.

She was livid at Matthew's latest attempt to manipulate her.

While Erianna and Gus were off talking Matthew began the unloading process for his horse. In preparation for the trip travel boots, which covered his legs from the hock to the coronet, had been fitted to the horse's legs for protection, thus ensuring that any sudden movement of the vehicle would not harm the animal's legs as he moved inside the trailer to brace and balance him during the trip. His tail had also been bandaged from the top of the tail to the end of the dock and a trailer blanket was snapped in place over the horse's back.

Matthew unlocked and pulled down the rear ramp. Then he climbed into the trailer, leaving the butt bar in place as he moved along the empty stall to the horse's head. He petted the black stallion, making sure that he was calm enough to unload.

When Gus reappeared Matthew untied his horse, but left the lead line through the ring so that the animal would think that he was still tied up.

"I think he's ready to unload," Matthew told Gus as he walked to the back of the trailer.

He made his way between the horse and the outside wall to his head. Erianna appeared just as Gus unhooked the butt bar, and they stood on either side of the trailer to help guide the horse as Matthew gently pushed him back. The black Arabian backed out and down the ramp without incident, and Matthew rubbed the horse's chin to settle him as he took in his new surroundings.

He tied the lead rope to the side of the trailer and took off the horse's travel boots while Gus worked to untie the strings and remove the tail bandage. With that task accomplished Matthew removed the trailer blanket, untied the lead and began to walk his horse in a wide circle.

Gus and Erianna both examined the Arabian to check for any injuries he may have sustained during the trip.

"Well," Gus said, "he looks none the worse for wear."

He was a magnificent specimen and Erianna was slightly intimidated by his size. "How tall is this horse?"

"He stands a little over sixteen hands high."

That was nearly sixty-six inches tall, taller than any other horse in her barn.

She suddenly came up short. "This horse is a stallion," she declared.

"That's right," Matthew replied.

She turned to Gus. "Where are we going to put him?"

They moved away and began a quiet discussion, and when she finally nodded Gus moved off to prepare the agreed-upon stall.

Matthew continued to walk his horse for several minutes as Erianna stood and watched. When she heard Gus's shout she addressed Matthew in a professional, businesslike tone.

Okay, we're ready. Bring him—what's his name?"

"Ráfaga," Matthew supplied.

Erianna thought about that and asked, "How does that translate? Something like storm? Or black clouds?"

"Actually it's more like 'a gust of wind.'"

"Oh. Well, bring him along with me."

She headed into the breezeway as Matthew led his horse behind her. She stopped several times along the way, letting the new arrival get a chance to see and smell his new stablemates.

They moved slowly down the long, covered walkway. When they reached the T, Erianna stopped to let the horse look around. She had converted the last stall at the far end of the center aisle into her office. Just across the way were Gus's sleeping quarters. This wing also housed the tack room, storage room and several additional horse stalls.

While the horse became accustomed to the accommodations she asked Matthew more questions about the black stallion.

"The end stall on the east side will work best for us. Does he tolerate an end stall, or is he usually boarded in a middle stall?"

"An end stall is fine. At his previous boarding facility he was in a barn with only three stalls."

"Okay." They were moving again. "We'll keep the stall next to him empty until the dust settles. I only have one other stallion in my barn, but he's well past his prime. So I don't anticipate any major hurdles on that front."

As they came to Daisy's stall she looked out and whinnied several times, throwing her head and demanding attention. Ráfaga stopped and looked over. Daisy threw her head again and whinnied.

"Uh oh, this could be a problem," Erianna murmured. She took another lead line off a nearby hook and clipped it onto the other side of the stallion's bridle.

"Let's see what happens. Just follow my lead," she told Matthew.

He nodded in agreement. They let the black move closer to little Daisy, a bay Caspian pony. The mare threw her head several times and then blew softly. Ráfaga drew his nose toward the little pony and they greeted each other without incident. They spent several moments together as the pony assessed the new arrival. Finally, Daisy nodded her head in approval. It seemed as if the monstrous black stallion and the little bay pony had decided to become friends.

Erianna settled Ráfaga into the last stall on the east side of the barn. But when they moved off the pony became indignant that the stallion was leaving her and she began to kick her door. So Erianna went back to collect the distressed pony. She led little Daisy into the stall next to Ráfaga, and both settled happily into their new digs.

When Gus rounded the corner he noticed that Erianna was moving the ten-hand high Caspian into the stall next to Matthew's stallion.

"She's gonna need a shorter door," he called out.

Erianna nodded. "I'll switch them out in a minute."

Matthew would normally have offered to perform that chore, but decided not to volunteer. This was her domain. He had established a precarious foothold, but his status was far from secure and he didn't want to rock the boat.

As Erianna left to retrieve a cordless drill for the stall hinges Matthew walked beside her until she turned down the center aisle, and then he continued toward his trailer to collect Ráfaga's tack.

With the horse finally settled he left, grateful to Pap for his suggestion. Erianna had tolerated his presence, if only for a short time. It was progress, but there was a long road ahead.

Over the next few weeks Matthew visited several times, riding his horse around Erianna's cross-country course and schooling him in the ring. He ran into her a number of times, but they kept their conversations short and spoke only in generalities.

On the last Monday of the month Matthew took the day off and drove down to the farm. He pitched in and helped the young boys, who were on summer break, with their assigned chores. They were tasked that day with riding the fence lines south of Donovan Lane to check for breaches.

As they saddled up Matthew offered to ride along with them. Jamie and Theo headed out toward the southwest fence lines while Matthew and Ned rode the southeast miles of fencing.

Erianna happened to glance out of one of the open breezeway windows just as the group rode away. At first she thought that Matthew was going to break off from the boys and put his horse through the cross-country course, but when Jamie and Theo turned and headed west Matthew continued to ride along with her son.

What nerve! What gall! He thinks that if he ingratiates himself to my son that I'll change my mind about him. If it hadn't been for the fact that there were other borders in the area she would have whistled Ned back to the barn and put an end to them teaming up. *That man has no business interfering this way.* But, once again, she was forced to bury her displeasure and go on with her day.

As they rode along Matthew talked a little bit about himself with Ned, trying to let the boy learn something about the man who kept showing up and 'bothering' his mother, as Ned put it.

"Why are you a doctor, but you don't practice medicine?" he asked after Matthew pointed out that he had a medical degree. "Isn't that a waste of a lot of money?"

"I do earn my living from my degree," Matthew told him. "Just not in the conventional way. You see, when I was a junior in high school I started taking college-level classes in addition to my high school courses. I earned my college degree two years after high school and started medical school at twenty."

"Where did you go to med school?"

"I went to Northwestern and then did my internship in Chicago." Matthew chuckled. "That was a wake-up call, let me tell you. I wouldn't want to repeat that any time soon."

Ned nodded. "You must have seen it all."

"Yep."

"So if you don't practice, but you earn your living from your medical degree, what exactly do you do? I still don't get it."

"Okay, so here's how it went. I have a friend, his name is Chip. He was the red-headed man who was with me at your grandpa's house. After college he went to law school. We got together for a drink one Christmas when we were both home on break, and we got to talking about our futures and all that."

Ned made a face at that statement.

"Long story short, we decided to go into business together. He ran the start-up while I attended the Wharton School of Business at Penn, and I traveled back and forth to help as much as I could as we got our feet wet in the world of business. We now develop and sell medical devices and equipment. We look for the next generation of products and market them to doctors and hospitals to use when *they* practice medicine."

"I get it. Kind of like Dad, only he sold pharmaceuticals, while you sell equipment."

"Exactly."

Since Ned had mentioned his father, Matthew asked about him.

"Were you named after your dad?"

Ned looked over as they rode along. "That's kind of a long story."

Matthew was puzzled and asked Ned to explain.

"Well, my real dad's name was Edward. When I came along, my dad wanted to name me Edward Junior. But Mom said it would be too confusing, so she talked my dad into naming me Nathan Edward, and they call me Ned for short."

"That wasn't a very long story."

Ned giggled. "I wasn't finished."

"Sorry," he teased.

"My Grandpa Fowler's first name is Nielsen. Mom suggested we name me after both Grandpa and Dad, but apparently my grandpa threw a fit. He refused to let Mom name me Nielsen. Grandpa never liked his name, you see, and he just goes by Neil. Grandpa liked the name Nathan much better than Nielsen, so he asked Mom to name me Nathan. And she took the first letter from Nathan, N, and put it with Dad's name, Ed. Thus we get Ned, which is what everybody calls me."

Matthew sat back in his saddle and thought about what the boy had just said. "Nathan Edward, it's a very good name. I like it."

"Thanks."

"What exactly did you mean when you said your *real* dad?"

Ned looked askance at Matthew. "Well, you see, technically I have two dads."

"Two dads—you were adopted."

Ned smiled. *This guy is quick*. "That's right."

"I see. Now it all makes sense."

"Yeah, my sister and I are both adopted. And from the same mother and father. Grace and I are biological sister and brother."

"That's unusual," Matthew pointed out.

"I know. That's the long part of the story."

They rode along, stopping once to pull a small limb that had fallen from a tree on the adjoining golf course onto the fence. And little by little, the story came out.

Grace had been adopted by Erianna and Ed through a private adoption arranged by Neil Fowler, who was a gynecologist in Cleveland, Ohio. A local college student had become pregnant, and the couple decided to give the child up for adoption. Dr. Fowler was the young lady's obstetrician and he arranged for his son and his new wife to adopt the baby.

After college graduation the couple was still together, and so they married and moved to Columbus. The woman became pregnant with Ned, but she died in childbirth. And after trying to raise his son by himself for six weeks, the birth father realized that the best thing for his boy was to be with his biological sister. So he contacted Dr. Fowler again and the second adoption was arranged.

"His name is Phillip Keegan," Ned said. "We still see him, but not as much as before, because we live farther away now."

They continued to chat as they rode along until they met up with the Donovan boys, and then the four of them rode north in a string through the center of the property.

Matthew was brushing his black stallion after a long ride the following Thursday when the boys arrived to do their afternoon chores.

The ever-exuberant Theo ran up to say hello and told Matthew, "Today is Ned's birthday."

"It is? Happy birthday, Ned."

"Thanks."

"Did your mom make your favorite cake?"

"No, Doro did."

"Really?" Matthew feigned surprise, even though he'd figured as much. "What did she make for you?"

"Angel food cake. From scratch," Ned added. "Not the store-bought box kind that Mom used to make."

Matthew knew that his sister used a lot of their mother's dessert recipes, and her angel food cake was delicious. "Doro makes great desserts, that's for sure." He licked his lips. "Maybe I'll stop by and see if there's a piece left over for me."

"Sorry, you can't," Ned shook his head.

"Oh, well, that's okay."

Ned heard the disappointment in Matthew's tone and quickly clarified. "It's just that you can't come up to the house in those clothes. I'll bring you down a piece if you'd like. I always bring a slice of my birthday cake to Gus, so you can eat yours with him here."

"Do I need to dress up to come into your house?" Matthew teased the boy good-naturedly.

Theo giggled and Jamie scowled at his uncle.

"We can't wear barn clothes around Ned's house," Theo said. "Cause Grace is allergict to horses."

"Allergic," Ned corrected him. "Grace has allergies to animal dander."

"You're kidding!"

"Really," Jamie piped up. "She blows up like a blowfish." He puffed out his cheeks.

"How does she manage here with all these horses?"

"We have a clean-air filtration system at home," Ned explained. "When I go into the house, I come in through the basement 'clean rooms'. And when I'm done I change into clean clothes before I go upstairs."

"That's a clever idea," Matthew said.

"Mom and Grace came up with it. Grace helped Mom search online and they found a process that would keep the dander out of the house."

"Did you bring a change of clothes, Uncle Matt?" Jamie asked.

"Nope."

"Maybe you could borrow some clothes from Bob," Ned suggested.

"Yeah," the boys chimed up in unison.

"We're eating on our screened-in porch," Jamie said. "Let's go ask Mom if Uncle Matt can borrow some of Dad's clothes."

"Chores first," Ned reminded them.

"Ned?" Matthew cut in. "You should probably ask your mom if it's alright with her, too."

Jamie rolled his eyes. "Erin won't care. She's always saying 'the more the merrier'."

Ned nodded agreeably. "She won't mind, especially when I tell her that I invited you."

"Well," Matthew chuckled, "technically I invited myself."

They all laughed at that as they went off to take care of their chores.

When Ned finished he went looking for Matthew and found him sitting in his mother's office. "I'll get cleaned up and meet you behind the garage in fifteen minutes."

The boys took off for home. After asking permission and washing up as best as he could in Gus's small three-quarter bathroom, Matthew went to meet up with Ned.

"Go down these stairs," Ned began, pointing to an outside stairwell that had been excavated to provide direct access to the basement. The sloped steel storm doors were open and the concrete steps were sided by cinderblock walls.

"When you get inside, close the basement door behind you. There are three rooms, and each one has a printed instruction sheet. Just follow the instructions. When you get to the last room there'll be clean clothes for you to put on."

"Got it, thanks." Matthew started down the steps and entered the first room. After reading the instructions, he stripped off his dirty clothes and put them into a plastic bag with a drawstring closure. He put his boots into a second bag and stowed both in a cubbyhole near the outside door. Then he flipped a switch and a strong blower came on.

Erianna had installed an innovative filtration system to combat Grace's allergies, and Matthew was impressed by her ingenuity. He stood in the wind tunnel, which was preset on a timer. When the blower stopped he moved into the second room where he took a shower and dried off.

The last room, a half bath with a large locker-room style dressing area, was where he found the borrowed clothing and a pair of flip-flops. Once dressed, he headed through the basement rec room to the stairs.

He took a detour to his car to retrieve Ned's gift before heading next door. He had known that Ned's birthday was fast approaching, so he bought the boy a present and stowed it in his center console. As he walked along, Matthew made a mental note to start packing a complete change of clothes to keep in his trunk.

Chapter 7

The party was in full swing on Doro's back porch by the time Matthew arrived. Everyone was there, including Pap, who was sitting at the table in his wheelchair. Everyone, that is, except Gus Donovan, who was unwilling to participate in family gatherings to celebrate birthdays and other such special occasions.

Since the night that he gambled away his inheritance Gus had not touched a drop of alcohol. Pap told Matthew the story of how Erianna pleaded with his brother to stay in his life-long home, but Gus refused. He was packed and ready to leave his land in banishment, but she convinced him to stay when she told him that she could not run the stables without his help. If Gus didn't stay she would be forced to sell her newly acquired property and stay in northeastern Ohio with her children.

In his sobriety, Gus had been unable to face the shame of what he had done. He moved into his one-room quarters in the stables as a kind of self-imposed punishment. If not for Erianna's intervention he could easily have become a hermit, drifting from one place to another, unnoticed by others.

Matthew suspected that hanging out at the Hoot 'n Holler had been a regular occurrence for Gus in the past, and Matthew was glad that Erianna accompanied him for a night out twice a month. *It's funny*, he thought to himself. Erianna and Gus were very much alike in the sense that they preferred living semi-isolated lives.

Erianna seemed to be tolerant of Matthew's attendance at her son's tenth birthday party, and for that he was greatly relieved. He knew that she would not cause a scene, not here in front of the family, and he felt a little guilty about showing up unexpectedly, but not guilty enough to stay away. He would try every trick in the book to get back into her good graces, and if a little subterfuge was what was called for then so be it.

He kept to the background as the partygoers enjoyed their meal and each other's company. After the cake was served Ned opened his gifts. When he opened Matthew's present, Ned frowned slightly before he politely thanked the man. Then he showed the Popsocket to his mother.

"That's a very nice gift, Ned," she smiled encouragingly.

"What is it?" he mouthed the words.

Matthew offered an explanation. "It's a Popsocket phone grip for the back of your cell phone. You can pull out the handle and use it as a phone stand, and it pops flat when you don't need to use it."

Ned grinned as he thanked Matthew once again. Pap cleared his throat loudly and Grace rolled her eyes. The younger Donovan boys began to snicker, but Erianna turned and frowned at them. And then Bob laughed out loud, which set the whole group off. Before Matthew knew it everyone was laughing.

He was clueless. He turned to look at his sister with one eyebrow slightly raised. She finally relented.

"Ned doesn't have a cell phone, you imbecile. He's only ten."

"No phone?" He looked over at Erianna.

"None of us do," Ryan, the oldest Donovan son, told him. "Until we get our driver's license none of us is allowed to have a cell phone."

Matthew slapped his palm against his forehead and more laughter erupted. Only this time he joined in the merriment.

Ryan finally turned to Ned and said, "I'll take it. I've got my temps and I'll be able to use it a lot sooner than you will."

Before he headed to the stables the following Saturday morning Matthew pulled into Erianna's driveway and knocked on the wooden screen door from the garage into the house.

"Who is it?" he heard her call out.

"It's Matt. I have a present for Ned. Is he here?" he answered as he let himself in.

She peeked around the corner into the hall. She was tempted to lie and say that Ned wasn't home. The last thing she wanted was to have Matthew think that he could just drop by the house whenever the mood struck him. It was bad enough that she had to tolerate his presence at the stables. This was beyond the pale.

But, once again, fate intervened when Ginny came through the open door from her suite at just that moment and answered before Erianna had a chance to tell him to get lost.

"He's in his room," she said.

"Do you mind if I go up?"

"Sure." She turned to Pap and said, "Will you let Ned know that Matt is on his way up?"

Finally, he had made his way back into the house, but not by Erianna's invitation.

On the fourth of July Matthew and Doro's mom came down to visit. They all spent the day at the Berrington Country Club where Grace was now officially employed. She was still too young to be a paid employee. But that small technicality did not stop the junior entrepreneur. She had jumped into the pool to help one day when the swimming instructors were short-handed. From there it had been simple for her to brainwash everyone into believing that she was a member of the regular summer staff.

The owner, Harlan Connelly, who had a daughter Grace's age, called Erianna just the day before and worked out a quid pro quo arrangement with her. Grace would continue to assist with morning swim lessons and help at the snack bar for the lunch rush, and in exchange she would not be charged for use of the club facilities.

Both Grace and Ryan now spent the first half of their day employed at the Berrington Country Club, which bordered Berrington Farm on the eastern boundary line. Grace would, as usual, go to her swim team practice at dawn, while Ryan worked at the golf course starter's shack from sunup until midday. It was an ideal location for summer jobs, and Erianna was glad that they were learning the value of a day's work.

It was an easy walk to the country club from home, but Matthew noticed that Grace usually drove a golf cart and that she wore a filter mask over her mouth and nose when she scooted past the stables on her electric cart, always with a friendly wave as she rode by. Grace didn't seem to mind that she couldn't go near the horses. She was happy working and hanging out at the club.

Matt, Bob, Helen and Grace all played a round of golf before lunch that day. Everyone else gathered in the grassy area around the pool. Doro and Helen brought picnic baskets filled with an assortment of sandwiches and side dishes which were laid out on a picnic table. A large blanket was spread out on the lawn next to it under the shade of a maple tree where the children could sit and eat.

The boys ran around in their swim trunks and cavorted in the pool as the lazy day progressed. When Ryan walked over after a double shift, Helen and Doro served up slices of good old American apple pie for dessert.

Grace sat next to her mother on the blanket as they ate. She hounded her about the unfairness of the arrangement she had made with Mr. Connelly.

"I really think I should be paid the money you're saving in dues, Mom," she started up again. "You're profiting from *my* toil. How is that fair? This arrangement is inequitable. You didn't even ask me if I agreed. You've farmed me out as an unpaid summer intern," Grace pled her case.

To which Erianna replied, "I worked all the time when I was growing up. And I was never paid one red cent. Don't talk to me about inequitable." She tilted her head just a little. "I learned that hard work has its own rewards. It taught me responsibility and was a character-building experience."

When Grace objected Erianna shut her down. "Need I remind you, young lady, that you aren't even old enough to work here legally? Mr. Connelly is being very generous *letting you volunteer* here. And I'm not about to start paying you to be a volunteer."

Grace realized when she made the plea that her cause was all but lost. She may have been able to bluff her way onto the summer staff at the Berrington Country Club, but her mother was not such an easy mark and her argument fell on deaf ears.

Matthew leaned over and mumbled, "Give up yet?"

Grace sighed in defeat. She had practiced her speech several times before confronting her mother, but it was all for naught. "Yeah, I'm sunk. Mom's a hard sell and that was the best I had."

Matthew offered her a small smile. "Better luck next time." He patted her shoulder in commiseration.

And once again, Matthew managed to ingratiate himself with her child. By now both had accepted him as a regular visitor and a nice guy to hang out with. Unfortunately, the wall that Erianna had built was also starting to crack.

Erianna went to the stables to look after the horses just before the fireworks began that night. Some did not like the noise and bright flashes of light, so she and Gus needed to be onsite in case one or more of the animals acted up in their stalls.

Matthew strolled over just as the fireworks began, and she grew wary when he showed up. Her mind conjured up images of the last time she had been alone with him.

"The view from this vantage point is just as good as from the Country Club," he observed, but she didn't reply. He could sense that she was a little bit skittish, just like some of the horses were likely becoming.

They watched the display in uncomfortable silence. When the finale began several of the horses acted up and Erianna went to calm them.

Matthew soothed Ráfaga with a gentle head rub as Daisy whinnied softly to her stablemate. The black stallion settled as the crescendo ended and the echoes died off. Then he said goodnight to Erianna as he passed by her on his way out to his car.

He spent the whole ride home praying that Erianna would come to see that nothing was going to happen between them without her invitation. He was certain now that she had no memories from her seventeenth year. But he did.

He remembered everything, including the fact that she had loved him. Every bit as much as he loved her. His memories hadn't been lost or forgotten. He felt the same way he always had. Matthew was madly in love with Erianna Fowler.

How do I go about winning her back? He had a lot of thinking to do. He needed to gain her trust, but how? Would it be possible to move forward if she couldn't remember the past, and how would that relationship manifest itself?

Erianna loved him once. Would he be able to rekindle those feelings in her now? Or would whatever trauma she suffered have buried those emotions so deeply that she would be incapable of ever loving him again.

Matthew was convinced that something dire must have happened. People didn't just lose their memory for no apparent reason.

He went to bed that night certain of his need for Erianna's love. There had to be a way to win her back, and he considered every possible avenue. He wracked his brain for a solution, some way to help her recover those long lost memories.

He needed her, but Matthew was afraid. The stakes were high and he had everything to lose if she spurned him. A long and difficult road lay ahead, but failure was not an option. He was unwilling to walk away. Because walking away meant giving up his future, his happiness, his life.

Flowers? Chocolates? Romantic moonlit walks? Matthew considered and rejected a whole host of ideas. He needed something personal, something intimate, something that might spark her memory. Erianna could easily be spooked, and he would have to bide his time and ease his way back into her heart.

Low key by nature, Matthew moved with a subtle style. Laid-back and easygoing, he was not overly animated or showy. His mother had pointed out once that his calm and steady demeanor was why he was so good with horses. That same approach was just what was needed here.

At last he chose a plan of action. Matthew could think of no better way to Erianna's heart than with his words. And so he decided to start writing to her. It was old-fashioned, he knew, but Erianna was a bit old fashioned and sentimental herself. Maybe relaying his thoughts and feelings in prose would spark her interest.

It would take time, but Matthew had one thing going for him. He was a very patient man.

While on a business trip to Seattle he wrote:

Dear Erianna,

When I look out at the dreary view from my hotel room as the rain pours in sheets across my window, I close my eyes and imagine the rolling hills of bluegrass and miles of fencing in your picturesque Village of Berrington. Each place I visit now pales in comparison to your little corner of paradise. I can think of no other place as peaceful and serene.

Maybe next Monday, if you have time, we could go for a ride. I need a good workout as much as Ráfaga. I look forward to it.

Matt

Erianna had no idea what to think when she received the hand-written letter. No one wrote letters and sent them through the mail anymore. What in the world did this mean? Was Matthew taking a page from her book when she wrote the note to Helen Prestwick?

He'd used his own stationery, just as Erianna had when she wrote to his mother. She doubted that he normally carried personalized stationery when traveling, and she was at a loss as to his motive. Did Helen Prestwick show the letter of apology to her son? Was that why he was writing to her in this manner?

This has to be some kind of ploy. But she could not make heads or tails of the tactic.

She re-read the letter several times over the next few days. Maybe Matthew was just homesick and made the offhand observation about the pastoral beauty of the area in passing, as one would complement the hostess of a party about her lovely home.

But his suggestion that they take a ride together was much more concerning. It could only be interpreted as an attempt to move from a professional relationship to a more personal one.

Erianna tried her best to figure out what Matthew was up to, but there were too many variables and she could reach no reasonable conclusion. So, in the end she made the decision not to acknowledge or respond to the letter. She would evade.

On Monday morning she took Ginny and Grace to Lexington for a day of shopping, dinner and a movie. By the time they got home it was dark and Matthew had come and gone without Erianna having to interact with him.

Two days later another letter arrived. Matthew wrote about the City of Prestwick and his grandmother, Lucinda.

> ...she has been widowed far longer than she was married. I often wondered why she never remarried, but I think that I understand her a bit more now. Although she rarely talks about Grandpa, I believe she loved him with all her heart and never found that passion again with anyone else.
>
> Do you believe in 'one true love'?
>
> Matt

Matthew showed up before dawn to help with morning chores.

"Good morning," he greeted her as he walked down the breezeway toward Ráfaga's stall. He didn't stop to chat and didn't ask if she'd received his letters. He just walked on by as though it was just another hum-drum morning.

Erianna was bewildered. She didn't like that he showed up whenever the mood struck him, and she certainly wasn't prepared to deal with his cool, laissez faire attitude. She stood outside the stall she had been mucking and watched him move off toward the opposite end of the stables, having absolutely no idea what she should do next.

Luckily, she was spared from dealing with Matthew Prestwick and his odd Jekyll and Hyde behavior. After morning chores he saddled his stallion and rode out to run Ráfaga through the jumps on the cross-country course. By the time he got back, washed, groomed and set his horse out to pasture Erianna was just starting a class.

He walked down the center aisle and stopped at the open barn doors to watch her in the fenced riding ring. The first thing he noticed was how quiet the group was. There were six children of various ages riding ponies and small horses around the ring. Two people, one on each side of the horse, were helping assist the students, and two of the ponies were on a lead line, one held by Ned and the other by Theo.

Each horse had been selected specifically for the age and size of the child. Erianna had a stable that included horses of various breeds and sizes, from ponies like Daisy to a quarter horse standing at sixteen hands.

This class was obviously some kind of therapeutic program for special needs children, although Matthew wasn't sure which group was represented here. He asked Erianna about it when the kids finished their rides and the horses were unsaddled and brushed.

"It's an equine therapy program for children with autism," she replied as she gave Daisy's coat a good brush. "I read an article about how the rhythmic movement of horseback riding helps autistic kids to focus better.

"I'm not a certified therapist, so I looked up the Kentucky Advisory Council on Autism website, and from there Grace helped me navigate through the process. We contacted Anita Tasker, a certified therapist from Georgetown. She does all the coordinating and brings a group for a lesson every other week, weather permitting. All I do is provide a free facility for them."

Matthew smiled, one of his bright, broad smiles that never failed to bewilder her. "That must be very rewarding."

Erianna looked up at him through her heavy bangs. "It's really not that much."

"It's more than most," he pointed out.

"Well, we should all try in our own small way to do what we can for others." She shrugged.

"To whom much is given, much is required," he said with a brush of his hand across her back. "I'll take Daisy for you and put her out to pasture with Ráfaga."

He took the Caspian's lead and with a nod he took off toward the pasture gate.

Erianna stood watching as he left, as nonchalantly as he had come. She could still feel the heat from his light contact on her back.

That Saturday night Matthew went to the Hoot 'n Holler. He'd been going nearly every Saturday since his first week and had established himself as a semi-regular at the club.

When she walked in with Gus that evening they made their way to their usual table and sat down with friends. Erianna glanced Matthew's way as she passed and he brought two fingers to the brim of his black hat in recognition of her arrival. Then he turned his focus back to the attendees at his standing table by the bar.

Bernice noted Matthew's greeting and her curiosity was peeked. She had suspected all along that his efforts to learn how to dance were due to his attraction to Erianna Fowler.

When Sally asked him for a dance Matthew happily agreed. "It would be my pleasure." Escorting her to the floor, he took her in frame. And when the song ended they returned to their table.

Matthew had continued his private lessons and found that he very much enjoyed country-western dancing. He was working on mastering the waltz, a much more complicated dance than the two-step, with Sharon Zimmer at the Silver Spur.

"I've been practicing my waltz," he said to Bernice. "Maybe later I'll get up my nerve and ask you to try it with me."

As it turned out Bernice, a widow, was his favorite dance partner. She moved very lightly on her feet for someone of her advanced years, and just like his private instructor, she helped him smooth out the rough edges.

She smiled at him. "Sure. But maybe you should ask that young lady over there for a waltz." She pointed in Erianna's direction.

Matthew followed her motion and then turned back with a hint of a smile. "I don't think I'm ready for that just yet."

"Afraid you'll flub it up and embarrass yourself?"

"Exactly. Sounds a little foolish, right?"

"Nope. It's refreshing. I can see how much you want to impress her."

Sally agreed. "If only my Yancy had been as romantic back in the day. Oh well, that's water under the bridge now."

"At least he doesn't mind when you come here without him," Bernice pointed out. "You're very lucky to have him. Most men would object to their wives dancing with other men. He really is a gem and you know it."

Erianna noted that Matthew danced several times with a few different women. He seemed to be feeling right at home and enjoying himself as he shot the breeze with a small group of people by the bar. She had the distinct impression that he'd met and talked with these people before.

When a couple walked past him, Matthew smiled and said a few words to them. The lady said something back and Matthew nodded. He followed them toward the dance floor, stopping along the way to ask a woman to dance.

"You gonna spend the whole night gawking?"

Startled, Erianna turned her attention back to Gus.

"Your food's getting cold."

She lowered her head and hid her blush from view as she began to eat. Until Gus had so bluntly pointed it out, Erianna had been unaware that she was staring. She couldn't help it. She'd always had a crush on Matthew and had often watched him surreptitiously from afar when they were in school.

But she wasn't a silly child anymore and her juvenile fantasies were pointless now. It was too late for such nonsense. Erianna was a grown woman with two children who had their own dreams of fairy tales come true. And so she made a concerted effort to put a stop to her musings and enjoy her night out with Gus.

Matthew was having a drink with Bernice and Sally when a Barnyard Mixer was announced. Erianna had just finished the previous dance and was standing with her partner near Matthew's table. The two women, escorted by Matthew and another acquaintance, partnered up and escorted the ladies to the floor.

Matthew somehow maneuvered his way to the spot on Erianna's left with Bernice, while Sally and her partner fell into line on Erianna's right.

"Hello," Matthew said with a friendly smile just before the music started. With Bernice's lead-in he began to dance the circuit in unison with the other couples, and Bernice was swung on to the next man as Erianna was handed off into his arms.

"Are you having a good time?" he asked her.

"Yes," she nodded, tilting her head down slightly to evade his scrutiny.

And off she went. With Bernice and Sally on either side of her, they completed several circuits on the dance floor. Sally's exuberant cheerfulness was catching and Erianna found herself thoroughly enjoying the dance.

When the song finally ended the band took a break, and the three women found themselves near Erianna's table on the opposite side from where they began. Bernice and Sally chitchatted pleasantly with Erianna as Matthew made his way through the crowd to join them.

"That was fun," he said a little breathlessly.

"Very," Sally agreed.

"Do you ladies know Erin Fowler?" he said by way of introduction.

"Yes," Sally extended her hand. "I've seen you here before. It's nice to put a name to your face. I'm Sally Holloway, and this is my friend Bernice Anderson."

"It's nice to meet you, Mrs. Holloway." Erianna shook her hand. "Hello, Mrs. Anderson. I believe I know you from church."

"That's right," Bernice shook the younger woman's hand. "I'm the organist at Immaculate Heart of Mary," she explained to Matthew. "It's very nice to meet you. Please," she added, "call me Bernice."

"Erin Fowler," Sally repeated the name several times. "Why do I know that name?"

Erianna's radar went off. When a local person began with that line what usually followed was a critical judgment about her 'stealing the land' from the Donovans. She was aware of the gossip and had been dealing with it since she moved here.

"Erianna owns Berrington Farm on the east side of town," he supplied, unaware that he was fueling the fire. "Have you heard of it?"

"Berrington Farm. Yes, I have."

Erianna braced herself for what would come next. She'd heard it all before.

"But I don't—" Sally frowned. "There's something else—" She tried to remember where the Fowler name had come up, and in what context.

Bernice cleared her throat. "Sally—" she cautioned her friend with a slight note of warning in her tone. Both Bernice and Sally were well aware of the gossip, but Bernice did not agree with the general consensus of many in the Village. From what she'd observed of the Fowler family they were upstanding citizens and pious worshipers at Immaculate Heart.

"I've got it!" Sally pronounced proudly. Erianna held her breath as Bernice placed a staying hand on Sally's sleeve.

"My granddaughter is in your son's class in school."

Bernice expelled an audible sigh of relief.

"What's his name? Teddy?"

"Ned," Erianna supplied.

"That's right," Sally confirmed with a clap of her hands. "My little Jennifer did a history project with your Ned. They got an A plus and she thinks that he is the smartest boy in the whole school. From what I hear, all the little girls are smitten with him," she finished with a cheery smile.

Matthew had picked up on the subtle change in mood and made a mental note to dig into what that was all about later. He excused himself and went over to say hello to Gus and a couple of his buddies who were shooting the breeze nearby as the ladies continued to chat.

From what he observed, getting out every now and again was good for Gus. Preferring to stay near his regular table, Gus didn't wander over to the bar. Instead, he sat and chatted amiably with patrons whom he had probably known for many years.

By the time the band resumed with the playing of a waltz Erianna had made her way back to her table. Matthew offered her his hand and she allowed him to escort her onto the dance floor.

"They're a very striking couple," Bernice observed as she and Sally watched Matthew dancing with Erianna. "It's a shame what people are saying about her."

"She's a lovely lady," Sally agreed. "Very demure and polite."

"Mmm," Bernice nodded. "Have you noticed the way he looks at her?"

Sally wasn't looking at his eyes. "Do you see the way he moves? Wow! He's one sexy hunk of male flesh."

"Pfft," Bernice made a dismissive sound. "You're a married woman, Sally."

"That don't mean I can't look."

They watched Matthew and his lady waltz by again. He led her with confidence and self-assurance through the dance steps, his restrained movements and easy, natural bearing reminiscent of men with much more experience on the dance floor.

"Does he remind you of anyone?" Sally asked after a time.

"Like who in particular?"

"Well, his subtle moves are deliciously sexy," Sally continued her earlier vein of thought. "And with that wide Stetson and those broad shoulders, he kind of reminds me of—a young George Strait."

"Mmm. I didn't notice until you brought it up. But I think you've hit the nail on the head."

"I wonder if he knows that he moves just like George Strait," Sally thought out loud.

"And I'm wondering if she notices it, too," Bernice added.

There was a note on his car seat when Matthew left Berrington on Sunday afternoon after a long trail ride with a group that Ryan had taken out.

Matthew,

I had a very nice time last night. Meeting your friends Bernice and Sally was a pleasure, and so was the dancing.

E

"I think there's been a break in the case," Matthew told Chip at the office the next day.

Chip and Nancy had been Matthew's confidants and were both supportive of his efforts to befriend Erianna Fowler.

Matthew pictured the personalized notecard with her name *Mrs. Edward P. Fowler.* Her beautiful flowing handwriting was a far cry from his bold block lettering.

"Maybe we should give her a call," Chip suggested when he heard the news. "Set up some kind of get-together. I bet I can sweet talk her into taking the kids for a trail ride. It might help to have all of us become friendly again."

"Good idea, but not yet," Matthew replied. "It's much too soon for that. One little note does not a victory make."

Chip laughed. "Well, keep on waxing poetic like you have been, my friend, and you'll have her eating out of your hand in no time."

"Very funny," Matthew mumbled. Chip laughed again, that infectious sound that made people around want to join in.

Matthew scowled at his friend.

It was mid-July and the heat was oppressive. Erianna and Doro had taken the three younger boys shopping for clothes and shoes, and then to baseball practice. But the heat was unrelenting, and the women decided to leave the boys at the ball fields and come home.

"I'll text Bob and ask him to pick them up on his way home from the clinic," Doro said. "It's too hot to sit on these metal bleachers."

Erianna happily agreed. She could use the time to catch up on her paperwork. Doro dropped her off and Erianna headed upstairs to stow Ned's new clothes.

On her way to the office she stopped at the dinette table and gathered up the paperwork from the stables' office that she had brought home earlier.

She walked down the hall and found Matthew in her office, sitting in the middle of the leather couch with his computer and work papers spread out over the coffee table. She listened in from the hallway door as he took a conference call, conducting his business with his assistant and two other gentlemen.

"Okay, Monday at ten. Will that give you enough time to put the presentation together?"

"Plenty," a nameless voice answered.

"Okay, I'll see you then." The line disconnected and a female voice spoke up.

"Matt, the jet isn't available for you on Sunday night. Chip is flying back from Vancouver on a red-eye flight and he doesn't land until eight o'clock Monday morning."

"That's alright. Go ahead and book a commercial flight from Cincinnati. And see if the company plane is available to bring me home. I'd like to swing by Travonelly Medical Technologies for a visit on my way back."

The plant manufactured a widely used medical isotope used in hospital Tomography machines. The startup company had been one of Chip and Matthew's first investments, and Travonelly was doing very well, both for the community and for their bottom line.

"Looks like that might be doable," the woman said. "I'll call Mr. Travonelly's assistant and let him know you're coming."

Matthew noticed Erianna standing in the doorway just then and he immediately wrapped up his call. "Thanks, Allison."

He stood up. "Hello."

"Hello."

She stood there waiting for Matthew to explain himself, which he did forthwith.

"I usually work from my car when I'm here, but it's just too hot today. Sometimes I set up shop in Pap's living room. But he said that you would be gone for most of the day and he thought you wouldn't mind if I got out of his hair and worked from here."

Matthew shifted his weight to one leg and looked back at the files spread out over her coffee table.

Erianna listened to his explanation as she surreptitiously cast quick glances at him. The last time they were in here—she couldn't think about that now. *Concentrate on what he's saying, for heaven's sake.*

Matthew waited, but Erianna still didn't reply, and he knew where her thoughts had gone. "You're home early," he pointed out, trying to shake those images from her mind and bring her back to the present.

She cleared her throat softly and finally found her voice. "Yes. I—" She suddenly remembered the paperwork she had clutched to her chest. "Actually, I came home early to get some work done myself."

"Sure. I'll just gather this up and let you get to it."

Matthew didn't try to press. She stood timidly in the doorway while he collected his things, and as he passed by his cell phone rang.

"Hey, Chip." Clutching his computer and jumbled papers in one arm, he walked down the hallway and over to Pap's place with his phone to his ear.

Erianna retreated into her office and closed the door. She leaned back against it and expelled a deep cleansing breath. She didn't like seeing him in here. He unnerved her.

Chapter 8

Everyone was gathering at Ginny's for supper. After finishing up with her accounting work Erianna went upstairs to wash up before she headed over to help Ginny with the large family-style meal.

Having been ousted from Erianna's office, Matthew once again set up shop in Pap's living room. The women worked alongside each other in relative silence so as not to disturb him while Pap read the latest mystery novel from a new fiction writer that Erianna had discovered on one of her regular trips to the library. This was the author's second novel and Pap was engrossed in the murder mystery.

Ginny stirred a pot of risotto cooking on the stovetop while Erianna worked on putting together a fresh tossed salad with sides in small vessels around the wooden salad bowl. The large wood platter resembled a sunflower, and each petal-shaped container was filled to the brim with julienned vegetables, small cherry tomatoes and various other accoutrements.

Bone-in chicken pieces baked in the oven and the aroma was irresistible. The atmosphere was homey and inviting. Matthew wanted this. He yearned to be a part of this lively, fascinating family. When he witnessed the camaraderie going on around him in the multi-generational family unit he realized how isolated and lonely he was.

"Dinner in fifteen," Pap announced to everyone over the ranch-wide intercom system at Ginny's directive.

Erianna set the salad and several bottles of dressing on the end of the bar and approached Matthew once again, standing quietly as he spoke on the phone.

"No, I think we should pass on that. There just isn't enough innovation to market that model. It's only a marginal upgrade and hospitals aren't going to invest in new equipment until their current machines become obsolete."

"Okay," Chip could be heard on the other end of the line. "I'll have the Research Department keep an eye on it, and I'll review it again in six months."

Matthew had watched her advance to where he was working. He couldn't help but notice. She was so lovely, he had to have been blind not to see how appealing she was. He hung up with Chip and sat back on the couch, spreading his arms across the cushions as she stood there.

Erianna had a timeless, classic elegance, with a flair for fashion and a unique style. Her sleeveless white button-up shirt was tucked into a pair of blue knee-length shorts, finished with a skinny belt, the style reminiscent of the early sixties. Matthew was certain that the outfit was her own creation. She had taken the best of the fashion from the time of *The Beatles* and brought it into modern day. He noticed that she never seemed to tug at her clothing and she always appeared to be cool and comfortable. She was a feast for his eyes.

"Um," Erianna started, and faltered.

"I'm in the way again."

She tilted her head down a little. "Well, it's just that we're about to eat and it's going to get quite noisy in here. Why don't you go back and work from my office, I can see how busy you are."

"Are you sure?" He couldn't believe she was making the gesture.

"I'm sure." She smiled just a little and leaned in so that he would hear her when, in a hushed voice she said, "I should have offered to let you stay there and work in the first place. I don't know what happened to my manners."

Matthew leaned forward and pressed a button on his computer. "I'm done for the day, Allison. You can go on home now."

"You have that eight a.m. breakfast meeting tomorrow, Matt."

"Okay. I'll stop in first and then walk over."

Erianna was surprised that his assistant was still on the line, but Matthew wrapped up quickly and shut down his laptop.

"Thanks for the offer," he smiled, showing just a bit of dimple in his left cheek. "But I'm about done for the day."

"Well, then, stay and eat," Pap inserted mere moments before the boys came barreling through the side door and bedlam ensued.

On Saturday afternoon Erianna found Matthew in her office once again. He and Grace were working from her laptop on the coffee table as they sat on the floor with their legs crossed. Papers were scattered all around them.

"Do your charges cover the cost of overhead?" he asked Grace.

"Where would I find that?"

"Here," he called up a page on the screen. "See how you can track your expenses from this spreadsheet?"

"Yeah, I get it."

Matthew asked her another question, to which she responded, "Won't I have to decide which is more profitable, filling my empty stalls with horses I own and can rent out or boarding horses and collecting the fees to cover overhead?"

"Overhead, plus a profit margin. Let's say for the sake of this example a ten per cent profit."

Grace followed Matthew's logic as he guided her and she posed several questions of her own.

"Okay. So I'd have to run the numbers both ways, right?"

"Right, it's called a cost benefit analysis. But I think that's a little advanced for you."

Grace's head snapped up from the papers she was studying. "What kind of crack is that?"

Matthew stopped short.

"Are you insinuating that girls aren't smart enough to understand cost benefit analysis reports?"

"No, no—whoa." He held his palms outward to ward off her remarks, but Grace had been insulted and was gearing up for a blow.

"I'll have you know that girls can understand *lots* of things—"

"Now just hold on a minute," Matthew snapped back. "You're putting words in my mouth, young lady."

"I'm not your young lady," she retorted.

And the sparring began. Matthew gave as good as he got, but Grace was an old hand at verbal debate and Erianna stepped in to put a halt to it before things got out of hand.

"Grace," she interrupted her daughter. "You're being disrespectful to your elder."

"But—" Grace stopped short when she looked up at her mother. She crossed her arms and sat back in a huff, but refrained from saying anything else.

Matthew tried one last time to rephrase his words as delicately as possible. "I only meant to say that it would be hard for me to explain that to you. I'm not a teacher and I'm not sure where to begin."

"You could go to the library and check out a book on the subject, Grace," Erianna suggested. "Give it a read through before you ask Dr. Prestwick any more questions."

He noted the use of his formal name, but wasn't sure why. Grace and Ned had been calling him Matt for a long time. Coupled with the 'elder' remark, he figured that Erianna was subtly reprimanding her daughter for her inappropriate behavior.

"That's not a bad idea, Grace," he said. "Not a bad idea at all. I could go with you. How big is your library? Maybe we could find a textbook that would help guide me."

"Guide *us*," Grace corrected. "I'm not sure what we will find, but maybe the high school will have an economics textbook we could borrow. Mom could get us in if we don't find what we need at the library. She's friends with the custodian and his wife."

They were off and running. Scooping up and securing all their paperwork and Grace's computer, they set off for the Berrington Public Library, and they didn't come home until after it closed at six o'clock.

"Are you hungry?" Erianna asked her daughter when they got back.

"No thanks, we stopped for fast food." With a wave of thanks, she headed upstairs with her arms full of books.

Matthew approached Erianna. "She's a natural-born businesswoman. She has a real head for numbers and calculations."

Erianna did not, and she admitted as much to him. "She's inquisitive, but I'm not a good mentor when it comes to business. She's been trying to help *me* with my finances, but it's like the blind leading the blind. I'm never going to understand the nuances. Grace is going to have to negotiate those waters without my help. All I can manage to do is to stick the numbers into the right columns."

This was the first actual normal conversation they had had since the night of the high school reunion. Matthew resisted the urge to jump in with an offer to help. Instead he made a simple suggestion.

"Why don't you start by subscribing to the Wall Street Journal? I'm pretty sure she would enjoy reading it, and she could pick up a lot of information that way. She really likes to learn."

Erianna smiled. "Yes. She does."

Matthew went for a long ride on Sunday and stayed for dinner with Erianna and the kids that evening. They ate at the rectangular dinette table positioned against the back of the couch. The kids sat side-by-side and Matthew took the seat opposite Erianna, who was sitting nearest the entrance to the kitchen.

He watched her school Grace in Latin and Ned in Roman History as they ate their supper.

"Are you working on summer school assignments?" he asked.

"No," Grace replied. "We're working on Mom's assignments."

Matthew was both surprised and impressed. Apparently, Erianna was homeschooling her children in addition to their regular schoolwork.

After supper he helped Ned clear the table as Erianna finished reviewing Grace's homework before she wandered off to her room.

Then Erianna pitched in, and the kitchen was cleaned and leftovers stored in no time.

Matthew had seen the Donovans tease Erianna about her 'marginal cooking skills', but she took the ribbing good-naturedly. She had served creamy scalloped potatoes with sliced smoked sausage in a béchamel sauce, and Matthew found it to be quite tasty.

"Thanks for letting me stay, that was a very good meal," he complimented the chef.

"Sausage and potato casserole was one of Dad's favorites, right Mom?"

"That's true." She gave Ned a little tug, and he gave her big hug in return.

"I'm going to my room," he announced. As he passed by, Ned offered Matthew a hug as well. He picked the boy up into his arms and gave him a huge bear hug. And then Ned scampered off.

Matthew collected his phone and keys from the kitchen counter. On his way out he paused to give Erianna a gentle side hug and brushed his lips across the top of her head.

"Thanks for the invite," he said. "I'm going to pop over and visit with Pap before I head home."

And with that he was gone, leaving Erianna to wonder what had just happened and how he had so shrewdly managed to crumble her defensive wall.

"She's amazing with those kids," Matthew said as he and Pap shared an after-dinner drink. "A subject comes up and they run with it. I've never seen anything like it."

Pap nodded. "Once Erin realized how smart they are she began fueling their minds. Those two are like sponges. They absorb everything.

"One time a while back I remember her saying how lucky she was. She said that Grace and Ned were better than anyone she could have reproduced."

Matthew blanched at that comment. "Jesus."

"I know. It was very hard to hear."

"She would have had beautiful, intelligent children." *She should have been my wife, and the mother of my children.* "Do you know why she and her husband adopted?"

"No. She's never talked about that."

"Do you mind if I stay overnight at Doro's?" It was the first Friday in August, the day after Erianna's birthday. Matthew had been out of town all week, and had flown back directly to the small airfield on the south side of Berrington where his car was parked.

"I was wondering if you, your sister and your mom would like to go bowling with me tomorrow, and maybe we could stop for a bite to eat afterward." Matthew addressed that question to Ned, although Erianna was sitting beside him on the couch.

Ned looked quizzically at his mother.

Erianna wasn't sure when or how Matthew had become such a regular visitor to the farm. She had grudgingly put up with his visits to her home, but she hadn't foreseen that he would ingratiate himself into their routine in so short a time.

She had been hoping that he would just get bored, or busy, and his visits would wane. But just the opposite seemed to be happening. Her children were becoming comfortable with him popping in and out, and she began to look forward to seeing him as well. He had made no overtures of a romantic nature and she could find no fault with his behavior.

"I could help you with chores tomorrow and then we could go out and bowl a few games. Have you ever been bowling?" he asked Ned when neither of them answered his question.

"I've been a few times." He looked again to his mother. "Maybe I could stay with Doro tonight, too, and we can we have a boys' night?"

Matthew looked at Erianna. She shrugged, got up from the couch and went to the open duplex doorway.

"Pap, do you know Doro's schedule for tonight and early tomorrow?"

"She's catering a wedding rehearsal dinner right now," Pap informed her. "I think it's a small job, but I'm not sure when she'll be home. And Bob and the boys went to a Reds game, so they won't be home until late."

"No. Sorry, Ned, no slumber parties tonight," his mother relayed the information.

Ned looked disappointed. So did Matthew.

"You could hang out here, I suppose," Ned offered, "until Doro gets home."

"Well, it sounds like they're all going to get home late. I can always come back tomorrow." He turned to Erianna. "Would you like to go bowling and then out to dinner?"

Matthew refrained from saying that it was a belated birthday dinner date, knowing full well she would turn that down flat. Ned sat watching his mother as she mulled over the invitation.

"We'll have to see what your sister thinks," she finally answered.

"Why don't I text her—oh, that's right. She doesn't have a phone." Matthew winked at Ned, who grinned widely.

"I'll go up and ask her," Ned volunteered. With a quick glance at his mother Ned was on his way up the stairs, taking them two at a time, just like she did.

Matthew sat back in the recliner, looking out the slider into the backyard as they waited for Ned to return.

Erianna was uncomfortable with the idea of being seen with him in public. She worried about what others might say and, as there was already enough gossip circulating about her, she was hesitant to add more fuel to the fire.

She had already decided not to renew his three-month contract at the stables, putting him on notice that he would have to find another boarding facility for his horse. She intended to notify him by letter that his contract with Berrington Farm would not be extended. It would be non-confrontational, which was just what Erianna wanted. She abhorred uncomfortable scenes, preferring to avoid them whenever possible.

It wasn't long before Ned came back downstairs and told them that Grace was in. Then he popped over to Pap's and asked him to put the outing on the schedule.

"Doro and the younger boys are going to Prestwick in the morning, so they won't be here for afternoon chores," Pap read the schedule off to Ned.

"I bet Ryan will help me out. And with Matt helping out, too, we should be able to finish in plenty of time."

Matthew suggested that they invite Ryan to come along and Ned volunteered to check with him. They began to work out details for the next day and finally, in a momentary lapse in judgment, Erianna suggested that Matthew just stay overnight on the built-in Murphy bed in the basement rec room.

"Okay, thanks." Matthew quickly jumped on that, agreeing before she could rescind her remark. He turned to Ned, gave him a little hug and said, "I'm going to turn in, little guy. It's been a long week and I'm bushed." With that he disappeared down the basement steps, closing the door behind him.

When the mail came the next morning there was another note from Matthew. Erianna knew he had sent it earlier in the week, but it was kind of creepy receiving a letter from him while he was on the property. It read in part:

> Erianna,
>
> "Parting from you is sad for me, but meeting you after parting is an amazing happiness."
>
> —Avijeet Das

He ended the note with a standard birthday wish. She was surprised that he knew it was her birthday. An introvert by nature, Erianna was uncomfortable being the focus of everyone's attention. She much preferred to have the day pass unacknowledged. She was certain that neither she nor her children had mentioned it to anyone, and she wondered how he had found out about it.

The family celebrated her birthday with a low-key dinner and a homemade no-bake cheesecake that the kids had made for her. Knowing of her aversion to large gatherings and parties in her honor, Grace and Ned each gave her a handmade card, and other than that no one on the farm was aware that it was her birthday.

Her father-in-law sent a card every year, but absolutely no one else, aside from her parents and sisters, who never gave her anything, were aware of the date of her birth. And so she hoped that Matthew didn't bring it up today. It was bad enough that he had wished her a happy birthday in the card. She could only pray that he would keep his mouth shut during the bowling trip that afternoon.

Although his letters still came by mail, Matthew never once admitted sending the notes. She wondered why he didn't bring it up and ask her if she liked the poetry he quoted. But she wasn't willing to open that Pandora's Box by mentioning it to him. *It's always better to let sleeping dogs lie*, she had decided.

Erianna Fowler was another year older. As she drove her Subaru toward the bowling alley with Matthew, her children and Ryan in tow she felt every one of her thirty-three years. Ryan was nearly sixteen, and as he sat chatting companionably in the seat next to Grace, she could see the man he was becoming. Tall and strapping, much like his father, Ryan laughed and carried on with Grace and Ned just as any teenage boy would do. He would be driving soon, and it wouldn't be long before he was off to explore the world on his own.

Grace, just a year behind Ryan in school, would also be gone before she knew it. Time was passing, and each birthday reminded Erianna of what little time she had left with her children.

Sitting next to her in the front passenger seat, Matthew and the boys rehashed the baseball game highlights from the night before. She worried her lower lip as they drove through town. Everyone was having a good time, but she couldn't seem to relax. This outing made her nervous and jittery.

Aside from biting her lip, Matthew could see no outward signs of distress from Erianna. And he knew, he knew that she felt trapped. But, he was sure that once they started bowling she would feel more at ease.

Erianna Fowler was not sedentary, which was exactly why Matthew had come up with the idea of a bowling date. Physical activity, he hoped, would calm her. And he felt certain that she would relax and have a good time with her family along for the 'date'.

She looked beautiful in a pair of slim leg dress jeans with a relaxed fit, short-sleeved knit tank top. The lower half of the pearl gray shirt, which was seamed around her natural waistline, fell in soft, supple ripples to mid hip. When she walked through the parking lot toward the bowling alley the folds of the lightweight shirt billowed slightly in the breeze.

Her hair was pulled back on either side of her head and secured with ornate barrettes, with her rich, honey masses falling heavily across her shoulders and down her back. Matthew longed to reach over and run his fingers through it.

Just as he had hoped, everyone had a good time bowling. With five people in attendance, they decided not to team up. It was every man for himself. Ryan won the first game, with Matthew and Grace right behind him. Ned beat his mother, who seemed to have taken several frames to settle down and find her line.

Erianna won the second game as Grace faltered, coming in last. Ryan was deferential and consoling, and Matthew realized that Ryan was enamored with Grace. He recognized the look. It was the same look he'd seen staring at him in the mirror these last several months.

Ryan had fallen for his neighbor's daughter. He had the look of a young man who had found his partner in life but was playing it cool, waiting for his time to come around.

It was quite obvious that Grace did not acknowledge or

reciprocate Ryan's feelings. She was definitely playing hard to get, whether by obliviousness or by design, Matthew wasn't sure. It was also obvious that Ryan was willing to wait.

Matthew glanced toward Erianna, wondering if she realized that Ryan was in love with Grace. Did she see what was happening?

The rubber game went to Ryan again and he was declared the victor. Matthew had ordered a pitcher of beer, but neither he nor Erianna drank more than one glass and the waitress took the half-full pitcher away when Matthew signaled that they were finished.

Before they left for supper at a local steakhouse Erianna and Grace went to the restroom to freshen up. Erianna added a second layer over the tank to dress up her look. The homemade cotton sweater laid perfectly over the tank top, falling just short of the under-layer at her hip. There were no side seams, but a back seam was open from her shoulder blades down and fell in an A shape to a ribbed bottom edge. The raglan sleeves, which Erianna had knitted separately, were stitched to the body of the lightweight pearl sweater.

"What do you think?" Erianna asked her daughter.

"That turned out really well, Mom. I like that you left the seam open, and that it's reversible. Maybe I could borrow it some time."

Erianna smiled. Grace was beginning to borrow her mother's clothes, even though she was still several inches shorter and more petite than her mother.

When they arrived at the restaurant Matthew managed to unobtrusively slip a note into Erianna's purse. As they were shown to their booth he placed his hand lightly on the small of her back and guided her in beside him. She felt the heat of his touch spreading through her body, making her skin flush a lovely pink color.

The kids scooted in on the other side, with Grace in the

middle and Ryan opposite Matthew on the outside. Ryan sat back lazily and put his arm across the back of the leather bench seat, and Grace cozied up next to him. They were a handsome couple, and as Matthew watched them interact he noted how relaxed and comfortable they were in each other's company.

Matthew turned to glance at Erianna. She, too, was watching the pair. Grace had her menu open and they were both reading from it. She looked up and asked what he had decided and Ryan told her that the New York Strip Steak sounded good to him.

As Erianna watched the teenagers a slight smile came over her face. Matthew knew she was thinking the same thing he was. He leaned over a little and whispered, "I see it, too."

Erianna looked at Matthew, knowing exactly what he was referring to. "I hope he doesn't get hurt," she murmured with a slight lift of one eyebrow.

She turned to help Ned with his choices and their orders were taken. They chatted amiably as they ate, and everyone was served individual birthday cupcakes that Matthew had pre-arranged for the occasion. He gave Erianna a belated birthday card, and the night ended when they got back and Matthew headed home.

All in all she had a very nice time, but was glad for the evening to end. When the kids were settled in for the night and she had locked up she went to her room, dumping the contents of her large purse onto her bed to sort through.

When she grabbed the birthday card to put it on her dresser alongside the others she'd received a stray piece of paper fell to the floor. She bent down and found another note. It was printed in large block letters and read only:

Do you like me?
Do you want to be my friend?

☐ Yes ☐ No

"What in the world—" Erianna's first thought was that Ryan had written the note to Grace, but she immediately rejected that notion. This wasn't Ryan's style. She knew who the note was from.

She sat down heavily on the bed, staring at the paper in her hand. It was written on a torn piece of ruled school paper which had been folded several times. A little crinkled and slightly worn, it had the look of a note that had been carried around for quite a while.

Erianna recognized the phrases from an old George Strait song about a schoolyard romance that blossomed into a happy marriage. But she couldn't remember the lyrics. After staring at the note for several more minutes she pulled her phone from the pile on her bed and listened to the tune on YouTube.

Holy cow! The song was very much akin to their childhood school days. Except that in this version the schoolgirl acts on her crush and her feelings are reciprocated, while Erianna had spent her days idolizing Matthew from afar.

And now he was sending her the note, asking for her response. Erianna was at a loss. She put it aside and went to bed, but she knew that she needn't have bothered, for she would get no sleep until she figured out what to do about the problem of Matthew Prestwick and her growing attraction to him.

Matthew was at his office going through his mail the following Friday when Chip came in and took a seat. Matthew had been in France for several days, and he was tired after the long flight home. The trip had been unscheduled, but there had been a 'fire' that he needed to put out and these short, stressful trips were an occasional necessity.

They talked about business as Matthew continued to sort through his mail. When he came across a letter addressed to him in Erianna's handwriting, Matthew sat up in his chair.

"Uh oh," he mumbled.

Chip stopped talking.

The envelope had been marked Personal, and Matthew quickly opened it. He pulled out the same note that he had left for Erianna.

He sat back in his chair. "Shit—"

"What is it?" Chip asked.

"The jig is up." Matthew shook his head. "I've been caught."

He passed the note to Chip, who read:

Do you like me?
Do you want to be my friend?

☐ Yes ☑ No

No, George, I'm not interested.
E

Chip looked at Matthew. "I don't get it."

"I left her this note last week, but I didn't count on her figuring out that it was a line from a George Strait song. I wanted her to think that I had been carrying the note around for a long time and had only just now gotten up the nerve to give it to her."

Chip laughed. "You're kidding."

"No, I'm not."

"You should have known better than to try to pull the wool over Erin Pruitt's eyes. You know how smart she is. And besides—it's really corny."

"Do you have any idea how hard this is? She doesn't remember having any romantic relationship with me. She only remembers us as classmates, and I thought this note might take her back, maybe jog a long-lost memory." He ran his fingers through his hair in exasperation. "If you have any better ideas, Mr. Wise Ass, I'm all ears."

Chip just laughed. "Well, you're up a creek now. I guess you're going to have to go back to the proverbial 'drawing board.'"

Matthew looked across the desk at his childhood friend and scowled.

That evening he sent off another missive.

Dear Erianna,

I never meant to mislead you. My offer of friendship was not deliberately stolen from a George Strait lyric, merely borrowed. Very much like the poetry I quote, the song reference was offered in much the same way. It was not meant to sound original, and I wasn't trying to be deceptive.

I apologize.

Matt

Erianna sent Matthew an official Notice of Non-Renewal, letting him know that his three-month contract to board Ráfaga at the Berrington Farm stables would not be extended. She sent the letter the week after her birthday, putting him on notice that he would need to make other arrangements for his horse. But to date he had not acknowledged receiving it.

As of September first, Matthew would no longer have any reason to come to the farm, and she theorized that it would put an end to these intrusive visits. She looked forward to the day when her life would return to normal.

Erianna was having trouble tamping down her feelings for Matthew. She just couldn't stop thinking about him. Her attraction was genuine, but such feelings were dangerous and she was having dreams that couldn't be repressed. Evicting him was the best idea she could come up with, and she hoped that his banishment would bring her some peace of mind.

Matthew read the Notice of Non-Renewal with amusement. She was giving it her best shot, and he had to hand it to her, it was inventive. He realized that she must be getting desperate to resort to such a tactic. He wished that she would just stop fighting and acknowledge her true feelings for him.

He was paying double the standard boarding fees in deference, he and Gus had decided when Matthew signed the contract, to the fact that Ráfaga was a stallion. And Erianna couldn't afford to turn away that kind of revenue. She was too level-headed a woman for that, business acumen or not.

He went down the hall to talk with Chip and found Nancy in his office.

"We were just going to lunch," she greeted Matthew with a quick peck on his cheek. "Want to come along?"

"Sure. I could eat."

They walked down the block and found an empty booth in a crowded downtown diner. Waitresses were bustling from table to table and the clatter of silverware and hum of chatter, typical of the lunch rush, swirled around the long, narrow restaurant.

Matthew brought Nancy up to date on the latest turn of events and showed the Non-Renewal Notice to Chip.

"What are you going to try now?" he asked. "Please don't tell me it's back to country western song lyrics."

Nancy turned toward her husband. "And why not? I thought it was sweet. If you sent me that kind of note I wouldn't have gotten mad about it."

Chip smiled at his wife. "But you're not Erin Pruitt, dearie. She doesn't want to admit that she has feelings for Matt. Whereas *we* knew that we loved each other when we were in grade school. You told me we did, remember?" he winked at her.

"Whereas—" she huffed. "Lawyer spiel." But she returned his teasing smile.

"You know," Chip turned back to Matthew. "George Strait may not have worked, but Tim McGraw might."

Matthew frowned. "How so?"

Chapter 9

Matthew had been in South Korea for the last ten days. By the time he dropped by the stables the kids were back in school. It was odd not having them running to and fro from their various summer activities, and the farm seemed much too quiet.

Erianna was working on cleaning and re-stitching the oft used tack that had been put off all season. The high volume of classes and many boarders who trained their horses for show competitions during the summer break had kept her schedule full, and she was finally getting around to caring for her tack.

That was where Matthew found her after his ride.

"Hey."

"Hey, yourself," she replied.

"Seems like a ghost town here."

"Mmm," she agreed as she continued to apply saddle soap and work it into the leather.

She had received several letters from Matthew while he was away on business.

One note with a South Korean postmark quoted lines from a poem by Pablo Neruda to describe the lush jungle vegetation surrounding his hotel. "*Green was the silence, wet was the light…*"

"Would you like some help with that?"

"No thanks. I'm enjoying my solitude."

Matthew ran his fingers through his hair and rubbed the back of his neck. He was tired of dancing around. He wanted to get things out in the open and declare his feelings and intentions toward her. But so far she hadn't acknowledged any of the notes he sent with regularity.

Matthew had been careful not to use the word 'love' in any of his missives up to now. But he had come across a poem which expressed his true feelings perfectly, and he included it in the letter he mailed a couple of days ago. He wondered if she had received it yet and hoped she wasn't too upset by the sentiment. Erianna was a long way from acknowledging such feelings, but he decided to take a shot and let her know how he truly felt.

"Well, I guess I'll wander up and say hello to my sister."

"She's not home."

"Oh." Matthew could think of no other reason to stay. "Okay, well, I guess I'll head on out then." He hesitated, but Erianna made no comment.

Finally, he turned to leave. "See you later."

"Goodbye." *And good riddance.*

Another letter came in the mail that afternoon.

Erianna,

"In my heart is a space
that is so sacred
and none can enter in but you.

And I shall wait for you,
though it takes forever,
Though my heart bleeds
and my all consumed.

I wait because I love you,
and love waits
for the only one
that it loves."

—Jocelyn Soriano

Matt

Erianna's heart skipped a beat. She held the note against her pounding chest and closed her eyes for a moment. And then, realizing what she was doing, she quickly refolded the paper and stuffed it into the envelope.

Shaking her head vigorously she grumbled, "Enough of these ridiculous fantasies. I'm giving you the heave-ho, Dr. Prestwick. And not a moment too soon."

On Wednesday morning, the last day in August, two pickup trucks, one with a horse trailer in tow, pulled down Donovan Lane. Erianna watched from her office window in the stables as they lumbered toward the stable yard. *Good. He's finally out of here.*

She noted that Gus went to help, so she decided to wait in her office until Matthew finished loading his horse and retrieved his tack. She thought she would be relieved and was surprised to note that her emotions were mixed. But Erianna was a pragmatic woman and she knew this was for the best.

As she worked on her books, her doorway was darkened by the appearance of Matthew and two others.

"Do you have a minute?" he asked.

She looked up. "Of course."

He came through the doorway, followed by a shorter man wearing a dark western hat. And bringing up the rear, Chip Neading came jaunting in.

"Hello, Erin. I haven't seen you all summer." Chip offered her a huge, cheerful smile. "And it's no wonder. It's just beautiful here." He advanced on her, bent down and gave her a peck on her cheek.

She was not happy with the familiarity of the kiss. "Hello, Chip."

"If I owned this land," he continued, "I would never want to leave it. You ought to rename this place Paradise. Wow!"

Always effervescent and flowery in his speech, Chip did not disappoint today. He was a sweet talker. There was no other way to describe him.

Trying his best not to chuckle, Matthew cleared his throat, drawing Erianna's attention. "I'd like you to meet our friend, Tim McGraw.

"Tim, this is Erin Fowler. We went through school together in Prestwick."

Erianna rose from her seat. She extended her hand, trying desperately not to let her astonishment show. "It's nice to meet you, Mr. McGraw."

He shook her hand. "Mrs. Fowler."

A stilted silence followed, so Erianna took up the mantle. "May I help you with something?"

"My stable manager and an assistant are here to pick up Matt's stallion," he replied. "I have a mare of breeding age coming into season."

"Oh, I see," she nodded. "Ráfaga had a vet check last weekend and was found to be sound and fit for transport. I'll get you the paperwork and then we can go supervise the loading process."

She was all business as she spoke politely to Tim. Matthew stood to the side and observed quietly.

"Do you mind if I look around?" Chip interrupted.

Erianna lowered her head slightly and glanced his way. "Be my guest."

With that he left to wander down the corridors and stroll around the area. As he passed Matthew's black stallion, Chip paused to admire the horse.

Erianna sat down and offered the men seats with a wave of her hand. "I think I have that paperwork around here somewhere."

She began to compile the sheets of paper from the August class attendance rosters that were spread across the top of her desk. Stuffing them haphazardly into a folder, she began a search for Ráfaga's file. She knew that it was somewhere on her desk because she had been working on it earlier in the day and she didn't remember re-filing it.

Matthew chuckled, which brought her gaze up from the mess on her desk. She looked questioningly at her nemesis, but with Tim McGraw sitting across from her Erianna did her best to remain composed.

"I'm sorry," Matthew said in a lighthearted tone, "but you're so organized everywhere else, I'm surprised your desk is such a disaster." He cleared his throat loudly and then added, "If you like, we can come back in about an hour or so. Maybe you'll have found the folder by then."

Tim watched the interaction between the two. Clearly, Erianna was not amused. She had become very still, looking at Matthew with a calm, neutral expression, waiting for him to continue his ribbing. Matthew, for his part, leaned slightly forward as if to challenge a response from her.

Finally, she spoke. "Feel free to go check on your horse, Dr. Prestwick."

Matthew smiled indulgently, then got up and patted his friend on the shoulder. "Want a tour?" he asked.

"No thanks." Tim remained seated across from Erianna.

"When we finish our business here I'll be happy to show you around the stables, Mr. McGraw."

Tim lowered his head so that his hat would hide the smirk on his face. Then he straightened and looked at the woman Matthew was in love with and said, "That would be very nice. Thank you." His tone was just as formal and businesslike as hers.

"Okay," Tim sat back after Matthew left her office and was out of earshot. "What was *that* all about?"

He posed the question such that Erianna could not play dumb and claim that she didn't know what he was referring to.

"I'm sorry," she replied with a deep, heavy sigh. "Matthew and I have differing views about many things and so it's difficult at times to interact in a civil manner."

She glanced down at her desk. "But he is right about one thing. I'm not a businesswoman, and I have a real mess here." She shrugged, trying to lighten the mood with a little harmless self-deprecation.

Tim took off his hat and crossed one leg over his knee. "There's a lot more to it than that, isn't there." It wasn't posed as a question, but a statement of fact.

When Erianna looked innocently at him, Tim stopped her. "Don't kid a kidder, Erin—can I call you that?" At her nod he continued. "There's a lot more going on between you two than just a difference of opinion."

She quickly lowered her head and hid her eyes from his scrutiny. "I'm sure you're mistaken." She pushed at the folders on her desk with nervous fingers.

Tim shook his head. "I know what I saw. He's nuts about you, but you're not giving an inch."

Erianna went still. He leaned forward, lowering his leg and resting his forearms on his thighs as he twirled his hat in his hands. Neither spoke for a time.

"Do you listen to my music?" he finally asked her.

"Yes, I do," she replied honestly as she began to search again for the appropriate folder. "I like a wide variety of music, from the classics and church music to the latest hits in a wide variety of genres, including country music."

"I hear you're a particular fan of George Strait."

Erianna's head snapped up. Her hazel eyes rounded and color rose in her cheeks.

He'd hit a nerve. Tim sat back again. "He's a very good performer. We have completely different styles, of course, but I admire his work."

Erianna was acutely embarrassed by the turn in the conversation. Finally, she found her voice. "Excuse me, Mr. McGraw—"

"Call me Tim."

"No, I don't think—"

"Come on, Erin," he interrupted. "You don't have to act all formal-like with me."

"I—"

"We're birds of a feather, you and me. I know how you're feeling."

Some of the rigidity left her and she raised one hand and rubbed the bridge of her nose with her fingers. "Obviously Matthew has been talking to you about us."

"Yeah, some. He's a good friend."

"May I ask how you happen to know him?"

"My wife's mother is related to Gail Neading," he supplied

"So you know Matt through Chip."

"Yeah."

"Yes, well, be that as it may, let's get back to business, shall we?"

Tim acquiesced, tossing his hat on the seat Matthew had vacated and pulling his chair closer to her desk. He began searching through a wire basket filled with folders as Erianna shuffled through the mess on her desk, looking for the errant paperwork.

"Why don't you want Matt to know that you like him?" he asked offhandedly.

Unwilling to discuss the matter or acknowledge her feelings, even to herself, she made no response.

"He told me that your first dance together was to a George Strait tune. I ribbed him a little about it and called him a traitor."

"I see." But she didn't, not really. How could Matthew have gossiped about her with Tim McGraw? She must be in some alternate reality, where discussing her private life in her dirty stable office with a world-renowned superstar was commonplace.

"If you *don't* have feelings for the guy, why don't you just tell him so?"

"Honestly, I was hoping the problem would just go away with the horse," she admitted sheepishly.

Tim huffed. "I hate to tell you this, little lady, but Matt has no intention of going away."

Erianna shrugged. "I'm not a confrontational person."

"Telling a man you're not interested isn't confrontational, it's the decent thing to do. But you can't do that, can you? Because deep down you *do* have feelings for him, and to tell him otherwise would be a lie. I can see it, even if you won't admit it. Why don't you give him a break? He's a good guy. You could do a lot worse."

She held up her left hand. "I'm not on the market."

He noted that she still wore her wedding band. "Oh. Well, that being the case, all the more reason to let Matt know."

She was ashamed of misleading Tim, but it couldn't be helped. Thankfully, she finally found the errant folder and they reviewed the paperwork before he went out to rejoin his friends. As soon as he left Erianna escaped to her house, jogging up the hill and away from prying eyes.

Every year since Matthew had purchased his condo in Mt. Adams, which overlooked downtown Cincinnati and the Ohio River, Doro and her family came to stay over and watch the Labor Day Fireworks. Matthew's condo boasted an unobstructed view of the river where the fireworks would be set off.

This year Doro and Bob had opted out, so Matthew extended an invitation to Grace and Ned, asking them if they'd like to join his nephews and watch the spectacle from his place. Erianna was miffed when her children came running in with the news and asking for permission to go, but she put on a happy face and consented.

Bob dropped the kids off around noon and they played pool and video games as they waited for the fireworks to begin. Matthew ordered pizza and sides from LaRosa's, and the kids scarfed it down as if they had never eaten pizza before. The fireworks display was spectacular and the kids had a blast.

The next afternoon he brought them home. His company driver drove them all to the Village. Matthew had a trip scheduled and he was catching a commercial flight from Lexington to Dallas. When they pulled into Pap's driveway the kids gathered up their things and headed off with words of thanks for the great weekend.

Erianna came out to meet the group. "Did you have a good time?" she asked her son.

"Oh, boy did I—" his eyes lit up. "Mom, you should have been there. The fireworks were unbelievable and Matt's view was probably the best in town."

With a wave Ned took off for Pap's side door, calling to the other boys, "I'll meet you at the stables."

Erianna turned to Matthew, noting how handsome and confident he looked in his business suit. "Thank you for inviting them. I hope everything went well."

"We had a great time. I'm glad they came." He smiled, showing that hint of dimple that Erianna found so appealing.

Matthew turned to leave, but hesitated. Looking back he said, "I love being with your children."

"Well, I'm sure the feeling is mutual," she replied sincerely.

And then Matthew did something unexpected. He drew Erianna into his arms and kissed her.

Needless to say, her dreams that night were filled with images of Matthew, looking tall and sexy in his business suit.

The scheduled one o'clock trail riding group was just heading out when Erianna noticed the horse trailer pulling into the stables parking area. Matthew's stallion was back, and she was steaming.

Prevented from doing anything at the moment, she turned to close the pasture gate after the last rider passed through. She sat glaring at the scene unfolding in the distance, frustrated and fed up. Tim McGraw had been right. It was high time that she had it out with Matthew Prestwick. This could not continue.

The trail ride seemed interminable. She did her best to shake off her sour mood, but her thoughts kept running to what she would say when she confronted him. One thing was certain, she would be crystal clear that he was no longer welcome on Berrington Farm.

When she came upstairs after changing in the basement cleanroom she found not only Matthew, but Grace and Ned sitting on the floor in her office. They were working on some kind of historic timeline. With Matthew's help Ned had input the information and Grace was running off copies at the printer on Erianna's desk.

"Hi, Mom. Matthew helped me download a program that runs long, continuous graphs for my timeline."

"It's an app he found online," Grace continued over the hum of the printer on Erianna's desk. "I wish I'd had this a couple of years ago. It would have been so much easier when I did that Early American project on the settling of the Scottish population in western North Carolina." Grace turned to Matthew. "Did they have this program a couple of years ago?"

"I'm not sure," he replied. "I think I downloaded it last spring."

When they finished Ned said, "Now all I have to do is draw in the scenes and color the background."

While most students would have settled for handing in the assignment as is, Ned, who had an artistic flare, went to his room to sketch various events along the timeline. Then he colored and shaded the renderings, expertly fading one scene into the next and filling in the background with watercolors.

Erianna left the group to their own devices and went to the kitchen to start supper. Matthew wandered in not long after.

"Would you like me to set the table?" he offered.

Erianna turned on him. "No! What I *would* like is for you to get out of my house and get that horse off my property. Immediately!" She advanced on him and would have said more, but her daughter came bounding down the hallway just then.

Grace stopped short when she saw her mother's aggressive stance. Unsure what to do, she said nothing. Her mother turned toward her, scowled and uttered a sound of frustration.

"Grace Margaret, set the table!"

Grace flinched. Her mother turned on her heel and stormed into the kitchen, leaving Grace and Matthew staring after her in shock.

Matthew stood sheepishly, rubbing the back of his neck as Grace glared at him, much the same way her mother had. He motioned toward the doorway to Pap's place. Without another word he retreated through the portal to the safety of the in-law suite.

Erianna went to the sink and grasped the lip as if she was holding on for dear life. She closed her eyes and slowly counted to ten. Ashamed of the way she had just spoken to her daughter, she needed to get a grip on her temper.

When Grace came into the kitchen her mother, much calmer now, gave Grace a quick hug as she passed by.

"Should I get out three place settings or four?"

Erianna sighed heavily. "I wish I could say three. But you probably should set four."

"I could uninvite him if you want, Mom."

Erianna patted her daughter's back and gave it a little rub. "Thank you for your offer. But I intend to put this matter to rest right after supper."

Grace set the table and went upstairs to fetch Ned. During supper both kids reviewed their homework assignments and Erianna asked questions that required more in-depth responses. But the meal was much more subdued than usual.

When Grace reported on her chemistry work Erianna said, "Well, I can only hope your answers are correct."

"They are," Grace nodded.

Erianna usually read chapters ahead in her children's schoolbooks and added additional research assignments for them to complete.

"You haven't been keeping up on your reading lately, Mom," Ned reprimanded her lightheartedly.

Erianna looked across the table, directly at Matthew. "I've been otherwise occupied."

Ned giggled and the sweet sound, so typical of little boys, filled the room. He looked conspiratorially at Matthew and, resting his elbow on the table, he put his chin in his hand. "Otherwise occupied doing what?"

Matthew searched for a suitable response. He couldn't make a sarcastic crack, that would upset Erianna even more so than she was now. And he couldn't be honest with the boy. That conversation would have to take place with his mother, not him. So he just sat back in his chair and shrugged noncommittally.

Ned snickered and Grace scowled. Both children's gazes

were focused directly on him. He turned to meet Erianna's gaze and found that she, too, was shooting daggers at him. Finally, she cleared her throat and rose from the table.

Matthew got up as well. "Thanks for feeding me. The meatballs were very tender and quite tasty."

"Thank you," she replied, making a Herculean effort to adopt a conversational tone. "Doro's homemade spaghetti sauce helped a lot. I cooked them on low all day in the crock pot and they absorbed all those wonderful flavors your sister puts into her sauce."

Erianna tried her best to defuse and lighten the mood in the room. Her children had both been passive aggressive toward Matthew, albeit in completely different ways. And her own behavior was not much better than theirs.

"I'm going next door to help Pap into his wheelchair," she told the kids.

Matthew followed her from the room. "I'll help," he said.

Pap was ready when they came in. "The girls are on their way down the lane," he informed them.

Doro and Ginny had catered a fiftieth birthday party for the father of a newlywed bride whose wedding she had catered last spring. Pap was on his way next door to eat leftovers with the Donovan clan.

"What did she make?" Matthew asked Pap.

"Pulled pork sandwiches. Man, they're good."

Matthew smiled broadly. "Bob's a lucky guy."

Pap chuckled. "I'll say. She sure captured my heart with her cooking. Come on over," he suggested. "Grab some leftovers to take home."

"Thanks. I think I'll mosey on over with you and say hello. But I'll just give my doggie bag to Gus."

"Good idea," Pap said as they left through the side door.

Very clever, Dr. Prestwick. He had managed to escape before Erianna could deliver her ultimatum.

* * *

Ned and Grace had gone upstairs to their rooms, and when Matthew returned Erianna summoned him to the in-law suite. She closed the door behind them. With Pap still next door they were finally alone.

"Dr. Prestwick," she began in a clipped tone. "You must remove your horse from my stables. Today. Immediately! I have a trailer in the equipment shed, and you can use that to transport your animal off my property."

"Erin—"

"You have one hour." She glanced at her wristwatch.

Matthew was not about to consent to that. "One hour—or what?"

"I'll have no choice but to involve law enforcement."

"I've had enough, Erin. It's high time we sat down and discussed this." He grabbed her by the arm and began to tug her toward the couch.

She resisted, pulling against him with all her might.

"Dammit, Erianna."

"Let—go of me," she demanded.

He did not. Somehow, he managed to wrangle her onto the couch. He sat beside her, turning his legs at an angle so as to imprison her there.

"Please, Erin, be reasonable. We need to talk about this in a civil manner."

She sat back and settled herself comfortably against the cushions. Glancing at her watch again she said, "Fifty-seven minutes."

Then she closed her eyes and settled in, paying her jailor no heed. She was an old hand at going deep into her own thoughts and tuning out the outside world. Matthew spoke for several minutes, but she didn't hear him.

Knowing that he was getting nowhere he got up and began to pace. Every so often she would glance at her watch, but that was the only movement she made as she sat, apparently cat napping on the couch.

"All right, Erianna. If that's the way you want to play this, fine. I'm calling your bluff."

His hour was up. Erianna rose from the couch and went into Ginny's kitchen, picking up the portable landline from its perch on the back counter. Matthew was sitting on a bar stool sipping a glass of bourbon, and as she walked past he got up and followed her.

She pressed the digits 9-1-1.

"Come on," he protested. "You're *really* going to do this?"

She hesitated, her finger suspended over the send button. Oh, how she longed to press down. But how would she explain her actions to her children. And how would the Donovan's react to the news that she had called the cops to have Matthew forcibly removed from the property.

"Please, Erin—"

It was all too much for her. With shaking fingers she reset the phone and returned it to its charging station. She lowered her head. Her mind was swirling and she felt off kilter, as though the earth was turning but leaving her behind.

Matthew waited at the entrance to the U-shaped room. The normally composed woman standing before him suddenly seemed fragile and vulnerable. He became alarmed. She looked as though she might collapse, so he moved forward slowly and took her into his arms.

"Erianna—" he murmured. He ran his palm across her back, pinning her against the wall of his chest. She shivered in his arms.

"Why won't you go away and leave me alone?" she mumbled against the material of his shirt.

"I can't," he admitted on a breathy whisper. He kissed the top of her head. "I want to be with you."

He thought about that statement for a second. "No. That's not the right word." Taking her face in his hands he looked into the watery depths of her hazel eyes and confessed, "I *need* to be with you, Erianna. I can't stay away. I love you."

She closed her eyes. "No—" she whispered forlornly.

"I love you. I know that frightens you. I'm frightened, too. I've never felt this way for anyone else. Only you."

She lowered her head, snuggling against the base of his neck. "Please, Matt. You need to stop this and go away. I have my family to think of."

Her words said one thing, but her actions another as she sidled against him and settled into the warmth of his embrace.

"We can't fight this, sweetheart. I promise you no one will get hurt. I would never let that happen. Just let me love you."

She shook her head in denial.

Matthew kissed her. Backed up against the kitchen counter, she could not retreat. His mouth worked its magic and Erianna was lost. She kissed him back, losing her will to resist as he sheltered her in his arms.

He ended the kiss when he heard Pap and Ginny coming along the path between the two houses. He stepped back just far enough to put a little daylight between them.

"Pap and Ginny are coming home."

Regaining her senses, Erianna walked out of the kitchen on shaky legs. She turned back saying, "I obviously can't stop you from boarding your horse here. But this," she motioned with her arm between them, "this has to stop. I don't want a personal relationship with you."

She walked toward the door to her home. "Stop writing me, Matthew. Do you hear me? All letters that come will be shredded—unopened."

With that last statement she went through the door and closed it behind her.

At eight a.m. the next morning Matthew slid into the pew next to Erianna at Immaculate Heart of Mary Church. She pretended not to know him.

He noticed that although she had her song book open and mouthed all the words to the hymns, not a sound came from her throat. It saddened him that she did not sing along with the congregation.

He spent the day on the farm. Erianna was grumpy and irascible and they exchanged not so subtle barbs. All pretense of civility between them had been suspended.

Grace wandered next door and sat down in Doro's enormous kitchen to visit with her and Ginny while they prepped Sunday supper. She mentioned the clipped, icy comments that had been exchanged between her mother and Matthew all day.

"I'm not sure what's going on, but I think he really likes her," Grace told them. "Has he said anything to you guys about Mom?"

Ginny piped up before Doro could reply. "No, but from what I see he's in love with your mother."

"We don't know that, Ginny," Doro cut in. "Have you talked to your mom about this?"

"No."

Grace filled in the details of their interactions the day before.

"That reminds me a little bit of your relationship with Ryan," Ginny pointed out.

Grace frowned. "How so?"

"Well, Matthew's nuts about your mom the same way that Ryan's nuts about you, but neither of you seem interested in reciprocating those feelings. Maybe Erin likes Matthew as much he likes her, but she just doesn't want to admit it."

"Enough of that, Mom," Doro admonished her mother-in-law. "The kids are much too young to be anything more than friends. And as for Erin and Matt, that's none of our business."

Grace rested her chin in her hand as she considered what Ginny had said. "Mom's relationship with Matt may have started way back in school, but they went their separate ways a long time ago.

"And I know how Ryan feels about me. I wasn't born yesterday, you know. Maybe someday he and I will settle down together. But, that's a long way off and we have a lot of growing up to do before that time comes."

Doro was relieved by Grace's proclamation. She was a sensible young lady and Doro was reassured by her comments.

"You know what I think?" Grace added after a time.

"What?" Ginny replied.

"I think my mom has feelings for Matt, but she's pushing him away because of Ned and me."

"That's probably true," Ginny agreed. "But, you two won't always be living at home with her."

Grace nodded. "I don't want Mom to end up all alone. I don't want us to be the reason why she and Matt don't end up together. She's still fairly young and there are going to be a lot of lonely years ahead of her if she tells him to get lost."

"Whatever will be will be," Doro said. "You shouldn't get in the middle of this. Let the adults work things out for themselves, and don't either of you interfere."

Supper was served at Ginny's place that night. The group served themselves plates of roast beef and baked fingerling potatoes with green beans and succotash. Then they scattered to various locations to eat their meals.

After supper Ginny served slices of marble sheet cake, each with a scoop of vanilla ice cream. Sitting at the counter, Erianna declined dessert and sat quietly as she watched Ned dig into his sweet treat.

"You know, Mom," Grace spoke up as she helped Ginny store the leftovers into plastic containers. "We could use another desk in your office."

Erianna was surprised by that statement. "Another desk?"

"Yeah. Somebody or other is working in there quite a bit, and a second desk would be very helpful. And Matt really needs a proper work space. He can't continue to work from the coffee table."

"There isn't room for another desk, Grace." But what she really wanted to say was that Matthew wasn't welcome in her office, or anywhere else, for that matter. She would rather that he take a hike and leave them all alone.

"Well, if we took out one of the easy chairs and the coffee table it could work."

Erianna did not like the idea of sharing her office. It was her space. "I don't think a second desk is necessary—"

"I disagree," Grace cut in. "It would have been a lot easier for Ned to work on his timeline if he'd had a desk. And I, for one, am getting a little too old to sit on the floor with paperwork scattered all over the carpet."

"You each have a desk in your rooms, and there's a table in the upstairs library."

Grace was prepared for that argument. "That's true, but there's no printer upstairs and we have to run back and forth to print out research papers and homework assignments. Besides, Matt works in there a lot and he could set up his laptop at the desk instead of on his lap."

"Or in my living room," Pap added, warming up to the idea.

Grace looked at Pap and said, "I was thinking that a curved desk would work best. It would take up less space and have more surface area to work from."

"That's not a bad idea, but you'll need to take some measurements before you commit to a purchase."

"Now just hold on a minute—" Erianna tried to stop the train from rolling out of the station.

Grace returned her focus to her mother. "It would have been so much easier for Ned to put his timeline together if he had a larger worktop."

Ned looked at his mom. "I don't mind sitting on the floor," he admitted with a little shrug.

Grace ignored him. "I already did a quick search online. There are several interesting possibilities that might work."

"We could go shopping next weekend," Ginny joined in, always up for a shopping trip. "We could spend the day in Lexington."

"Or Cincinnati," Doro suggested. "There's an Ikea store I've been dying to check out. And we could stop at the supply outlet so I can stock up on autumn and winter decorations for my catering jobs."

"And Mom will probably want to go to the fabric stores. Could we stop at the butterfly exhibit at the conservatory while we're there? I'd really like to see it."

The three women began to chatter excitedly as if the trip was a foregone conclusion. Erianna had obviously been overruled by the entire group. She sighed in exasperation and sat back, leaning against the wall. Ned, having lost interest, wandered off to his room after thanking Doro and Ginny for supper.

Erianna looked off toward the front window and noticed Matthew standing in her peripheral vision. She made eye contact with him and her lips thinned in disapproval. Her mutinous expression spoke volumes.

He couldn't be sure, but Matthew suspected that Grace had decided to become his ally. And he would take any help he could get in his battle to win Erianna's heart.

Chapter 10

"Welcome to the second annual Autumnal Treasure Hunt," Grace announced.

With Pap's help Grace had organized the event and the stables had been closed to the public on this first Sunday of the fall season. The Fowlers and Donovans were ready to start. They had packed various items into backpacks, hoping they would have the things they needed to aid them on their quest, and everyone was gathered and in high spirits in Pap's duplex.

The hunt would be run on horseback this year and they were saddled and ready for the beginning of the afternoon escapade.

"This year you will run the course in pairs, so you guys need to choose your partners."

Matthew came through the door just then.

Grace hadn't expected him. "Hi, Matt. We were just about to start a treasure hunt."

"A treasure hunt?"

"Yeah. We did it last year, and everybody had a great time. But we're going to break off into pairs and run it on horseback this time."

"Oh. So I take it you're not participating?"

"No. Pap and I put it together."

Grace looked around. With Matthew's appearance the numbers were odd, and she wasn't sure what to do about the problem. "It seems we have an odd number."

"That's okay, Grace," he said. "I don't want to throw a monkey wrench in the works. I'll just sit this one out."

"Don't do that, Uncle Matt," Ryan objected. "It was really fun last year. You don't want to miss out, do you?"

"Matt can take my place," Ginny volunteered. "I can stay

back and help monitor the race." She turned to Grace. "You told Pap that you were spread thin, so maybe I can help you at one of your posts."

"I don't want to put you out," Matthew said. "Why don't I help her instead?"

"Nonsense," Ginny waved a hand. "I'm getting too old to spend an entire afternoon on horseback, and this will work out better in the long run. Whoever got me for a partner was bound to come in last." She laughed. "I'd much rather sit back and watch the goings on."

"Are you sure?" Grace asked her.

"I'm positive."

"Is everyone alright with that?"

Everyone agreed, and Pap called down to the stables to ask Gus to saddle Matthew's horse.

"Okay, so now we just have to figure out the pairings."

After a lot of discussion, the teams were finally chosen. Bob and his youngest son, Theo, teamed up, while Ryan and Ned joined forces. Matt and James made up the third pairing, with Erianna and Doro forming the fourth.

When everyone was ready Grace handed out the first clue to each team. "This year time penalties will be assessed for any infractions to the posted rules. There is a laminated Rules card inside your clue boxes, so I don't want to hear that you didn't know what the rules were when you get back."

Grace pulled out one of her swimming stop watches and handed it to Pap. She put a second one around her neck and Pap started the countdown.

"Ten, nine, eight..." at the word 'Go' each team opened the boxes containing their first clues. The Rules card rested on top of a group of puzzle pieces.

Doro and Erianna ran for her office, closing the door behind them as they dumped the pieces onto the coffee table.

"Clever girl," Doro commented, "making the first clue a puzzle. How many pieces do you figure there are?"

"Looks to be about a hundred to a hundred and fifty, I'm guessing."

They set to work and it wasn't long before the picture emerged, a scene of an oak tree with a yellow ribbon tied around it. As Doro continued to work, Erianna tried to place where the oak tree might be located.

"Let's fill in the background and forget about the pieces of the tree," she suggested. "There are lots of oak trees on the property. We just have to figure out where this one is."

Just then they heard the screen door to the garage slam shut.

"I wonder who that was," Doro said. "Maybe we should just follow them."

"That's against the rules," Erianna replied as she scanned the laminated card.

"Who cares."

Erianna grinned. To a fault, each and every one of the participants was competitive. "I think this looks like the cornfield at the south end of the property line. And this bit here might be the golf course on the east side, but I can't be sure."

"Let's ride out to the southeast corner and have a look around," Doro suggested.

They took off for their horses and set out in that direction. Bob and Theo were right behind them. They reached the area in tandem and spotted the tree at the same time.

Attached to the yellow ribbon was the next clue. Grace was stationed nearby, wearing her filter mask and a pair of swim goggles.

To find the next clue on your hunt for the treasure, you must add the year of Tom Sawyer's author's birth and the year he met St. Peter at the 'pearly gate'.

Erianna and Doro moved away from Bob to discuss the clue without being overheard. Just then Ryan and Ned rode in.

"Mark Twain, or rather Samuel Clemens, wrote Tom Sawyer," Doro supplied. "But I have no idea when he lived. Do you?"

"Well, I know he died in the early nineteen hundreds, but I have no idea when he was born."

"Do you know how old he was when he died?"

"No, but his wife died before him and he outlived most of his kids. So if you figure the average life span for people in the eighteen hundreds at about, maybe sixty years?" she suggested. "And you factor in that he lived much longer than average, we should be able to figure this out."

"Okay," Doro said. "So let's say that he died in about nineteen 'o five."

"That sounds about right," Erianna agreed. "And let's say that he lived what—about twenty years longer than average? That would make him somewhere around eighty when he died."

Doro pulled out a notepad from their backpack, and subtracted 80 from the year 1905. "Okay, that gives us the year 1825. And when you add 1825 and 1905, you get 3730." Doro looked askance. "I don't get it."

Ryan and Ned rode off almost immediately. Erianna re-read the clue out loud. "What does the number 3730 have to do with the pearly gates?"

"I don't know. There are gates all over the place. But there aren't thirty-seven hundred of them."

Erianna watched Ryan and Ned head northwest across the cross-country course. And suddenly it came to her.

"It's not 3730. It's 3745. Our address. Pearly gates must mean the front entrance gate. The clue has to be around the front gate or the mailboxes." They quickly remounted and rode out, leaving Bob and Theo in their dust.

Matthew and Jamie had yet to be seen, and Erianna surmised that they had been the first ones out the door. That meant she and Doro were currently in third place.

When they reached the fence dividing the lane from the cross-country course at the front entrance of the property no one was there except Pap, who was obviously monitoring the area for infractions to the rules from his electric wheelchair.

Erianna had read thru all the rules earlier and she knew that they could not ride the horses on Donovan lane. The rules stated:

1. No following another group without figuring out the clue for yourself.
2. Both partners must be present at each clue location.
3. No riding horses onto Donovan lane.
4. No riding horses into the yard.
5. No taking horses off property.
6. Obey all additional rules posted along the course.

So they dismounted and tied their horses to the fence rail and ran together to the front gate to look in the mailboxes. They found two remaining manila envelopes, thus reinforcing the fact that they were in third place.

The clue read: *In order to make a man or boy covet a thing, it is only necessary to make the thing difficult to attain.* There was a paintbrush enclosed in the envelope.

"What does that mean?" Doro was stumped.

"The quote is from *The Adventures of Tom Sawyer*, and it references how Tom hoodwinked his friends into whitewashing his Aunt Polly's picket fence."

"Well, we don't have any white picket fences, so now what? Are we supposed to paint something?" She turned the paintbrush over in her hand without really looking at it.

"Let me see that," Erianna grabbed for the paintbrush and took a good look at it. There, on the metal piece where the brushes were held together was a taped piece of paper with the words: *Daisies may be growing.*

"Come on," Erianna said.

"Where are we going?"

"To the pasture where Daisy is grazing." She filled Doro in as they rode toward the stables.

Bob and Theo were pulling in as they left.

"How do we know which pasture Daisy is in?" Doro asked.

"We don't. But she usually grazes with Ráfaga in the northeast pasture beyond the stables. Let's just hope that Grace didn't move Daisy to another location to throw us off. If she did, we could be searching far and wide for the pony."

They rode to the stables and dismounted, tying their horses to the hitching post out front just as Matthew and James rode through the far gate at the entrance to the riding trails. Wet Paint signs were posted at regular intervals along the fenceline. Ryan and Ned were in the pasture, trying without success to corral Daisy. The little Caspian pony was tracking Matthew's mount, her stablemate, at the far end of the pasture.

"Come with me," Erianna commanded, grabbing Doro's arm and tugging her through the open stable doors at the center T. They ran down the aisle to the metal gate at the end of the east wing.

"Get out that apple we packed," Erianna instructed as she pushed open the gate. She let out a series of loud whistles, calling for the pony.

"Here Daisy," she whistled again. Daisy turned and began to trot toward them. Ryan and Ned tried to coax the animal toward them by dangling a carrot at her, but Erianna took out her pocketknife and cut the apple in half, holding it out and whistling shrilly.

"Here Daisy," she called as she walked slowly toward the mare, holding the apple piece in her outstretched hand.

Daisy paused long enough to grab for the piece of carrot that Ryan offered her and Ned grabbed the next clue from her halter. Then both boys jumped over the fence and opened their clue.

"Rules violation!" Gus shouted. "You boys touched the 'wet paint' on the fence."

"Cheaters," Doro called out as Erianna was still trying to entice Daisy to come to her.

"How much is the time penalty?" Doro asked Gus.

"No talking to the judges," Bob piped up as he and Theo came up next to her. "Theo, go out with Erin and see if you can help her catch Daisy."

"Okay, Dad."

Doro and Bob watched from the gate as their partners approached the pony.

"How the hell was I supposed to know when Mark Twain lived?" Bob asked his wife.

"I know. It took us a while to figure that one out, too."

"I'm afraid of what Grace has in store for us next," he admitted.

When Erianna finally caught hold of Daisy's halter, both husband and wife went out to join their partners so as not to incur any penalties in obtaining their next clues.

Bob and Theo ran for their horses as Erianna and Doro opened their next clue in the pasture. It read: *Where Tom and Becky were trapped for three days.*

"They were trapped in a cave," Doro stated. "Grace must be sending us to that little cave along the riding trail, right?"

"Right," Erianna agreed.

It wasn't really much of a cave, being only about five or six feet deep, but it was the only so called 'cave' on the property.

Doro started toward their horses, but Erianna stopped her.

"I have a better idea," she said as she ran toward the far side of the stables. "Let's cut through the gully."

"The gully?" Doro shook her head. "Isn't that against the rules?"

"I don't think so. The rules don't say anything about having to *ride* to the clue locations."

"But—"

Erianna shut down any further protests when she took her teammate's hand and tugged her along. They ran up the rise and into the backyard between their houses.

Both yards were fenced across the back by a six-foot chain-link fence that had been installed to keep their children from accidentally falling into the gully. About a hundred yards wide, the grassy play area was lined by a fence on the far side which had two inset gates so that a push mower could be used on the other side to cut the additional eight feet of grass along the edge of the drop off.

Pap was sitting in his electric wheelchair with a pair of binoculars in his lap. He had obviously moved to this location after the last group of contestants left the front gate so that he could monitor the teams across the way.

Doro took one look at the vertical drop off and balked. "Erin, we can't get down that hill, it's way too steep."

"Yes, we can. I'll help you." She reached into the backpack and pulled out two pairs of work gloves, and leaving the pack in the yard they sat down at the edge.

"I don't know about this."

"Trust me," Erianna assured her. "Just slide down slowly on your backside and dig in with the heels of your boots. I'll go first."

With surprising agility Erianna reached the bottom quickly and stopped near the trunk of an old elm that had toppled across the gulch years ago when it had succumbed to Dutch elm disease. It was located directly under the cave on the far side.

"Okay, Doro," Erianna called out. It's your turn. Just take your time."

Doro did as instructed, albeit not nearly as gracefully. They traversed the large stump and scrambled up the opposite side, which was not nearly as steep. When they got to the cave they found a pole wedged horizontally inside. There were four clues dangling from the pole by a bit of fishing line affixed at the top with an S hook.

"We're the first ones here," Doro announced excitedly, just as they heard the sound of riders approaching.

"Let's get out of here," Erianna told her. She tucked the clue into her shirt and the two women made their way back down the hill and across the tree stump bridge.

Doro took one look up the steep grade above her and said, "We're never going to get back up that hill."

Erianna was worried as well. The location offered no handholds to grasp, so she scanned the slope on either side. "Look, over there. There's a small tree growing near the top. And I see a couple of decent-sized rocks below it. We can use them for footholds. Let's try to climb up there."

They moved along the gully to a place about twenty feet to their left and began to climb. Doro slipped several times and

Erianna had to help her along. The higher they climbed, the steeper the grade became.

Doro stopped at the last rock. "I—can't do this," she panted.

"We've made it this far. You're not giving up on me now."

Just then they heard Jamie call out from across the way.

"That's cheating, Mom."

Doro, shaky and winded shouted back, "Shut up, Jamie!"

Both Matthew and Erianna laughed, the gay sound echoed through the gully. Erianna sobered quickly and reassured her partner, who seemed ready to retreat.

"We're more than halfway to the top," she pointed out. "I'll help you, Doro. You *can* do this."

Doro took several deep breaths and tried to settle her quaking nerves. Finally, she nodded. "Okay, I'm ready."

Erianna went first, pulling herself up until she could reach out and grasp the base of the tree clinging to the side of the hill. She let herself hang there.

"Okay, try to climb up and grab hold of my foot."

Doro did as instructed, using Erianna's leg to pull herself level with her teammate. Erianna helped her ascend until Doro was standing with one foot secured against the base of the tree. Then she climbed up level with her partner.

"Okay. We're almost there."

Doro looked up. "But this last section is nearly vertical."

"It just looks that way from here, but it's easily doable. I'm going to hoist you up this last bit. We can do this," she declared with confidence. "It's a piece of cake."

Erianna used every bit of her strength to shove Doro up, up, up, nearly to the top. With both arms stretched above her head, she managed to hold Doro's foot until she finally pulled herself over the edge and rolled onto the grass, where she lay gasping for air.

"Are you alright?" Pap called out.

Too exhausted to answer, Doro lifted one hand and gave him a thumbs up.

Erianna tried several times to scale the last bit of the slope, but failed. Finally she called out, "Doro, I can't get up. I need your help."

She crawled to the edge and peered down. "I don't know what to do. Should I run and get a rope?"

"No. Just lay flat and put one leg over the edge. I'll grab your boot and pull myself up."

"I'm afraid you'll pull me back down," Doro admitted. "This was a terrible idea. We should have taken the trail like all the other teams."

Erianna spoke to her patiently, just like she did with her children. "I promise I won't pull you down. Just plant your other heel and use your arms to hold yourself firmly to the ground."

When Doro sat at the edge and bent her knee so that her foot dangled, Erianna corrected her. "No, Doro. You need to lay flat."

She did as she was instructed, and Erianna made a lunge for Doro's overhanging boot. At last, after several failed attempts, she was able to grasp her partner's boot and haul herself up and over the edge onto level ground.

Pap clapped enthusiastically. "Bravo!"

Doro wanted nothing more than to lay in the grass and rest, but Erianna pulled her up into a sitting position. Finally gaining their feet, Doro and Erianna moved back through the gate and secured it before they opened their next clue.

What do Tom Sawyer and a Panda have in common?

Doro looked at her father-in-law. "What the hell does that mean?" She leaned heavily against the fence.

Pap smirked.

"I give up. Let's call it a day and go take a nap."

"No way," Erianna decreed. "We're in the lead and I'm not quitting now."

"This is way harder than last year."

"Come on, Dorothy," Erianna said as she handed her friend a bottled water from the backpack. "Help me think." She repeated the clue.

"I don't know," Doro whined. "They're both bears? They both like to hibernate?"

"Bears," Erianna mused. "Tom Sawyer and a bear—" She scratched her head, trying to make the connection.

Doro took another swig of her water and offered some to Erianna. "I'm hungry," she announced. "Let's stop and get something to eat."

"No time to eat," Erianna told her as they began walking toward the stables. She stopped suddenly. "No time to eat," she repeated.

Doro looked askance at her. "What—"

"Eat. Pandas eat bamboo."

"So?"

"Bamboo—Doro, you're a genius. Come on."

Too tired to object, Doro followed her partner. When they reached their horses, Erianna helped her mount up and they rode out.

Finally, Doro questioned her. "Where are we going?"

"To the pond."

"The pond? The golf course pond?"

"Yep. And we have a *huge* lead."

At Doro's look of puzzlement, Erianna elaborated. "Panda bears eat bamboo. And we're headed to the pond." She let that statement sink in.

"Tom Sawyer fished with a bamboo pole?" Doro finally caught on. "Wait—" she pulled her horse to a stop and Erianna pulled up beside her.

"There's another pond on the golf course. On the west side, near the trail cabin."

"That's true," Erianna agreed. "But that pond is too close to the last clue. And I'm betting Grace wouldn't send us there."

"Are you sure?"

"No, but so far she's sent us from the southeast corner of the property to the front gate on the west side. And then she took us east to the pasture, and then past the cabin at the northeast corner and around to where the cave is. I'm betting that she'll take us back here," she pointed in the direction of the pond beyond the old ranch house, "to this pond."

She had been right. As they neared the golf course pond located just across the fenceline they noticed Grace's golf cart parked nearby. They tied their horses to the fence and walked to the pond where they found eight bamboo poles, fishing line and hooks resting on a cloth tarp laid out in the grass.

There was a stake in the ground with a posted set of instructions:

Go fish for your next clue.
You must pull in two bobbers,
one red and white bobber,
one blue and white bobber,
before you can open the clues.

There where eight bobbers floating in the water.

"Have you ever been fishing?" Doro asked.

"No, never."

"Me neither." She grabbed one of the bamboo poles. "How the hell do we attach the fishing line to the pole?"

Erianna had an idea. She pulled off her backpack and grabbed a role of duct tape. "Let's use this."

Doro nodded. They found one end of the fishing line and Doro held it against the edge of the pole as Erianna wrapped a piece of the tape around the line to secure it in place.

"Rules violation," Grace called out through her filter mask.

Erianna turned on her daughter. "How so?"

"Tom Sawyer had no tape to use on his pole," she said.

"Well, damnit!" Doro swore.

"And Tom Sawyer never used a bamboo fishing pole, if you want to get technical about it," her mother shot back. "There was no bamboo growing in Missouri back then."

Grace laughed. "That's true, technically—But you're still accessed a penalty for the duct tape."

Erianna sat back on her haunches to think. She studied the end of the pole, and finally reached into her backpack for her pocketknife. She tried to poke a small hole in the side of the pole, but cut a large gash instead. Turning the pole, she tried again, but could not manage the task.

"Well, this isn't working. Do you have any ideas?"

Doro sat and thought for a few minutes. "We could try to make two cross slashes, wind the line through and around it and tie it off somehow."

Erianna stood up and put one end of the pole between her boots to hold it in place while she sawed down on the top of the pole with her utility knife. When that was finally done, she turned the pole and made a cross cut on the piece of bamboo.

"Okay, here, try and string the line on this one while I cut the other pole."

Doro did her best to pull the line through the gashes in the bamboo, wind it around the pole and tie the line securely. By the time she was finished Erianna had the other pole cut. She handed it off so that the process could be repeated.

Erianna sat in the grass and tried to tie one of the fishing hooks to the other end of the line. When she had one hook secure she got up and cast the line into the water. But instead of seeing the line fly, it caught up in the grass behind her.

"Do you know how to cast off?"

"No idea," Doro replied.

Grace, who was sitting nearby in a folding chair, was thoroughly enjoying the spectacle. She chuckled now and then as the inept fisherwomen tried to complete the task at hand. At the rate they were going they would be here for the rest of the day.

When her mother finally managed to cast the line into the water she immediately realized that it was too short to reach the bobbers in the middle of the pond.

"Well, shoot." She turned to Doro. "This line is too short. Don't use so much line when you wind it around the pole," she instructed.

"Too late. I just finished this one and I tied it the same way I did with the one you're holding."

Erianna frowned. Then she scooted as close to the edge of the water as she could before she recast the line into the pond.

Watching her mother and Doro try to fish for the bobbers was like watching babies learning to walk. They tried again and again, but weren't even close to successfully pulling one in.

The other groups appeared, one by one, and the women were still floundering.

They had been the first to arrive at the pond by a wide margin, but the last to leave. Ironically, Bob and Theo, who were the last arrivals, made short work of the task and left in first place, followed by Matthew and Jamie.

Finally, the women managed to pull in their bobbers with their clues attached. The first one was a quote from the book:

Huck Finn and Tom Sawyer swears they will keep mum about this and they wish they may drop down dead in their tracks if they ever tell and rot.

They opened the second clue: *Injun Joe got off scott free for the murder of Sawbones.*

"We need to go to the old graveyard across the road from the southwest boundary line," Doro said.

Erianna agreed, and they rode out, pushing their well-rested mounts into an easy lope across the pasture. By the time they got to the graveyard all the other teams had left.

"Look for a headstone with the name Robinson," Erianna told her partner. "I think that was the doctor's name."

They made short work of the task and found the next clue, a rolled-up piece of parchment paper tied with a ribbon. It was a map of the cross-country course with X's marking spots where keys would be found and a circle around the location of the 'buried treasure'.

The women followed the map and collected four keys, then headed for the stables where they dismounted and led their horses through the center aisle to the practice ring. There, under the mounting block, they located the last of four strong boxes. Using the keys to open the box, they found two chocolate coins wrapped in gold.

"Time." Grace and Pap both stopped her swimming watches and Grace noted the time on her clipboard.

Doro collapsed in the dirt, hungry and exhausted. Everyone but Gus was gathered there. Erianna asked her daughter who had won.

"I have some calculations to make," she announced to the group. "We'll meet at Pap's and I'll make the announcement there," she said through her mask and swimming goggles as she turned to head up the hill.

Matthew approached Erianna. "Are you all right?" he asked her. "I got worried when I saw you trying to scale that slope."

"I'm fine," she waved a hand in dismissal. "But you should probably ask your sister how she's doing."

They looked down at Erianna's teammate, who was lying unresponsive in the dirt. Matthew and Bob managed to pull her to her feet.

"I'll help with the horses," Matthew advised Bob. "I think your wife could use a shower and a comfy chair to collapse in."

Gus, who had just arrived in his truck from his station at the graveyard, helped the others tend to their horses. Forty-five minutes later, after everyone had cleaned up and gathered in Pap's duplex, Grace and Pap had tallied their results and were ready to announce the winner.

Ginny served up bowls of Cowboy Stew with crusty bread as Grace stepped forward.

"The official results for the second annual Autumnal Treasure Hunt are in," she announced. "Bob and Theo finished with the fastest time," she informed the group. "However, they incurred a ten-minute penalty for not figuring out the clue at the oak tree on their own."

"Matt and Jamie finished with the second fastest time, but they were assessed a four-minute penalty for not bringing in all four keys from the treasure map leg of the race, plus an additional three-minute penalty when Jamie cantered his horse in a trot zone on the trail."

"That's not fair," Jamie objected. "We got the key that opened the box. We didn't need all four keys. And besides, I was just trying to keep up with Uncle Matt's horse on the trail."

Ginny had been assigned to monitor the trail paths on her four-wheeler. They were marked with walk, trot and canter zones. "If you couldn't keep up with your uncle's horse you should have called out for him to slow down."

"Nice try, James," Grace added. "But you missed the fourth key, and the clue clearly showed that you had to collect all four. So you incurred that penalty as well."

Jamie scowled. "Well, Mom and Erin cheated. They cut through the gully instead of riding the trail to the cave."

There wasn't anything in the rules stating that you had to ride to the clues," Grace clarified. "So technically they didn't cheat."

"But—"

"Don't be a sore loser, son," Bob admonished the boy.

As Jamie sulked, Grace continued. "Ryan and Ned had the third fastest time. They incurred a three-minute penalty for climbing the fence which was clearly marked 'Wet Paint'.

"And in fourth place, Mom and Doro." They incurred a two-minute penalty for trying to use duct tape on the fishing pole."

"We took it off," Doro mumbled from her recliner.

Erianna glanced at Pap and grinned. "Don't mind her," she told Grace. "She's been put through the ringer today and she's exhausted."

"Yeah, I heard about your shortcut."

"So who actually won?" Ned asked his sister.

"Okay—drumroll please." The boys complied. "The winners of the second annual Autumnal Treasure Hunt are—" she paused for effect. "Ryan and Ned by a total of forty-four seconds over the second place team."

Ned pounded Ryan on the back. "We won!" he exclaimed.

Ryan picked up his partner and swirled him around and

around as Ned laughed with childlike glee. Everyone congratulated the pair on their victory, and when things finally settled down their prize was handed out. Pap did the honors.

"Ryan, Ned, come collect your prizes." The boys approached Pap's bed, where he was resting after his long day in the wheelchair.

"In honor of your victory I bestow on you these minted one-ounce gold coins."

Erianna gasped. "You can't do that, Pap. Those coins are worth a fortune."

He gave her a dismissive wave.

"Bob and Theo, you came in second," Grace announced. "Good work at the fishing pond."

Pap handed out two one-ounce silver coins to the teammates. "Congratulations."

The honorees graciously accepted their coins.

"Matt and James earned the third-place distinction."

Pap looked at Jamie. "Come here, James," he told his grandson. Jamie did as he was told.

"The third-place prize is usually a bronze medal, but I decided to give the third place finishers silver-minted coins as well." He handed the prize to his grandson, but took hold of his arm as he placed the coin in his hand.

"I'm not happy about your behavior, young man. But, you did earn the third place position and so I'm going to let your poor sportsmanship slide. This time," he added. "I hope that in the future you learn to be a more gracious loser."

Jamie hung his head. Then he cleared his throat and turned toward Grace. "I'm sorry for being such a sore loser."

Grace came up and gave him a reassuring hug. "That's okay, Jamie. I'm sorry that you lost. But did you have fun?"

"Yeah, I really did," he admitted with a small grin.

"Well, that's what's most important."

Matthew stepped up to receive his coin and turned to thank Grace.

"On behalf of my teammate and me, I'd like to thank you for

the wonderful adventure we had today. And in honor of your hard work I'd like to give you my third-place prize."

Grace shook her head, but Matthew continued. "It's obvious that you put a lot of hard work into this and you deserve a prize of your own."

Grace looked at him for several moments before accepting his offer. "Thanks, Matt."

Bob, too, offered her his coin, and once again she objected.

"You should give that to Pap. He worked just as hard as I did."

"No, sweetheart," Pap shook his head. "You deserve it."

Grace blushed prettily and Pap chuckled. "Three cheers for Grace."

"Hip, hip, hooray," everyone chimed in. "Hip, hip, hooray. Hip, hip hooray."

Chapter 11

Matthew was exhausted, both mentally and physically. While everyone else pitched in to clean up he went next door and sat down in the family room recliner. He needed to close his eyes for a few minutes. He'd been burning the candle from both ends, and his battles with Erianna had taken a mental toll.

He pulled the footrest up and settled in. *I need a vacation.* As he drifted off he fantasized about spending time at the beach with a beautiful, golden-honey blonde running in the sand and frolicking in the ocean with him.

Ned and Grace had gone to their rooms for the night and the Donovans went home right after supper. Erianna helped Ginny with Pap's nightly ablutions. She offered him a peck on his cheek as she made ready to lock up for the night. But Pap stopped her, reaching out to take her hand in his giant paw.

"You look frazzled." He raised one eyebrow. "What's troubling you?"

"Nothing—" she started. But Pap was an intuitive man and she knew he couldn't be fooled. She shrugged. "Things are getting a little out of control."

He nodded in understanding and gave her hand a gentle, reassuring squeeze. "He's really a very nice guy. I'm sure he doesn't mean to complicate things for you."

It was the second time that she'd heard Matthew described that way. She looked toward the doorway between the two units.

"Maybe *you* should adopt him. Let him live over here and see how long it takes you to lose your patience."

Pap grinned widely. "Touché."

Erianna locked up and turned to find Matthew fast asleep

in her family room. She let him nap while she went upstairs to tuck Ned in for the night and look in on her daughter. When she came back down to pack school lunches for the morning he was still sound asleep.

All set for the next day, Erianna went over to wake him. "Matt," she bent down and lightly touched his shoulder. "It's time for you to go home."

He roused a little without opening his eyes and mumbled, "Five more minutes."

Erianna stood over him, watching as he slept. His features were softened in repose and he didn't seem as menacing as when he was awake.

"I know you're a nice guy," she murmured, "but I sure wish you'd go be nice somewhere else."

She reached down again. "Matt, you need to wake up now. It's late."

He sighed deeply and began to squirm in the chair. "Mmm, five more min…" his words trailed off.

"Matthew—"

One moment she was leaning over him and the next she was in his lap. She wasn't sure how it had happened.

"Mmm," he mumbled. "Go home—" he moved a bit to get more comfortable. "Five more minutes—" With that he was sound asleep again.

It was clear that he was in no condition to drive home safely.

Erianna perched stiffly against him, but he was out for the count and she doubted that he knew she was sitting on his lap. She relaxed a little and readjusted herself in his arms. Closing her eyes, she drank in his tantalizing scent. *Oh lord, you smell good.* It felt so natural to be in his arms that she was reluctant to get up.

Truth be told, Erianna did enjoy his company. She always had. He fit well into the family dynamic and got along with everyone, including Gus, who was a hard man to win over.

Maybe someday, long after the kids were grown and gone, maybe then they could become a couple. But for now, she would strengthen her resolve. There was no room in her life for a romantic fling, and she had made that point very clear to him, time and again. She was sure that in time he would accept that she was not interested in him and he would move on to greener pastures.

Erianna woke an hour later, still snuggled up against him. She yawned and stretched, and Matthew sighed sweetly when felt her movements.

"Love you," he murmured in his sleep.

Erianna grew very still. Carefully, so as not to further rouse him, she got up and backed away from the recliner.

She clutched her fist against her heart, worried that the pounding in her chest would wake him. She was sure that the sound was echoing around the room, and her ears were filled with the sound of the blood rushing through her veins.

When she finally managed to make her feet move she covered him with a crocheted afghan throw and went upstairs to her room. She undressed and climbed into bed, but sleep eluded her. She missed the warmth of Matthew's body against hers.

Dear Erianna,

I dreamed last night that I slept with you in my arms. Your heavenly scent lingers on my clothes and I'm tempted to never wash them again. Instead, I want to pillow them against me and hold on to that wonderful image.

Now that I've found you, I think of all the time lost when we could have been together.

I've yearned for you, my honeybee, and I now rejoice.

Matt

The note had been left on her desk in the stables and she found it when she went down to do her pre-dawn chores. Well, he had gotten around her decree that she wouldn't read any more of his missives. She wrote a response on the paper and placed it in an envelope along with a copy of the newly signed contract she had drawn up for Ráfaga that would be mailed to his office.

Matthew,
"You could have found me.
You could have seen me.
But I have always been the invisible one."
—Jocelyn Soriano

Let go, Matthew. It's too late…
E

Early the next week a card arrived in the mail. It was addressed to Grace, but was written in Matthew's handwriting. Erianna wondered what he was up to this time. When Grace came home she opened the card.

The front pictured two Panda bears munching on bamboo, the inside was blank. Matthew had written:

Dear Grace,
Thank you for inviting me to participate in your Treasure Hunt. I had a blast.
Matt

That same week the new office desk arrived. After searching through the Ikea store and shopping online Grace had finally decided on a semi-circular desk with the right dimensions to fit the space. Removing one of Erianna's sitting area chairs and the coffee table, they positioned one end of the desk against the bathroom wall directly across from Erianna's desk. In addition, they purchased a small file cabinet that fit perfectly under the end of the desk that butted up against the bathroom wall.

All in all, the new piece did look nice in the room. Grace, who had taken charge of the project, had done a very good job and Erianna approved of the result.

Matthew came to visit that Friday and was thrilled that Erianna had consented to allow him to work from her office. Grace showed him the new furnishings and asked him what he thought.

"Um—" he hesitated.

"Oh, you don't like it." There was disappointment in her tone.

"That's not true. I love it. But—"

She was puzzled. "Did you have something else in mind?"

"No, Grace, it's perfect. But where's the chair?"

She giggled. "Sorry. I forgot about the chair. That was pretty stupid."

"Don't worry about it."

Erianna came in just then.

"We forgot about a chair, Mom."

"Indeed, we did." She wished she could have forgotten about the desk, too, but that was water under the bridge.

"That's okay," Matthew told her. "A chair will be easy to find. It really is a nice desk. Thanks for doing this."

"It'll be easier than you think to find a chair," Erianna informed them. "Follow me, guys."

She led them upstairs to her room and through the master bath to the far side of the suite. Opening a door that he assumed was a closet, she turned on a light and stepped aside to allow Grace and Matthew to pass. Then she left them to their own devices.

He found himself in a large attic space, which was obviously located above the two-car garage. They rummaged around and found two office chairs on rollers under a dusty sheet.

"Why don't we sit in them and decide which one is more comfortable?" Grace suggested.

They tried out both and found that one had a crack in one of the legs that gave way when Matthew tried to sit on it.

"Well, it looks like this is our only choice," Grace laughed when he almost tipped over in the broken chair.

They lugged the piece down and took it out to the garage to clean it. By the time they had it in position Erianna called everyone to dinner.

* * *

Throughout the month of October Matthew became a regular visitor to Berrington Farm. When Erianna realized that his accumulation of spare clothes was stacking up on the pool table in the rec room and he was doing his laundry in the basement machines she brought down a small dresser from the attic for him to store his belongings.

How and when she had made peace with Matthew's presence, Erianna wasn't sure. He rode along with them when Gus and she went to the dance club and he became a regular attendee at Sunday morning mass. He also went to Ned's soccer games and watched Grace's tennis matches whenever he could.

Matthew had made no further romantic advances, but he did touch her casually, offering little hugs and brushes across her back as he passed. And he was fond of brushing her bangs to the side when she tried to hide her eyes from him.

They would often gather in the family room to play board games or team up for a round of Euchre. Ned was especially good at chess and he welcomed the competition that Matthew gave him. Ned had long surpassed his mother and Grace's abilities, and he was glad to have a worthy opponent in Matthew.

Some evenings he would sit opposite Erianna on the couch and rub her feet, which more often than not put her to sleep. By the end of the month she was allowing him to kiss her again. He would offer her a friendly goodnight kiss when he stayed over, but he never pushed her to the point where she became uncomfortable.

The Saturday before Halloween dawned with bright, clear blue skies. They were enjoying Indian summer with temperatures expected to be in the low eighties. It was a perfect day for a group trail ride and picnic at the trail cabin.

Chip Neading had booked the day for his family to visit Berrington Farm. They arrived just as Erianna was coming back on her four-wheeler from the small trail cabin where she had dropped off the picnic lunch Doro packed for the excursion.

"Good morning," she greeted them. Erianna was not pleased that she would have to entertain Chip and his family, but paying customers were paying customers, so she put aside her resentments and adopted a friendly, albeit professional attitude.

"Hello," Nancy replied. "The weather is just perfect, isn't it? We really lucked out."

"You really did," Erianna agreed with a pleasant smile.

"Kids, this is Erin Fowler. She grew up on the same street as your dad and me and we went to school together."

The children were distracted by the horses poking their heads out of their stalls and Erianna could tell that they wanted to explore.

"This is our older son, Trey," Chip began the introductions. "And his younger brother is Seth. Patsy is our youngest."

"Hello, Trey." Erianna reached out and shook his hand. "How old are you?"

"I'm eight."

Next she shook hands with Seth. "And how old are you, Seth?"

"Seven."

Patsy was clinging to her father's leg so Erianna went down on one knee to put herself on the little girl's eye level. She offered the little girl a friendly smile. "And you must be Patsy. Is that right?"

She nodded shyly, still clinging to her father's leg. Erianna held out her hand, and after several moments of deliberation, the little girl took a step forward. Erianna took Patsy's hand in hers and said, "I'm guessing you must be about—" she pretended to ponder for a moment. "About five. Is that right?"

Patsy smiled. She held up five fingers. "I'll be five on November tenth."

"Are you going to have a big party?"

She nodded enthusiastically.

"That will be fun, and just think of all the presents you're going to get."

Ned came around the corner just then and called out to his mother. “The kids’ horses are saddled. My mount is ready and Gus is finishing saddling Leona for you.”

Erianna rose and turned toward her son as he walked toward the group. “Thanks, Ned.”

When he reached them she made the introductions. “This is my son, Nathan Edward. We call him Ned.”

After the introductions were completed Ned asked his mother which horses she wanted saddled for the adults.

Erianna turned to Nancy and inquired about her riding experience.

“Well, I’m not what you’d call an expert, but I’ve ridden quite a bit over the years. I’d say I’m a competent rider and am comfortable in the saddle.”

“Okay,” Erianna responded. “Good.” She turned to Ned. “I think Rowena will be a good fit for Mrs. Neading.”

“Rowena, that’s an unusual name for a horse,” Nancy remarked

“I suppose. Rowena means ‘white-haired’ in Welsh. The mare has very light coloring, with a white mane and tail. There really is no such thing as a white horse, as all horses with white coloring are really grays, but the name fits. She’s easy to ride and sure footed. You won’t have any problems with her on the trail.”

“What about Mr. Neading?” Ned asked.

“You can call me Chip. I rode a lot with Matt as a kid. But I haven’t had any formal lessons.”

Ned looked questioningly at his mother, and she shrugged.

“Do you mind if I ask how tall you are and how much you weigh?” the boy inquired.

“Not at all. I’m six foot one and I weigh in the neighborhood of two ten.” He looked over at his wife. “Okay, okay,” he smirked. “More like two twenty. But I’m going to get that off,” he assured his wife.

She threw him a disbelieving look and he laughed.

Approaching the group, Gus had overheard the conversation. After an extended discussion between Erianna and him, they couldn't seem to come to an agreement on which horse Chip should ride.

"We could let him ride Matthew's horse," Erianna said. "But Ráfaga has only been on the trails once or twice and I don't know how he will fare with Chip aboard."

Gus disagreed. "He really should be riding Archie."

"I'm not sure Chip can handle Archie," Erianna countered. "You know how he hates that steep trail hill. I don't usually take him when we go to the cabin for just that reason."

"Well, what's it gonna be? I don't have all day."

"Okay, I'll deal with Archie. Saddle him up."

Then she turned to Ned. "Go saddle Rowena for me please."

The boys were getting antsy and Erianna turned her attention back to the children. She knew that they had had a long car ride and probably needed to use the bathroom before they started, so she escorted the family to Gus's sleeping quarters so they could use the bathroom, which she had cleaned earlier that morning.

Matthew appeared just as the children were coming out. Patsy spotted him immediately and ran as fast as her little legs could go, launching herself into his arms.

"Patsy cakes!" he hugged her against him. "How's my little sweetie pie?" He smacked his lips against her chubby cheek and she squealed in delight.

"I'm going on a horse ride, Uncle Matt."

"Are you sure you're old enough?" he teased. "Didn't your dad say you had to be five years old before you could ride a horse?"

"I'm almost five," she declared.

"That's right," he said as he tickled her. She giggled and squirmed.

"Are you coming with us, Uncle Matt?"

He looked to Erianna, who nodded her assent, so he left to saddle his horse. Nancy went to their car to collect the children's riding helmets.

* * *

While Erianna and Ned worked with little Patsy to get her accustomed to riding Daisy the others, under Gus's supervision, were settling in on their mounts in the far riding circle of the fenced figure 8 practice rings.

They stood on either side of the young girl as she took her first horseback riding lesson.

"This is a western saddle," Erianna began the tutorial. "It's just the right saddle for a little girl like you. See here?" she grabbed onto the saddle horn. "You can keep one hand on this while you ride and in the other hand you hold your reins."

She gave Patsy the reins to hold.

"That's perfect, Patsy," Ned encouraged her. "I bet you already knew that from watching your brothers when they take their lessons, didn't you."

"Yep. I watch them a lot."

Patsy didn't seem the least bit frightened and Erianna was relieved.

"Daisy just loves little ladies. Don't you, girl?" She cooed to the pony, who nickered and threw her head a little, as if nodding in agreement.

"She'll do whatever you ask her to do. You just have to know how to talk to her."

"That's right," Ned agreed. "When you want her to walk you just say, 'walk Daisy' and she'll do just what you say."

The little girl nodded in understanding.

"Do you want to try it?" Ned asked.

Patsy nodded and said, "Walk Daisy." The pony, standing a mere ten hands high, dutifully began moving around the ring, and Patsy seemed quite at ease in the saddle. She had good balance and looked comfortable and relaxed.

"Okay, Patsy," Erianna continued the lesson. "Now you need to learn how to make the pony go where you want her to go. We steer ponies the same way your dad steers his car. When your dad wants his car to turn, he moves the steering wheel and the car turns. The same thing happens here." Erianna reached up and placed her hand over Patsy's little fingers. "Which way would you like to turn first?"

"I want to go that way." Patsy took her hand off the saddle horn and pointed to the right.

"Do you know which direction that is?" Ned asked her. "Is that a right turn or a left turn?"

"Mmm."

"Which hand is your right hand?" Ned prompted.

"This is my right hand," Patsy supplied with ease.

"So which direction are you pointing?"

"Right."

"Wow. I can't believe how smart you are," Ned smiled happily. Patsy preened.

"Okay," said. "So if you want Daisy to go right, all you need to do is take your reins and move them in that direction, just like your dad moves his hand when he wants his car to turn."

"Do you want to try it?" Ned asked.

Patsy nodded confidently and moved the hand holding the reins to the right. Daisy immediately made the maneuver and Patsy screeched with glee. "Mommy, Mommy," she called out. "I told Daisy to turn right and she did."

"Good job!"

Erianna and Ned walked alongside Daisy as Patsy turned her, first in one direction and then the other.

As they walked Erianna continued. "Okay, Patsy, you've learned to walk Daisy and you can turn her wherever you want to go. Now, what if you want her to stop? What do you think you should do?"

"I say 'stop, Daisy.'" The pony stopped and Patsy beamed.

"And you can also pull back a little on the reins to get her to stop. Would you like to try that?"

After showing Patsy a few more essential points and having a try at trotting, which she handled very well, Erianna was comfortable enough to begin the trail ride with the group. They moved their mounts into line in the near ring.

Ned took the lead on his Pinto, Boswell. The gelding, standing thirteen hands high, was accustomed to leading riding groups.

Trey was next in line riding Flossie, a chestnut pony. Erianna guided Nancy's mount into position behind Trey. Rowena stood a little under fifteen hands and was a veteran trail horse. Following her, Chip moved into line on Archie, a solid brown quarter horse with a white blaze. Archie stood sixteen hands high. A solidly built gelding, he could easily handle Chip's height and weight.

Behind Chip, Erianna brought Seth into line on Toby. The unflappable Caspian pony, a sibling of Daisy's, stood twelve hands high and would be unperturbed by Archie's antics if he started to act up. Daisy came into line next, following her brother.

Erianna moved Leona into position behind the Caspian siblings. Her mare, a Bright Bay Arabian with a rich, reddish-brown coat, black mane, tail and lower legs, and a white stripe on her face stood just over fifteen hands high. She was Erianna's favorite trail horse.

Bringing up the rear, Matthew was mounted on his stallion.

When Gus saw how Erianna had lined up the horses he shook his head. "You're gonna have trouble."

He was exactly right. Daisy refused to follow Toby. Normally accustomed to riding behind her brother, she would not cooperate today. Gus walked alongside Patsy as they tried to walk single file around the practice ring. But Daisy kept falling out of line, trying to move toward Ráfaga.

"You're gonna have to let her follow the black," Gus said. "She's not staying in line."

He led Daisy to the end of the line and the little pony happily fell into step behind her stablemate. Erianna moved back to follow Patsy, and most of the horses settled in. Gus grumbled and scratched his whiskered chin, still not happy with the order. He grabbed Chip's horse by the chin strap and moved him to the very end of the line.

After several more circuits around the ring, Gus was finally satisfied. He opened the gate and Ned walked his horse out of the ring, followed by Trey, Nancy, Seth, Matt, Patsy, Erin and Chip. They walked their mounts along the wide riding path, which was fenced on both sides, toward the gate to the riding trails.

Erianna walked on foot beside Patsy and spoke softly to her, reassuring her that she was doing great.

"Uncle Matt's horse is really big," Patsy said. "Isn't Daisy afraid of it?"

"Not at all," Erianna replied, telling the little girl the story of how Daisy and Ráfaga had become best friends. "Do you want to know a secret?"

Patsy, much like her mother, was intrigued by the notion of learning a secret. She nodded, and Erianna leaned over a little and said, "Daisy is the boss of Ráfaga. But don't tell Uncle Matt."

"She is?" Patsy wasn't convinced.

"Yep. She really is. Their stalls are right next to each other, and when Ráfaga tries to misbehave Daisy makes him stop being bad. Ráfaga thinks that Daisy is his mother and he doesn't do anything bad when she's around. So you don't have to worry about following such a big horse. You're as safe as can be riding behind your Uncle Matt. I promise."

They were nearing the far gate and Erianna jogged to the front of the line to open it. The horses moved through in single file.

"Hold back, will you, Chip?"

He stopped his horse just beyond the gate. Erianna quickly closed it and remounted. She moved Leona into line behind Daisy, with Chip bringing up the rear as they entered the densely wooded trail.

Chip had heard Erianna's discussion with his daughter. As she passed him he simply said, "Thanks."

"No problem. She's very bright and very brave."

"And very bossy," he added with a chuckle.

The group rode the trail for about ten minutes. When the path widened and the trees thinned, Ned held up his hand. "Riders Ho-o," he called out in a sing-song voice.

The boys giggled as they followed Ned's instructions.

"Wait here," Erianna told Chip. "And take your mount in hand. He may try to turn back toward the barn."

She moved to the front of the line of horses and dismounted, tying her mare to the hitching post at the bottom of a steep hill.

"Okay everybody, we're going to ride up this hill one at a time. All your horses are used to walking up the hill, so you don't have to worry."

Just then she noticed that Archie was becoming restless, so she walked to the back of the line of riders to deal with the recalcitrant quarter horse.

Ned continued with the standard spiel given to all trail riding groups.

"When you go up a steep hill on horseback, you need to give your horse his head. Loosen your reins in your hand so that your horse can move freely as it walks up the hill."

Ned demonstrated before continuing the tutorial. "Grab hold of the saddle horn and lean forward, like this." Again, he demonstrated. "Your legs should move back toward your horse's flanks. That will help it stay balanced and help you stay in the saddle."

With the exception of Matthew and Chip, everyone practiced the position Ned had described. Meanwhile, Erianna dealt with Archie. The gelding shied as she neared, but she pulled a piece of carrot from her breast pocket and offered it to the quarter horse. She grabbed the cheekpiece of the western bridle as the gelding reached for the carrot. Then she took up the reins under his chin.

"You'll need to dismount here, Chip. Archie hates to be ridden up this hill. I don't know why."

Chip dismounted and Erianna led the obstinate horse to the hitching post where she tied him securely next to Leona. Daisy was standing next to Ráfaga and the others who had gathered around Ned.

"We're ready here, Mom."

"Good. Let's get started."

Ned turned his horse toward the hill and showed the group how to ascend, and then Trey followed on Flossie. When he reached the top, Erianna turned to Matthew.

"Would you mind going next?"

"Sure, he agreed.

"Hold on a minute." Erianna turned to Patsy. "Daisy is going to follow Ráfaga up the hill," she told the youngster. "But I'm going to have you ride up the hill with me."

"I can do it myself," Patsy protested.

Erianna lifted her from the saddle and she pouted unhappily. She held the girl on one hip as she looped the western-style reins across Daisy's neck near her withers.

Patsy protested a little louder and tried to wriggle free from Erianna's hold. At her nod, Matthew started up the hill with Daisy in his wake.

"You're mean," the child hollered.

"Patricia Neading," Chip admonished his daughter, taking her from Erianna's arms. "Shame on you."

Apparently, those particular words were devastating for the child and she buried her face in her father's shirt.

"You straighten up and apologize this minute. We *do not* behave this way in public."

While Chip dealt with little Patsy, Ráfaga and Daisy safely reached the top of the incline. Seth was sent up the hill next, followed by Nancy. Then Chip, with Patsy riding piggyback, traversed the hill on foot. Still unwilling to apologize, Patsy was set on a large rock at the top of the hill, Chip's version of a time out spot.

Erianna was alone at the bottom of the hill with the two remaining horses. She untied Archie from the hitching rail and turned him toward the hill, but the gelding pulled back. Grabbing him by one ear, she stared him down.

"You're going up that hill, you old codger. I'm not putting up with any more of this nonsense."

The horse seemed to understand her threatening tone and he grudgingly allowed Erianna to walk him up the hill. Clearly unhappy, he snorted and blew when he reached the top.

"Good boy," she soothed him as she rubbed his chin and jowls. "Good boy. You're just a big baby, aren't you fella." Her tone settled the animal somewhat, and she felt comfortable enough to hand his reins to Chip.

Erianna walked back down the hill and remounted Leona. By the time she reached the top, Ned had everyone remounted, lined up and ready continue the trail ride. She called out, "Riders Go-o," in the same sing-song tone that Ned had used and they were off.

They spent their morning riding the trails. The group trotted their mounts in the flat, open areas and Ned stopped to let the boys explore the cave. By one o'clock Ned had led the group into the clearing where the cabin was located near the northeast boundary line. There was a large, fenced pasture next to the little cabin and Erianna rode ahead to open the gate. Several jumps were scattered around the perimeter of the enclosed area and as the boys and men rode through, Erianna asked them to stop for a moment.

"You can run your horses and have all the fun you want here. But do not try the jumps. None of your mounts are jumpers and we don't want to risk injuring them. Okay?"

"Yes, ma'am," Seth agreed. "We won't."

With that the boys were off to play, pretending they were pony express riders handing off mail from one rider to the next.

Patsy wanted to canter her horse just like the boys. Erianna looked to Nancy for advice.

"I don't think so, young lady," she told her daughter. She dismounted and moved to her daughter's side, placing her hands on her hips. "You haven't apologized to Erin yet, have you?"

"Oh, I forgot. I'm sorry, Erin."

"Thank you, Patsy."

The child was not experienced enough to try to canter her pony, so Matthew offered to take her up on his lap, which Nancy okayed. This time Patsy did not object as Erianna lifted her off her horse and into Matthew's arms.

After they entered the pasture Erianna closed the gate. She and Nancy led the horses to the small paddock where Erianna loosened their saddles and drew water from a pump well and sloshed it into a trough for the animals to drink.

They walked to the cabin. A wide screened-in porch fronted the structure. There was a living room / kitchenette area, with another area sectioned off for a full-size bed with a small half bath.

Erianna would sometimes retreat to this cabin for a few hours of peace and quiet, times when her life seemed overwhelming and she needed a respite from the hustle and bustle of her hectic life. She had come across it not long after she first arrived and immediately set to work restoring the dilapidated structure.

"This is lovely, Erin."

"Thank you. I like it."

The women set out the picnic lunch, a variety of sandwiches with Doro's homemade bowtie pasta salad.

One by one the riders wandered in and sat down to eat. When everyone was finished Matthew helped her clean up and repack the picnic basket. Then they went out to watch the Neadings play cornhole and swing on the tire swing hanging from a branch of the large maple tree in the yard. They sat companionably in Adirondack chairs, and after a time Matthew reached for her hand.

"I love you, Erianna," he said when she looked over at him.

Her eyes rounded and she shook her head ever so slightly.

"You are the most adorable woman I've ever known."

She tried to look away, but there was something so compelling in his expression that she couldn't. She studied his handsome face, from his liquid brown eyes that seemed to sparkle with life to his strong jawline and the oh-so tempting shape of his mouth.

She longed to kiss him. She wanted to run her fingers through his dark, wavy hair and trace the shell of his ear with her fingertips. She wanted to be held in his arms and cocooned in his tender embrace.

Matthew brought her hand up and brushed his lips across her knuckles with a featherlight touch. She shivered in response. Oh, how she wanted this man. She'd never known these kinds of feelings, and she longed to throw caution to the wind and return his sentiment. It was so tempting, so very tempting.

Thankfully, Patsy came running up and climbed onto her Uncle Matt's lap. Erianna was ever so happy to have been interrupted. She got up from her chair and walked over to the horseshoe pit, challenging Chip to a game.

Ned had been doodling in his sketchpad, which had been packed in the picnic basket, and he wandered over and plopped down at Matthew's feet. "Look here, Patsy, and I'll draw a picture of you. Would you like that?"

She nodded happily, and Ned began a portrait of her with his sketching pencil. The sound of horseshoes clinking echoed in the air, joined by the sounds of the boys swinging on the tire swing.

"You two make a mighty handsome couple," Chip said to her.

"Knock it off, Chip," she growled.

Chapter 12

The group arrived back at the stables late that afternoon. Ryan was there to help groom and stable the horses, and James ran down the hill just as everyone was dismounting.

"My mom wants to know if you guys would like to stay for supper. We're grilling out hot dogs and hamburgers."

"I'm sure the Neadings would like to get on the road, Jamie."

"I haven't seen Matt's sister in quite a while," Nancy said. "Are you sure it won't be too much trouble?" she asked the boy.

"Mom says it won't be any trouble at all. It's a nice day for a cookout and she said to tell you that there's plenty of food for everybody."

Erianna pointed out that they would need a change of clothes and Nancy told her that they had, indeed, packed spare outfits.

"Matt told me about your daughter's allergies, so I packed clean clothes for everyone, just in case."

Of course, he did. What a buttinsky. Erianna had no choice but to give in. "If you'll show Jamie where your things are, he'll put them in the basement for you."

Jamie followed Nancy to their mini-van and collected the bags of clothes and shoes. After Patsy said goodbye to Daisy Erianna escorted Nancy and her daughter to the clean room and explained the procedure.

By the time the women were finished the men came up and took their turns, and within the hour everyone was gathered at Doro's house. Bob and Matthew put the meat on the charcoal grill and the women set out plates and side dishes on the Donovan's screened-in porch.

Pap and Ginny joined the group and they listened as the Neading children regaled them with stories about their exciting trail ride. Ned finished his portrait of Patsy and gave the picture to the youngster.

Nancy was astonished by the talent Ned showed in his artwork. "That's a very good likeness, Ned. I'm going to frame this. Would you sign it for me?"

Erianna sat on her porch watching the others playing wiffle ball under the backyard floodlights. Little Patsy had fallen asleep on the two-cushioned glider and Erianna sat with her as the others teamed up for a game.

Her thoughts wandered back to Matthew's profession of love. She closed her eyes and imagined herself saying those words to him, wishing that she could tell him how much she loved him in return.

There was no denying it, no fighting it. He'd won her heart and she longed to tell him so.

Sitting quietly, she imagined sharing her innermost secrets with him, whispering of her childhood infatuation and her fantasies of a lifetime together. She shivered at the thought of making love with him and of waking in the morning wrapped in his arms.

It was such a lovely thought. *If only—*

Caught up in the mists of her daydreams, she felt a warm hand on her cheek and she sighed. "If only," she murmured.

"If only what?" a deep, soothing voice replied.

Erianna opened her eyes to find Matthew on his knees before her.

"If only you could tell me that you love me, too?" he suggested in a soft whisper.

Still hovering between fantasy and reality, she answered, "Yes."

Matthew brought his lips to hers and kissed her sweetly. "I love you, Erianna."

"I love you, too," she whispered.

He kissed her again, oh so tenderly. She was swept away, reveling in his love and flush with the pleasure of the fairytale moment.

"Will you marry me?"

"Mmm. Marry you," she murmured with a nod.

"Oh, my honeybee, you make me so happy. So happy."

Erianna drew in a deep breath and opened her eyes again, shaking her head a little to clear the cobwebs. She tried to move away from him, but Matthew drew her to her feet and held her in his arms. He kissed her, and she felt a rush of heat spread throughout her body. She was helpless to stop the flood of emotions washing over her.

Erianna was floating on air as Matthew lifted her off her feet. She heard the sound of his laughter and was caught up in the joy of his reaction. It all seemed so surreal—was this just a young girl's fantasy? Was she Cinderella? Had her Prince Charming finally found her?

When he set her back on her feet she felt dizzy.

The sudden sound of Chip's voice congratulating the couple brought her back to reality.

Chip had come to check on his sleeping daughter, and he stood quietly at the doorway watching the exchange between Matthew and Erianna. She had just agreed to marry his best friend and he was thrilled for them.

"Wait," she finally managed. "Wait a minute."

But it seemed that neither of them heard her. They were pounding each other on the back and talking nonstop, only Erianna couldn't seem to make out the words. She turned and ran for her office.

Surprised by her sudden flight, both men followed her, reaching the door before she could shut it and lock them out.

Matthew cautiously approached her, but when he reached out she shied away.

"What—what just happened here?"

"It's simple. We love each other. We're in love and we're going to be married." He pulled her into his arms and kissed her.

Erianna could not deny her love for this man, but it was all happening too fast.

"Let me go," she demanded, and he complied, albeit reluctantly. She stood before him, studying his face.

"Erin?"

She squeezed her eyes shut and rubbed her fingers along the bridge of her nose. When she finally looked at him again she realized that she could not convincingly retract her declaration.

"It's true. I do love you. I always have."

Matthew smiled and the hint of dimple appeared in his cheek. "And I love you, too. You have no idea how much."

She turned and began to pace. Matthew stepped back and perched on the edge of her desk. Back and forth, back and forth, she seemed to pace for hours, although in reality it only seemed that way to him.

Finally, she stopped and turned toward Chip. "This is all your fault." She pointed her finger at him.

"My fault?"

"Yes, your fault."

He would have said more, but Erianna stopped him.

"Don't even try to deny it," she hissed.

She resumed her pacing, mumbling under her breath. Chip moved into the room and took up a position behind her desk. With Matthew leaning against the opposite side he felt a little less vulnerable if she decided to launch another verbal attack.

"Get up there and sing, Erin," she quipped. "You wouldn't leave it alone. You had to push. Always pushing me—you just wouldn't leave me be."

Matthew tensed. Erianna was referring to the night of the Senior Dance. She was finally remembering the night before graduation. He started to rise, but Chip put a staying hand on his shoulder.

"You and Nancy, you had to have your own way, no matter what. It didn't matter what I wanted. Nooo. It was always your way or the highway."

She snorted. "Moon River—what a joke. You set me up for

all kinds of grief. I'll bet you had a jolly good laugh, making me the butt of all those jokes."

Suddenly, with her back to them, Erianna stopped short and stiffened. She stood rigidly for several beats. Matthew wanted to go to her, but once again Chip stopped him. Finally, she turned toward the men. But she wasn't focused on the here and now, she was looking back, remembering.

"Moon River." She shut her eyes for a moment. "I sang Moon River."

"Yes," Matthew murmured. "It was beautiful."

She turned away. "Everyone jeered.

"That summer—your car." With a loud gasp, she pivoted back. "My father," she clutched at her throat as her face lost its color. "He found out! He found out about us..."

Her eyes rolled back and she fainted, slipping toward the ground. Matthew sprang forward and caught her in his arms before she hit the floor.

"Erianna!" He clutched her to him. Looking over at Chip, he swore. "Jesus!"

Chip ran over and went down on his knees beside Matthew. "Oh, God. What have I done—"

"Go fetch the medical bag from my trunk," Matthew ordered. "My keys are on the kitchen counter."

Chip was out the door like a shot and running down the hallway, grateful to have something to do. When he ran into the room Nancy and Ginny were standing at the doorway to the porch.

"There you are," Nancy scolded him. "We were wondering where you went off—"

"Go see if Matt needs any help," he commanded in his most authoritative tone.

"Chip? What's going on?" He *never* spoke to her that way. Something was terribly wrong.

"Erin fainted." He grabbed Matthew's keys. "Ginny, will you watch Patsy?"

She nodded. "Of course. What—"

"I'll explain later. They're in the office," he called to his wife as he ran out the front door to Matthew's car.

"Where's the office?" Nancy asked Ginny.

"Down the hall," she pointed. "Last door on your left."

Nancy found Matthew settling an unconscious Erianna onto the leather sofa.

"Go into the bathroom," he instructed her, pointing to the adjoining door. "Wet a washcloth in cold water, wring it out and bring it to me."

Nancy quickly followed his instructions. By the time she handed the cloth to Matthew, Chip had come back into the room. Bending down, he handed his friend the medical bag.

"Close the door," Chip told his wife.

She obeyed, and stood there quaking as she looked down at Erianna, who was a pale as a ghost and unresponsive to Matthew's voice. "Should I call 9-1-1?"

"No," Matthew told her. He placed the compress across her forehead and reached into his bag to grab a capsule of smelling salts. He cracked the vial to release the aromatic spirits of ammonia and waved the cotton-soaked capsule under Erianna's nose.

"Erin," he cooed. "Come back to me, sweetheart." He passed the cotton across her nostrils again and she jerked her head away from the foul smell.

"You're okay, Erianna," he whispered softly. "Everything's okay. I'm here with you, sweetheart. You're safe with me."

Once again, he passed the vial under her nostrils. Erianna inhaled and moaned, lifting her hand to try and push the foul-smelling odor away. Her eyes fluttered and opened.

Chip, who had run for another cold compress, returned and handed it to Matthew, who replaced the first cloth with the cold one.

"Matthew?" she whispered.

"Yes, I'm here."

"What happened?"

"You swooned, just like a true southern bell," he teased.

"I did?" She closed her eyes.

He chuckled. "Yes, you did. And I don't mind saying you gave us quite a scare. Do you know where you are?"

She opened her eyes again. "Yes, I'm in my office."

Greatly relieved, he kissed her lightly on her cheek.

"I'm okay now. Can I get up?"

Matthew moved off the floor and lifted her just enough to sit down on the couch and reposition her upper body against his. "Let's take it nice and slow, and make sure you don't get dizzy again."

"Okay," she agreed. "I do feel a little lightheaded."

"That's to be expected. You've had quite a shock."

She looked over at Chip, who was wheeling her office chair over toward the couch. Once he settled himself he smiled at her, taking her hand in his.

"I never saw anyone faint before," he kept his tone light. "My heart is still pounding."

Erianna closed her eyes again and sighed deeply. "It's a first for me, too."

"Erin, do you remember what you were saying before you fainted?" Matthew asked her.

She looked up and saw the tension etched on his face. "Yes, I remember."

"Moon River—"

"Yes, I sang that song the night of the Senior Dance. I remember now."

Raising her a little higher in his arms he hugged her lightly.

Chip glanced at Nancy, who was still hovering by the door. He winked at her and she smiled brightly. She had finally caught on.

Noticing the quick exchange between the two, Erianna moved off the couch and onto Chip's lap. "I'm sorry." She kissed his cheek. "I'm so sorry."

He cuddled her in his arms. "Sorry for what? There's nothing to be sorry about."

"I've been horrible to you. You and Nancy both. You guys were always so nice to me and I was a real bitch about it."

Chip threw his head back and laughed. "I've been known to be a bit pushy—from time to time."

"Maybe, but you never meant me any harm. I don't know why I didn't see it."

"I've always thought of you as a good friend, Erin. I still do. And so does Nancy."

Erianna took his face in her hands. "My friend," she agreed. And with that, she kissed him on the mouth.

Momentarily shocked, Chip quickly regrouped and gave her a lecherous grin. "Your friend, now and forever." He kissed her back.

Matthew cleared his throat. "That'll be enough of that. I'll thank you to unhand my fiancé."

"Your fiancé?" Nancy repeated. "Oh, how wonderful. I'm so happy for you."

Erianna found herself once again enveloped in Matthew's arms. She welcomed the feeling of security he offered her. She was safe with him. The pretense was over and she could finally, blessedly, openly acknowledge the depth of her love for him.

Closing her eyes, she said, "Matthew?"

"Yes, sweetheart?"

"I want a Prenup."

The room was suddenly filled with laughter, a welcome sound after the tension of the minutes before.

Do you feel like talking about what happened?"

"Yes. I'm okay now." She nestled against Matthew's chest.

Nancy took a seat on the arm of the leather sofa as Erianna began to recount the events on the day of her eighteenth birthday.

"My mother and sisters were at the grocery and I was vacuuming the living room rug when my father came home unexpectedly and attacked me. He grabbed me by the throat and pinned me against the wall. He started punching me in the gut as he screamed at me, saying that I had been 'whoring for that Prestwick bastard'."

She paused, thinking back. "It's funny. I remember that the vacuum was running the whole time. It's odd, how I remember that.

"Anyway, I could hardly breathe. He was choking me as he punched and punched, again and again, driving his fist into me. There was so much pain. Then he pulled a screwdriver from his utility belt and shoved it up inside my skirt, inside me, asking me how I liked it. He said, 'after I'm through with you that Prestwick bastard will never want you again'.

"There was so much pain, but I couldn't scream. I couldn't breathe. The room started spinning. His fingers tightened around my throat and then everything went black. I thought I was dead."

They had heard enough. Matthew held her tenderly as she spoke, but his eyes reflected the rage that consumed him. It was all he could do to tamp down his thirst for revenge and focus on Erianna's needs.

Nancy wiped a tear from her cheek, and Chip moved to his wife's side as she whimpered quietly.

"Oh, my God." Erianna suddenly shot up. "I left Patsy alone on the porch."

"Ginny is with her," Chip assured her when Matthew refused release his hold on her.

He reached into his bag and pulled out a prescription bottle. Shaking out two pills, he gave them to Erianna. "I'm going to get you a glass of water and I want you to take these."

"I'll get it for you," Chip said. "Nancy and I need to get the kids rounded up and head for home."

He helped his visibly shaken wife to her feet and they left the room. When he returned with the water, Chip asked if they needed anything else and was assured that everything was fine.

"We had a wonderful time today, Erin. I'll give you a call and you can let me know what you want in the Prenup. I'll prepare it for you, no charge," he flashed a grin at her.

"Thanks for nothing," Matthew snarled.

"You might want to take one of those yourself, my friend," he said, pointing to the bottle in Matthew's hand.

With a wave, Chip was out the door.

Erianna took the pills as instructed and Matthew held her for a time, waiting for the medicine to take effect. She was beginning to feel lightheaded again. "What did you give me?" she finally thought to ask.

"Just a mild sedative. You'll be right as rain in the morning."

He helped her to her feet, guided her to her bedroom and helped her settle into bed, staying with her until she fell asleep. Then he went downstairs.

Matthew found Grace and Ned sitting at Ginny's kitchen counter waiting for him. He explained that their mother and he were engaged and asked their permission to marry her.

Grace was quick to approve, but Ned had misgivings. They talked for quite a while and Pap was helpful in reassuring the boy.

Finally, Ned said, "If Mom tells me she's okay with this, I'll go along with it. I'll go ask her."

"She's asleep. She's had quite an eventful day and she was very tired."

"You can talk to her tomorrow," Grace assured her brother. "C'mon, let's go to bed. I'll tuck you in."

After they went upstairs, Matthew closed the door between the units. Ginny poured them each a stiff drink and Matthew finally relaxed enough to talk about what had happened. He told them how Erianna's memory returned and that she had fainted as her recollections suddenly came pouring back. And then he told them about Clyde Pruitt's brutal attack on Erianna's eighteenth birthday.

Ginny was appalled. "Can he be prosecuted?"

"I don't think so," Pap answered. "There's probably a statute of limitations that has long since expired."

"That man is a monster," she declared.

Matthew choked back a sob. "I never knew. *I never knew*. If I had known I would have killed the bastard myself."

Ginny offered him a much-needed hug. "It's not your fault," she assured him.

"I don't understand how she managed to survive," Pap said.

Matthew didn't understand it either. "There are still a lot of unanswered questions. I need to talk to my mother and see if she can fill in any of the details."

He rubbed his tired eyes, which felt like sandpaper. "It was all I could do not to tear up in front of her."

Grace called Pap on the intercom just then. "Ned is asleep and I checked in on Mom. She's sleeping, too. I'm going to bed."

Goodnight, Grace. Thanks for taking care of them," Pap replied.

Matthew climbed the stairs and went into Erianna's bedroom to check on her. He settled himself on her old couch in the sitting room, but sleep was elusive and filled with vivid nightmares.

The next morning he went down to the stables to help Bob and Gus with the morning chores, filling them in on the events of the day before, but omitting the details of her attack. Knowing that Erianna would likely sleep past mass time, he asked Bob to take Grace and Ned with him to church. He also cautioned both men not to tell anyone about their engagement.

While she waited for her children to get home from mass, Erianna thought about the events of the day before and wondered how it had all come to pass. How in the world had she found herself engaged to be married? Was this what she truly wanted?

How did this happen?

She knew the answer to that. Everything changed the moment she recovered her memory and realized how much she loved Matthew. Then—*and* now.

I love him. I've always loved him and I always will.

But, was this just an unfulfilled childhood fantasy that she had carried into the present day? What had happened to her vow not to disrupt her 'well-ordered life'? And why would she even consider changing the status quo?

She had made the decision all those months ago to shut him out, and yet here she was, engaged to Dr. Matthew Prestwick, heir to the Prestwick fortune and a man of considerable wealth and prestige in his own right.

He fit her so well, and her children obviously liked him very much, but did she want to give up her freedom and independence?

Will I be giving up my freedom?

Matthew had advanced degrees and was a world traveler, but never once had he made her feel inferior. Not once had he undermined her decisions or interfered in her life. Not when it came to the important things. All he had ever done was fight for *them*, for their love and their future together.

She understood now why he had pushed so hard against her efforts to chase him away. But it was a huge leap from acknowledging that she loved him to finding herself engaged. It made her head spin. She thought of the expression 'whirlwind romance' and understood now how it could happen.

Matthew had waited a long time to find love and make a commitment to a woman. And so she understood his desire to begin their life together.

But am I ready? I've been married once. Do I really want to navigate these waters again?

As she pondered, it finally came to her.

Yes, we're engaged. But that doesn't mean we have to walk down the aisle tomorrow. We have plenty of time to get to know one another again, and we'll see how it all works out.

Erianna settled herself in Pap's recliner and waited until Ginny fed the kids their breakfast before talking to them about her engagement. She explained that she and Matthew had dated and fallen in love the summer after her high school graduation, but after an accident she lost her short-term memory and had no recollection of their relationship.

She told them that for some reason, she wasn't sure why, her memory of that time had been triggered by an offhand comment Chip made the day before.

They spoke about her desire to marry Matthew and she put to rest any doubts that Ned had. She also promised her children that she would not move forward unless they were comfortable with the idea of Matthew becoming a permanent member of the family. They had a say, she assured them, and she would not marry again if they did not approve.

"Mom?"

"Yes, Ned?"

"Does this mean that Doro and Bob will be our aunt and uncle?"

"Yes, it does. And the boys will become your cousins."

Ned frowned. "Then I vote no."

"Why?" Pap asked the boy.

"Because. If we become cousins then Ryan won't be able to marry Grace someday. He won't like that one bit and I know he'd want me to vote no."

"You're an idiot, Ned," his sister quipped impatiently.

"Please don't talk to your brother that way, Grace."

"Well, he is."

Pap spoke up. "You won't be cousins by blood, Ned. Just by marriage."

"What's the difference? Cousins can't marry cousins. There's a law against it."

Pap explained, and when he was finished Ned nodded in understanding.

"Besides," Grace told him. "Who says that I'm even interested in getting married? I might decide to travel the world and never get married at all."

They all laughed at that statement.

"Well, I might. You never know."

"Alright. I think we've talked about this long enough. Nothing has to be decided today. We have plenty of time to think things over. There's no rush."

"Okay," Ned agreed.

The kids started to disperse, but Erianna stopped them with one last thought. "I don't want you to discuss this matter with anyone else." She looked at her son. "I mean it, Nathan. Until we decide to move forward, this is a family matter which is not to be discussed with anyone outside this room."

"Not even Matt?"

"Yes, you can talk to Matt, but absolutely no one else. You *must* obey me on this. Do you understand?"

"Yes ma'am. I understand."

That afternoon Chip called and they discussed Erianna's wishes for the Prenuptial Agreement.

After seeing to his fiancé's needs that morning Matthew headed home. He stopped at the office to catch up on some paperwork, but after several unproductive hours he found himself driving to his mother's house.

Helen took one look at her son and knew something was terribly wrong. He was disheveled and looked as though he'd slept in his clothes. His eyes were bloodshot and his hair greasy and uncombed.

"Come into the kitchen. I'll get you something to eat."

"I'm not hungry."

Helen slipped her hand into his. She led him toward the paneled family room adjacent to the kitchen. Like a walking zombie, Matthew allowed his mother to guide him to the couch. Pouring a scotch for herself and a double shot of Jack Daniel's for her son, she joined him, waiting patiently until he spoke.

"I'm engaged to Erin Pruitt." He hung his head and rubbed the back of his neck, then downed the alcohol and set the tumbler aside.

Helen said nothing. She didn't understand why he seemed so miserable. His somber tone did not gel with such happy news. Marriage to Erianna had been his heart's desire. So why the apparent melancholy? She settled back, quietly sipping her drink.

Finally, he straightened up and gazed heavenward. "God help me, I don't know what to do."

"Do about what, Matthew?"

He expelled a shaky breath and intertwined his trembling fingers. "Tell me what you know about Clyde Pruitt's attempted murder of Erianna."

Helen was shocked. Taking another sip of her scotch, she tried to digest her son's words. She had kept the news of Erianna's near-fatal attack from her son and now, after all these years he'd learned of the brutal assault. But, no one knew for a fact that Clyde had been the perpetrator.

Matthew got up to refill his glass. "I need to know, Mom. Why didn't you tell me what he did to her?"

"How do you know it was Clyde?"

"Erin told me."

"I'm sorry, son."

He turned on her. "Don't hand me that *I'm sorry* crap. I want the truth. All of it."

Helen wasn't happy with his tone. But, she supposed he had every reason to be upset.

"Sit down and let's talk about this."

He downed another shot. Helen worried about his drinking so heavily on an empty stomach. She tried to keep her voice modulated as she said, "Please, Matt. Come here and sit with me."

He poured one last shot and sank heavily onto the couch next to his mother.

"Has Erin regained her memory?"

"Yes."

"And she told you it was her father who attacked her?"

"As if you didn't already know that."

"I assure you, Matt, I didn't know for certain. Clyde *was* a suspect, but he had a solid alibi, and no one saw him coming or going from his house that morning."

"Well, from what she told me, her father jumped her at home when no one else was there. Frankly, Mom, I don't understand how she survived. That mother fucker beat her within an inch of her life. He had her pinned against the wall and he shoved a screwdriver up inside her."

Helen swiped a hand across her eyes. "Oh, my." She reached for her drink and took a healthy swig, choking as the fiery heat went down her throat.

That fucking son of a bitch—"

"Language, Matthew."

He waved that off. "I don't give a damn. Come clean, Mom. I need to hear what you know. And I want the truth, goddammit."

Helen got up to refill her glass, refraining from offering him another. When she returned to her seat she turned toward her son. "I'm not sure where to begin."

"I know about the assault. What happened next? How did she survive?"

"It really was a miracle. If her mother hadn't come home when she did—"

Helen took one last sip of her drink and set it aside. "I'll tell you everything I know. But I want you to sit back and listen without flying off the handle."

Matthew grunted. "I can't promise you—"

With a warning glare she shut down any further protestations.

"Colleen Pruitt found Erin unconscious when she came home from grocery shopping. The girl was bleeding heavily and was barely breathing. Colleen called for an ambulance and tried to give Erin CPR, but she had no idea what she was doing. The younger girls ran outside, screaming for help.

"Chuck and Gail Neading happened to be driving by and Chuck stopped to see what was going on. He was the one who administered CPR until the ambulance came. If he hadn't been there, Erin surely would have died.

"When the paramedics arrived Chuck managed to intubate her. Gail told me that Erin's throat was so swollen that the paramedics had trouble passing the breathing tube down her windpipe, but Chuck stepped in and was able to intubate her."

"Oh my God, Mom. What were the odds that Doc Neading would be driving by at just the right moment."

"Yes, it was serendipitous." Helen took a beat before continuing. "Erin was losing a lot of blood. We found out later that her uterus had been ruptured."

"It was the screwdriver," Matthew told her.

"They packed the area to try and staunch the bleeding, but it had little effect. She was given multiple blood transfusions at the emergency room. Chuck stayed with her the entire time because Colleen refused to leave her precious younger girls home alone."

"Jesus!"

Helen nodded. "She's a real piece of work, that one. How she let Clyde treat Erin so cruelly is beyond comprehension."

"This is all my fault. Her father stuck her with that screwdriver because of me. Erin told me that Clyde found out about us dating and he blamed me for taking her virginity. It's my fault that he attacked her."

"Stop it, Matthew. You know better than that."

He sighed heavily. "We never made love, Mom. Not once. I swear. She was still a virgin."

"I believe you, son. This wasn't your fault."

"I know you're right, but I can't get past the guilt. She can't have children because of me."

"No, son. She can't have children because her father is a violent, deranged megalomaniac."

"Why wasn't he prosecuted?"

"Because, although he was the prime suspect, there wasn't enough evidence to bring charges against him. When Erianna finally regained consciousness ten days later at the hospital in Cincinnati she had no memory of what had happened."

"So how did she end up married not long after?"

"I don't know. Your father and uncle went over to talk to her parents, and when the men saw that Erin had been living in a curtained-off section of their dank, chilly basement they refused to let the girl return home.

"Your dad made arrangements for Erin to go live with Colleen's sister, Wanda, in Gainesville. Gail Neading, your Aunt Agnes and I flew down to check out her aunt, and when she was well enough to travel your father and Chuck accompanied Erin by private jet to Florida.

"She was enrolled at the University of Florida. Your father paid her tuition for the first two years of her attendance."

"She never went to college, Mom. She married a man from Cleveland and adopted her daughter, Grace, the following February. Erianna was just eighteen when Grace was born."

Helen shook her head. "I don't understand that. Your father insisted that he get a copy of her class schedule each semester. He paid her tuition, Matt. I'm sure of that. We thought she was safe and happy in Gainesville."

"I don't know how they managed it, Mom. But they scammed you. They must have found a way to enroll her in classes and then cancel her courses within the next twenty-four hours for a refund. They pocketed those funds, goddammit."

"We never suspected anything was amiss. I assure you of that. And then when your dad got sick her junior year, I admit that we lost track of her. I'm sorry."

He could take no more. Matthew broke down. With his head resting in his mother's lap he cried as she rubbed his back, trying to sooth her son. When she finally managed to get him on his feet she guided him to his old room.

"Take a shower, Matt. I'm going to get you something to eat and then you're going to bed."

She went downstairs, and with each step she cursed Clyde Pruitt and his good-for-nothing wife.

Chapter 13

The weather was worsening by the minute, with heavy rain pelting her windshield and a strong wind blowing from the northwest. But Erianna managed the drive up I-75 into downtown Cincinnati without incident. The rain didn't start until she got to the I-275 bypass south of town in Northern Kentucky, and she was surprised by the severity of the storm.

She parked her car in the underground garage across the street from Matthew's office and arrived a few minutes early for her appointment with Chip Neading. As she exited the elevator she was greeted by a friendly receptionist who looked to be no more than eighteen years old.

"Please have a seat and I'll let Mr. Neading know you're here," the pretty brunette told her.

"Thank you." Erianna turned toward the waiting area where two other visitors were settled on ultra-modern vinyl-covered couches.

She took off her leather gloves and shrugged out of her trench coat, brushing absently at her black A-line wool skirt. The black dress boots she wore had a two-inch tapered heel, and the leather harness strap at the ankle gave the look an equestrian-inspired aesthetic.

Erianna reached up to make sure her classic French twist had not come undone in the wind, and she was just about to take her seat when a woman approached her.

"Mrs. Fowler?"

"Yes."

"I'm Eleanor, Mr. Neading's assistant. If you'll follow me, I'll show you to his office." She took Erianna's coat as they walked down the hallway.

Chip's office door was open, but he was on a call, so as the women waited Eleanor remarked, "That's a beautiful blazer."

The textured jacket was a kaleidoscope of jewel tones in a brilliant shimmering print. Blue, purple and deep bronze tones blended against a deep, rich coffee-colored field.

"Thank you," Erianna replied politely just as Chip wrapped up his call. She was escorted into his office and he rose from his chair and walked over to greet her.

"Hello Erin. I'm surprised that you made it here in this weather. It's getting really nasty outside."

Rain was pelting the bank of windows that looked south toward the Ohio River, but Erianna made no comment other than to offer a polite nod of agreement.

Chip's assistant laid Erianna's coat over a chair near the door and he showed her to a seat opposite his desk. He tried to make small talk, but she was in no mood for chit chat. She wanted to be done with this business and start for home as soon as possible.

"So, were you able to put together the Prenuptial Agreement for me?"

He wasn't surprised by her business-like air. He knew she was none too pleased that this meeting was taking place. After their discussion on the phone he realized that she was still trying to come to terms with the fact that she was engaged. So he decided to follow her lead and get down to business.

"Yes, I've drawn up a draft of everything you requested." He opened a folder on his desk and removed the Prenuptial Agreement, of which there were two copies. He pushed one of the copies across the desk and Erianna picked it up and began to read.

"I can take you through it—"

"No, thank you," she interrupted. "I can read it without your help."

He nodded. Erianna was an intelligent and independent woman and he knew she was fully capable of interpreting the legal jargon in the document.

"Alright. I'll just give you some time to review it and when you're ready we can discuss any changes you might want to make."

With that he got up and headed out the door, closing it softly behind him.

Erianna settled back in the chair as she read. The further she got the more distressed she became. While Chip had followed her directive that Matthew could make no claim to any of her belongings, he did not include the same stipulations when it came to Matt's holdings.

Erianna thought she had made it very clear that she wanted no part of Matthew's wealth. She told Chip that she wanted the Prenup to stipulate that her money was her money and his money was his alone. But this document clearly stated that upon their marriage she would receive an equal share of all Matthew's assets.

There were also stipulations for her children to be provided with large cash settlements upon their twenty-fifth birthdays, along with funding set aside for their college educations.

The more she read the angrier she became. This was not what Erianna had proposed, and there was absolutely no way that she would agree to this Prenup as written. She was angry with Chip and anxious to get home, and she considered this trip a complete waste of time.

How dare he!

As Chip waited in the outer office for Erianna to read through the draft Matthew returned from an appointment. He came around the corner and stopped when he saw Chip standing by Ellie's desk.

"Did Erin make it?"

"Yeah. She's in my office now reading through the draft."

"Okay. Let me put my things down and I'll pop in and say hello."

He headed toward his office, which was three doors down from Chip's. Just as he reached his assistant's desk Erianna emerged from Chip's door and confronted him.

"Is this a joke?" he heard her say. "*Is this a joke*?" she repeated a little louder. "Do you actually believe I would ever consent to these terms?"

From the tone and timbre of her voice Matthew knew that she was gearing up for a blow. He quickly divested himself of his coat and briefcase, tossing them onto a chair beside Allison's desk, and headed back toward Chip and Erianna, who were facing off beside Ellie's desk.

"If you think I'm going to sign this you've got another thing coming," she hissed.

"Let's go into my office and discuss it," Chip tried, but Erianna would have none of it.

"I made it perfectly clear that I wanted nothing to do with Matthew's money," she spat. "This is a total waste of my time. I'm going home. Where's my coat!" she looked around, trying to remember through the fog of her anger where it had gotten to.

"Hello, honey," Matthew greeted her with a calm, friendly air. He put his hand on her elbow with every intention of ushering her back into Chip's office and out of the view of his employees, but she jerked herself free from his grasp.

Suddenly all her anger was directed away from Chip, who immediately retreated toward his office door in obvious relief.

"Don't you *honey* me," she said through clenched teeth. "I made it perfectly clear to Chip that I don't want any of your money. You put him up to this, didn't you?"

"Let's just calm down and discuss this—"

"No!"

Matthew looked toward Chip, who shrugged in defeat and backed through his doorway.

"I'm no gold-digger," she stated in a low, threatening tone. "I don't want one red cent of your money. I couldn't have been clearer, and I'm *not* interested in discussing it."

Matthew began to move toward Chip's office door and Erianna followed him, railing at him as he backed away from her. He didn't want this scene to play out in front of his staff, and it was obvious that Erianna was unaware of her surroundings as she continued her tirade.

"Do you know what people will say?" She didn't bother to wait for Matthew's reply as she continued to castigate him. "Everyone in Prestwick will say that I married you for your money. They'll say that the girl from the wrong side of the tracks got her hooks into you and took you for everything you have. I don't want any part of that."

By this time Matthew had successfully lured Erianna through Chip's door and Ellie shut it behind them. Matthew breathed a sigh of relief. At last he could counter her remarks without the scene being played out for all to see.

"I don't care what anyone thinks or says," he told her. "What people think has nothing to do with us and you very well know it." He stopped retreating and stood his ground.

"Well, I care," she countered. "I care!" She turned and began to pace. "You just don't get it," she declared, her anger clear and her frustration mounting.

"I've worked all my life, from the time I could push a broom and carry a bucket. I wasn't born with a silver spoon in my mouth. While you were out golfing and swinging a tennis racket around a court, I was mopping floors and washing windows. I never took anything from anyone. I've worked hard for everything I've earned. And I won't have people saying I married you for your money. *I won't!*"

Matthew and Chip stood silently as she continued to pace and vent. Matthew realized that her pacing was a form of running away, as she had always done from these kinds of confrontations when she could. It was obvious that she was fearful about marrying him and she was hiding her fear in anger.

He let her go on until she had had her say. She evidently felt backed into a corner and, like a she-wolf, Erianna was fighting against what she perceived to be an untenable situation. Matthew, on the other hand, had no such misgivings. He didn't feel the least bit guilty about manipulating her into agreeing to marry him. He only knew that, come hell or high water, he was going to make her his bride.

More than anything in this world, he wanted a life with her, permanently and irrevocably. And the sooner he got her to the altar the better. He loved her, and he knew that deep down, despite her fear, she felt the same way about him.

Matthew and Chip exchanged several glances as she paced. At one point Chip shook his head in disbelief at something she said and the small movement caught her eye. She turned on him.

"This Prenup isn't worth the paper it's printed on." She held up the papers she still held in her fisted hand. Walking over to where he stood at his desk, she crumpled the Agreement and threw it at him.

"*You* are the bane of my existence."

"Me?"

"Yes, you. What ever happened to 'I'm your friend, now and forever'? You just can't leave well enough alone. You're still pushing and prodding me. You still think you can manipulate and control me. It's your mission in life to get into my business, isn't it?"

She took a breath before adding, "No wonder you volunteered to draft this for me. It's just another way for you to interfere."

"That's just not true, Erin. I honestly volunteered to write the Prenup because I care for you and want to look out for you."

"Well, no one asked you to look out for me. I don't need looking after. I couldn't attend my own commencement exercises because of what you did. Do you think I could show my face at graduation after the humiliation I endured the night before? Did you think my father wouldn't find out about what happened?"

She was running out of steam and she turned her back on the men.

Matthew finally spoke up. "You may not have participated in the commencement, but you *were* at graduation. I saw you there."

She turned back. "I would know if I was there Matthew, and I assure you that I was not. My diploma arrived in the mail a couple of weeks later."

"Oh, you were there, all right. You finished in the top ten in our class and should have been sitting in your cap and gown in the front row with us, but you weren't. But I did see you, up in the back of the auditorium, right below the unlit spotlight. You were with your two younger sisters. I remember—they were sitting next to you, almost hidden from view. I'm sure I saw you," he said. "And when I gave my speech I spoke directly to you."

Erianna wanted to discount his statement, but couldn't. He watched as a pensive look came over her face. She turned and went to stare out the window as she thought about his declaration. Finally, she turned back to the men.

"That's right. I remember now, too. I *was* there and I did hear your commencement speeches. I wonder why I didn't remember that. My parents banned me from participating in the graduation ceremony. They went out of town for the weekend and I had to stay home and babysit my sisters. I brought coloring books for them and we snuck up to the lighting balcony to watch from there."

She hung her head, dejected.

Matthew went over and took her into his arms. "I'm sorry, honey. I never meant to upset you."

"It's not your fault," she murmured. "This is all a huge mistake, Matthew. I don't think you should marry someone who doesn't have all her faculties intact. Why would you want to chain yourself to an unstable woman?"

"You're not unstable," he countered, lifting her gaze to his with his fingers. He studied her face as she looked up at him through her long bangs. His heart lurched as he took in her forlorn expression.

She broke away from his hold, taking several steps back in order to gain some distance and perspective.

"I cannot marry you, Matthew." When he started to object she held up a staying hand. "You don't know me at all. And the fact is that I really don't know myself. We have no idea if we're even compatible. We haven't been—" she searched for an appropriate word. "Intimate yet, and you don't know if I'm any good in the sack." She turned away. "And I don't know if I even like it.

"No, we shouldn't be jumping into this. We need to open our eyes and face reality. I can't give you children and God knows you deserve someone who can give you heirs."

Matthew was shocked by her statements. What did she mean 'if she liked it?' They needed to have a private conversation and get to the bottom of these strange, incomprehensible remarks. As she turned and gazed unseeing out the window into the gloom beyond, he slowly approached her, brought her to his side and wrapped his arm around her. They both peered into the semi-darkness and he gradually pulled her tighter against him, trying to ease her fears and bolster her flagging spirit with his indomitable strength.

After a time he took her hand in his. "I think we should talk privately."

He guided her toward the door. Leading her past Chip's desk, he reached out for the second copy of the Prenuptial Agreement. Quickly and efficiently, he folded the document and tucked it into his suit jacket pocket.

When they walked into the outer office Chip's assistant rose from her seat and offered Erianna a reassuring smile as she passed.

Erianna paused, and then turned back, retracing her steps to the assistant's desk.

"Miss—I'm sorry, I don't know your last name."

"I'm Eleanor Porter. Please, call me Ellie. Everyone does."

"Erin," she echoed with a soft smile. "Ellie, I want to apologize for my inappropriate outburst earlier."

Ellie held up a hand. "Please, don't. There's no need for that." She came around her desk and leaned in toward Erianna as if to relay a juicy bit of gossip. Erianna suppressed a grin at the age-old female gesture.

"Honestly," Ellie whispered, "it's about time someone stood up to those two. I feel honored to have witnessed it."

Erianna was amused by the admission. "Well, nevertheless, I was wrong to make such a public scene. One should never address another person so disrespectfully in full view of other people. I'm sure that the news has already spread like wildfire. And for that I'm a little ashamed and disappointed in myself. I hope you will accept my apology."

"Of course. Please be assured that I have not and will not repeat anything I see or hear in this office. That's just not my style. Unlike most women," she chuckled, "not everything that goes into my head needs to be spewed out of my mouth."

Ellie could see that Matthew was ready to move on, so she gave Erianna's arm a reassuring squeeze and stepped back so that they could pass. "If there's anything I can do for you or any assistance you may need, please feel free to call me."

"Thank you, Ellie. That's very kind of you," Erianna replied. Then she returned to Matthew's side and he guided her to his office.

"Allison, would you step in here please?" Matthew beckoned his Executive Assistant. She followed the couple through the office door and shut it quietly behind them.

He guided Erianna to a small, oval conference table and showed her to a seat. "There are a lot of things we need to discuss," he said. "But first, let's just take a beat and gather our thoughts."

Erianna nodded in agreement closed her eyes for a few moments. When she reopened them she felt more centered—until she met Matthew's gaze. Her heart immediately skipped a beat and she quickly averted her gaze.

Matthew waited, sitting calmly and studying her body language, looking for a sign from her that she was composed enough to begin. Finally, when she could look at him without discomfort or embarrassment he graced her with a soft smile of reassurance and cleared his throat.

"How about we start again and talk about the Prenuptial Agreement?" he suggested as he removed the document from his coat pocket.

"Okay."

Allison took her cue from the slight movement of Matthew's head and approached the table, taking a seat across from him.

"Is there anything else in the Agreement, aside from the provisions for the distribution of my holdings, that you think we need to talk about?"

Erianna looked down at the Prenup and then back up at him. She pondered the question for a time, and then picked up the papers and began to scan the pages again. "Do you have a pencil?" Allison supplied her with one, which she used to quickly scan the paragraphs, making a few notes in the margins.

"I didn't read it word for word," she said when she finished. "Matthew, maybe we should set this aside. I don't think—"

"Listen to me, honey. Regardless of what you just said in Chip's office, nothing and no one is going to change my mind about us. We *will* be married, even if I have to spend a lifetime convincing you."

She still had misgivings. He could see it in her eyes.

"Come on, humor me. You came here to go over the Prenup. Let's just concentrate on that for now. The rest will work itself out over time. Okay?"

"Okay," she agreed. "Well—" she took up the paperwork again. "I don't know much about legalese. I understand enough of the language to be able to follow the text. And from what I read, I don't take issue with the Agreement, minus your provisions."

Matthew nodded, encouraged by her willingness to discuss it with him. She made no further statements about not being wed and the knot in his stomach began to ease.

"Is this all that a Prenuptial Agreement usually contains?" she asked.

"I haven't seen a Prenup before," he answered honestly. "Tell me what you're thinking and we can make decisions together about additional language to the draft."

That seemed sensible to Erianna and so she continued. "Do we need to spell out where we will live?" She paused. "I mean, well—we haven't really discussed it," she finished lamely.

"I was hoping to move in with you and the kids in Berrington," he told her. "Would that be okay with you?"

"You'd be willing to do that?"

"Absolutely."

"Won't it be inconvenient? It's a long commute from the farm to the office."

"Inconvenient?" he chuckled good-naturedly. "Are you kidding me?" He graced her with a huge smile. "I would love nothing more than to be welcomed into your home, into your arms, and into the wonderful world you've established there. I know of no other place on this blue planet that would please me more than to live with you in Berrington."

"Really?" Erianna was thrilled, although she did her best not to show it.

"Really."

"What about that long commute?"

Matthew leaned forward in his seat and rested his elbows on the table. "I can easily work from my car during the commute. Henry will drive me. All I need is my computer and my cell, and wherever I am that's my office. I work offsite quite a bit. I've long since adjusted to that reality."

"Henry?"

"Yes, Henri LaRue. He's my personal assistant.

"I do intend to keep my place here in the city, though. There will inevitably be times when I will have to stay overnight in order to attend an early-morning meeting or catch a flight out of town. Much as I don't want to be away from you for even one night, we both know that there will be times when I'll be gone for several days."

Erianna understood that necessity and she quickly reassured him. "My first husband traveled regularly for work and I'm accustomed to living with a man who travels for his living. It will be no hardship for me to adjust to your schedule."

Matthew nodded. He looked toward his assistant to confirm that she was taking notes. "Please include language in the Prenup stating that I will make no claim to the Fowler residence. That is to stay in Erin's name only."

Allison nodded.

"Is there anything else?"

Erianna ruminated on the question. "There might be other points that may need clarification, but for the moment I can't come up with anything that's pressing."

"Okay. Good. Now, are you willing to tackle your objections to the provisions I laid out in the Agreement?"

"You won't like what I have to say, Matt. Can't we just state that your money is your money and mine is mine. I don't want any support from your personal holdings—"

"You can't honestly believe that I will agree to that, can you?"

"I don't see why not," she declared.

"Erianna, I want you for my wife. And I was raised to believe that a man has a duty to support his wife and family. It's not like I'm trying to take over your mortgage or car payments, but if you think I'm going to live solely off your largesse you are sadly mistaken."

"I don't have a mortgage or car loan," she commented off-handedly.

"There's no reason why my assets can't come into play in our future lives together. I'm a responsible, successful adult, and I *will* contribute to the household finances. You can continue to pay your property taxes and business expenses. I won't interfere with that. But there is absolutely no reason why I shouldn't pay the household bills such as the utilities, groceries and other monthly incidentals from my salary."

"That's an antiquated notion, Matthew."

"Well, then I'm an antiquated man. I don't care what label you put on it, I insist that you allow me to support you and the children after we're married."

"But—"

"No buts," he snapped. "It's clear that you want to be an independent woman, I get that. Shouldn't I be afforded that same courtesy? I won't be a *kept man*, Erin. Surely you can understand that I have my pride, too. Try to put yourself in my shoes."

He made a good point and Erianna finally acquiesced.

They spent the next half hour going through the Prenup section by section, discussing objections and working through several impasses. Erianna agreed to allow Matthew to pay the household expenses from a joint checking account, although she vowed that she would never accept any portion of his business holdings.

Having finally convinced her that his earnings would be allocated for the monthly bills, Matthew felt that he had won a small victory and conceded the point about her making no claim to his assets. He made a mental note to just rewrite his will and name her as the sole beneficiary of his estate when he died.

The final roadblock came when they began the discussion of Grace and Nathan's section of the Prenup.

"My children will not benefit from your wealth, Matthew." Erianna was adamant on that point and would not budge.

"I have to say that I don't like your use of the phrase 'my children,'" he told her tersely. That statement brought her up short. "I love those kids, and if you keep referring to them as *yours* instead of *ours* it will be a deal breaker for me."

He waited several beats for that remark to sink in.

"I—" she was at a loss, unable to think of any response. The children had always been hers and hers alone. Ed had never taken any interest in parenting and Erianna was accustomed to thinking of Grace and Ned as her sole responsibility. She did not know how she felt about co-parenting. She wasn't even sure if she could comprehend such a notion.

Neither spoke for several minutes as each weighed the importance of this decision. Then a heated debate began, with neither of them willing to give an inch.

"Don't give me that 'born with a silver spoon' crap," he replied in a clipped manner when she began to wax poetic about self-made individuals. "You, Erianna Pruitt Fowler, are a real snob."

"I most certainly am not!"

Matthew couldn't help but smile. "You are, too. You just won't admit it. You believe that anyone who has been afforded a life of financial security in his or her childhood is undeserving of any success they achieve on their own as adults. But you fail to understand that wealth is neither an automatic guarantee of success nor a recipe for failure. Each individual's successes or failures are not automatically predetermined by any lack of or abundance of money in their formative years. And your viewpoint, to my way of thinking, is the classic definition of a personal prejudice. Jesus Christ, Erin, I hate to think how you really feel about me."

"That's not fair—"

"It's not only fair, it's absolutely true. I may not have paid out-of-pocket for my education or incurred mountains of debt in student loans, but I've earned every cent I've made, with no injection of funds from my parents' coffers. And by the way, my undergraduate degree was paid for by scholarship funds that I *earned.* And had you applied, you may very likely have received scholarship and grant monies yourself.

"I consider myself to be a self-made man. I have no controlling interest in my mother's and grandmother's holdings. That will come to me in the future, as well as to my brother John and Dorothy. But we support ourselves, the three of us, from the benefit of our educations and the sweat of our brows."

Matthew sat back in his chair and crossed his arms defensively. He had worked tirelessly for every success he had garnered. And he'd be damned if she thought she could judge him solely on his family's wealth.

"Look," Erianna tried again. "The fact is that I've already set aside funds for Grace and Nathan's higher educations. There's absolutely no need for either of them to go to Harvard or Notre Dame. With the money I have saved my kids will receive a first-rate education at a reasonably priced university."

Matthew brought his fist down on the conference table,

startling both Erianna and Allison. "Dammit, Erin! You make me so mad."

He catapulted from his chair and began to pace. "There you go *again*. *My* kids. *My kids*." He raised his hands heavenward in frustration, hoping for guidance from above. None was forthcoming.

He turned to face her. "Give me one good reason why I can't at least match the funds you're so proud to have stashed away. And explain to me, my dear, why I'm not entitled to match those funds with my own hard-earned money."

He raised a hand to stop her from responding. "And if you say that they aren't our children, they're your children one more time I'm going to throttle you right here and now."

Erianna did not speak as he loomed menacingly over her. Although she kept her expression neutral, she was secretly amused by his empty threat, believing from the bottom of her heart that she could trust Matthew with her life. He would never harm her, of that she was certain. He was trying to intimidate her with his height and masculine bravado, but she wasn't the least bit frightened.

He was so dear. Even in his anger he drew her to him. His unwavering strength and the magnetic force of his personality were irresistible.

Matthew waited, but no response was forthcoming as she quietly weighed the validity of his argument. He could glean no hint of her thoughts or feelings. But he waited, calling upon every ounce of self-control he could muster not to drag her from the chair and shake some sense into her. He clenched and unclenched his fists and watched the woman he loved as she took her time to respond.

"Please," she finally motioned to his chair. "Sit down with me, please."

Begrudgingly, he complied.

"We're going to be married?" she posed the question to him once again, as if it wasn't a foregone conclusion.

"For the rest of our long lives," he solemnly assured her.

She sat back and seemed to relax, accepting the finality of his statement.

"Then I'm going to ask for your patience, Matthew." She paused before continuing. "I was wrong not to see the importance of co-parenting in our future as a married couple. But it's going to be a difficult adjustment for me, learning how to co-parent. I've never done that before.

"I agree that you should freely participate in the rearing of Grace and Ned and provide them opportunities that only you can give them. Grace would dearly love to visit New York and I can't think of anything I would hate more.

"I realize that you will be a wonderful, loving father to them during these next formative years. As their sounding board and advisor, guidance counselor and teacher, you can offer the children knowledge and experiences that I will never be able to give them. There is no one else, Matthew, no one that I would accept as Grace and Nathan's father but you. So please, try to be patient with me."

He let out a sigh of relief, knowing how much courage it had taken for her to say those words. "I love you so very much, Erianna. Your family dynamic is fascinating and unique. And I can't wait for the day when we're married and I become an official a member of the family. I love those kids."

She smiled shyly. Matthew leaned across the table and brushed his lips softly across her cheek.

"By the way," he murmured. "If one of *our* children decides to go to Harvard, then Harvard it will be. I don't care what it costs."

"Well," she said with a soft laugh, "that's a discussion for another time."

Chapter 14

Erianna glanced at her watch. "Oh my," she rose from her chair. "It's five-fifteen." She made eye contact with Allison. "I'm sorry to have kept you this long."

With a dismissive wave of her hand she said, "Think nothing of it."

Allison Maddox was a very pretty woman, and obviously pregnant. Erianna guessed that she was somewhere in her second trimester.

"When are you due?"

"In mid-March."

"Is this your first?"

"No. I have two sons. My husband is a free-lance writer and he works from home. He looks after our growing brood."

"We're done here for now, Allison," Matthew advised her. "These changes can wait. There's no rush. Be careful on the drive home."

"I will," Allison replied as she gathered up her notes and headed to her desk. "Do you need anything else before I leave?"

Erianna scanned the room. "Do you happen to know where my coat is? I need to get going—"

"The storm is getting nastier by the minute," Matthew cut in. "Why don't we get something to eat before you leave? Maybe by the time we finish the weather will have improved."

Erianna was hesitant. She really did not want to stay in town. She wanted to go home.

Matthew followed Allison to the door and spoke to her quietly. "See if you can get us a dinner reservation nearby. With this foul weather it should be easy enough to find something close." Allison nodded and left the room.

When she opened the door Chip, who had been loitering in

the hall with Erianna's coat in hand, waited for Allison to pass and then came into Matt's office. "Is everything alright?"

He nodded. "Allison will give you the changes we made to the Prenup next week. We've come to a tentative agreement, but once you make the modifications I'll go over them with Erin again and we'll tweak it if necessary."

Chip nodded. "I'm sorry, Erin, but Matt insisted—"

"Give it a rest, Chip. I'm not going to apologize to you again."

He smiled impishly. "What could I do? He's my business partner and my best friend."

"Yes, well. You were supposed to be representing *me*, not your buddy here. I'm very disappointed in you."

Chip couldn't help but chuckle. "Sometimes you say the funniest things."

"Funny—you think this is funny? Well, Mr. Neading, I'm glad that you find me so amusing."

"Don't start, you two," Matthew interjected. "Go home, Chip."

Taking his cue, he placed Erianna's coat over a nearby chair and with a friendly wave he said, "See you tomorrow."

"I need to get going, too. I don't want to leave Grace and Ned home alone," Erianna said. "They have school tomorrow and I need to get back."

"Let's call Pap and see how things are going on the home front first," he suggested.

He reached for his cell and placed the call, but could not make a connection. So he walked over to his desk to call from his landline to Pap's landline. Even in this weather, he knew it would go through. Pushing the speaker button, they listened as Pap's phone rang twice before he answered.

"Donovan's."

"Hi, Pap. This is Matt Prestwick."

"Well, hello, Matthew. Is the weather as bad there as it is here?"

"It's raining cats and dogs."

"Has Erianna left yet? We're very worried about her driving in this storm."

"No, Pap, she hasn't. We're here in my office. I'm a little concerned myself, but she's anxious to get home. How are things in Berrington?"

"We've hunkered down and settled in. Bob came through here not long ago. He was on his way to the stables to help Gus with the horses. He told me he's going to check on them periodically until the storm blows through, so tell Erin not to worry. We have everything under control here."

"That's good news," Erianna spoke up. "But the kids have school tomorrow and I'm going to start home as soon as the rain and winds let up a little."

"Do you know what the weather reports are saying?" Matthew asked. "Have you heard when worst of this is supposed to let up?"

"From the reports I've seen it's not supposed to blow itself out until around midnight."

Matthew looked at Erianna. "I can't stop you from trying to make a run for it, honey, but I really wish you would consider staying with me tonight here in the city."

"No, that's a very bad idea. Thank you for the invitation, but I'll pass. I need to get home. I have responsibilities to my family and my business."

"Nonsense," Pap huffed. "Why are you even considering taking such a chance? Grace and Ned have already lost one parent in a car accident. Why take a chance with your life trying to get home in this gale? That's a very dangerous decision you're making."

Ginny had been listening in and she added her two cents. "Erin, please. I can handle getting the kids off to school. And Bob doesn't mind a bit checking up on things at the stable. We're just fine here. Please err on the side of caution."

"But—"

"We'll hear no more of this now," Pap said. "You let Matthew get you safely settled at his place for the night and you can start home at first light."

"Good. It's all settled," Matthew quickly agreed. "Let the kids know that they can call and check in with their mother if they want. Goodnight, Pap."

He broke the connection before Erianna could say anything else and began to absently tidy his desk. "I won't be long here. What do you think of my office?"

He posed the question casually, hoping to distract her from the fact that he had just hoodwinked her into staying overnight with him. He didn't look up, but continued to sort and put away the files scattered across his desktop.

Matthew was relieved that the ploy worked when she began to peruse his office.

Matthew's desk, on the left side of the room and closer to the bank of windows than the door, was positioned facing into the room. A long credenza sat against the wall at his back. Though large in scale, the mid-toned wood desk was not ornate or heavy. With unadorned lines, it was neither contemporary nor antique. It was a timeless piece and she wondered where he had found it. The glass-covered top was scattered with various stacks of files and other common office supplies, and she decided that it suited both the space and his personality.

The white Lucite conference table where they had been sitting was located across the room from his desk. Instead of the standard vertical blinds, the bank of windows sported a solid, light-filtering shade which closed from either the top or the bottom by a remote, handheld device. In addition, heavy forest green drapes could be drawn to block out all sunlight.

As she moved through the space, she noticed a lack of knick-knacks in the room. It was clear that Matthew preferred not to work in an overly cluttered space.

She turned to walk across the soft, light beige carpeting to an area where a classically tailored, three cushioned couch anchored the space along the far wall to the right of the office door. It was covered in a muted green linen print with piped seams and skirted legs. She imagined him napping on it after longs hours of work. The glass coffee table and two wood-legged chairs upholstered in a green and beige design with button tufting completed the vignette.

A landscape hung on the wall over the couch and Erianna moved closer to examine it. Matthew glanced up as she looked at the framed panel.

"Do you like it?" he asked.

"Very much. It's a beautiful print. Interesting."

"That's an original Andrew Wyeth," he casually remarked.

Erianna spun toward him. "An original? An original Wyeth. An *original* Andrew Wyeth painting. *You* own an Andrew Wyeth painting?"

Matthew straightened to his full height and looked directly at her. "Don't go there," he stated emphatically.

That brought her up short.

"And I don't technically own it. It belonged to Grandma's sister, and Lucinda inherited it after my Great Aunt Elizabeth died. She knew Wyeth personally and she commissioned the piece from him. It's never been shown publicly or lent to a museum, so very few people know of its existence.

"And it's on *loan*," he chuckled. "Grandma knew how much I admired it and when we opened the business here I asked her if I could borrow it and hang it in my office."

"Your grandmother is very kind to have consented."

He huffed. "You know very well that there's not one *kind* bone in her body. But," he shrugged, "the scene reminds me of home. It takes me back to my childhood, and when I explained that to the old battleax she loaned it to me."

Erianna smiled. She knew about the Prestwick matriarch's reputation and could not fault Matthew's opinion of her.

She turned back to the work of art. She was not well acquainted with the works of Andrew Wyeth, but she seemed to remember that he had completed many landscapes depicting trees. This was obviously one of those pieces.

The scene was anchored by the thick, broad-reaching limbs

of a sycamore tree. Devoid of leaves, it seemed to have been painted in what was probably late autumn. The softness of the cloudy, mid-day light supported that theory. Barren limbs showed white areas where bark had peeled away and dropped. A massive, gnarled trunk with exposed roots at its base revealed the advanced age of the fully mature tree. Brown and cream hues dominated the rendering of the tree.

Aligned in the left side of the pastoral scene, the sycamore looked down onto rolling farmland with a small stream meandering through the valley below.

"Do you know the title of this piece?" she asked.

Matthew rocked back and forth on his heels and put his hands in his pockets as he tried to remember. "To be honest with you, I don't know if this piece was ever named. I'll have to ask Grandma the next time I visit."

"Tell me about your office," she prompted as they arrived at the elevators in the reception area. "I see that there's another occupant on this floor. Do you lease your space by the square foot?"

"Actually, no. Chip and I lease the entire floor. We occupy seventy-five per cent of the square footage and we sublet the western exposure to an accounting firm.

"So you collect rent?"

"No, we don't. They occupy the space rent-free." The elevator doors opened and they rode down to street level as Matthew explained. "When we began the start-up for this business Chip and I decided not to staff a dedicated accounting department. For a couple of years we sent our accounting work off-site. At the time there was a law office leasing the space. I wasn't very fond of the firm," he looked at her, "they specialized in divorce law. When their lease expired we chose not renew with them."

Erianna wrinkled her nose. "I can just imagine the kinds of melodramas that took place in the reception area."

Matthew nodded. "Exactly."

The doors opened and they walked together into the lobby. Matthew pulled out his cell and shot off a quick text, but Erianna didn't mind. It was common for him to send and receive texts, but he never lingered over his phone when he was with her.

He continued. "An accounting firm was interested in leasing the space, but they were worried about the expense. So Chip and I decided to let them have the space rent-free, and in exchange they would handle our accounting work at a substantially reduced rate. In essence, we have a semi quid pro quo arrangement."

"That's a fancy way of saying that you barter for services, Mr. Ivy League," she quipped. "And you don't need an advanced degree to figure that one out."

Matthew threw his head back and laughed, the sound so pleasing to her ears.

When they reached the lobby door she looked out to a torrent of rain. "Do you Uber?" she asked him.

"Rarely, you?"

She looked up at him with a wide smile. It was a silly question. "I'm willing to make a dash to my car if you are," she offered.

Just then a black SUV pulled over to the curb. "No need," Matthew told her. "My driver just pulled up."

Matthew escorted Erianna through the front door and they ran to the car. Even with the awning sheltering the sidewalk between the office entrance and the curb, they were nonetheless pelted from the side by the wind-driven rain. Blocking her from the worst of it, they gained entrance to the car without becoming too soaked.

Erianna slid over to the seat behind the driver and Matthew climbed in next to her as the door shut automatically. They settled in and buckled their seatbelts.

"Erin, this is Henri LaRue, my driver. Henry, I'd like you to meet my fiancé, Erianna Fowler."

Henry made a motion with his hand and Matthew said, "He's very happy to meet you. Henry doesn't speak."

"Oh, by the way. Where did you park your car?"

"I'm in that underground garage right there," she pointed to her left as they moved slowly along the rain-soaked streets.

Matthew made note of it, as did Henry.

The Italian restaurant was just a couple of blocks from Matthew's office, and when they pulled up he guided her to the entrance. They hurried down a cement stairway set off by an arched brick portico and a wrought-iron railing on the street side. He guided her through the door of the rustic subterranean trattoria and out of the pouring rain.

"I hope you like Italian," he said as they shed their damp outer layers and handed them to the attendant at the coat check.

"Ymmm," she whispered back.

She inquired about the location of the powder room and he directed her. While she was freshening up he secured a booth in a quiet corner of the restaurant. When she returned to the public area the hostess showed her to the table where Matthew was waiting.

She was led past a sunken wine rack which was visible from above. A circular iron railing kept patrons from accidentally falling into the display. The wine rack was laid out in a concentric circular honeycomb configuration. Erianna was fascinated and paused to get a closer look before joining her fiancé.

Matthew rose from the soft leather seat of the booth when she arrived. She slipped in opposite him with a nod of thanks to the hostess. They were in the last booth at the end of this section of the restaurant where he had taken the seat against the back wall.

"Are you all dried off?" he inquired.

"Yes, I'm just fine and dandy."

Their waitress appeared with menus. "Would you like to start with a cocktail?"

Matthew looked to Erianna. "What would you like?"

She wasn't much of a drinker and she hesitated, unsure what she should order.

"Would you like a beer, or a glass of wine?" he suggested.

Erianna turned her attention to the waitress. "Do you have Kentucky Bourbon?"

"Yes, we do."

I'll have bourbon over ice, please," she decided.

Matthew ordered a beer on tap and they turned to their menus. Erianna studied it for quite a while, but was unwilling to admit that she didn't understand many of the selections, as they were written in Italian.

When the waitress returned with their drinks Erianna was tempted to ask her for assistance, but she worried that she would embarrass her fiancé. She seldom ate out, and when she did it was usually at a chain restaurant friendly to family dining.

"Are you ready to order?"

"No, not yet," Matthew replied. "We'd like some time to decide."

With a nod, the waitress turned and left.

"So. How hungry are you?" That was a silly question. He knew she had a healthy appetite. "Why don't we start with Antipasti, and then have our main course."

"Antipasti, appetizer," she surmised.

He nodded.

Erianna was accustomed to pinching pennies. "What looks good to you? Is there something we could share?"

"There's a buffalo mozzarella with tomatoes and basil," he pointed to the item on her menu. "It's very tasty and I order that quite a bit. We could get it and the blue oven tortano bread and share. Would you like that?"

She nodded, and then guided her through the main course offerings.

"The majority of these main course items have some kind of pasta. There is, of course, spaghetti, everybody's favorite. I'd tell you about the tagliolini con funghi, but I know you don't like mushrooms, so that one's out."

She was surprised that Matthew remembered her aversion to mushrooms. Maybe what she said earlier in Chip's office wasn't true. Maybe he knew her better than she thought.

He quickly explained the various dishes on the menu and she decided to try the rigatoni and broccoli raab. He chose the bombolotti and signaled to the waitress, who came to take their order.

Erianna was grateful that he had smoothed the stormy waters with the menu and she settled in to enjoy her night on the town. Fine dining was new to her, and she couldn't recall ever being asked to dinner by anyone other than Matthew. Looking back, she thought about some of their dinner dates during that short summer after graduation.

"What exactly do you do?" she struck up the conversation as he sipped his beer.

"Well, we invest in companies in medically related fields. We search for new innovations and help bring them to market."

At her puzzled look, he expanded his explanation. "Basically, among other things, we help start-up companies patent their inventions and produce, sell and distribute them to hospitals and doctor's offices. We invest in a variety of companies who manufacture medical supplies, such as Bone Density Test Scanners, as an example. We employ a large staff in our research and patent departments, and we guide inventors through the testing and approval process for their patents."

Erianna was impressed. She had no idea his work was so varied and complex. "Einstein started in a patent office," she murmured.

Matthew raised one eyebrow. "Do you think maybe his line of work called for an advanced degree?"

"Touché."

Deciding to use this opportunity to shift the conversation, Matthew began by asking how her first husband made his living, although he already knew through his conversations with Ned.

"He was a Pharmaceutical Sales Representative," she told him. "His father, Neil, the children's grandfather, is a Doctor of Gynecology and Obstetrics in Cleveland. Ed, my husband, earned a bachelor's degree in pre-med, but he decided that he didn't want to follow in his father's footsteps, opting instead to take a sales job."

With Matthew's prompting Erianna told him more about their married life.

"Ed loved to travel. He was on the road more often than he was home. His sales area included Ohio, Michigan, Pennsylvania, West Virginia, Kentucky, and Indiana.

"It sounds like he was gone a lot. That must have been difficult."

"Not really. I'm used to being alone," she admitted. "And besides, I have the kids to take care of, and they keep me pretty busy.

"It was Ed's father who arranged for our adoptions of Grace and Nathan. He's a wonderful man and a loving grandfather to the kids. We still visit him a couple of times each year."

Matthew knew the story of how Grace and Nathan came to be with Erianna, but he didn't want the conversation to veer off in that direction. And so with great care he redirected her.

"Ed's passing must have been very tough for you and the kids."

Erianna was becoming uncomfortable with the direction their conversation was taking. She didn't want to talk about how she felt when her husband passed. Taking several small sips of her bourbon, she sat quietly, concentrating instead on the liquid swirling around the ice in her glass.

But Matthew kept pressing. "Were you in love with your husband?"

"Of course." She tried to sound convincing, but fell far short.

"Did you have a satisfactory marital relationship with him?"

Her head snapped up and she set her drink down with a decided clank. "Matthew, why are you asking me about this?"

"Because, honey, earlier in Chip's office you made a reference to a lack of intimacy with your husband and I'm just trying to understand what you meant."

She blushed profusely and lowered her head, breaking eye contact and hiding behind her bangs.

"Why did you say that you don't know if you like making love?" he pushed.

Erianna was flummoxed. "Honestly," she snapped. "I don't want to talk about that here."

Their antipasti were served just then, but the question hung in the air. Matthew ate in silence and Erianna played with her food as she sat in the suddenly uncomfortable booth.

When the waitress returned to clear their first course she asked, "Was everything to your satisfaction?"

"Oh, yes, it was delicious," Erianna lied, offering the woman a friendly smile. In truth, she had barely tasted the food.

She sipped her drink while they waited for their main course. Erianna was working on her second tumbler of bourbon, and she made a mental note not to accept a third. And when Matthew tried to continue his questioning in the same vein she shut him down.

"This is not the time or place for such a personal discussion. It is highly inappropriate dinner conversation. Suffice it to say that Ed was gone a lot and leave it at that."

Matthew reached for her hand. "I'm sorry. I don't mean to make you uncomfortable. Why don't we wait until later to take this up again."

"Or drop it altogether," she retorted. "Besides, I just misspoke in the heat of the moment."

Not bloody likely. Matthew let the matter drop—for now. She was right. This was not the place to have such an intimate discussion. But he silently vowed to get to the bottom of the mystery before the night was over.

"Have you noticed that I argue with you a lot?" she said from out of the blue after their entrées were served. "That's something that I need to rein in."

"There's smooth sailing ahead," he assured her. "We just need to get to know each other again and become comfortable with one another."

"I suppose," she sighed.

Matthew leaned forward and rested his forearms on the table. "Erianna, look at me." He could finally see her eyes as she complied, albeit through the thick curtain of her bangs.

"Considering that you've never really been properly courted, the fact that you suddenly find yourself engaged must be quite unsettling. I intend to *date* you," he teased. "That's one reason why I hoped that you would stay for the night, so that we could go out to dinner and then head back to my place to talk, just the two of us."

She blushed. But she made a concerted effort to relax and enjoy the rest of her meal. They ate in companionable silence and Matthew was relieved when she commented that she was enjoying her rigatoni.

Then Erianna struck up another topic for discussion. "Could you tell me something about your driver?"

Matthew was happy to oblige. "He's much more than just a driver. Henri LaRue is my right-hand man."

When the waitress appeared to clear their plates and ask if they needed anything else, Matthew ordered another drink for Erianna. And then he continued the story of how Henry came to work for him.

"I met Henry on a business trip to Paris. He had been injured in a horrific terror attack and never fully recovered. Once a successful midlevel businessman, Henry was unable to return to his previous employment. I had known him casually and I ran into him on the street after a meeting one day.

"Henry can hear, but he can no longer communicate verbally. Luckily I know enough sign language that we were able to strike up a dialogue and I learned that he was in dire straits. Long story short—oops," he winked at her. "Too late?"

She smiled indulgently.

"Well, he had no hope for a career in France. I knew how intelligent he is, so I decided to offer him a position working for me.

"I understand and speak passable French, and Henry is fluent in English. It's been a good fit, the two us. He lives with me at the condo, which is in his name as well as mine. It is his home now, too, and will continue to be. He has the security of knowing that he will always have a home here in Cincinnati."

Matthew sat back. "That reminds me. I'll probably need to either include a notation in the Prenup naming him as the inheritor of the condo upon my passing or file a Transfer on Death Declaration with the county. I'm not sure which."

"I'm sure your best buddy will be able to advise you."

All kidding aside, Erianna was moved by his story. "What exactly does a 'right-hand man' do?"

Matthew smiled broadly. "That's just a term I used in order to give you some idea about our association with one another. Basically, Henry handles everything from shuttling me around and taking care of the condo to offering me business advice. He and Allison handle my schedule, and Henry travels with me sometimes on business trips. He is my mentor and my friend."

"I see. Henry is there whenever you need assistance, whether its work related or personal. And you are there for him. But how does he communicate? Through sign language?" She took a beat. "Not many people know how to sign. Maybe I should learn, and the kids, too."

"Henry would be thrilled that you're willing to learn. But he also has an app on his phone that speaks what he types."

She smiled. "Cell phones do everything these days. It's a wonder how we ever got along without them."

"They do indeed," he agreed. "You'll probably be seeing Henry a lot. He's a family member to me and he'll be a part of our daily lives, I hope."

"I'd like that very much."

He leaned forward a little. "I love you, Erianna. You're an incredibly compassionate woman."

His declaration warmed her and she blushed.

"We're going to have such a wonderful life together," he murmured huskily as he leaned further across the table. "I'm so happy—there aren't words."

* * *

Matthew shot off a quick text and signaled for the waitress. After paying the bill they collected their coats and ventured once again into the wickedly cold night. Henry was waiting at the curb. He drove through the now nearly deserted streets and pulled into the underground garage where Erianna had parked her car.

"Where are you parked?" Matthew asked when Henry made several motions with his hands.

"Matthew, I've had too much to drink," she confessed. "I don't think I should drive. Why don't we just leave my car here for the night?"

"Sorry honey, this lot doesn't stay open all night. After closing, all non-stickered vehicles will be towed."

"Oh." She guided Henry through the rows to her Subaru.

"Will you give me permission to drive your car? I know the roads like the back of my hand and I only had one beer. I won't have any trouble driving home."

She nodded and pulled the keys from her purse, handing them over to him as he ushered her to the passenger side door.

Henry was pulling away as Matthew started the Outback. He looked over at her as she buckled her belt, shrugged and said, "If I could drive home without having to change your seat settings I would, sweetheart, but I need much more legroom than you do."

"Be my guest. We wouldn't want you to be uncomfortable," she teased.

At his wicked glare she couldn't help but laugh.

They set off through the dark city streets toward his nearby condo. He drove through what she believed was the Mt. Adams area due east of downtown Cincinnati, but she wasn't sure of her surroundings in the pouring rain. In truth, she actually knew very little about the Queen City, and on this pitch-dark night she could locate no landmarks to aid her.

In no time at all Matthew turned her car into the garage of a residential condo high rise. He parked in one of his assigned spaces, ushered her to an elevator, inserted a key that unlocked a private car, and they rode to the top floor. There was only one button in the elevator, and it read PH. Erianna bit her tongue and composed herself.

As the elevator rose she wondered about the man she would someday marry. Not once had Matthew referred to his place as a penthouse, preferring either condo or apartment.

Penthouse living didn't come cheap, but Matthew seemed to play down his wealth. He never bragged or boasted about living so stylishly. In fact, he never spoke about it at all. Either he just didn't see it or he didn't care about labels. He certainly didn't behave like a rich man. He never had.

Erianna's last thought before the elevator doors opened was to wonder if her fiancé was, in fact, just an ordinary guy, your average Joe.

Chapter 15

The elevator opened, not into a hallway that led to the main entrance door, but directly into Matthew's condo. He took her coat and hung it with his in the vestibule closet.

"Welcome to my humble home," he said in all sincerity.

"Thank you." She offered him a beautiful smile.

"It's just a few rooms, not the expansive property you have in the country. But—" He paused, as if searching for the right words.

"But it's your home sweet home," she supplied as she sidled up against him.

Erianna looked around. "It's remarkable," she mused. "If I lived here I would have chosen exactly the same décor. You know? Decorated the place the same way you have and given it the same ambiance. It's just lovely." She looked up into his handsome face.

Matthew smiled. "Mmm. I love your taste and you love mine," he agreed with a slight lift of one eyebrow. The deliberate double entendré hung in the air, but Erianna did not take the bait.

Suddenly he grabbed her around her waist and pulled her up against him. He tried to kiss her, but Erianna resisted.

"Don't."

"Why not?" He brought his lips toward hers.

She placed her hands on his shoulders and tried to push away, but his hold tightened around her waist.

"Matthew, please—"

Turning her face one way and then the other, she tried to elude his advances. She pushed with all her might, but he was single-minded in his pursuit.

"*Please* don't."

"Why not?"

"Because—when you kiss me I lose all rational thought."

"Just one kiss," he countered. "Then I promise to stop."

The moment his lips caught hers she surrendered. He kissed her passionately, and her hands moved of their own volition to his hair. She ran her fingers through his thick, wavy locks and then settled them at the base of his neck, clinging to him as the long, hypnotizing kiss continued.

When at last he ended the searing kiss Erianna was breathless and she struggled to regain her senses. He held her lightly until, at last, she recovered her equilibrium and then, as promised, he began the tour of his condo.

"This is the landing area, the catch-all space."

Erianna took note of a corner handkerchief table to the right of the elevator. A colorful blown-glass bowl rested on top and Matthew took her keys from his pocket and dropped them there.

He took her elbow and ushered her down one step as they moved into the heart of his home. The entryway floor, which was covered with a marbled ceramic tile, gave way to wall-to-wall carpet in a soft, pearl gray.

"The architect referred to this area as the 'great room', but I prefer to call it the living room."

The condo design was well planned and executed. Beautifully appointed, the space was warm and welcoming in shades of blue, gray and cream, with splashes of orange here and there. From the spectacular, highly polished oak bar on her left to the stylish, comfortable furnishings in a mixture of textures and tones, the hardscapes and contrasting softscapes blended together seamlessly.

Though not vaulted, she guessed that the ceilings were around twelve feet high. They gave the room a light, airy feeling, and yet the space was warm and cozy. Matthew had good instincts and very good taste.

There was a hallway on her right which led, she assumed, to the bedroom area. Opposite the hallway entrance padded stools were tucked under the bar on her left.

They walked into the living room and Erianna looked approvingly at his choice of couch and scattering of chairs and side tables. Nothing matched, and yet the space came together in perfect harmony.

The great room included a living area with a gas fireplace, a dining room, where an oval glass table had been placed near the southwest corner, and the bar. The dining table sat four, and she noted that the padded chairs were mismatched, but finished with the same fabric on the cushioned backs and seats. A corner hutch with glass shelving was lit by under-mount lighting, and its soft glow lent a soothing ambiance to the far corner of the room.

Matthew explained that, although not visible now with the drapes drawn, the bank of windows were bisected by sliding glass doors to balconies on both the southern and western exposures.

"I have a great view of both the Ohio River and downtown Cincinnati," he told her.

Erianna frowned slightly. "Don't you feel like you're living in a fishbowl when the curtains are open?"

"No. These are one-way vision windows. They are coated with a film that allows me to see out, but stops others from seeing in."

As her tour continued Matthew pointed out the doorway to the kitchen. "Beyond that are Henry's private quarters."

"Private quarters?" She questioned the oddity of the phrase.

"I know," he grinned. That's how he refers to his bedroom and bath. I believe it's a common European phrase."

He led her down the interior hallway and pointed out his office on the left. It, too, had a large window with a view of downtown. A guest bedroom and bath was also accessed from the left side of the hallway.

Matthew then opened a door on the opposite side of the hall and turned on the lights. "This," he motioned with his arm, "is my man cave."

Erianna laughed out loud.

The paneled room was expansive, and the moniker was spot on. This was a man's room. Matthew's room. Wherever she looked she could see his personality reflected there.

He grabbed a remote from the coffee table and pressed a button. The far end of the room was suddenly awash with light.

"There's the pool table, and over on the far side I have a nautilus machine and weights."

The center of the room boasted a game table and chairs, and Erianna suspected that he probably hosted a poker night now and again in this room.

"And right here is where I watch TV."

A built-in entertainment center ran across the entire wall. It was filled with a myriad of gaming systems that would rival those of even the most dedicated teenage nerd. The huge, big-screen TV and surround-sound audio system would make any young boy drool, and nearly every shelf was filled with a plethora of gadgets and sports memorabilia.

The large leather sectional and a recliner faced the TV and an old, beat-up coffee table was scattered with remotes and newspapers.

"Guessing by what I see," Erianna commented with a hint of sarcasm, "this is where you hang out."

"Guilty."

Matthew then showed her his bedroom suite at the far end of the hallway. When they returned to the living room Henry was at the bar, and he signed to Matthew.

"Henry would like to know what you would like to drink."

"Oh," she paused to think. Then she went over, pulled out a stool and took a seat. She spoke to him directly.

"I really think I've had enough to drink this evening, Henry, but thanks just the same."

He reached for his translator and typed rapidly. And through a speaker in the unit a male voice spoke. "We have a well-stocked bar. Might I tempt you with an after-dinner liqueur, or how about an Irish coffee? It might help warm you up on a cold night like this."

She smiled. "Thanks just the same, but I probably should stick to water."

Henry nodded and typed again. "Would you like ice? Lemon?"

"A squeeze of lemon would be fine, if you have it. I don't want to put you to any trouble."

He waved his hand casually as if to say that it was no trouble at all.

Erianna settled in to survey the shelves. "You weren't joking, were you?"

When he turned with a questioning look, she smiled. "The bar certainly is well stocked."

The highly-polished oak bar was well-crafted and shaped in a U. An impressive display of bottles with a wide variety of spirits sat on glass shelves mounted in rows against the mirrored back wall. A small stainless-steel sink was tucked under the shelves along the low counter.

To her left, at the curve of the U, a floor-to-ceiling hutch housed beautiful Waterford leaded crystal stemware and tumblers. There were also several decanters and various serving pieces on display.

When he brought her the water Erianna spoke up. "Henry, what is the sign for water?"

He paused.

"If you'd prefer not to show me that's fine," she assured him.

He held up his index finger and wagged it as he shook his head. From that small motion she surmised that he was willing to show her. He held up his right hand, encouraging her to mimic him, which she did. With three fingers raised he formed a W. Then he tapped his index finger against his mouth two times.

Erianna followed suit. "That makes sense," she said. "Your fingers make a W, for water, and you bring them to your mouth to show a drinking motion."

Henry smiled shyly and acknowledged her understanding with a quick nod.

They talked for several minutes before Erianna realized that Matthew had disappeared. She looked around, wondering what she should do. Henry tapped lightly on her shoulder to gain her attention and typed a message.

"Matt just went to change out of his suit. He'll be back in a minute."

By the time he returned from changing his clothes and turning down the bedding Erianna and Henry were chatting like old friends. She was obviously pleased that he was willing to talk to her. And Henry seemed to have taken an immediate liking to her.

Matthew came up to the bar and sidled up next to his fiancée. In rapid-fire French, of which she understood nothing, he spoke to Henry, who nodded in response.

"Why don't we go sit down in the living room?" Matthew suggested.

"Okay."

"Let me take your blazer for you, and I'll turn on some music."

Henry came over with two tumblers and set them on coasters on the coffee table. As he passed Matthew he signed something.

"Ok. I'll tell her. Good night, Henry."

After he left Erianna asked, "What did he say?"

"He said that that it's a pleasure meeting you and that he's going to bed."

They sat down on the overstuffed couch. Matthew handed her the drink and once she was settled he reached for her legs and drew them across his lap. Pulling off first one boot and then the other, he tossed them to the floor.

Erianna was wearing thick wool socks, and Matthew pulled them off and began to massage her feet, knowing full well how much she liked it. With a heavenly sigh she took a sip of her drink. It was just like evenings at home in Berrington where they would settle in and relax on the couch in her family room.

"How was your day?" he asked her.

"You mean besides the inappropriate scene in your office?" she remarked lightheartedly. "It was a hectic day, trying to get everything taken care of before I had to leave for my appointment with Chip. Other than that it was just your typical work day."

"Do you feel better now about what happened at my office?"

Her only response was a slight shrug.

Finally, Matthew broached the subject that was uppermost in his mind. "I'm still wondering why you said that you don't know if you like making love?" He paused for several beats. "I really don't understand what you meant."

"I didn't mean anything. Can't we just drop it?"

She couldn't believe that she had spoken those thoughts out loud, but the truth was that she had. In actuality, she didn't recall exactly what she had said. But she was, as Ellie so succinctly put it, obviously guilty of letting what was on her mind escape from her mouth.

Matthew was not about to let the matter drop. "Erin, did you and your husband ever make love?"

She squirmed in her seat and tried to pull her feet off his lap, but he held fast and continued to rub her toes.

"I don't want to talk about this." She reached out and grabbed her glass. Taking a healthy swig of her drink, she choked as the fire burned her throat.

"That's too bad." He toughened his tone somewhat and got straight to the point. "But I'd like to know what you meant. Have you ever had intercourse?"

She set the drink aside. "No, I haven't. Okay? Are you satisfied now?" She was mortified. All the liquor she had consumed was taking its toll and she realized that she was buzzed.

Matthew was flabbergasted. "Was Ed gay?" He couldn't help asking the question.

"Listen, I really don't want to discuss this—"

"I'm sorry if I've offended you or your late husband. But really, Erin, you need to help me understand why a healthy heterosexual man wouldn't want to make love to you."

"Maybe not all men are horn dogs," she shot back.

"If you're insinuating that I'm some kind of pervert for wanting to make love to you—"

"I didn't *insinuate* any such thing. Don't you go putting words in my mouth."

He sat back, rubbed his hand across the back of his neck and took a beat to regroup before he continued. "Let's start again. Ok?"

"I've already answered your question. The answer to your question is 'no'."

He was lost. "Which question?"

"No, Ed was *not* gay. Are you satisfied now?"

Matthew didn't know what to say. He couldn't think of an appropriate response.

"Maybe you should think twice before agreeing to marry a thirty-three-year-old barren virgin," she muttered indignantly. "If you want out of this engagement, now you have a perfectly good reason to call it off."

"Dammit, Erianna. I—don't—want—out. I'm just trying to wrap my head around all this."

"Frankly, I don't see how it's any of your business—"

"None of my business? Of course it's my business."

"Well, I don't know what to tell you. Ed was never interested in sexual intimacies. We did try a couple of times, but he would lose his erection. Maybe I just didn't appeal to him in that way. But I assure you that he wasn't gay."

"Maybe it was medically related," he suggested.

"That's possible. His father told me that Ed was born with no testicles."

Matthew had learned about the condition while he was in medical school. It was called testicular agenesis.

"But Neil said that Ed was being treated with medications to replace whatever hormones the testes produce. I don't know about such things. I'm not a doctor." She shrugged. "The bottom line is that Ed wasn't a sexual person. End of story."

Matthew sat back, contemplating his next move. They listened to the music as he digested all he had learned. It was unfathomable to him that his fiancé had never had intercourse. He decided that it was time to put this matter to rest, time that she be introduced to the pleasures of the flesh.

Sliding his arm under her knees, he scooted toward her and lifted her into his arms. Holding her securely, he walked toward the hallway to his bedroom.

"What are you doing? Where are you taking me?" she asked with trepidation. Her head was spinning from the effects of too much alcohol.

"You know exactly where I'm taking you," he replied as he nuzzled her neck. "And you know very well what we're going to do."

As they crossed the threshold to his bedroom he paused and kissed her. Then he carried her to his bed and laid her down gently, as though she was precious cargo.

"I love you with all my heart," he professed. "And I'm going to make love to you so that you will know what it's like to be intimate with me."

He began to undress as she lay unmoving on the bed. She was floating, helplessly trapped in a dreamlike state that was neither sleep nor wakefulness, but a combination of both. Erianna was caught between two worlds and she knew that all the alcohol she had consumed was playing a major part in her current state.

After he rid himself of everything but his boxers he sat down beside her. She was so beautiful, but she looked so frightened. His heart skipped a beat and then began to race. He leaned down and kissed her sweet, luscious lips.

Erianna was reluctant and unsure, and he needed to take great care with her. His hands began to explore as she lay there, and when he reached down to her waistline to locate the zipper on her skirt she instinctively turned to her side to give him better access.

Before he removed her skirt and panties, Matthew reached for the sheet and covered her to the waist. Then he eased her garments off and set them aside. Erianna was now naked from the waist down.

"Matthew, this is a bad idea—"

"No, it's not, my little honeybee. We've waited long enough. If we don't do this now you'll just wonder and worry."

"But—"

"No buts."

He lifted her into a sitting position, bringing her up against his torso. Reaching up, he took the pins from her hair. Her sweet-smelling locks cascaded down her back. Tugging gently on her honey-colored masses, he tilted her head back so that he could begin an exploration of her jawline and neck. He kept his ministrations light as he brushed his lips across her sensitive flesh.

Moving his fingers to the hem of her fine-gauge knit sweater, he slowly pulled the garment off and laid her back on the bed. Erianna was a precious gift and he unwrapped her with great care.

Her head was spinning as overwhelming sensations enveloped her. She was floating on a cloud of wonder and delight. Letting go of the last of her inhibitions, Erianna brought her arms around his neck and murmured, 'Matthew' in so sweet a tone that he was lost.

Everywhere he touched her skin tingled. His hot, passionate kisses thrilled her. When his lips began a lazy exploration of her ear and the side of her neck she purred in delight. She shivered when he whispered words of love, his endearments softly spoken in his deep, rich baritone.

Matthew knew from experience that she wore front-closure bras, and he worked the clasp and artfully released her from the last of her clothing. Still wearing his boxers, he moved into bed beside her. *One step at a time*, he told himself. There was no need to overwhelm her.

He moved over her, spreading her legs a little and settling himself on top of her. Slowly, torturously he moved his lips down her body.

"Mmmm," she uttered when he kissed her hardened peak of her nipple. He pulled and sucked slightly with his lips and she responded by arching her back. "Ohhh."

He brushed his lips across her breast until he reached her other pink peak, and taking her into his mouth, he nipped lightly with his teeth. Erianna sucked in a deep breath and moaned seductively.

He moved his hand ever downward, his fingertips tickling her skin as he lightly stroked her ribs and marveled at the firmness of her flat belly. When he reached the juncture of her thighs he pressed his palm against her, and she aided him by opening her legs a little wider. Slowly, so as not to startle her, he inserted a finger inside her, searching her face for any adverse reaction.

"Does that hurt you honey?"

"Mmmm," was her only response.

He moved his finger a little deeper. "Does that feel good to you?"

"Ahhh."

Matthew took that to mean she liked it.

"Would you like me to stop, sweetheart?" he whispered. His husky voice sent shivers down her spine.

"Oh, yes," she answered as she began to squirm under him. "Stop, Matthew. Oh please, please stop."

Only she didn't mean stop. Instead she spread her legs further and bent her knees slightly. She was hot, and moist, and ready for him.

With a minimum of fuss, Matthew efficiently divested himself of his boxers. Then he repositioned himself and slowly entered her. She clutched at his shoulders and gasped as his velvety hard length filled her.

He made no further movements, waiting until she became accustomed to the feel of him inside her. It was torture, but he called upon every ounce of his self-control to take things slow until, suddenly, she opened her mesmerizing, multi-colored hazel eyes and looked up at him.

"Is there more?"

"Yes, my darling, there's much more."

He withdrew slightly, but Erianna objected. She wrapped her legs around him and brought her hands down to the base of his spine. He smiled as he once again slid into her, this time a little more deeply.

"Ohhh." She closed her eyes.

"Do you like that? Do you want me to stop?"

"Oh, yes. Please stop."

He chuckled quietly. Then he began a slow rhythm, each time thrusting himself a little deeper inside her.

"Oh, Matthew," she whispered. "Oh, yes."

He kissed her with all the pent-up lust that he'd been so long denied. She answered with a hunger of her own. He took her higher, increasing the tempo and force of his thrusts. She was climbing with him toward the peak, their movements growing more fevered as they made love for the first time.

When he brushed his lips across her jawline to the pulse point just below her ear her body stiffened and she threw her head back against the pillows, arching into her release. Erianna's orgasm was intense, her spasms clutching the shaft of his manhood. And when the white hot heat of his seed filled her she cried out.

Matthew nestled his fiancé against him as she slept in his arms. He never imagined it would be like this. He would never tire of her, for he knew that she was the woman of his dreams, his one and only love. He wanted to give her everything she desired and make all her dreams come true. He would love her until his dying day.

When she awoke the next morning the sun was trying to peak out from the thinning clouds. Her mouth was dry, her eyes gritty and Erianna realized that she had a hangover. She looked to the side and noticed that a glass of water and two Bufferin tablets were sitting on the bedside table, and she gratefully took them.

Then she glanced at the clock. "Nine-thirty!" she exclaimed in surprise.

"I was beginning to think you were never going to wake up."

Erianna snapped her head around. The movement sent pain shooting through her skull, and she brought one hand to her forehead to try to stop the pounding.

Matthew was dressed and sitting in a chair beside the dressing table across the room from the end of the king-size bed. "Good morning."

She closed her eyes again. "I overslept."

After a few more minutes of just lying there waiting for the aspirin to take effect, she finally moved toward the edge of the bed and dropped her feet over the side, stopping short when she realized that she was naked. She glanced over and found Matthew still sitting in the chair.

"I need to get cleaned up and on the road."

"Go ahead. I'll wait."

She blushed. "I'm not wearing anything."

"I know," he leered as he wiggled his eyebrows suggestively.

She was not about to go prancing around the room in her birthday suit. "I need some privacy, Matthew."

"Don't mind me."

Obviously, he was thoroughly enjoying this, but Erianna was in no mood to spar. Her head was throbbing and her stomach was queasy. She raised one arm and pointed toward the bedroom door. "Out!"

Matthew did not follow her command. He was having much too much fun harassing her.

Finally, after a silent standoff in which neither spoke, she jerked on the top sheet until she had it untucked and wrapped around herself. Scowling at him as he sat smirking, she got up and managed to trip her way along until she reached the bathroom doorway. But before she had a chance to pull the trailing end of the sheet through the door Matthew lunged forward and yanked on it, pulling the cloth from her grip.

With a shriek she slammed the door shut and quickly turned the lock. A shrill catcall whistle filled her ears.

* * *

Erianna took a quick shower and brushed out her hair. She wrapped herself in a terry robe she found hanging from a hook on the back of the door. As she cleaned up and made ready for her day, memories of what she had done the night before bombarded her. Not sure how to feel about what had taken place, she paused to think.

Glancing at her reflection, Erianna wasn't surprised by the heightened color in her cheeks. At long last, at the ripe-old age of thirty-three, she'd finally been intimate with a man. And not just any man, with Matthew Prestwick himself. She couldn't believe it—her childhood dreams *had* come true.

She'd always wondered what making love would be like, and it didn't disappoint. *It most certainly lived up to all the hype.*

"Was it only this good," she wondered aloud, "because it was with Matthew?"

On the rare occasions when Ed had tried to have marital relations with her it became awkward and uncomfortable, which left her feeling worthless and disillusioned.

"Was it so great because I was drunk? Did that have any impact on the outcome?"

She couldn't remember ever being so inebriated. Sure, she'd toked up a few times, but other than that she couldn't recall overindulging. She never cared much for the taste of alcohol or its intoxicating effects.

Having lingered long enough, she put her thoughts aside and headed for the door. Opening it just a bit, she peeked into the bedroom. The bed had been made and her clothes lain out. And, thankfully, Matthew was no longer in the room. So she made a mad dash for the bedroom door and locked it.

Relieved to have been left alone at last, she began to dress, but she couldn't seem to find the wool skirt she had worn to the city the day before. Instead, a pair of women's jeans had been substituted for the skirt.

Erianna held up the boot-cut pants. They were obviously

well-worn and looked to be about her size.

Whose jeans are these, and what the hell happened to my skirt?

Did Matthew have a collection of clothes he kept from 'the ghosts of girlfriends' past'? And if so, why in the world would he think that she'd be interested in wearing any of their cast-offs. She was just about to start rummaging around in his dressers when she stopped herself.

Quickly assessing her options, she made the decision not to go snooping around. As her mood worsened, and with her skirt nowhere to be found, she slipped into the jeans. Jeans that some random former girlfriend had obviously discarded.

Matthew came around the corner from the kitchen and found Erianna standing in the living room, apparently lost in thought.

"I hope you're hungry. Breakfast is ready."

"No thanks."

She couldn't face him.

He went to her, took her in his arms and kissed her. Erianna blushed a deep pink and looked at the floor. Shoving her hands into the pockets of the repulsive jeans, she rocked back and forth on her heels.

Taking her arm, he guided her to the kitchen and held her chair as she took a seat at a small table that was set against the window. Deciding to leave her to her thoughts, Matthew served up two plates that had been kept warm in the oven.

"I wasn't sure how eggs would work for you so I opted for waffles and a few strips of bacon."

"Sounds fine," she mumbled.

He actually felt sorry for her. She was obviously feeling the embarrassment and distress of a virginal bride on the morning after her wedding. At thirty-three years old, Erianna had finally been introduced to the pleasures of lovemaking and she was clearly feeling a bit shy with him after the intimacy of their coupling.

* * *

"Thank you for breakfast," she said as she helped him clean up.

They gathered their things and headed out the door. Although her headache had improved and her stomach had settled somewhat, Erianna was still miserable. When they exited the elevator into the parking area she noticed that her SUV was not parked in his assigned space.

"My car's not here."

"I'm going to take you home."

For the first time that morning she realized that Matthew wasn't dressed in business attire. He obviously wasn't going into the office today, but that didn't explain where her Subaru was, and he wasn't forthcoming.

He ushered his sullen bride-to-be to his Buick LaCrosse. They left the garage and headed east on Columbia Parkway. Erianna sulked as the still wet roads glistened in the morning sunlight. She continued to sulk, unaware of where Matthew was going until they pulled up to a hangar at Lunken Municipal Airport.

"Where are you taking me?"

"Home," he said. "I didn't think you'd be up for a long car ride."

They boarded a leer jet and he showed her to a seat.

"Can I get you anything?" he asked her after they were airborne.

"No."

"Erin, I wish you would relax and talk to me."

"You want me to talk to you? Okay, Dr. Prestwick. I'll talk to you. Whose jeans am I wearing? An old girlfriend's?"

Matthew smiled indulgently. "They're your jeans, sweetheart. I found them this morning in the back of your car."

"Oh." She was being childish and jealous and had assumed the worst. She looked out the window.

"Erin?"

"What—"

"I love you."

She felt like crying.

Chapter 16

Henry was waiting by her car when they landed at the airstrip just outside the Village of Berrington. He handed the keys to Matthew and then got into the LaCrosse and drove off.

"Is your headache any better?"

"You shouldn't have plied me with so much liquor, Matt."

She was still grouchy and irascible. They made the remainder of the ride in silence. When he pulled into the garage Erianna exited the vehicle in a huff. She walked stiffly into the house and made a beeline to the basement to change and head to the barn.

Matthew went over to Pap's suite. "Did the kids get off to school alright?"

Pap assured him that they had. They chatted about the storm for a few minutes before Matthew left to join Erianna at the stables.

He found her standing in the bed of her Ford pickup. She was lugging bales of hay into the lofts above the horse stalls. During the cold winter months the layers of hay helped insulate the stalls and keep the horses a little more comfortable.

She struggled with the task, lifting each bale to the top of the truck cab then climbing into the loft and pulling the bales up into the cubby. Matthew jumped into the flatbed and began to lift the bales directly onto the ledge in a single, fluid motion. When the outer edge filled he climbed up to help Erianna stack them into place. They worked on their knees as the headroom was limited.

"I don't need your help. I can handle this by myself."

When she tried to reach past him to reposition a bale he stopped her.

"Hey—" he took hold of her arm. "Come on. I'm not the enemy."

She stilled and lowered her gaze. "I know," she mumbled unhappily.

He lifted her chin with his fingertips. When she finally made eye contact with him a look of torment came over her and she jerked her head away.

He closed the distance between them and took her in his arms. He kissed her, rubbing his hands down her back in an attempt to comfort her. But she broke away from the kiss with a strangled cry.

"Erianna," he rasped. "Please—don't be so downhearted. I don't like it when you're unhappy."

"Oh, Matthew," she whispered. "I don't know how to act. What we did—I'm not sure how to behave."

"Behave?"

She made another sound of distress and buried her face in his coat.

"Erin, do you think there's something wrong with what we did?"

She didn't answer.

"We're in love, and we're going to be married. We've made a commitment to one another. When we made love it was a natural expression of those feelings. I know you enjoyed it. You had several orgasms."

She cried out, mortified by his remark, and tried to escape.

"Not so fast my blushing bride-to-be." He pulled her back against his chest. "Talk to me."

With her head once again buried in his coat she finally mumbled, "You know that I liked it. But—did you?"

"Did I?" He crushed her to him. "Oh yeah—I sure did. I liked it very much."

He pulled on her ponytail, lifting her face away from his coat and took her mouth in a searing kiss, slashing his lips across her soft, sweet mouth. When he thrust his tongue inside she moaned with pleasure.

He fumbled with the buttons on her jacket and pulled it none too gently from her arms. Their movements became hurried as they removed the thick layers of their outer clothing. When he finally succeeded in unbuttoning her flannel shirt, he turned her around so that her back was to him. Reaching around, he unzipped her jeans and tugged them down.

"Erianna," he moaned as he bent her over a hay bale and entered her from behind.

"Oh—my—god," she cried out.

They set a rapid pace, with Erianna's rhythmic motions matching Matthew's thrusts. The sound of their coupling filled the air, and when they reached the pinnacle he groaned in pleasure.

Finally redressed, he sat with his back against a hay bale and his long legs extended, cuddling Erianna to his side.

A deep voice broke the silence. "Go somewhere else to take care of business, you two. You're disturbing the horses."

Erianna's eyes rounded and she clamped a hand over her mouth. Gus could be heard grumbling impatiently as he walked away.

They looked at one another and then, in unison, broke into shameless, unrepentant laughter.

Once they had sobered she asked, "Will it always be like this?"

"What do you mean?"

"Um," she searched for the words. "Is lovemaking always so—pleasurable?"

"I believe it is, when the couple is in love."

"Hmm."

"What are you really asking me, Erin."

"Well, I was just wondering. This experience wasn't anything like last night, but I had just as good a time as I did then. Is that—normal?"

He smiled. "There are many ways to make love, sweetheart. Slow and tender, fast and hard. Oh, yeah, there are lots of ways to make love, and they are all enjoyable."

She sighed sweetly. "Well, I certainly have enjoyed myself so far."

He kissed the top of her head. "I'm glad you feel that way. But darling, I'm in a bit of a quandary here."

She turned to face him.

"I made a promise to myself that I wouldn't make love to you until we were married—out of respect. The only reason I broke that vow last night and again today was to assure you that intimate relations between us will be pleasing and gratifying, and that you needn't worry about our compatibility—in the sack."

She studied his expression as she digested that statement. He seemed to have spoken in earnest, but she was surprised that he was willing to wait until marriage to begin their sexual relationship. As far as she knew, most men would never agree to wait so long to satisfy their carnal lust.

"If you want to abstain until we're married I'll respect that. But, don't men have—needs? You know, sexual needs that they can't repress?"

"Most men do, I suppose. But Erin, I want to do this right. I want to show you that I love and respect you. And I don't want you to think I want to marry you just for the sex."

"Oh, Matthew. You are the dearest man."

"So you understand?"

"Yes, I understand. Thank you for showing me how wonderful it will be. And I'm willing to wait if you are."

He graced her with a broad, captivating smile. "So, no more sullenness?"

"No."

"No more embarrassment or shame?"

She shook her head. "No more embarrassment. I love you, Dr. Prestwick. Til the end of time."

The note came on Tuesday.

My dearest Erianna,

Home. At long last I have found my home. Not just four walls and a roof over my head, not a place of respite where I can lay my head at the end of the day. Home for me is where we are sheltered together from the incoming storms of life.

You have my heart, and in your heart I have found my home. Wherever you are, when I am with you, I am home.

All my love,

Matt

Erianna was in the kitchen on Thanksgiving morning when Matthew arrived. She was in sweats and had large hot rollers pinned in her hair. He grinned. How she could look so beautiful in curlers he hadn't a clue, but he thought she was the sweetest, loveliest creature he'd ever laid eyes on.

"Good morning."

She glanced up. "Hello."

Ned and his mother were working on wriggling the crock pot into a cozy so it would stay warm for the trip to the Prestwick estate. Once they completed the task Ned was sent upstairs to get changed.

"You're early," Erianna said as she blew a stay lock of hair off her face.

"Yeah, a little, is there anything I can do?"

"I think it's pretty much under control."

"What's in the crockpot?"

She glanced at the electric appliance on the countertop. "Oh, that's sage crockpot dressing. I called your mother to ask if I could bring it. I wasn't sure what kind of stuffing she serves and Ned would be disappointed if he couldn't have his favorite Thanksgiving dressing. She seemed to be okay with my bringing it." She shrugged.

"Don't worry. I'm sure she won't mind. Mom loves to cook and she loves to try new things. She'll probably ask you for the recipe, especially now that we're all family."

Erianna stilled for a moment. "She's going to be family. I hadn't thought of that." She focused her full attention on her fiancé saying, "Be patient with me, Matt. I'll get there, but I just need to ease into this."

He tilted his head down and looked into her beautiful, upturned face. "I love you."

She smiled, still a little shyly, and Matthew was bewitched.

Ned came downstairs just then dressed in church attire. His mother reached for the car keys and tossed them to the boy. "Go get your good coat out of the front closet, run outside and start the car so it'll warm up."

"Okay." He took off.

"What can I do for you?" Matthew asked.

"You can keep an eye on the pie for me. I'll go change and hurry Grace along."

When Ned came back in the front door he found Matthew looking through the oven window at the crumb-topped apple pie.

"Do you know what this pie is supposed to look like when it's done? Your mom told me to keep an eye on it, but I don't know what to look for."

Ned rolled his eyes, an endearing childish gesture and said, "It's on a timer. You don't have to stand there and stare at it."

The children helped their mother in the kitchen as a matter of routine and knew what they were doing. "When the juices begin to ooze up the outside edge it's done," he informed Matthew with authority. He went to the oven and peered in. "It's not ready yet."

They began to pack the items being taken to Prestwick for Thanksgiving dinner into shallow cardboard boxes that Erianna had procured from Doro. They put the crockpot in one and stuffed crinkled newspaper around it to keep it from shifting as they drove.

Erianna had gone to the Village the day before and picked up an arrangement of autumn flowers which were resting in the wide mouth of a small cornucopia. Matthew chose the cardboard box with the lowest lip and set the arrangement in the center. Once again they carefully stuffed newspaper around it.

"Mom usually covers this kind of stuff with sheets of newspaper over the top, too."

Matthew glanced over by the boxes and noticed that there was white tissue paper lying there. "There's some tissue over there. Why don't we cover it with that?"

"Good idea," Ned agreed.

They used tape to secure the paper in a loose bubble over the top of the flowers. Ned stepped back to survey the result. "Good job. I think it's well protected and it doesn't look too bad."

Ned went back and looked at the timer. Then he went to the intercom and buzzed his mother's room. "The pie has four more minutes, Mom."

After a short pause she responded, "Thanks, Ned. Keep an eye on it for me."

Erianna changed into a bronze-colored knee length fit-and-flare dress with flecks of gold shot through the fabric. The soft, lightly-puckered texture of the material would resist wrinkling and she hoped she would look presentable when they arrived. The rounded neckline sat against the base of her collarbone and three-quarter length sleeves completed the fully lined, home sewn dress.

She grabbed a brown, two-inch-wide inner circle belt and fastened the oversized hook and eye closure around her waist. Finally, she rummaged in her closet, wondering which shoes would work best with the dress. Deciding to take a conservative approach, she slipped into a pair of black pumps with a tapered heel.

"Mom!" Grace shouted from her bedroom door. When her mother appeared in the hallway Grace asked her, "Ballet flats or loafers—which do you like better?"

She was wearing one of each, and she waited for her mother's opinion.

"I like the loafer better than the flat. Did you try the dark blue lace-up Keds?"

"Good idea, I'll try that."

"Two minutes, Grace."

"Yeah, yeah, yeah."

Erianna smiled and turned to hurry downstairs. She had kept her hairstyle simple, opting to pull it back from her face with a wide, cloth-covered headband. She had applied mascara to the tips of her blonde lashes and added a bit of semi-gloss lipstick to her lips.

When she came into the kitchen Matthew's heart skipped a beat. She moved gracefully to the oven and looked at the pie.

Ned came up beside her. "It looks to me like it's just about to ooze a little on the left side."

"I think you're right. Let's get out the foil, and when Grace comes down we'll take it out and pack it."

Ned nodded. "I sure hope they like it, Mom. I never had a better apple pie, not even Doro's."

Erianna smiled brightly and gave her son a hug. "Happy Thanksgiving, Nathan."

Like a whirlwind, Grace came bounding down the stairs. She was becoming a beautiful young woman. Her rich brown hair had auburn highlights that complimented her lively green eyes. Unlike her mother's peaches and cream complexion, Grace's coloring was a warm silky mid-tone. She looked long-legged and stylish in a navy slim-leg windowpane pant. The dark blue background was broken by a thin white pattern of crisscrossing squares. She had paired it with a deep cranberry colored cable knit sweater. Under its bulky weight she wore a navy turtleneck.

"I decided on the loafers, Mom."

Her mother turned to look. "Good choice. You look very nice."

Erianna then directed her next comments to both of her children. "I hope you remember to mind your manners today, no matter what anyone says or does. Matthew has explained how his grandmother can be, but we will not let that get to us. Come what may we will conduct ourselves with decorum at all times."

She turned to Matthew. "That includes you, too, Dr. Prestwick. None of your shenanigans, do you hear?"

The kids chuckled as he smiled innocently. "Yes, ma'am."

* * *

They pulled into the circular drive, having made good time on the roads. Erianna silently worried about not arriving on time because of heavy traffic, but Matthew had taken State Route 27 north from the Village to I-271 in Alexandria, Kentucky. They crossed the Ohio River and exited, turning right onto State Route 52, and just a short time later arrived in the city of Prestwick, right on time.

They unloaded their wares and approached the door. Erianna held the crockpot in her arms and Grace the pie. Ned brought the flowers. Matthew opened the door for them, stepping aside to let them pass. Helen came to greet them.

The formal entryway was two stories high. Ned craned his neck to take in the space. A wide, slightly curved stairway led to the upper landing and a huge crystal chandelier splashed light over the area.

Ned stepped forward. "These are for you, Mrs. Prestwick. They're flowers."

"Why thank you, Nathan." She took the box from the boy. "Would you help me open it?"

He tore away the tissue and Helen smiled when the arrangement was revealed. "Why they're just lovely. Let's take them to the dining room. I think they'll look just right on the buffet table." Ned fell in step and they went through the hallway toward the room to the right of the front door.

Grace glanced to her left. Beyond the wide threshold to the formal living room stood a stately grand piano with the lid raised. Sunlight poured through the front window and spotlighted the instrument, and her fingers itched to play it.

From childhood Grace had played the piano. When they lived in Hudson she had taken formal lessons, but since moving to the Village of Berrington she practiced on her own on the small spinet piano nestled under the front window in the living room.

Matthew ushered Erianna and Grace down a hallway to the kitchen. The room was massive, as were most of the rooms in the Prestwick mansion. Black and white squares of cork flooring were laid and the walls were painted white. Marble countertops rested on dark finished lower cabinets. The uppers, also shaker in style, were white, and several had frosted glass insets.

After they deposited their boxes Matthew took their coats. The women began to unpack the crockpot and pie, and by the time he returned they had completed the task.

"Should I run and put these boxes in the back of the car?" Erianna asked him.

"No. I'll just stow them in the pantry."

Erianna removed the warming cover from the base of the crockpot and plugged it in just as Helen came into the room with Ned in her wake.

"Is that the sage dressing?" she asked the boy.

"Yes," he nodded vigorously. "It's really good."

"Can I have a taste now?"

"Sure." He followed Helen as she opened a drawer, and they each took a fork. Ned went over and got ready to lift the lid. "We don't want to keep the lid off for too long. Are you ready?"

She nodded. He lifted it back just enough for each of them to grab a forkful and then he quickly closed it.

They stood side by side and tasted the stuffing. Helen let the flavors roll over her taste buds as she considered.

"What do you think?"

"It's delicious. No wonder you like it so much. That's *really* good." She turned to Erianna. "You'll have to give me the recipe."

"I'd be happy to." She looked at Matthew and they laughed.

More guests were arriving by the minute. The Fowlers were introduced to Tom and Agnes Lattimore and their two children. Agnes was Helen's younger sister and the baby of the Collier siblings.

Helen's older brother, Broderick Collier, a retired business tycoon from New York City, was staying with Helen and he came downstairs just as his baby sister arrived. Introductions were made all around and everyone moved toward the back of the house to the family room.

When Grace learned that Uncle Brock, as they had been instructed to call him, lived in New York City she struck up a conversation with him. They sat on matching chairs at the far end of the room near the hearth of the gas fireplace where a warm fire glowed.

Drinks and snacks were served and Matthew turned on the football game. Not long after, Matthew's older brother, Monsignor John Prestwick of the Cathedral Basilica of the Assumption in Covington, Kentucky came in and took a seat to watch the game. The Fowlers had met him several times before when he visited his sister in Berrington and they were comfortable being in his presence.

The afternoon was spent in pleasant company. At halftime Grace and Ned went downstairs to the finished rec room to play pool with Agnes's children, Andrew and Victoria, who were both in college. Andrew was finishing his dissertation for his Ph.D. in economics and was fielding offers from several universities for a professorship. Vicky was in her last year of nursing school at Vanderbilt where she had met and fallen in love with a handsome medical student.

Matthew and his Uncle Tom, who was the CEO of the Prestwick Foundation, joined the group in the basement and they teamed up for a mini-pool tournament. The television was turned on, and the first game had just ended when they came back went upstairs to join the others.

Lucinda, the Prestwick matriarch, finally made her appearance and Matthew introduced her to Erianna and her children.

"Grandma, I'd like you to meet my fiancé, Erianna Fowler. And these are her children, Grace and Nathan. Erin, this is my grandmother, Lucinda Prestwick."

"It's a pleasure," Erianna said. "Thank you for inviting us. You have a beautiful home."

The children said hello, then remained quiet as the adults

conversed. Ned slipped his hand into Matthew's and Lucinda took note of the familiarity in the gesture.

"So, you're my grandson's choice of bride." She looked at Matthew. "I would have thought it more appropriate to meet the lady long before you became engaged."

"Grandma—" he warned in a cautionary tone.

She turned her gaze back to Erianna. "You grew up here in town." The remark was a statement, not a question, but Erianna responded nonetheless.

"Yes, I did."

"I understand that you're a widow."

"Yes, ma'am."

"Such a shame." Her tone softened somewhat. "I lost my husband many years too soon."

"We're ready to eat, Lucinda," Helen informed her mother-in-law.

As Matthew escorted his grandmother and Erianna to the dining room the older woman said, "You come with a ready-made family, I see. Do not think that your children will have any claim on the Prestwick holdings."

Matthew shot her a warning look, but Lucinda was not finished.

"My grandson deserves a wife who can produce a legitimate heir to the estate."

"That's enough, Grandma. You have no voice, nor will I permit any opinion of yours to interfere with my choice of a bride. I can't believe how rude you're being."

"I speak my mind, boy—"

"Well, stop," he interrupted her. "Jesus, Grandma. Could you be any more vulgar?"

"It's alright, Matthew," Erianna murmured.

"No, it's not alright. It's Thanksgiving, for Christ's sake. Who appointed her—"

"Language, Matthew," Helen scolded. "Enough of this, you two. Let's eat."

The dining room was twice the size of Erianna's formal dining room at home and beautifully appointed. Lucinda took her place at the head of the table, which was set for twelve, with Monsignor John at the foot. Matthew sat beside Grace, with Erianna and Ned opposite them.

Blessings were given by the Monsignor and they shared the Thanksgiving meal as casual conversation flowed. There were no more uncomfortable moments with Lucinda, and Matthew was happy to have his family members welcome Erianna and her children into the fold.

As was customary at Prestwick family Thanksgivings, dessert was not served immediately after supper. The women cleared the table as the men gravitated toward the television in the family room to watch second game between Washington and the Dallas Cowboys.

Erianna and Helen were in the dining room clearing the last of the dishes when someone began to play the piano.

Lucinda, who was still sitting at the head of the table, pounded her cane on the floor. "What's that?" she demanded.

Erianna stiffened and dropped the serving bowl in her hands. "I'm so sorry. That's probably Grace. I'll go tell her to stop."

She moved swiftly through the dining room archway and ran through the expansive hallway to gain access to the living room beyond.

"Erin, wait—that's not necessary," Helen called out as Erianna rushed away. Helen followed her as Lucinda rapped her cane on the floor again.

"Stop that, Grace," Erianna spoke quietly as she ran into the room.

Helen had just reached the living room entryway when the music stopped. "It's alright. You don't have to stop," she assured the teenager. "She's welcome to play," she told Erianna. "Don't make her stop."

Helen came over and sat down beside Grace on the bench.

"Please continue. What was that you were playing, Brahms?"

"No, it was Mendelsohn." Grace paused. "I'm sorry, ma'am. I should have asked permission."

"Nonsense," she said. "You play beautifully. And please, call me Helen—for now that is."

Grace was unsure what to do next. Helen encouraged the teenager to continue with the piece she had been playing.

Erianna hovered near the piano, looking across the entry hall and back, as if unsure what to do. When Grace finished, Helen assured Erianna that everything was fine and suggested that she help the others in the kitchen.

Erianna left, slowly and with great reluctance. Unwilling to face the Prestwick matriarch alone, she opted to bypass the dining room and walked toward the hallway to the kitchen.

There was little left to do, so Erianna gravitated toward the family room. She caught Matthew's attention and he got up and came to her. He knew by the expression on her face that something was wrong.

Taking her elbow, he guided her to his mother's office, closing the door quietly behind them. "What is it?"

She told him that Lucinda had become snappish when Grace began to play the piano.

"I'm not sure what to do? Your mother is with her and Grace is still playing. But I'm sure that your grandmother disapproves."

"If Mom is with her I'm sure it'll be alright."

"No, Matthew. Please go in there and make her stop. She can play at home."

He took note of her distress. "Okay, I have an idea. Wait here a minute."

He left the room, and after several excruciating minutes he returned with a drink in his hand. "Here, take this."

She pushed his hand away. "No alcohol."

He thought about insisting, but shrugged instead and drank the shot himself.

"I sent my brother in to run interference. Lucinda won't cause a scene with the Monsignor in the room."

"It would be better if we broke it up." She wrung her hands.

"Let's go in and monitor the situation. I can step in if there's trouble, okay?"

She nodded nervously and looked toward the door.

"Remember," he said. "We need to behave with decorum."

"Right." Erianna pulled her shoulders back to correct her posture, taking several deep, cleansing breaths. Then they left the office and walked sedately down the hall and into the living room.

Matthew's grandmother was sitting in a side chair to the right of the doorway and his brother was standing beside the piano. Matthew led Erianna to the couch and they took a seat.

When Grace finished the seasonal tune she was playing Monsignor John was ebullient in his praise. "Do you know any church hymns by heart?"

She took a moment to think. "Well, let's see. This Sunday is the Feast of Christ the King."

She began the introduction to the hymn *To Jesus Christ, Our Sovereign King.*

The Monsignor sang the words:

> To Jesus Christ, our Sovereign King,
> Who is the world's salvation.
> All praise and homage do we bring,
> And thanks and adoration.

Helen joined in the refrain:

> Christ Jesus, victor,
> Christ Jesus, ruler,
> Christ Jesus, Lord and redeemer.

They continued with the second verse and the final refrain.

All seemed well and Erianna began to relax. The Monsignor sat down in a chair beyond the couch as Helen and Grace played a short duet. Then Lucinda rapped her cane on the leg of her chair, demanding their attention.

"Play a Rosemary Clooney song."

Grace looked at Helen with a questioning expression on her face.

"I probably have some sheet music for that." They both stood and Helen opened the piano bench lid. She pulled out a large bundle of sheet music and perched the pile next to the music rack on the upper edge of the fall board. When she found the piece she'd been searching for she handed it to Grace.

"*Hey There*," Grace read the title out loud.

"That's a good one. Play that," Lucinda ordered the teenager.

Grace quickly scanned the piece before beginning. Helen sang along.

"*Hey there, you with the stars in your eyes.*"

Broderick and Agnes wandered in just then and sat down to listen. When the song ended everyone, with the exception of Lucinda, clapped in appreciation.

"Do you know anything by Henry Mancini," Brock asked. "The theme song from Pink Panther was always my favorite."

Helen searched but couldn't find any sheet music for that song. So she pulled out another piece composed by Mancini, telling her brother, "I don't have that one, but I have another song by Mancini. Grace, would you do the honors?"

Grace began the intro and then played the composition of the song *Moon River*.

Brock smiled in delight. He rose from his chair. "Come on, Aggie, dance with me."

Erianna was beside herself. There was that song again. Would she never escape it? When Mathew rose from the couch and pulled her into his arms she blushed profusely.

They danced cheek-to-cheek as Helen watched them. She knew the special meaning behind this particular tune. She had been in the crowd the night Erianna sang it for her classmates.

Grace played the piece beautifully and as the couples danced Erianna began to relax. She closed her eyes as the haunting tune took her back, enveloping her in the mists of the past.

When the last phrases of the song were reached, Matthew looked into her eyes and sang. "*We're after that same rainbow's end, waiting, round the bend, my lover and my friend,*" he used her rephrased words from long ago. "*Moon River, and me.*"

Erianna was captivated. She lost all sense of where she was and who was around her.

"I didn't do this properly the first time," Matthew murmured as he touched his forehead to hers. Then he went down on one knee, holding her left hand in his.

"Erianna Fowler, I love you with all my heart and soul. Will you marry me?"

Erianna's happy expression met his and she uttered the response he longed to hear.

She had finally stopped wearing her wedding band when they became engaged, and he took a square-cut diamond ring from his pocket and placed it on her finger. The one carat stone was offset by small diamonds and sapphires that glittered in the light.

Erianna's eyes widened at the unimaginable sight of the diamond on her finger. All the color drained from her face.

"I hope you like it. I picked it out especially for you," he professed as he got up from his knees.

"I chose it for the girl," Lucinda barked.

Matthew did not hear her. His focus was on Erianna alone. She shook her head and stepped back a little.

"My grandfather gave this ring to my grandmother many years ago. It was an anniversary present. From the moment you and I reconnected I've pictured you wearing it."

She took another step away from him. "I don't want this, Matthew. I can't understand why you pictured me wearing it. People of my station don't wear jewelry like this."

"Erianna—"

"No, Matt. No! After all this time, you still don't know me at all."

She took the ring from her finger. "I cannot accept your grandmother's ring. What will people think?" Tears threatened to spill down her cheeks. "She doesn't even like me. She doesn't approve."

A sob escaped. She turned to flee, and as she passed Lucinda she dropped the ring in the dowager's lap.

She started for the front door.

"Erin, wait!" Matthew called out.

She paused at the sound. Then, in a panic, she turned and dashed through the entryway to the stairs, making her escape to the second floor.

Chapter 17

Matthew's feet were glued to the floor. He was mired in quicksand and each small step took a colossal effort.

"You made my mother cry," Grace threw out the accusation as she stood by the piano bench with her hands on her hips.

Matthew looked her way. "I'm sorry."

"My mother *never* cries."

Matthew hung his head in shame.

"Well, clearly she is *not* the woman for you," Lucinda stated. "That woman is obviously unstable and her manners are deplorable. She is certainly not worthy of the Prestwick name."

"Lucinda!" Helen cried out as she moved toward her son.

"Don't you dare disparage my mother," Grace declared in a low, threatening tone. Her hands fisted as she stood fearless in defense of her mother. "You will never know a more honorable person than my mother. She is the most unselfish, loving and caring person you will ever meet. Unlike you, you dried up old biddy."

"How honorable can she be," Lucinda shot back, "raising an ill-mannered, foul-mouthed whelp like you? How dare you speak to me in such a manner. Obviously you have not been taught to respect your elders, which is another shortcoming of your mother's."

John stepped up. "The girl is right, Grandma. Respect is earned, not acquired by age. Your inappropriate and insufferable statements are inexcusable."

Helen came forward and took her son's face in her hands. "I'll go talk to her. I think this needs a woman's touch." She went up on her tiptoes and kissed Matthew's forehead.

He stood in abject misery as his mother left the room.

"Come with me, Grace." Agnes took the teenager by the hand and led her from the room. She guided the agitated teenager to the morning room in the east wing and closed the door behind them.

John embraced his brother. "She hasn't called off your engagement," he pointed out reassuringly. "She just rejected the ring. And who can blame her?" he scowled once again at Lucinda.

"That's right," Brock agreed. "Your mom will calm the choppy waters. Don't beat yourself up about this."

Matthew shook his head. "She's so worried about appearances. I don't know what to do."

"Get rid of her and good riddance."

"You shut up, Grandma! People like you are exactly the kind of cruel, judgmental people she fears." Matthew was screaming, his sudden rage expelled with each word he fired at her. "I *hate* you and your narrow-minded prejudices!"

Without another word Lucinda rose from her chair, walked into the hallway and took the elevator to the second floor to her room.

Helen came back into the living room just then. "I can't find her, Matt."

He ran his fingers through his hair. "She's an expert at disappearing."

He turned and left the room, taking the stairs two at a time to the upstairs landing. One by one he opened every door as he searched for his fiancé.

When he eased open the door to the guest bedroom his Uncle Brock used when he visited, Matthew detected the faint scent of Erianna's perfume, but in the darkness he could not see her. He slipped inside and quietly closed the door, standing still as his eyes searched in the dark.

Erianna finally moved, resuming a pacing path on the far side of the room. When she became aware of his presence she moved to the corner and turned her back to him. Hugging her arms around herself, she stood unmoving.

Matthew went to her and enveloped her in his arms. They stood together for a time, until he turned her around and brought her against his chest. She pressed her body against him, seeking out his comforting warmth, and he buried his face in her golden hair.

Neither spoke. Words were not necessary.

When, at long last they left the room, Matthew sheltered her against his side as they headed toward the stairs.

Lucinda sat in her room thinking about her grandson and his fiancé. The young lady hadn't spoken two words to her all evening, and Lucinda considered her to be a timid, uninteresting woman who was afraid of her own shadow, not at all suitable as a Prestwick, whose women were strong and self-assured.

She wasn't sure what Matthew saw in the girl. But she was impressed that Erianna had rejected the ring. It was clear that she was no gold-digger and that the couple was very much in love.

As they passed her open doorway Lucinda called out to her grandson. "Matthew, come in here. And bring your young lady with you. I want to speak to you both."

"Not now, Grandma."

"Please, Matthew. Come in."

Lucinda never used the word 'please', and her tone was deferential as she made the appeal. He looked to Erianna for guidance. She nodded, and they walked hand-in-hand into the dowager's room.

She was sitting in an armchair covered in a floral silk challis. Her cane rested on a round side table which was covered with a tatted doily that had seen better days.

Lucinda came right to the point. "My grandson has suggested that I may have been hasty in my judgment of your suitability as his wife. While I'm not happy with his method of delivery," she paused to frown at him, "I have, nonetheless, decided to take his statements under consideration."

Erianna stood stoically beside Matthew and he gave her hand a gentle squeeze.

"Matthew, leave us. I wish to speak to Erin in private."

"No, Grandma. I'm not leaving her alone with you."

Lucinda focused her gaze on her grandson. "Leave us!"

He would have made further protestations, but Erianna stopped him. "I'm alright."

Those were the first words she'd spoken since she had run from the living room in tears. Matthew studied her face. Her eyes were a bit puffy, but she offered him a small reassuring smile.

With extreme reluctance he started for the door.

"Close it behind you," Lucinda told him.

He paused and turned back to Erianna. "I'll be right outside," he assured her.

Directing his next statement to his grandmother Matthew said, "You *will* be respectful to my fiancé, Grandma, or I swear—" He left the rest of that threat unspoken.

When the door shut behind him Erianna turned to face the old woman. She'd been through this scenario more often than she cared to admit. Lucinda would have her say and then Erianna would be summarily dismissed.

"Sit down, my dear." An armless wooden cross-back chair was positioned opposite her, but Erianna declined.

"No, thank you. I prefer to stand."

"Young lady, I detest talking to people who are hovering over me. Come and sit down."

Erianna took a moment to consider. Then she went over and perched on the seat, her spine ramrod stiff and her hands resting in her lap.

"Go ahead and speak your mind, Mrs. Prestwick. I won't stop you. And when you're finished I'll leave. Any future visits I make to Prestwick will be few and far between, so we won't have a repeat of this distasteful tete-a-tete."

Lucinda sat back, considering. "You're a very pretty girl. I can understand Matthew's attraction to you. And your daughter is quite talented on the piano, although she needs to learn how to mind her manners."

Erianna could only imagine what had taken place in the living room after she ran out. No doubt Grace had given this woman a piece of her mind.

"I understand that your son has an artistic flair. You must be very proud of your children."

She didn't bother to respond. Erianna knew what would happen next and wasn't fooled by the insincere compliment, meant only to soften her up before the fatal blow was landed. She would be required to sit and listen silently to whatever diatribe was coming. Erianna couldn't begin to count the number of times she'd been subjected to just such a castigation.

"My youngest grandson is my only hope for Prestwick heirs." Lucinda's eyes became unfocused as she looked away. "I always wanted a large family. But when my husband's fighter jet was shot down in Korea I was left with only one child, my David.

"I understand now, after witnessing Matthew's proposal, the depth of his feelings for you. Your rejection hurt him terribly." She paused to take a drink of water.

Turning her steely brown eyes back to Erianna she said, "I don't like seeing my grandson hurt."

And here we go. Erianna wanted this tongue lashing over and done with as soon as possible.

The dowager reached over to the table and took the rejected engagement ring in her fingers. "This was the last gift my husband gave to me. It carries great sentimental value. Matthew asked me for the ring early last June. Does that date hold any significance for you?"

Again, Erianna did not deign to answer, so Lucinda continued.

"When I learned that you are barren I admit that I was extremely upset. And so I decided, sight unseen, to disapprove of your union."

Erianna's eyes narrowed, but she remained seated in the hard, uncomfortable chair.

"I've learned a valuable lesson tonight, young lady. I've seen with my own eyes the love Matthew has for you and you for him."

This was not what Erianna expected. Was Lucinda actually bending a little?

Lucinda looked at the ring she was holding. "In my dotage, I think back more and more to my Frank and the all-consuming love we had. I witnessed that same love tonight in the two of you, and it gave me pause.

"I was wrong to judge you before I had even met you."

Erianna looked away. She had been on an emotional roller coaster all day and she was about to topple over the edge into the depths below. She reached up and rubbed her fingertips along the bridge of her nose, and when she realized what she was doing she returned her hand to her lap.

"I want you to have this ring, my dear. Not just as a symbol of Matthew's love and commitment, but also as my blessing of your marriage."

"No. I cannot accept that ring," She rose from her chair and began to move away, but Lucinda's cane shot out, blocking Erianna's path.

"Don't leave yet," she ordered.

Erianna was tired. She felt weak-kneed and she sank back down on the chair.

"Tell me why, besides your obsessive concern over appearances, you won't accept this ring? Explain to me why it's so distasteful to you."

"Because—I didn't earn it."

The rigidity in her posture left her and she collapsed against the back of the chair. Her shoulders slumped.

"Matthew doesn't understand or he won't accept, I'm not sure which, the guilt I feel when I receive something that I haven't earned on my own." She looked across the distance between them and caught Lucinda's eye.

"I wish that you, and he, could understand. I don't want his money. His love is all I need. We had a colossal fight when I insisted that we sign a Prenup stating that I will make no claim to the Prestwick fortune, for myself *or* for my children. I don't want a penny from him, or you. I have my pride too, you know. You Prestwicks haven't cornered that market."

Lucinda's admiration of the woman rose several notches as, at last, Erianna made her feelings clear.

"As I understand it you were given the property in Berrington. You didn't *earn* that."

"That's true. I tried numerous times to return the land to its rightful owners, but they adamantly refused to accept the deed. And I've worked every waking moment since then to deserve the gift I was given. It hasn't been easy. All my time and energy is split between running the farm and caring for my children. And now Matthew, of course."

The dowager leaned forward in her chair. "You're an independent woman. I admire that, and I like you more and more with each passing minute. It took guts to sit here and talk to me."

Erianna closed her eyes for several seconds and when she started to get up Lucinda stopped her once again.

"Before you go, I want you to reconsider. Just this once, bend a little. It would mean the world to me, knowing that you have this ring. I've waited a long time for the right woman to come along who would be worthy of it, and Matthew believes you are that woman.

"I know my Francis is smiling down on us. He would have loved you and admired your courage and fortitude."

Erianna faltered. This was all too much. Their conversation hadn't gone at all the way she'd expected and she was tired of talking.

Lucinda's cane rapped on the wood leg of Erianna's chair and Matthew came hurriedly into the room. She rose from her seat and approached her grandson.

Depositing the ring into the palm of his hand she said, "Try again." With a pat on his cheek she offered him a rare, genuine smile and added, "I insist."

And then she was gone from the room.

* * *

After Matthew, Erianna and the kids headed home, but before the other guests left for the night, Helen addressed her concerns to the group gathered in her family room. She gave them a brief history of Erianna's formative years, of her growing up in Prestwick with very abusive parents.

"Erin does not want Clyde and Colleen to learn that she has become engaged to Matt."

"I don't understand that," Broderick said. "She's a grown woman, what could they possibly do to her now?"

"Trust me Brock, those people are masters at physical and psychological warfare. And her father absolutely *hates* the Prestwicks. If he finds out that she's engaged to Matt it'll cause no end of grief for her.

"I will say this, I have no idea how she managed to survive her childhood and become such a lovely, accomplished woman. They tried everything they could to break her, but somehow she managed to rise above."

The ride home was interminable. Erianna tried to convince Matthew that she was fine and perfectly capable of driving her family home, which was the original plan. But he insisted on driving them.

Truth be told, Matthew was just as disconcerted as she. Ned napped on the bench seat while Grace sulked in silence.

Helen and her sister, Agnes, had talked at length with the teenager in an effort to reassure her, but Grace's anger was still simmering. She had been livid when Lucinda implied that her mother was not worthy to marry her grandson.

Helen assured Grace that nothing could be further from the truth. "Your mother is a wonderful woman. Every one of us loves her and we're thrilled that they're engaged."

"Everyone but his grandmother," Grace pointed out.

The children, ever their mother's champions, were quick to come to her defense.

"She'll change her tune in time," Helen told her. "Lucinda is old and rigid, and set in her ways, slow to accept new people and ideas."

"Her age is no excuse," Grace countered. "What's the expression, 'the wisdom of the ages'? There's no justification for what she did."

Try as they might, Grace's opinion could not be swayed. Helen had managed to help the girl understand Matthew's distress and sorrow when Erianna refused to accept the engagement ring. And yet, as she sat brooding in the car, Grace couldn't help but feel resentful about the fact that her mother was, nonetheless, wearing the diamond ring.

"I don't understand you, Mom. I can't believe you're wearing that ring."

Erianna turned in her seat. "Mrs. Prestwick and I had a long heart-to-heart. She's such a lonely, frightened old woman."

Grace huffed and crossed her arms defensively.

Erianna extended her left hand so Grace could see the ring. "Did you know that this ring was Matt's grandfather's last gift to her before he went off to fight and was killed in the Korean conflict?"

"No."

"Her husband died when she was about the same age I am now and Lucinda never really recovered from her loss. All that brazenness and false bravado is just a defense mechanism. I realize now how lonely she is."

Matthew glanced toward Erianna. "Well, that's quite an act she's perfected. I'm with Grace on this one. My grandmother is a miserable, nasty, vicious old woman."

"Well, you can hold onto your shared opinions and waste your time and energy resenting Lucinda. I, for one, choose to let go of my negative feelings and embrace a positive attitude toward her. And I will include her in my prayers. She's very misunderstood, and if you ever bother to scratch under the surface of her hard outer shell I believe you will find a very fine lady."

* * *

On Monday evening, the night before the Feast of St. Nicholas on December sixth, Grace and Ned hung their stockings from the mantle in the family room. After staying for a long weekend, Matthew was getting ready to head home, but he stopped when he noticed that a cross-stitched stocking with his name across the top had been hung with the others.

The Santa Train stocking depicted sleepy town buildings and a church with a steeple shrouded by snow in the background at the top of the stocking. Below, red train cars with green roofs rode along curved tracks. Several gondola cars were filled with evergreen trees, while others were passenger cars.

The train cars became larger as they turned and descended into the foreground at the foot of the stocking. A coal car was attached to the red, green and gold engine, and smoke puffed from the smokestack. Santa peered out the engine window waving his hand merrily.

"I wasn't sure if you preferred Matt or Matthew," she told him.

He pulled her against his side, smiling brightly and showing a bit of dimple. "I would have preferred 'Dad.'"

Erianna blushed and pushed him away, then went to sit on the couch.

"Have you finished your paper on St. Nicholas?" she asked Ned.

"Yes." He began his report. "St. Nicholas of Myra was a Christian bishop who lived during the time of the Roman Empire in the fourth century."

"Where is the city of Myra located?"

"It's in Asia Minor on the Mediterranean Sea. I think it's in modern day Turkey. He was born in the city of Patara—it's in the region of Lycia on the coast in Asia Minor. He learned to read, which was unusual for that time period.

"After becoming a priest he went on a pilgrimage to Jerusalem, and when he returned to Lycia he decided to live a life of quiet reflection, so he entered a monastery. But the Lord came to him and showed him another path."

"What path was that?" his mother asked.

"The Lord wanted St. Nicholas to work among the people of the region and to help those in need.

"There's a widely accepted story about how he helped a poor man with three daughters. They had no dowries and their father had no choice but to sell them into slavery because he could not secure good marriages for them without a dowry. But on three separate occasions a bag of gold was tossed into the man's home to provide the dowry for each daughter. The legend says that the bag of gold was tossed through an open window and landed in stockings or shoes left by the fire to dry. That's how the modern tradition of filling stockings with gifts came into being."

"Can we get gold coins in our stockings, Mom?" Grace teased.

Ned continued. "St. Nicholas, the Bishop of Myra, is commonly pictured with a white beard and a cassock, miter and crozier, the garments of a Bishop."

"What are a miter and crozier?" Matthew asked.

"A miter is a pointy headdress worn by bishops and a crozier is a bishop's staff. Like a tall walking stick."

"What else do you know about him?"

Ned turned back to his mother. I know that he participated in the first Ecumenical Council. Can you believe that? Pretty cool—"

"Who convened the first Ecumenical Council?"

"That was the emperor Constantine."

Erianna continued with more questions for her son. "To become a saint he had to have been found to perform at least three miracles. Can you tell me anything about that?"

"Yes," Ned nodded. He looked at his report. "One was the deliverance from death of three men unjustly condemned for the crime of stealing. St. Nicholas stopped the executioner by grabbing his raised sword before he could kill these men. Then he went to the Governor and condemned him for ordering their deaths, and the Governor was repentant and begged St. Nicholas for forgiveness.

"St. Nicholas is the patron saint of children and sailors. December sixth is the commonly accepted anniversary of his death, somewhere between the years of 330 and 342. There's some differing information in the articles I read about the actual year."

"When was he canonized?" Erianna asked him.

"Actually, Mom, I couldn't find a specific date, but it was somewhere in the late tenth century. Back then, long before the Roman Catholic Church standardized procedures for the canonization of saints, the local bishops verified miracles attributed to a person and canonized him or her themselves. By the late eleven-hundreds when the Church finally brought the process under a centralized system, St. Nicholas was already accepted by the Church as a saint."

"That's very good, Ned."

"Did you know that the tradition of placing a large orange in the stocking is symbolic of the gold he gifted to the father of the three daughters?"

"No, I didn't," Erianna admitted.

"You know, Mom, only cities with strong German populations like Cincinnati and Milwaukee hold to the tradition of hanging stockings on December sixth."

"Yes, I know. But I think it's a nice tradition, don't you?"

He nodded.

Matthew worked alongside Erianna at the stables on a dreary Saturday afternoon in December, one week before Christmas. She went home to change and run to the grocery, and Matthew stayed to finish up with Gus. When he finally left the sun was setting.

As he dressed in clean clothes he heard music playing and assumed that the kids were hanging out in the rec room. So when he opened the bathroom door and found them working from a collapsible table in the unfinished laundry area he paused to listen.

"We need to figure out a way to make a small slit in the birchwood so that we can insert the O-rings," Grace said.

"We could try a utility knife, but the angle isn't right and I think the slit might be too wide."

Grace and Ned had spent a great deal of time working on homemade Christmas ornaments to give as gifts. They ordered several dozen birchwood hearts online, as well as small jewelers O-rings. The metal rings needed to be inset at the dip in the heart so that they could thread thin cording through them to use as hangars for the ornaments.

The hearts were two-and-a-half inches wide by two-and-a-half inches high and a quarter inch thick. Half were painted red and the other half gold. Ned had used his electric wood-burning soldering knife with an angle tip to draw designs into the wood.

Several red hearts depicted the star of Bethlehem with rays of light streaming down, and some had an outline of a manger burned into the base color. Others depicted Christmas wreaths and candy canes. Ned had also outlined several gold hearts with the petals of poinsettia plants, and Grace had painted the petals in red.

They finished the ornaments with glitter markers in red and gold to accent their designs. Some ornaments' outside edges were burned in equidistant lines around the hearts, while others were highlighted with red or gold slashes, depending on the base color of the heart.

No two hearts were the same, and when they were finished there were forty decorated ornaments.

Matthew moved closer. "What are you guys up to?" he asked.

Grace and Ned turned in unison to look at him.

"Stop!" Grace commanded. "Don't come in here." She turned the music down.

Ned shot out of his chair and ran toward Matthew, his arms extended to ward him off. "You can't come in here, Matt. We're working on Christmas gifts."

"Okay. I won't come any closer. But it sounds to me like you need an exacto knife."

"I know," Ned agreed. "But Mom won't let me buy one. She's

afraid I'll slice my finger off."

Matthew ran his fingers through his still slightly damp hair. "Well, if you don't mind me helping a little, I have a scalpel in my medical bag. It's probably just the right shape and width you guys need to make the slits."

Ned frowned. "Wait here," he told Matthew.

He went over to his sister and they began a discussion, whispering to one another as Matthew waited patiently.

"If we let you help us then you'll know what you're getting for Christmas," Ned called out.

"That's true, but I don't mind finding out a week early if you don't."

The siblings put their heads together again and finally came to the conclusion that they had no other options.

"Okay," Grace agreed. "But you have to try *not* to look at the designs and you absolutely *can't* tell Mom that you helped."

"I promise," Matthew stated.

He went out to his car to retrieve the medical bag from his trunk. By the time he got back the kids had covered the hearts with a cloth. Matthew sat down at the table and Ned handed him one of the ornaments.

"Can I see an O-ring? That way I'll know what size slit you need."

Grace complied and Matthew set to work making the cuts in the hearts. It didn't take long. Ned handed him each heart, and Grace took it and covered it when Matthew finished.

The minute Matthew was done he got up and stepped back. He asked the kids, "How are you going to seat them in place? With superglue?"

Ned looked at Grace. "That's a great idea. We can use needle nose pliers to hold the O-rings. That way we won't glue our fingers to the rings."

Matthew left them to their work.

Their final step was to dip the hearts into clear acrylic and hang them to drip dry. They had already come up with a plan for that step. Several clothes hangers were suspended from the horizontal pole in the laundry room and they used metal wire ornament hooks to dip and suspend the hearts on the hangers.

Once they dried Grace and Ned removed the wire hooks and threaded thin braided cord through the rings, slip tying them together. Then they boxed the ornaments and cleaned up their workstation.

"We'll wrap them later in my room," Grace told Ned, who nodded in agreement.

"I'm hungry. Let's go see if supper's ready yet."

Preparations were in full swing for the Christmas holiday. After Sunday Mass the Donovan clan and the Fowlers, along with Matthew, drove to a nearby Christmas tree farm to choose their trees. Pap and Ginny no longer decorated live trees, opting instead to use an artificial tree that had already been put up and decorated.

Erianna chose a tall, narrow short-needle pine whose size wouldn't overwhelm the living room. The tree was positioned against the wall separating the living and dining rooms between the lower stairway landing and front the entrance to the dining room. Multi-colored mini-lights adorned it and a wide variety of ornaments graced its branches. Shimmering silver tinsel rained down and completed the beautiful tree and a handmade tree skirt was placed around the stand.

A homemade wreath of red and silver balls hung on the wall above the couch across the room, and a variety of nutcrackers stood sentinel on the top of the piano at the front window. Poinsettia plants spilled down the side of the three steps along the lower landing.

Erianna stepped up into the hallway, turned and surveyed the room from afar, pleased with the results.

The family room had also undergone a transformation. The fireplace mantle was decorated with an artificial swag that spilled over the edges and fell gracefully down the sides of the stone fireplace. The garland, abundant in cypress leaves and evergreen foliage that were lightly dusted in gold glitter, had mini-poinsettia flowers interspersed along its length. Red and gold berries were scattered throughout, as well as mini ball ornaments, both solid and striped, in red and gold. Clear LED lights braided through the garland glowed softly.

The cross-stitched stockings were rehung, but would not be filled. They were merely for decoration.

A nativity crèche rested atop the antique marble-top table just inside the back sliding door, and a star-shaped sconce hanging on the wall above spilled beams of light onto the scene below.

The hardwood floors in the dining room, which was one step up from the sunken living room, were polished and they gleamed in the light from the front bay window. An Oriental rug in a blue and cream design anchored the rectangular cherry wood dining table. Erianna covered it with her best Irish linen tablecloth and added a red and green plaid runner along the length of the table.

Presents were wrapped, and the women spent a day baking cookies at Doro's house.

On Tuesday morning Erianna slipped away and was gone for most of the day. Matthew was working from her office, and when he noticed her absence he asked Ginny where she had gone.

"She went shopping," was her vague reply.

When Matthew came in after work on Thursday evening he brought Erianna a low-profile tabletop centerpiece of red roses.

She was thrilled. "I've never gotten roses before," she admitted.

"Never?"

"No, never. They're beautiful, Matthew. Thank you."

"Oh, my honeybee, you deserve roses every day for the rest of your life."

She blushed. "That would be overkill, don't you think?"

Erianna placed the centerpiece on the dining room table and then got out her Waterford candlesticks, placing one on each side of the arrangement. She found white tapers in a buffet drawer and inserted them into the candlesticks.

"What do you think?" she asked him.

"I think it's just perfect." He turned to her. "Our first Christmas."

"Our first Christmas." She couldn't be happier. She moved into his arms and kissed him. They were locked in a passionate embrace in the semi-seclusion of the dining room when Ned walked by the hallway entrance to the room and noticed them.

"Yuck!" he cried out in typical little boy disgust.

They broke the kiss and looked at Ned's odious expression.

"You guys are gross," he declared as he turned on his heel and left.

By Friday afternoon the preparations were complete and they were ready for Christmas. Early Saturday morning, Christmas Eve, Erianna and the kids drove to Prestwick. They stopped at her parents' house for a short visit and to drop off their gifts.

Erianna looked at the wall in the living room where her father had tried to kill her. She had trouble tearing her eyes away from the spot of the horrific beating she had taken. Lowering her eyes to the floor, Erianna called upon every ounce of her strength not to dwell on the gruesome scene playing over and over in her mind.

The children placed the presents for their grandparents and aunts under the tree. The Pruitts, as usual, refused to open the gifts in their presence. Why, Erianna could not venture a guess. Grace and Ned received gift certificates and Erianna, as always, received nothing.

Within the hour, their duty complete, they went home to the Village of Berrington.

Chapter 18

Soft music played and the tree was lighted when Lucinda and Helen Prestwick arrived with Matthew that afternoon. Erianna had spoken to his mother several times on the phone since Thanksgiving. She extended an invitation to the Prestwick women, welcoming them to join the Fowlers on the farm for Christmas Eve.

A plan had been agreed upon wherein they would join Erianna and her children for a gift exchange in the late afternoon, and then the women would go next door to eat and visit until they all left for midnight mass celebrated by Monsignor Prestwick at the Covington Cathedral.

After mass, Matthew, Erianna and her children would head home to the Village while Bob, Doro and their brood would drive to Prestwick to spend the night and celebrate Christmas Day with Doro's extended family at the estate.

"Welcome to my humble home," Erianna greeted the women. "I'm so happy that you could come."

"Thank you, dearie," Lucinda patted Erianna's cheek as she crossed the threshold. Apparently, the dowager's attitude toward Erianna had softened considerably.

The children were waiting to take the women's coats. Matthew followed his mother through the door and paused to take in the sight of his fiancé.

She had paired a soft, shale green ruched turtleneck with a black, fully-lined wool straight-leg dress pant and unadorned black leather ankle boots with a two inch heel. An abstract wrap of soft-focus plaid completed the ensemble. Multi-colored in shades of shale green and dusty slate blue with sapphire and aubergene undertones, the cashmere wrap was anchored at her shoulder by a small round pewter pin.

Erianna had swept her hair back in a loose chignon and small wisps of her blond hair fell softly and framed her face.

Matthew drew her into his arms. "You look beautiful. Merry Christmas."

Erianna blushed, as usual, and he wondered if she would ever outgrow the youthful assuetude.

Henry, who had driven the group from Prestwick, came in through the garage door, and when Erianna heard the basement door open she hurried into the hallway.

"Please, join us," she told him. "You shouldn't spend Christmas by yourself."

The women were given a tour and then they went to Pap and Ginny's suite where drinks and canapés had been laid out for everyone to sample.

"You have a beautiful home, Erin," Helen said.

Thank you. It's a well thought out floor plan, but I can't take credit for that. It was Bob and Doro's design. I just added my personal touch to the place."

"Well, it's changed a lot since Doro lived here and I love what you've done with the place."

When it was time for the gift exchange Matthew helped Pap into his wheelchair while the others settled themselves in Erianna's living room. Henry sat unobtrusively on the step between the living and dining rooms, and Grace and Ned, who had been designated to play Santa for the evening and pass out the brightly-colored gifts to everyone, took up their stations on the floor by the tree.

Pap and Ginny joined the others in the living room, and they were ready to begin.

"This one is for Mrs. Prestwick," Ned said as he pulled the first gift from under the tree.

"Which Mrs. Prestwick?" Matthew chuckled. "You're going

to have to start calling them by their first names or we'll be here all night."

He looked to his mother. "It's alright, Ned. Just read the tags off as they're written."

"Okay. It says 'to Grandma, from Matt.'" The gift was passed to the dowager, and she opened the it to find a beautiful jewel toned silk scarf."

"Thank you, Matt."

The next present was given to Helen, from Erianna. The box was quite large, and she opened it to find a red and green tartan plaid throw blanket on an off-white field.

"I thought it would look nice in your family room during the holiday season."

Helen looked carefully at the knitted afghan. "Did you make this yourself?"

Erianna nodded.

"It must have taken you forever to knit this. Thank you."

"All of the Fowlers' gifts are handmade," Pap pointed out.

"Is that true?" Helen asked in surprise.

Grace spoke up. "Mom says it's more personal to *make* our gifts. Not everything is homemade, of course, but we try to give at least one present to each other that we made with our own two hands. It's our tradition."

"Why, I never heard of such a thing," Lucinda exclaimed.

"Grandma—" Matthew warned.

She waved a hand in dismissal. "No one goes to the trouble of giving homemade gifts anymore." She turned to Erianna. "That's an admirable tradition, my dear."

Matthew expelled a deep breath and relaxed. It was clear that Lucinda had decided to be on her best behavior, and the evening progressed without incident.

Grace and Ned handed out their wrapped presents to everyone in the room at once. The heart-shaped ornaments were opened and they all gushed over the beautiful designs. Each box contained two ornaments, one red and the other gold. When

Henry was handed his he seemed momentarily taken aback.

"That's for you," Grace assured him.

Everyone began to compare their ornaments.

"Look, Pap. Mine has a candy cane." Ginny showed her husband her gold heart with a red and white candy cane design.

Lucinda and Helen compared theirs and both were highly impressed by the quality of the workmanship.

Pap and Ginny received a handmade tree skirt from Erianna. And then Erianna unwrapped her gift from Helen, a pair of dress gloves that matched her coat.

Lucinda gave Erianna a beautiful new watch. "You shouldn't wear a cheap, ten dollar watch when you're in dress clothes. The band on this watch is reversible. One side is gold and the other silver. It will do double duty and you can match the color to your outfit."

"Thank you, Lucinda." She glanced at the old leather-banded Timex on her wrist. "Other than my watch I don't normally wear jewelry, and it never occurred to me to have a dress watch." She went to sit next to Lucinda and the dowager showed her how to turn the band. They chose the silver side to complement the outfit she was wearing and she took off her old Timex and slipped on the new watch.

Then Erianna went to look for a specific gift under the tree. When she found it she offered it to Lucinda. "Merry Christmas."

The wrapping was torn away and the box opened to reveal a tatted doily set. One was round and the other a long dresser runner.

"Don't tell me you made these," Lucinda sputtered.

Erianna nodded. "I noticed that the doily on your sitting room table was quite worn, and I thought you might like a new one. Helen measured the circumference of the table for me, so I think it should fit."

"Oh, my word. I can't believe this. I've never heard of anyone tatting their own doilies. Wherever did you learn—"

"I picked it up somewhere along the way." She shrugged.

Helen opened her purse and pulled out four envelopes, which were handed out to Matthew, Erianna, Grace and Ned. "Open these together," she advised them.

Inside the envelopes a Christmas card held handwritten notes:

You are cordially invited to accompany me to New York City next spring break.

We will stay with my brother Broderick at his home in Manhattan

and attend a Broadway show, visit museums and dine at fine restaurants.

I will escort you around the city and visit any places of particular interest to you.

Love,
Helen

Graces' mouth opened in an astonished 'O'. "New York City? I've always wanted to go there." She looked at her mother. "Can we really go to New York?"

Erianna was hesitant to agree, but she plastered a smile on her face. "How can we say no?"

Matthew reached for her hand. "We'll fly there in my plane and you can shop at that fabric store you're always talking about. What's the name?"

"Mood," Erianna supplied, her interest picking up.

Grace got up, ran to Helen and hugged her. "Oh, thank you so much. I've always wanted to go to New York."

Helen laughed. "I know. Uncle Brock told me."

"Ned will love the museums," Grace stated excitedly. "And I can't wait to see a Broadway show."

She began to chatter excitedly. "I wonder what shows will be playing. Where's a school calendar? I want to look up the dates for spring break."

Erianna sat back and enjoyed the spectacle as her children ran to find the calendar on the bulletin board. She glanced at Helen and Lucinda, who were sitting side-by-side on the couch. The women exchanged knowing glances and the gift exchange was put on hold until the children had calmed down and returned to their posts on the floor by the tree.

Ned found two matching gifts and handed them to Matthew and Henry. "These are the same for both of you, so you might as well open them together."

Matthew went over and perched next to Henry on the step to the dining room as they opened their gifts. Handmade nutcrackers, each finished with different coloring and each sporting different hats and capes were unwrapped. Matthew translated as Henry signed his ebullient praise for Ned's craftsmanship. He thanked the boy, and Matthew seconded the sentiments.

Grace rummaged around and found another gift for Henry. It was a cross-stitched stocking with a nutcracker design. The multitude of soldiers of various sizes encompassed the entire stocking, and Henry's name was stitched across the top.

"I didn't know which spelling you would prefer, so I opted for Henri. I hope that's okay," Erianna said.

"That's perfect," Henry signed as Matthew translated. Once again, he thanked Erianna for her thoughtful gift.

Then Matthew took a position on the floor next to Ned and pulled out a small, rectangular box. "This is for you, from me."

Ned opened his gift. Inside were tickets to two Bengals football games. "The tickets are for next year's season," Matthew explained. "I hope you don't mind waiting that long. One is a home game in Cincinnati against the Cleveland Browns. The seats are in a suite, so we can enjoy the game with all the amenities. And the other is the away game in Cleveland. Those seats are on the fifty yard line."

"Oh, wow! Thanks Matt."

"Don't spill the beans, but I got tickets for Bob and the boys as well. We can all go together, but you have to keep that under your hat until tomorrow."

"I will. I promise." He gave Matthew a hug and turned to show his sister the tickets.

"You're next," Matthew told Grace as he sorted through the remaining gifts. "Here—I hope you like it."

Grace tore the paper away to find the book *The Adventures of Tom Sawyer.* She opened the front cover of the hardbound book and gasped. "It's a first edition!"

"I had so much fun on your treasure hunt, I went on a hunt of my own."

Grace couldn't speak. She launched herself into Matthew's arms and hugged him fiercely. He patted her back saying, "You're welcome."

"See if you can find my gifts to the children," Lucinda told Matthew.

Ned received a poster showing the position of each planet and other orbiting bodies in the solar system on the day, hour and minute of his birth. Then Matthew handed a still visibly shaken Grace his grandmother's brightly wrapped present.

It was a Desiderata wall plaque. The dowager hoped that Grace would understand the significance of the words written on the plaque.

She took her time reading it. When she finished she looked at Lucinda, but said nothing for what seemed a very long time. Everyone remained silent as the two protagonists faced off. Finally, Lucinda spoke. "You are a child of the universe, Grace. And wise far beyond your years. The essay reads, 'As far as possible without surrender, be on good terms with all persons.' I would like to be on good terms with you and I offer my amends for my behavior."

Without a word Grace went over and knelt in front of the dowager. She offered her hand and Lucinda reached out with gnarled fingers and took it.

"Peace," Grace stated simply.

"Peace," Lucinda agreed.

There were two presents left under the tree, Matthew's gift to Erianna and hers to him. She opened hers first. Two vintage hairs combs rested in the tissue. The bronze metal combs were decorated in a floral cloisonné design. The brightly colored enamel combs, separated by thin strips of flattened wire, were just Erianna's style and she was thrilled to receive them.

Finally, Matthew opened his gift. A five by seven tri-fold frame held images of his mother and father, grandmother and grandfather, and the center picture was of Erianna and him. All were head and shoulder shots in sepia tones. Matthew looked at Erianna and brought his hand to his heart.

"I noticed that you don't have any family pictures in your office, and I thought you might like it."

"I love it. Thank you." He smiled broadly. "This explains the pictures the kids took of us after mass several weeks ago."

Matthew sat on the floor between Grace and Ned. "These are my grandparents, Francis and Lucinda Prestwick." Frank was dressed in his Air Force uniform, and a young and vibrant Lucinda smiled sweetly for the camera. "Grandpa Frank died when his plane was shot down in Korea.

"And here," Matthew pointed to the picture on the opposite side, "are my parents, David and Helen. I'm not sure when this picture was taken," he admitted.

"That was just after John was born," his mother supplied.

"Where did you get these pictures?" he asked Erianna.

"Your mother and grandmother let me rummage through old photo albums from their attic. I had a wonderful time listening to them reminisce."

Matthew and Erianna chose to go to the Hoot 'n Holler for New Year's Eve. Neither was willing to stray too far afield, as both considered it dangerous to be out on the roads with so many drivers under the influence.

The next morning Erianna was on a call in her office when Matthew wandered by. He paused outside the door to listen when he heard her raised voice.

"I don't have that much and you know it." She listened as the person on the other end spoke. "No. I gave you fair warning.

You should have applied for student loans. I can't continue to foot your bills."

Gus came out of his room just then. "Bloodsuckers," he mumbled as he passed the office door, continuing down the wide center aisle.

Matthew fell in step beside him. "What's that all about?"

"Her parents are bleeding her dry. Those fuckers have had their hands in her pockets since she moved here."

"You mean she's giving them money?"

"Yeah, that's exactly what I mean. At first it was just a little now and then, but as time has passed they've become greedier. Now they call every month, and the amounts they demand are getting higher and higher. They've got her paying for her sisters' college tuitions. Can you believe that?"

Every month? How much is she dolling out?"

"I don't know for sure, but I'd venture a guess that she's laid out in the six figure range by now."

Gus stopped. "Did you know that she leases the land beyond the south fenceline for farming? She had planned to build a jumping arena and dressage ring there when the leases expired. She was hoping to bring in business by hosting junior class three-day events."

He huffed. "Now she'll be lucky if she manages to hold onto that land. I should have agreed to transfer the deed back into my name when she asked me to. I had no idea at the time what she was up against. Those people should be tarred and feathered."

With a wave of disgust, Gus walked off toward his truck. He started the engine to warm it up while he waited for Erianna to join him. Then they headed out to the feed store to pick up supplies.

After they left Matthew snuck into her office to look at her books. He quickly searched through the computer records.

Gus was right. There were monthly payments transferred to an account that he assumed was her parents' checking account. Included was an outlay of five thousand dollars just this morning.

Matthew went back through her old records. Erianna was running in the red each month and had been since she came to Berrington Farm. He couldn't believe what he was seeing, but there it was in black and white. Clyde and Colleen Pruitt were bleeding their daughter dry.

He finished quickly and left her office long before she came back, then went to the house to talk to Pap. He needed to ask him about the situation and what, if anything, Pap might know.

The following Saturday Matthew was in the kitchen cooking supper for the Fowlers. Erianna had been ensconced in her office for hours. When she finally came into the family room and plopped down on the couch she had the look of a harried, anxious woman.

She dozed as Matthew and the kids got supper on the table. When they finished eating, Grace asked her mother, "Did you finish your paperwork?"

"No. I'm stuck."

"Stuck how?"

"I can't figure out if I should close the month, then the quarter, and then the year, or just close the whole year."

"Which accounts?" Grace asked. "Business or household?"

Erianna shrugged. "Uh, well, both I guess."

Grace expelled a long-suffering sigh and said, "What did you do last year?"

"I don't remember."

"Okay. Do you want to sit down and show me?"

"Sure. Go turn on my laptop. I'll be right there."

Grace went down the hall as Erianna finished clearing the table. Matthew stood nearby, fascinated by the interaction between the women. He ran his fingers through his hair and shook his head and Erianna, who had brought a washcloth over to clean the table, noticed the gesture.

"What?"

"Nothing."

She continued her chore, and when the kitchen was cleaned she walked back into the room, intending to join Grace in the office. But Matthew was still standing in the same spot, apparently lost in thought.

"Is something wrong?"

"No," he assured her. "Far from it. You guys are fascinating, the way you all work as a team and learn from one another."

"Well, I'm glad you brought that up," Erianna said. "I've been thinking—"

He couldn't help but chuckle. That brought Erianna up short and she stood silently, studying him.

"I adore you," he said. "Do you know that I had a placard made for my desk that says, 'I've been thinking…'?"

"Mmm." Erianna was sure there was some kind of subliminal message there, but she wasn't sure what it was.

He realized that she thought the joke was on her. "I'm sorry, but you do say that quite a bit."

"Oh. I didn't realize that. I'll try to refrain from using that particular phrase in the future."

Matthew grabbed her up into his arms. "Don't do that, honey. It isn't meant as a criticism. It's just that every time I hear you say 'I've been thinking', I know what follows will be a fabulous adventure. You, Erianna, are unlike anyone I've ever known."

Like I haven't heard that a thousand times before. "Yes, well, that has been pointed out to me a time or two."

He sobered. "Come on. Being unique is not a bad thing. I happen to love that about you. It's a particularly delightful quality to possess."

Erianna relaxed in his arms. She brushed the back of her fingers across his cheek. "Thank you."

She turned, intending to head down the hall, but Matthew held her fast in his embrace. "You never finished your thought."

"Yes, that's right. I was interrupted."

He smiled. "What were you thinking?"

"I was thinking that you should get into the act." She patted him on the cheek, much like Lucinda so often did.

"What act?"

"Step into the waters, Matt, and get your feet wet. You're far more knowledgeable than I am. Your interactions with the children will be welcomed."

"Me? I'm not a teacher."

"Neither am I. Just start the ball rolling and let them run with it."

"Like I did when Grace was working on her business plan?"

"Exactly."

And with that she headed down the hall and disappeared into the office.

Matthew was in the basement getting ready for a trip when Erianna came downstairs to start a load of laundry. There were two separate laundry areas, one for their everyday clothes on the first floor opposite the office, and another in the basement for items worn to the stables.

"You look handsome," she remarked when she saw him in his business suit.

He smiled. "I'll be gone most of the week. Henry will be here in an hour to pick me up."

Matthew's business trips were routine and everyone had accepted the status quo.

After starting the laundry she came into the rec room, which was now considered Matthew's bedroom, and smuggled a note into his bag. They continued the 'tradition' of writing to one another, despite their semi-cohabitation.

"Do you have a few minutes?" he asked.

"For you, I have all day."

They sat down together on the couch.

"What's up?"

"Well, I've been thinking—" Matthew wiggled his eyebrows.

"Fun-eee," she quipped in a sing-song voice.

He sat back. "Seriously, I did want to talk to you about setting a date."

"A date?"

"Yes. A wedding date."

Erianna sobered. "Oh."

"We're settled into a comfortable routine now and the kids seem to have accepted me. So I think it's time to have a discussion about getting married."

Erianna grew introspective. "I suppose you're right. I hadn't really thought about it."

"Well, I have. It's on my mind—a lot. Most of the time. *All* the time."

Erianna smiled. He was so dear. She knew what he was implying.

"Nothing has to be decided today," he assured her. "But we need to put our heads together and come up with a plan."

"We *could* just go to the courthouse—"

"No."

She frowned. "This is my second marriage, Matt. It wouldn't be appropriate to have a fancy wedding with a lot of guests."

"We're not going to the courthouse, Erin. I want a church wedding."

Erianna took a minute to think. "My parents are going to be a problem. You do realize that, don't you?"

He nodded.

"This isn't as simple as just picking a date."

"I know. Why don't you think about it? It's my understanding that women dream about their wedding days from the time they're little girls."

"I hate to dispel that myth, but I never once dreamed about my actual wedding day. Frankly, I never thought marriage was in the cards for me. My main focus was on surviving my childhood."

"Sweetheart," he rasped. "I'm sorry."

"I'm not looking for sympathy. I'm just telling it like it was."

He ran his fingers through his dark hair.

Erianna got up from the couch saying, "There's a lot to think about. And you're right, this can't be decided today."

He stood up and took her into his arms, but Erianna suddenly wasn't in the mood to cuddle.

Matthew's letters arrived with regularity, especially when he was out of town. He would tell her about the cities he visited and often quoted snippets of poetry from poets such as Byron, Dickinson and the like.

They made plans for a date night on Valentine's Day. Erianna looked forward to joining Matthew in Lexington for dinner. He would be flying in from Atlanta, and Henry would drive her to a downtown hotel where they would meet.

She was surprisingly apprehensive about the date, and she spent quite a bit of time trying to figure out what to wear. She had already decided that she would wear the red, stiletto-heeled shoes that Matthew found on her shoe rack one day when he was helping her try to open the small wall safe that Dorothy had installed in the master bedroom closet.

Erianna wanted to store her engagement ring and dress watch in the safe because she didn't wear them when she was working. But try as she might, she could not get the combination Doro had written down for her to open it.

"Wow," he had exclaimed when the shoes caught his eye. He pulled them from the rack, practically drooling as he imagined Erianna wearing the sexy high heels.

She had never worn them, but when she happened across the Christian Louboutin's on a closeout rack at a department store in Cleveland she just couldn't resist buying them.

The only question was what to wear with the shoes. She considered whipping up a red dress, but rejected that idea. Red was not a very good choice with her coloring. In the end Erianna decided to go with every woman's staple—her little black dress.

* * *

On Tuesday afternoon she went to her room to get ready for her date. She showered and took her time styling her hair, first curling it with hot rollers, and then sweeping it to the crown of her head in a loose, messy updo. Tendrils were left to fall haphazardly around her face, with the bulk of her hair falling in riotous, curly layers down the back of her head and onto the nape of her neck.

She took one of the cloisonné hair combs and worked it into the updo, stepping back to examine the result. Turning her head this way and that, her curls danced in the mirror and she was pleased with the result.

She stepped into her black dress, an elbow length frock that fell just above her knees. The wide, square neckline revealed just a hint of the upper swell of her breasts, and the dress followed the natural curves of her slim figure. A small slit at the center back seam eased the slim-line skirt and aided her movement.

She slipped on the red high heels and put on her engagement ring, opting to forego the dress watch. When she went downstairs to check in with Pap and Ginny, who would be sitting for the kids, Henry was in the suite waiting for her.

"You look beautiful," Pap told her. Ginny agreed and Erianna blushed.

Henry tapped out a message on his phone. "The weather is supposed to turn stormy. Maybe you should pack rain gear so you don't ruin your lovely outfit."

"Good thinking," she replied. "I wonder if you would mind running down to the basement and grabbing a pair of barn boots for me."

While he was gone Ginny rummaged around in a junk drawer and came up with an old-fashioned accordion-pleated rain bonnet in a vinyl pouch.

Erianna tried not to giggle. "I haven't seen a rain bonnet like this in years," she said. "What other treasures are you hiding in that drawer?"

"Don't make fun," Ginny retorted. "You never know when something like this will come in handy. It won't take up any room in your small evening bag and it will keep your pretty hairdo from getting ruined if it rains."

Traffic was surprisingly heavy and they were late arriving at the hotel. The skies let loose when they were just three blocks away.

"Oh, my. Can you see where you're going?" she asked Henry.

He signed in the affirmative.

Their late start was Erianna's fault and she apologized for their current predicament. "It looks like I'm going to need my barn boots after all."

Henry nodded. When they finally pulled into the front drive of the hotel he reached back to grab the boots. She unbuckled her seat belt and bent down to take off her shoes, tucking each one into a pocket of her trench coat. After pulling on the boots she reached into her purse and pulled the clear plastic rain bonnet from its pouch.

"This isn't how I imagined my entrance would be," she said, raising her voice a bit in order to be heard over the din of the wind and driving rain. "I wish this hotel had a covered entrance drive."

"Me too," he signed. Henry tapped out a message. "It's only 'til we get you inside. Wait here while I come around with an umbrella."

He jumped out and handed the car keys to a waiting attendant. They made their way toward the entrance door, but just as they reached the automatic glass sliders a gust of wind took hold of the umbrella and turned it inside out.

Erianna dashed through the doors while Henry paused, trying without success to pull it back into place. Giving up his futile struggle, he backed through the doors with the broken umbrella in hand.

Matthew had just emerged from the elevator at the far end of the lobby when the entrance doors opened and a woman hurried through. Outside the rain was coming down in sheets. He scanned the room, looking for his fiancé. When the lobby door opened again, the woman quickly moved aside, seeking sanctuary from the storm driven winds.

Matthew watched as Henry wrestled with an umbrella. He looked over at the woman again, realizing that it was Erianna.

Henry looked at her and raised his shoulders in a gesture of defeat. The umbrella had beaten him. Erianna threw her head back and laughed. Matthew could not hear her, but he was charmed nonetheless. She pulled off the old lady rain bonnet and shook out her curls. *Beautiful.*

Henry joined her, propping the broken umbrella in the corner where they stood. Erianna pulled something from her pockets before Henry took her coat. Then she sat down in a nearby lobby chair.

Laying the wet trench coat over the chair next to where she was sitting, Henry knelt in front of her to help remove the boots. Though he couldn't see, Matthew assumed she put on the pair of shoes that she had taken from her coat pockets. Henry handed her a handkerchief and she appeared to dab at her face and legs.

When she finally stood, he handed her an evening bag that he pulled from his coat pocket. As she brushed at her dress he tapped out a message and she nodded and said something in reply. Henry pointed and Erianna turned and headed to the center hallway toward the bank of elevators where Matthew was lingering.

She moved with a natural grace, and as she closed the distance between them Matthew wondered how she could move so gracefully in the red stilettos. He watched as she drew near. Never in his life had he been so consumed with desire for a woman. She was the most alluring creature he'd ever seen.

When she finally met his gaze Erianna stopped and graced him with a mesmerizing smile. His eyes swept over her, moving from her face to the décolletage of her black dress, and then downward to her red, high-heeled shoes.

In a perfect imitation of Dorothy Gale when she realized she was wearing the ruby slippers, Erianna turned her feet this way and that in a sexy, feminine display that held Matthew in her thrall.

He brought both hands to his heart, his broad smile leaving no doubt of his love and admiration.

"Hello," she greeted him.

"Hello yourself."

"Some storm."

"I hadn't noticed. I was busy taking in another sight."

She raised one eyebrow. "Do tell," she teased.

"Maybe we should forego dinner and get a room."

She smiled sweetly. "I'm hungry."

"So am I," he replied in a deep, husky tone.

Erianna blushed and leaned in slightly. "You're embarrassing me, Dr. Prestwick." She glanced to the side where another couple appeared who were also waiting for an elevator.

Matthew looked down at the upper swell of her breasts. "Oh, my darling. You do tempt me so."

Her lips thinned slightly and Matthew capitulated. He took her hand and tucked it into the bend of his elbow. When the doors opened he escorted her into the elevator. The other couple joined them. The man pushed the button for the top floor where the restaurant was located. He looked at Matthew.

"Same," he said.

As the floors ticked by he murmured, "You look lovely tonight."

"Thank you."

"Did you make that dress?"

"Yes."

The woman overheard and turned to look. "You made that?"

Erianna stiffened ever so slightly and nodded.

The woman took a closer look. "Are you a professional seamstress?"

"I used to be."

"You're very talented," the lady said. "I never would have guessed you made that."

Thankfully the elevator doors opened just then and Erianna was spared any further discussion about her homemade garment. She slipped into the powder room to freshen up before joining Matthew at their table.

As their drinks were served the rain pelted the windows, precluding any view of the Lexington skyline. They ordered their meals and as they ate the storm finally abated and the waning gibbous moon appeared in the night sky. Lights shone from nearby buildings and the view was like that of a Hollywood movie set.

Erianna was enchanted.

Chapter 19

The ride home was uneventful, and when Henry pulled into the driveway Matthew escorted Erianna inside through the garage door. She hung her coat on a hook just inside the laundry room door and walked down the hall to check in with Pap.

Matthew waited in the family room and when she closed the pass-through door for the night he pounced. He grabbed her and backed her against the wall just to the left side of the low kitchen counter where the corkboard was hanging.

He kissed her with the passion of a starving man. He couldn't get enough. He was like a man possessed. He lowered his mouth to the upper swell of her breasts, wanting more. Trying to tug her dress from her shoulders, he grew frustrated when he couldn't free her breasts from the garment.

Reaching behind her, Matthew fumbled for her zipper and yanked it down. He pulled her dress down to her elbows and finally freed her breasts. Sucking and nipping her swollen peaks, his hands grasped her buttocks and rubbed her rounded cheeks.

As quickly as the onslaught began, it stopped. Gasping for breath he backed away, and kept retreating until he bumped into the breakfast room table. Reaching up, he rubbed both hands across his face, trying desperately to resist what his body was craving.

Without a word he turned to leave.

"Matthew—don't go."

He turned back. "If I don't go now, I never will." He expelled a tortured breath. "Set a date, Erianna. A man can only take so much."

As he walked down the hallway she heard him say, "I'm no monk, for Christ's sake."

* * *

Erianna didn't see Matthew again until the following Monday afternoon. She was in the kitchen when he came in. He dispensed with the niceties.

"Come over here, Erin, and have a seat. I need to talk to you."

His tone, one which she had never heard from him before, had the hairs on her arms standing on end. She did as she was told, sitting gingerly on the edge of her seat.

He came right to the point. "I can't do this anymore."

"Oh."

She assumed by his tone and his words that he was calling off their engagement. Her heart was breaking, but she kept her expression neutral.

With a slight tremor in her voice she said, "I'll go upstairs and get you the ring so you can return it to your grandmother."

"Do you think I'm breaking up with you?" he snarled.

"Umm. Well—"

"I'm not calling it off, Erianna. I can't believe you would think that."

She lowered her head and hid her eyes from view.

"Don't do that, goddammit. Don't hide from me. We need to talk."

Erianna stood up and went to the kitchen. She brought him a sports drink and a granola bar. She'd never seen him wound so tight. Maybe if he put something in his stomach he would feel better.

Matthew glared at her, but he opened the drink and downed a healthy amount before shoving it aside.

"What did you want to talk about?" she began, hoping that his mood would lighten a bit.

"We need to set a date. I can't go on like this any more."

Erianna wasn't sure whether to feel relief or trepidation. "Okay," she said in a noncommittal tone. She got up again and brought over the calendar from the corkboard. Sitting down, she flipped through the months.

"How about late October or early November. It's beautiful that time of—"

"No."

"No? Well, then how about September, after the kids are back in school and things have calmed down around here."

"No, Erianna."

She sighed in frustration. "Well, what did you have in mind?"

"Mother's Day."

"Mother's Day—" Erianna's eyes rounded in disbelief. "I don't think that's possible, Matt. It's a Sunday."

"People get married on Sundays. I talked to my brother and he'll be happy to perform the service for us."

"At the Covington Cathedral? It's way too big."

Matthew reached out and snatched her arm. "Come with me."

Without another word he dragged her through the door to the duplex, out the side door, and across the path to Doro's house. When they went inside, Doro and Ginny were sitting at the kitchen table. Doro had a binder opened in front of her and Ginny had a pad and pen at the ready.

He pushed Erianna into a chair and sat down at the table. "Now," he stated authoritatively. "Let's get down to the nitty gritty. We're not leaving the table until this has all been hashed out."

"Really, Matthew. I don't like your tone."

"I don't give a damn!" he shot back. Taking a deep breath, he ran his fingers through his hair. "Okay, okay—I'll moderate my tone. But you have to understand, we need to come to an agreement—now."

He was clearly irritated and she understood his surly mood. "Alright, let's discuss this. Calmly. When is Mother's Day this year?"

"May fourteenth," Doro supplied.

Erianna nodded. "And you want to get married in Covington?"

"No. Actually, my brother will come here, to Berrington. We'll have the ceremony at Immaculate Heart of Mary. I made an appointment and spoke with Father Reinhardt this morning. We had a conference call with John and worked out all the details."

"I see. Well, I guess it's all set then. What's there to talk about?"

He scowled at her again. "You can be so annoying sometimes. Do you know that?"

"I don't mean to be."

Doro could see that a fight was brewing, so she stepped in before things got out of control.

"The proposal would be to have the wedding ceremony at the small chapel on Sunday, May fourteenth at one o'clock. The chapel doesn't hold more than fifty people max, so we'll keep the guest list small, just like you wanted."

"You all put a lot of thought into this, haven't you."

Matthew wanted to throttle her, but with supreme effort he kept his tone modulated. "Yes, a lot of thought. *Every waking thought.*"

Doro cleared her throat. "I can handle all the details for you if you like. I'll be your wedding planner, so to speak. That way you won't have to sweat the details."

Erianna smiled impishly. "How much do you charge?"

Matthew's fist slammed down onto the table, startling all the women. "Dammit, Erianna, this is no joking matter."

"Matthew Prestwick, you control yourself. What's gotten into you?" Ginny declared.

"I think it's called pent up sexual frustration," Doro replied with a smirk.

The meanness went out of him and, folding his arms across the table, he dropped his head in defeat.

Erianna reached over and stroked his hair. "If it will help, we don't have to wait any longer."

Matthew raised his head. "No, I made a promise and I intend to keep it." He looked Erianna in the eye. "But there'll be no more date nights until after we're married. I won't survive another one."

She offered him a sweet, knowing smile and he sprang to his feet, kicking the chair out behind him.

"And no more smiling at me like that," he shouted. "Do you hear me?"

He stormed from the room, leaving a slack-jawed Erianna in his wake.

"Maybe we should just elope," she suggested to the women.

"He'll survive," Doro answered succinctly.

The next hour was spent discussing wedding plans. After Matthew returned, much less combative than when he left, they discussed flowers and decided on pink peonies, which were Erianna's favorite, and small white tea roses. Doro pulled pages from her binder with examples of arrangements that the local florist could have delivered and set up in the chapel.

A photographer was chosen and Doro volunteered to handle the food for the small reception in the church grotto after the service. The so-called grotto, which in actuality wasn't a natural grotto per se, was an open area on the east side of the church just beyond the wooded copse. Generations before the level area had been chosen to erect a grotto of St. Mary, and fieldstone had been used to build the semi-circular alcove where the life-size statue rested.

Ginny asked about her wedding dress and Erianna told her that she did not want to marry for the second time in a long white gown.

"I have an idea in mind. I'll just make my own dress."

Matthew was not happy with that idea. "I don't want you to have to make your own wedding dress."

"Why not? You seemed pretty happy with the last homemade dress I wore." She smirked.

"You little—"

They squared off.

"Don't start up again, Matt," Doro warned.

"I can't help it. She's a god dammed tease."

"I am not a tease," she shot back. "All I did was put on a simple black dress. It wasn't cut down to my navel or hemmed up to my derriere."

"That's enough, you two," Ginny snapped.

"Well, honestly," Erianna directed her words to Ginny. "What does he want me to do, walk around in a burlap sack?"

Doro quickly brought the discussion back on track. "What about the guest list? Have you thought about who you'd like to invite to the wedding?"

"Um. Well, that's going to be tricky. You see, when my parents find out about this there's going to be hell to pay. That's why I've tried to keep our engagement a secret all this time.

"Oh, that reminds me. I should probably call my children's—" she pivoted toward Matthew. "Our children's birth father to let him know what's going on. I have very few relatives, and the kids and I consider Phil and his wife, Laurie, to be family members."

Matthew reached for her hand. "That's an excellent idea. We *should* invite them. I'd very much like to meet Phil. What about their grandfather? Does he know that we're engaged?"

"Yes, I spoke to him after Thanksgiving. He seemed happy enough about the news and I've written to him several times since then, letting him know how the kids are doing and keeping him in the loop."

"Do you think he'd like to come?"

Erianna thought about that for a minute. "I really don't know."

"Would you mind if I got in touch with him?"

"No, I suppose not. Remind me later and I'll give you his number."

"Okay," Doro said. "So far we have your parents and sisters, plus Phil and Laurie. And possibly their grandfather. Who else should we invite?"

"Do we really have to send out formal invitations? Is there any way we can get around that? I'm really dreading the grief that's going to come down on me when my parents find out."

Doro glanced at her brother. Some secret communication passed between the siblings and Erianna tensed.

Matthew nodded, and Doro looked to Erianna. "I hope you don't get mad at me, but I know about the situation with your father. Matt and I talked about it for quite a while, and the reason we came up with the idea of a Mother's Day ceremony was to disguise the actual nuptials."

Erianna frowned. "I don't follow."

"Well, here's the idea." Doro took a deep breath. "We'll invite family and close friends to a special mass celebrated by my brother, John, in honor of Mother's Day. But we won't tell anyone that it's actually going to be your wedding ceremony. That way we can get your parents here without them knowing that you're getting married. I know that its subterfuge, but we just couldn't think of another way."

"So you intend to pull off a surprise wedding?"

"In essence, yes. Of course, certain people will have to be told. But for the most part, no one will know until the mass begins."

"What do you think?" Matthew asked her.

"Do you actually think we can pull it off?"

He nodded.

"Then I think—I think it's brilliant."

Matthew became a relative stranger to Berrington Farm. He and Erianna spoke on the phone nearly every day, but he chose to lay low and refrain from any further overnight stays at her house until they were married. He attended mass with them at Immaculate Heart of Mary nearly every Sunday and went with Erianna and Gus to the Hoot 'n Holler on Saturdays, but on the rare occasions when he did stay over he slept at his sister's house.

The first Tuesday in April dawned crisp and clear. The children were on spring break. Everyone was packed and ready for their trip to New York City. They drove up and met Matthew and his mother at Lunken Airport on the east side of Cincinnati.

Grace and Ned were excited to be flying on Matthew's company Lear jet. Erianna, on the other hand, was not looking forward to this trip. She was not a fan of big cities and large crowds.

The kids were effusive in their gratitude for Helen Prestwick's generosity. They sat in the last row around a built-in table, playing cards with Matthew. Erianna sat in the front row opposite Helen, and they talked about the various sights they would visit while they were there.

They arrived at Broderick's brownstone on the upper west side near Riverside Park late that afternoon. Brock was a gracious host. He escorted the group around the city and secured tickets to the Broadway hit "The Lion King".

While avoiding most of the tourist traps, they did go to the top of the Empire State Building and also visited the 9/11 Memorial and Museum. Brock and Helen took Grace and Ned to the Guggenheim Museum designed by Frank Lloyd Wright. As they entered Ned craned his head back to see the skylight at the top of the rotunda.

Taking an elevator to the top floor, they moved down the gentle slope of a continuous circular ramp around the open rotunda. Both Grace and Ned were amazed by the architecture, as well as the works of art.

While the group was visiting the Guggenheim, Matthew took Erianna to Mood on 37th Street where she spent a small fortune on fabrics and notions. Ned had made a sketch of her idea for a wedding dress and an employee helped her find the fabrics she needed.

Matthew was banished to the front entrance area while she shopped, and when she was finished he insisted on picking up the tab. Rather than cause a scene Erianna deferred to his wishes.

The next day Matthew and Erianna took the kids to the Museum of Modern Art. They saw such works as Van Gogh's "Starry Night" and Picasso's "Girl with a Mandolin". Erianna's favorite was "Christina's World" by Andrew Wyeth. Since seeing the landscape in Matthew's office she had become a particular fan of Wyeth's works.

By far the highlight of Erianna's trip was their visit to the main branch of the New York Public Library in Bryant Park. They climbed the steps at the 6th Avenue entrance, walking past two lion sculptures called Patience and Fortitude.

The moment Erianna walked through the entrance door she was enthralled. Without thought to the others she wandered off saying, "I'll meet you back here in a couple of hours."

Matthew smiled and murmured, "I should have known."

That evening over dinner at a restaurant near Broderick's brownstone Erianna gushed about their outing that day.

"Did you see the Gutenberg Bible in the rare books section? Did you know that only forty-eight copies survive today? James Lenox bought a copy printed on paper in 1847. He was the first American to acquire one. It was just beautiful," she breathed in awe.

"So have you changed your mind about New York City?" Matthew asked.

"Well, I wouldn't want to live here, but I did enjoy my visit." She looked at Broderick. "No offense intended."

"None taken."

Erianna spent the following weeks working on both her wedding dress and the dress Grace would wear. Doro and Ginny were handling the plans for the mass celebrating Mother's Day, freeing up Erianna's time and keeping her stress levels in check, as this was not her purview. The women were lifesavers. They knew exactly what they were doing and how to accomplish each step in the process.

Erianna was chatting with Matthew on the phone one evening after the trip to New York City and he mentioned that his friends Faith Hill and Tim McGraw were on tour with their Soul2Soul concert series.

"Do they usually tour together?"

"Yes. Faith started as Tim's opening act, and after they were married they began touring as a duo act. Did you know that they also threw a surprise wedding?"

"No, I didn't."

"That's how I came up with the idea. I ran into Tim on one of my business trips and let him know that we're engaged. He told me about their surprise wedding, and that started me thinking that it might work for us."

As they chatted, Erianna mentioned that she'd never been to a live concert. Matthew was surprised by that admission.

Easter Sunday was a happy day. The kids' Easter baskets were filled with all kinds of goodies, and the two families attended Sunday mass and then went to brunch at a local restaurant. Late in the afternoon as Matthew was preparing to leave he pulled Erianna aside.

"How would you like to go to see the Soul2Soul concert in Louisville on the twenty-eighth?"

Erianna frowned slightly. "I don't know. All the tickets have probably been sold by now."

"Don't worry about that. I can get my hands on a couple of tickets. I'd really like to take you."

She thought about it and then said, "Won't that be a 'date'? I thought you said no more dates until after we're married."

"I did say that, but I'd really like to take you and it's not that far away. Tim will give us backstage passes and you can meet Faith. I think you two will really hit it off."

Erianna wasn't sure. She didn't want a repeat of what happened after their Valentine's Day date. "I don't think it's a good idea, Matt."

"Well I do. We're going. And I *promise* to be on my best behavior."

It seemed that the decision had been taken out of her hands. Matthew set the plan in motion and on the Friday afternoon of the concert Henry came to pick her up. He drove her to Louisville and she met Matthew at the Galt House, a hotel right next to the Yum Center in downtown Louisville. They had dinner and then walked over to the concert venue.

Matthew told her not to dress up, so she wore a pair of jeans and a white camisole with a lightweight, relaxed-fit popover tunic that had a faux front wrap and an offset tie. The pale green tunic fell to mid-hip and looked fresh and comfy, the perfect choice for a spring concert.

Matthew escorted Erianna to their seats, which were located to the left side of the stage in the lower section 116, the first row on the aisle.

Erianna was stunned. "These seats are fantastic. How did you manage to get them at such a late date?"

He smirked. "I have connections."

The concert was phenomenal and Erianna had the time of her life. After the show Matthew led her backstage where Faith and Tim were greeting other fans who had secured passes.

They waited for most of the crowd to thin out before approaching the couple. When Tim spotted them he raised a hand and waved them forward.

Matthew walked toward the couple with Erianna on his arm. "That was a great concert."

"Thanks. I'm glad you could make it," Tim said. He turned to his wife. "Faith, I'd like you to meet Matt's fiancé, Erianna Fowler. Erin, my wife, Faith."

"I'm happy to meet you." Faith held out her hand.

"Hello."

"Matt has talked so much about you, it's nice to finally put a face to the woman he gushes about in such glowing terms."

Erianna blushed to the roots of her hair. "Don't believe a word he says. You know what they say, love is blind."

Tim laughed. "I don't know. After I met you last year I'd have to say that he was spot on in his praise."

"Matt says that you have a beautiful singing voice," Faith continued. "He even went so far as to imply that it's better than mine."

Erianna's eyes rounded and she stiffened. "I'm not a singer. I'm sorry that he gave you that impression."

"Believe me," Matthew cut in. "She has the most beautiful voice you'll ever hear. When she sings *Somewhere over the Rainbow*, if you close your eyes you'd swear that Judy Garland was in the room."

Erianna looked at him. "I don't know what you're thinking, Matt. It sounds like you're deliberately insulting Miss Hill."

He frowned. "I'm not trying to insult her. I'm just complimenting you, honey. I know how much you enjoy singing and I only meant to let them know how talented you are."

"Have you thought about taking it up again?" Tim asked.

"I'm not a singer. I don't sing."

He was confused by her matter-of-fact-statement. "Why not? Matt says that he fell in love with you the first time you got up on stage and sang in front of your high school classmates."

"I see." She turned once again to face her fiancé. "Well, if that's the kind of woman you want, I suggest that we call off our engagement so that you can continue your search for your perfect mate. *I* am not that woman. Maybe Miss Hill knows of someone who can meet your requirements for a wife. Someone in the industry."

She turned back to the couple. "We've taken up enough of your time and there are others waiting to talk to you. Good night."

With that she turned to leave. Matthew reached out and grasped her wrist. "Erin, wait."

She stared at the hand holding her prisoner. Slowly, she lifted her gaze to his. Matthew took one look at her expression and immediately let go of her wrist. And without another word she walked away.

Matthew looked at his friends.

"Let me talk to her," Tim said as he took off after Erianna.

He caught up with her before she could get very far and hustled her into a room off the long hallway. Erianna found herself in what she assumed was a music practice room. An old, beat-up piano and a scattering of folding chairs and music stands were the only furnishings in the room.

She moved to the center of the room, keeping her back to Tim. Clutching her arms around her waist, she hugged herself protectively.

Tim gave her a minute before he said, "What was that all about?"

Erianna turned enough to show her profile to the country music superstar. She let out a small sound that Tim could not interpret.

"Talk to me, Erin."

After several beats she said, "I only just now realized that Matt doesn't love the woman I am. What he really wants is the girl I was."

Faith and Matthew were just coming into the room just then and heard what Erianna said. She turned her back and moved to the far side of the room near the upright piano. Matthew started toward her, but Faith stopped him. Closing the distance between them, she went to Erianna. Reaching out, Faith gently drew her into a supportive embrace.

"Men can be so exasperating. Sometimes they want a chef and a maid, and other times they want a nanny and a chauffeur. But all they really need is a lover and a friend."

"And sometimes they want what a woman can't give them," Erianna replied. "I can't be all things to Matthew. I can't give him children of his own and I can't sing for him. Not anymore. That was stolen from me a long time ago."

"All he wants is you, Erin. He loves you."

She wrenched herself free from Faith's embrace. "No, no, no—He deserves to have it all, just like Tim has. Matt is such a wonderful man. He deserves someone more like you. I can't take that from him. Don't you see? Someday he'll wake up and realize that he made a horrible mistake."

"No!"

Both women turned to look at him.

"I love *you*, and that's no mistake."

Erianna shook her head.

Matthew's fists clenched and he turned and put his boot through the wall. He yanked the door open and stormed out, leaving the others speechless in his wake.

A security guard appeared. "Is everything okay in here?"

"Yeah," Tim said. "We're fine."

With a nod to his wife, Tim led the guard from the room and shut the door behind them. He went back to dutifully greet his fans while Faith stayed with Erianna. Matthew was leaning against the hallway wall with his head lowered and his black Stetson blocking others' view of his face. He had one knee bent and his boot flat against the wall behind him as he leaned back, hands in his pockets. Another security guard noticed Matthew's odd behavior and approached him to investigate.

"Excuse me a minute, folks," Tim said. "I'll be right back."

Then he went to run interference for his lugubrious friend.

At Faith's insistence Erianna glossed over the details of the summer of 2001. She told Faith about her memory loss and of her chance meeting with Matthew last summer. When Tim poked his head in the door several minutes later Erianna said, "Go ahead. If you don't mind, I need a few minutes by myself."

"Take all the time you need," Faith told her.

On her way out she murmured to her husband, "Her father strangled her and left her for dead."

Tim came back into the room about ten minutes later and found Erianna sitting back on her heels examining the hole in the wall. He hunkered down next to her.

"This is an easy fix," she said. "I just need to cut away the damage and insert a small piece of wood behind the plaster. A few screws will hold it in place, and then all I need to do is cut a new piece of drywall to fit the opening. With a coat of spackle and some paint no one will know that the wall was damaged.

Tim smirked. "Don't worry about it. These things happen all the time." He helped her to her feet.

"Have you ever put your foot through a wall?"

He chuckled. "I plead the fifth."

Tim led Erianna over to the piano and they sat down side by side. Though he didn't play, he began to tinker with the keys, playing basic cords with one hand.

"How long did it take you to get your voice back?" he asked.

Erianna was not surprised by the question. She assumed that someone told him what had happened. "I'm not sure. I really don't remember."

Tim experimented until he found a few chords that sounded similar to those in the tune *Moon River.* "Have you tried to sing since then?"

"No," she admitted with a shrug. "I can't."

"Will you try with me?"

She shook her head.

"Come on. Give it a try with your old pal, Tim."

She started to get up, but he put an arm around her shoulder and gave her a reassuring hug.

"Moon River," he began. "Wider than a mile."

She remained mute, so he continued. "I'm crossing you in style someday. We're after— " he paused. "I don't remember the rest. Help me out."

Erianna swallowed. "...that same rainbow's end— " She shot to her feet. "I can't," she whispered.

He stopped tinkering with the keys. "Does it hurt?"

She shook her head. "No."

"Erin?"

She couldn't look at him.

"Your voice is beautiful. Just beautiful. You have a lovely, clear tone and your vibrato is perfect. You *can* sing, Erin. It's just a matter of overcoming the mental and emotional trauma associated with your attack. I know something about that. I'm sure you know my story."

She finally turned to him and nodded.

"I was pretty messed up for a while and I took to the bottle."

"How did you overcome your demons?"

"I learned to accept the things I could not change and to find the courage to change the things I could. Like it says in the Serenity Prayer."

Lost in thought, Erianna stood beside the piano as Tim absently played a few chords.

"It takes strength and determination to overcome your fears," he admitted. "I did it because I didn't want to lose my family."

He got up and took her hand in his. "I think our better halves are waiting for us."

"I've kept you much too long," Erianna agreed. "It's late. Thank you, Tim. You've been a good friend."

"Are you okay now?"

"I'm all right, but I have a lot to think about."

As they walked arm-in-arm toward the door he asked her, "Do you know my wife's song, *This kiss?*"

"Yes."

"I happen to know that it's one of Matt's favorites. If you ever decide to sing for your husband, sing that to him. I know how much it would mean to him to hear you sing again."

Matthew was lingering in the nearly deserted hallway when Erianna emerged from the room. They thanked the couple and headed out, where a car and driver were waiting for them. They rode in silence to Bowman Field. Matthew's jet was fueled and ready to leave. After takeoff, Matthew unbuckled Erianna's belt and pulled her across his lap.

He kissed her and murmured sweet nothings, assuring her of his love. "I'll never change my mind about us," he whispered as his lips traced the shell of her ear. "I love you."

"What if you never hear me sing again? You seem to want that very much. And what about children? All men want children of their own."

"Erianna, stop. It doesn't matter to me that you can't sing. I only wanted that dream for you. You spent your entire childhood singing, but we're grown now and I love you for who you are."

"Are you sure?"

"I'm positive. I'll never mention it again. And as for children, we can still have children of our own. You still have your ovaries, and all we have to do is hire someone to carry the baby for us. People do it all the time now. It's commonplace."

She'd never thought of that possibility. "I just need to know that you love me as I am, warts and all."

He did, and he spent the remainder of the short flight showing her how much.

Chapter 20

Mother's Day dawned bright and clear. Erianna slept in. Bob and Ryan volunteered to do her morning chores and she awoke, not to her alarm, but to the morning sunshine streaming in through her bedroom window.

Everyone on Berrington Farm was now aware of the wedding. Grace and Ned were told just the week before. On Saturday afternoon everyone met at the chapel for a rehearsal. Erianna and Doro worked out the seating arrangements and the Donovan boys were designated to act as servers for the mass.

Erianna met with the organist, Bernice Anderson, whom she knew quite well by now from her nights out at the Hoot 'n Holler, several times during the week before the wedding to go over the song list. Bernice was sworn to secrecy, especially from her friend, Sally Holloway, who did not know the meaning of the word secret.

Matthew was given the task of greeting the guests and guiding them to their pews without letting on that there was a specific reason for the seat assignments. He had also been in touch with Phil and Laurie Keegan and they had accepted his invitation to the wedding, although Neil Fowler had declined. In all, there would be thirty-four people in attendance, a number with which Erianna was quite comfortable.

Aside from the Keegans, the only other people who were made aware of the surprise Mother's Day wedding were Chip's parents, Charles and Abigail Neading. It was their job to get Erianna's family to the mass.

The chapel was decorated with beautiful, fragrant flowers, and Ginny and Doro had worked out a post-communion processional to the statue of the Blessed Mother. They placed a circular wire holder around the base of the statue in the chapel that would be filled with nosegays of white tea roses with blue ribbons intertwined in the bouquets.

Erianna relaxed in a bath for a time before getting ready. She styled her hair much the same way as she had on Valentine's Day, adding a touch of Baby's Breath to the updo for a more formal look. Then she slipped into her dress and flesh-toned shoes, standing at the mirror to survey her appearance.

She had used fabrics she bought in New York to sew her wedding dress. The sleeveless top was made from a silk, four-ply crepe in a light orchid pink color. The soft, lightweight silky top billowed loosely to her ribcage, where it was sewn into to a pleated, tightly cinched white silk Carmeuse cumberbund at her midriff.

The attached straight skirt, which was hemmed at her knee, was sewn from a refined woven linen blend that would resist wrinkling. The medium shade of orchid pink, slightly darker than the silk crepe, blended perfectly with the blousy top of the one-piece dress.

Erianna was pleased with how the dress turned out, deciding that it was just the right look for the small chapel wedding. She eased her arms into a collarless jacket, made from the same orchid pink linen as the skirt. Cut in a bolero style with a rounded bottom edge, the jacket fell to the bottom of the cumberbund and complimented the overall appearance of her 'wedding suit'.

"Well, I guess I'm ready. This is as good as it gets," she said to herself. She switched her engagement ring to her right hand and went to check on her children.

Ned was not in his room, so she assumed he was dressed and ready to go. Grace was just slipping into her soft green swing dress when her mother appeared at her door.

"Wow, Mom, you look great."

"Thank you." Erianna turned a full three sixty to let her daughter see the finished dress. "Do you think Matt will like it?"

Grace laughed. "Yes, Mom. Quit worrying, you know he likes everything you make."

"Your dress turned out well," Erianna said. "I'm glad we went with that shade of soft green. It's a very good color for you."

The women went downstairs to Pap's suite. Bob and Ryan were helping him get ready for the mass, as Ginny had gone over to assist Doro with the set up for the reception. Ned was in his Sunday suit and was sitting on the floor shining his shoes.

"Oh, boy. You guys look fantastic," Ryan exclaimed. Only he wasn't looking at Erianna. He had eyes only for Grace.

Shortly before noon Henry pulled into the driveway. The plan was to meet Matthew at the church an hour early to take pictures. As they rode toward Immaculate Heart, Erianna's nerves began to tingle. But when they pulled up and Matthew opened the door for her, she calmed herself. With the man of her dreams by her side there was no need to worry. Come what may, they would be together. He would always be there for her, from this day forward.

Matthew took her hand. "Let me look at you." He stood back and then gifted her with a bright, broad smile. "I've never seen a more beautiful creature. Never in all my life."

Erianna reached up and ran her hand along his silk tie. "You look quite handsome yourself, Dr. Prestwick."

"Oh, honey, you make me so happy."

"Okay, okay," Grace interrupted. "Let's dispense with the gush and get the ball rolling."

Matthew laughed out loud and grabbed Grace in his arms, twirling her around and around.

"Hey, knock it off! My skirt is flying up." She shoved at Matthew and he finally relented. Ned giggled.

They made their way toward the chapel to the right of the church and met the photographer, who took pictures both inside and outside on the grounds. Azalea bushes were in full bloom and Dogwood trees, of both pink and white varieties, were flowering. Bees hummed and birds chirped on this beautiful Mother's Day.

When the first guests pulled into the parking lot Matthew made his way to the entrance as Erianna and her children retreated to the sacristy.

Chuck and Gail Neading pulled up to the curb in front of the Fowler home. Clyde was sitting on the front porch when they came up the walk.

"Good morning, Clyde," Gail greeted him.

"Humph. What's so good about it?" he grumbled.

"It's a beautiful Mother's Day. The skies are a brilliant blue and it's not too hot," she replied, not bothering to pay him much heed. She knocked on the screen door and called out to Colleen as she let herself in.

"Are you ready?" Chuck asked.

"I don't see why we have to go to this damn blasted mass," he grumbled. "I'd just as soon stay home."

"It won't hurt you to go. After all, we are honoring our wives, the mothers of our children. You can at least give them this one day and celebrate their hard work with a special mass."

He was still grumbling when Gail and Colleen came out.

"Where are the girls?" Chuck asked.

"They couldn't make it," Colleen replied succinctly.

They made their way to the car and Chuck drove east along Route 52, picking up I-275 and crossing the bridge into Northern Kentucky. When he turned south on I-75 near the airport Clyde spoke up.

"I thought this mass was in Covington. You should have turned north, not south."

"Didn't you know?" Chuck replied. "The church is a little south of town in Harrison County. It won't take long and it's a beautiful day for a drive."

"I never agreed to this. Where the hell is Harrison County?"

"It's not far, Clyde."

When they drove into the Village of Berrington Gail shot off a quick text. They pulled into the parking lot at five minutes before one o'clock. Matthew made himself scarce while Chuck and Gail ushered the Pruitts into the first pew on the left.

The bench was slightly inset so that those with wheelchairs or special needs could sit, as Pap was sitting in his wheelchair across the aisle from the couple, with Ginny by his side. Clyde rested his walker next to him at the inset and Colleen sat to his left.

At the last moment Brock, Helen and Lucinda came up the aisle and took their seats just behind the Pruitts. Neither turned to look behind them as the opening hymn began.

"On this day O beautiful Mother,
On this day we give thee our love.
Near thee Madonna, fondly we hover,
Trusting thy gentle care to prove."

Ryan led the processional as the cross bearer, followed by James and Theo, who held lighted candles. All wore the cassock and surplus of servers. Grace and Ned followed them, holding the offertory gifts of bread and wine. Matthew, with Erianna at his side, carried the Bible which he raised above his head as the processional continued to the opening song. Finally, Monsignor Prestwick came down the short aisle.

Erianna slipped into the pew behind Pap and Ginny as the others moved forward and placed their offertory gifts and the Bible in the designated places. They returned to join her in the pew in front of Chip and his family, with Chuck and Gail right behind their son.

Laurie and Phil Keegan were in the last pew on the right, while Matthew's relatives, including Doro and Bob, and Agnes and her family, took up the pews on the left side behind Lucinda, Helen and Brock.

The mass began, Scripture readings read, and the gospel was read by Monsignor Prestwick.

After the gospel the congregation took their seats to listen to the homily. Monsignor Prestwick moved to the front of the altar and stood on the step of the small chapel, with the statue of Mary to his right.

"I'd like to begin by welcoming you to the Immaculate Heart of Mary chapel on this beautiful Sunday afternoon as we celebrate Mother's Day. Mother's Day is a special day set aside to honor all mothers who work so diligently throughout the year, raising their children, feeding them, teaching them and keeping them safe and sheltered on their way to becoming independent adults."

He spoke for a few minutes about the vital role that mothers play in the lives of their children before he moved on to another subject.

"There are two other reasons that make this day special. It was fifteen years ago this month that I was ordained a priest in the Catholic Church. My ordination has allowed me to celebrate mass, to perform baptisms and to anoint the sick and dying. I am humbled by those I minister as they bring life into this world and as they pass into the hands of the Lord.

"The most joyous of my duties as a priest is the celebration of wedding ceremonies for young couples making a commitment to each other before God in the Church. Marriage is a most auspicious occasion, and I have performed more wedding ceremonies than I can count.

"But today is a very special day for me, as I have the honor of performing the wedding ceremony for my brother and his bride to be."

A collective gasp went up through the chapel.

"When Matthew asked me to perform the ceremony I was delighted. He and his lovely fiancé, Erianna, will make their vows to love and honor each other here today. So at this time I would like to invite the couple to come forward to exchange their wedding vows."

The Monsignor turned to look at Ryan, who brought him the hard cover portfolio containing the script for the marriage ceremony as Matthew, Erianna and the children rose and moved forward.

The couple had added their own words to the traditional wedding vows. Matthew made his vows first.

"I, Matthew, take you, Erianna, to be my beloved wife. I promise to be true to you, forsaking all others. You are my one and only love, my soul mate, and my friend. I give you my heart. I will comfort you in times of sorrow and rejoice with you in times of joy. I offer you my love and devotion. From this day forward you shall not walk alone, for I will be ever at your side. I will love your children as my own. I will cherish, honor and keep you all the days of my life."

"I, Erianna, take you, Matthew, to be my beloved husband. I promise to be true to you, forsaking all others. I have loved you always. You are my rock, my shelter from the storm. I give you my heart. I will comfort you in times of sorrow and rejoice with you in times of joy. I offer you my love and devotion. All that I am, I give to you. I will cherish, honor and keep you all the days of my life."

They exchanged the rings that the Monsignor blessed and finally, the words were spoken.

"And now, by the power vested in me by the Holy Catholic Church, it is my honor and privilege to pronounce you husband and wife."

Matthew took his bride in his arms and kissed her with reverence and love. The congregation stood and clapped. All at once Matthew turned and grabbed Ned, hoisting him into the air and catching him to his chest. He planted a kiss on the boy's cheek and hugged him fiercely.

Erianna turned to Grace and they embraced as the witnesses continued to clap. All, that is, except Clyde and Colleen. Ned was set on his feet and sent to his mother. He hugged her waist and Erianna bent down and kissed his forehead. Matthew went to Grace, and she wrapped her arms around his neck as they hugged. He kissed her cheek and softly patted her back.

They returned to their seats and the others settled as well. Chip reached forward and squeezed Matthew's shoulder as the mass continued. The offertory song, Sing of Mary, was sung by all.

At communion, Monsignor Prestwick walked to Pap and Ginny's pew to offer them the communion wafer. When he moved to the opposite side, Clyde and Colleen refused to take communion. He moved back to the center and the others filed forward to receive the body and blood of Christ.

After communion the Monsignor sat for a minute, offering a silent prayer before standing. "At this time I invite all the women and girls to join in a special acclamation to the Virgin Mary. If you would, please join Dorothy at the back center aisle."

The organist began playing as the women left their pews and walked to the back of the chapel. Erianna paused to wait for her mother, but Colleen did not join her.

"Mom?"

Colleen refused to look at her daughter.

Lucinda poked Colleen. "Get up," she ordered.

Colleen began to rise, but Clyde grabbed her arm and pulled her back down beside him. Erianna looked at Lucinda, who waved her hand in dismissal. With a heavy heart Erianna started down the center aisle behind Lucinda and Helen to join the others.

She happened to glance up, and there in the small loft above the vestibule were Faith Hill and her husband. Erianna intertwined her fingers and raised them slightly. *Please,* she mouthed.

Faith nodded and got up from her seat to join the women. Erianna motioned to Tim and he followed his wife down the narrow stairway to take a seat in the back pew.

Doro and Ginny handed each of the ladies a nosegay of white tea roses as well as a small index card with the lyrics to the song they would sing. They took their places in pairs as directed, with Grace alone at the front of the line. She carried a small crown of flowers with pale blue ribbons streaming down the back. Faith stood to Erianna's left, where her mother should have been.

"Just follow my lead," she whispered.

When all the women were ready the music for *Queen of the May* began. Both the women and the men began to sing.

"Bring flowers of the rarest
Bring blossoms the fairest..."

Grace moved slowly forward as the processional began. Doro and Ginny followed her. When Grace reached the step up to the altar she continued forward while the other women stopped. She moved to the back of the statue of Mary where a three-step stepstool had been placed. Ryan was waiting there.

He took her elbow to help keep her steady as she ascended the first two steps, holding the crown in both hands. Then he repositioned his hands at Grace's waist to help her balance as she climbed to the top step. She extended her arms up as far as she could reach and placed the crown of flowers on Mary's head as the attendees sang.

"Oh, Mary we crown thee with blossoms today,
Queen of the angels, queen of the May."

Ryan helped Grace step down as the song continued. He moved the stool to the side and then Doro and Ginny moved forward. They placed their nosegays in the floral holder at Mary's feet. The women stayed by the statue as Lucinda and Helen approached next, handing their bouquets to the women, who placed them into the wreath.

Erianna and Faith waited until the Prestwick women moved to the side aisle, and then they approached the statue. Erianna was not singing, but she mouthed the words as Faith's voice rang out. Faith followed the Prestwick women from the altar to the side aisle and Erianna moved to the opposite side of the chapel. She stopped beside the organ near the side door exit where Bernice was playing.

Agnes and her daughter, Victoria, moved forward next, followed by Nancy and Patsy, and finally Gail and Laurie Keegan. The song ended just as the last pair left the altar.

Bernice began the introduction to Schubert's *Ave Maria* and Erianna took one step forward. She began to sing the lyrics in Latin.

"Ave Maria."

Her voice was strong and clear. Taking few breaths, she held the notes with a professional vibrato.

"Gratia plena
Maria, gratia plena
Maria, gratia plena
Ave, ave dominus
Dominus tecum"

Erianna closed her eyes as she sang. She'd practiced the song several times with Bernice and had memorized the words. As she began the second stanza she looked across the chapel to the now beautifully adorned statue of the Virgin Mary.

When she reached the last 'Ave Maria' she held the note as long as she could before letting the note fade as the song ended.

There was a moment of silence before the guests began, once again, to clap. Erianna looked at her husband. Tears streamed down his cheeks. She moved into her pew from the side aisle. Grace rose and threw herself into her mother's arms and Ned stood up on the bench, hugging his mother as well.

Suddenly, Clyde slammed his fist down on the wooden bench of his pew. The thunderous crack echoed ominously throughout the chapel, but Erianna did not look at her father. She knew what she would see. Rage.

Matthew, Erianna, Grace and Ned were the first to leave the chapel by the side door as the recessional music played. Doro and Ginny had snuck out after the final blessing and made their way down the path to the grotto where the small reception would be held.

Henry and Lucinda's driver, Garrett, also left. They were tasked with driving the two golf carts brought over for the afternoon to aid those guests who needed assistance getting down the winding, tree-lined path to the grotto.

The newly married couple and their children took their positions along the walkway for a receiving line as the others waited until the music ended before leaving their pews. Gail approached Clyde and Colleen, making sure that they went out the side door and not the back entrance door.

The Pruitts were the first to exit. Navigating the handicap ramp, they moved toward the receiving line. Lucinda and Helen were next, followed by the others. As the Pruitts approached the newlyweds Colleen greeted her daughter.

"Mom, I'm so glad you came." She kissed her mother's cheek. "What happened to the girls?"

"They couldn't make it," was her rote reply. She moved on to say hello to Matthew and her grandchildren.

"Dad," she said. "I'm so—"

Clyde took his right hand off his walker and slapped Erianna across her face. The blow was so fierce that it knocked her sideways against her husband, lifting one of her feet off the pavement. She saw stars.

Erianna knew from experience what was coming next. She scrambled to regain her balance quickly in order to ward off his next blow. His fisted left hand shot out toward her midsection, but Erianna anticipated this move and she bent from her waist, thus enabling her to avoid the worst of the blow to her solar plexus. Nonetheless, her breath left her with an audible 'ooof'.

Matthew was stunned. He grabbed his wife and did his best to shelter her from her father's onslaught. There were screams and shouts from the guests as Clyde fisted his right hand for yet another attack. As his uppercut shot toward Erianna's jaw Matthew reached out and, quick as lightning, caught Clyde's fist in his hand. He squeezed her father's fisted paw, refusing to let go.

Chip, Tim and their wives were standing on the top step when the uproar began.

"My God," Chip snapped as he ran down the steps to intervene. Tim leaped down the stairs and took off after him.

They ran into the fray and took hold of the old man. Chip grabbed Clyde's left hand, which was holding onto the walker, and Tim reached for his right.

"You can let go now, Matt," he told his friend. "I've got him." Tim wrestled Clyde's hand back to his walker and held it in place by putting his hand over the old man's.

"Let go of me," Clyde shouted vehemently. But they did not.

He glared at his daughter. "You fucking bitch! You are the spawn of the devil," he spewed, spittle appearing at the corner of his mouth. "Think you're so high and mighty, do you? I told you what would happen if you took up with this fucking bastard."

"That's enough," Chip told the incensed man as Clyde was forcibly backed away from the newlyweds.

Her father continued his tirade as the guests watched and listened in dismay.

"Let him go," Erianna finally said in a slightly winded tone. "It's okay. Let him go. Please."

The men did as they were asked, albeit reluctantly, but they stayed by Clyde's side in case he launched another attack. Erianna slipped herself free from her husband's sheltering arms. Her eyes were watering from the force of the blow to her face, but she took a small step forward and stood fearlessly as she addressed her father.

"It must be very satisfying for you to have marred this blessed occasion. I can only imagine the pleasure you must feel, having all these witnesses on hand to watch you humiliate me. At long last you've taken your abuse public. What a thrill that must be for you."

"Don't you speak to me that way, you brazen hussy. You whore!"

Matthew put a hand on her arm. "I'm okay," she assured

him. "Children, say goodbye to your grandparents. This is the last time you will ever see or speak to them again."

Ned ran over and wrapped his arms around his mother, a small whimper escaping as he buried his face against her side. Grace, on the other hand, was livid and ready to attack. She shot forward, but Matthew grabbed her and pulled her back.

"*I hate you*," she shouted.

While the others were concentrating on the scene playing out between Erianna and her father, Lucinda watched Colleen, who wore a smug look of satisfaction as her daughter was assaulted. A small, nearly imperceptible smile appeared on her face and she watched her husband with a sense of pride.

Finally, Lucinda wrapped her cane on the ground several times, gaining everyone's attention. "Henry, Garrett, escort these people to my car. Garrett, see that they arrive home safely," she ordered. "You needn't come back. Bob will bring us home."

Tim and Chip hustled the Pruitts to the waiting golf carts and shoved them unceremoniously into their seats. Then Lucinda came forward, addressing Colleen directly. "Shame on you for allowing your husband to use your daughter as his personal punching bag. I should have put a stop to it years ago."

Colleen adopted an innocent look. "I didn't do anything—"

"That's right. You didn't. You let him take his rage out on your own flesh and blood. In fact, I think you encouraged him. By the time I'm through with you there won't be a single business in town that will accept your patronage. You're finished in Prestwick."

With a wave of dismissal the chauffeurs drove them to the parking lot. Colleen looked back with an expression of astonishment and then dread as she was driven away, with Chip perched on the side as her jailer.

Lucinda turned to the hushed crowd. "Agnes, Abigail—" the women came forward. "It's time Erianna learned the truth."

"Not now, Lucinda," Helen said.

"Yes, now. Right now. This has gone on long enough."

The three exchanged knowing looks and then Gail took Erianna by the arm. "Come with us, my dear."

Matthew was not inclined to be separated from his bride and Ned was still clinging for dear life to his mother's side. So Bob came forward and scooped the trembling boy up into his arms.

"Come on, Neddo, let's you and your Uncle Bob take a little walk."

"Are you alright?" Matthew whispered to Erianna.

"I'm fine," she responded with a tremulous smile.

The women took her, arm-in-arm, and started along the walkway that wound around to the front of the church. Matthew made to follow, but his mother stopped him. "She needs ice, son. Go find an ice pack."

Matthew nodded and took off toward the grotto, running as fast as he could. Grace stepped forward and took Lucinda's arm in hers. "Let me help you, ma'am."

Lucinda patted her cheek lightly as the two started down the beautiful flower-lined path toward the reception area. "Won't you call me Grandma?" she asked the girl.

"I'd be proud to, Grandma," Grace replied with an open, unpretentious smile.

Helen greeted the guests as they shuffled by. Henry returned with one golf cart and stopped to let Lucinda climb in. Grace stepped up on the floorboard and hung onto the vertical bar as they rode to the grotto.

Matthew came running up the path before they were halfway down the walkway. "Where did they take Erin?"

Henry stopped and signed, and Matthew took off through the trees on a straight-line route to the front of the church. By the time he found the women, Gail and Erianna were just sitting down on a park bench on the far side of Immaculate Heart of Mary, between the church and the rectory.

Agnes stood to the side as Matthew knelt on one knee in front of his wife, placing the ice pack gingerly on her cheek. It was bright red and he could clearly see the finger marks that Clyde had left on her face.

"Don't look so glum, Matt. It's our wedding day and I'm just fine."

"I'm so sorry," he said. "I didn't see it coming."

"How could you? I didn't expect it either. He's never hit me in public before."

As she held the ice pack on the left side of her face, Erianna turned to Gail Neading. "Did you want to say something to me?"

Without further ado Gail took her free hand. She looked at the young woman and came right to the point. "Clyde Pruitt is not your biological father."

Erianna's eyes rounded, but she said nothing.

"When your mother, Aggie and I were in college your mom was dating a man named Aaron Meecham. He was from Cincinnati. Aaron was in his last semester at the University of Virginia when we started our sophomore year at the College of William and Mary. He used to drive down to visit your mother on weekends and they were very much in love.

"Aaron's parents were wealthy, and he was planning to tour Europe for six months after early graduation and before he started law school the following fall. But your mother was afraid of losing him, so she got pregnant—deliberately."

Gail paused and Agnes picked up the story. "Over Christmas break, just before we were due back on campus, Colleen called Aaron and told him she was pregnant. He immediately drove to Prestwick to see her. It was New Year's Eve, and he was due to fly out the next day.

"We all went out to a party that night, and in the early morning hours on New Year's Day Aaron drove back to Cincinnati. He was less than ten minutes from his home when he was hit and killed by a drunk driver."

Gail squeezed Erianna's hand. "Colleen was pregnant and your father was dead. When her parents found out what she had done they refused to pay her college tuition. We—Aggie and I, went back to school, but your mother did not. I'm not sure how she and Clyde met, but by the end of January they were married."

"Oh my god," Erianna whispered. "She got pregnant just so that she could trap the poor man and force him to marry her?"

"Yes," Gail confirmed. "We were there when she took the home pregnancy test. When it came back positive she said, 'Thank God.'"

"That's despicable."

"We thought so," Gail agreed. "We knew that Aaron would cancel his European tour and marry her. He was a stand-up guy. And that's exactly what he agreed to do that night."

"He was a wonderful man and he had a beautiful singing voice," Agnes said. "You obviously inherited that from him."

"You also have his hazel-colored eyes," Gail added. "He was a very handsome man."

Erianna sat on the bench and thought about what she had just learned. "That explains why my father—why Clyde hated it when people called me Erin. My mother named me Erianna after my birth father, and when Clyde heard people shorten my name and call me Erin he would become incensed and beat me when we got home. It all makes sense now." She stood up. "Thank you for telling me, Mrs. Neading."

"For heaven's sake, young lady, don't you think it's about time you started calling us by our first names? You're an adult now and Clyde's ridiculous rules no longer apply."

"Yes. Of course, you're right. I'll try."

The women left and the newly married couple was finally alone. She took the ice pack from her face. "How bad does it look?"

"Well, I could lie to you and say that you don't have a mark on you, but the truth is that you're probably going to have a shiner tomorrow."

She sighed heavily. "It isn't my first," she admitted. "But it's certainly going to be my last."

They took a few minutes to themselves before Matthew escorted his bride to the golf cart that Chip had parked nearby for their use.

When he turned the last bend along the path to the grotto Matthew stopped. Erianna took off her bolero jacket, laid it on the seat, and they walked arm in arm to the reception.

Chapter 21

The guests slowly filtered down to the grotto. Everyone was talking in hushed tones about what had just happened. The Monsignor and the Donovan boys were informed about the incident and Phil checked in with Bob to make sure that Nathan was okay.

The mood at the grotto was somber. Clyde Pruitt had ruined what should have been a joyous occasion.

Tim and Faith had planned to sneak in and out of the surprise Mother's Day wedding unnoticed, but after Faith was enlisted to take part in the dedication to the Madonna they decided to stay long enough to offer their congratulations to the newlyweds at the receiving line. With the assault by Erianna's father, those plans were also abandoned and the couple joined the other guests in the grotto.

"This feels more like a wake than a celebration," Faith told her cousin Nancy.

Nancy turned to Chip. "Do something. Matt and Erin will be here any minute. Get up on stage and say something."

"What do you want me to say?"

"I don't know. Think of something. You need to lighten the mood. Tell a joke, dance a jig, I don't care. Just do something."

"I've got this," Tim said.

A DJ with a karaoke machine had been hired for the reception and a small raised platform had been set up for those who might want to sing. But, with what had happened Doro asked the DJ not to begin the music just yet.

Tim stepped up to the mic. "Folks, if I could have your attention, please."

The group quieted.

"For those of you who may not know me, my name is Tim McGraw. My wife, Faith, and I are friends of the newlyweds and we're happy to be here today to celebrate their wedding. I think my friends would appreciate it if we put the unfortunate incident outside the chapel aside and get on with the party. So I'd like to start off with a song for y'all."

He turned and spoke to the DJ. The music for his choice began and Tim stepped back to the microphone to sing his classic hit *I Like It, I Love It*. When he raised his hands and began to clap the guests followed suit. Grace and Ryan moved forward and started to sway to the music. Chip and Nancy joined them in the small designated dancing area. Before the song ended several of the guests were moving to the beat.

"Who's next?" Tim asked.

When no one volunteered, Monsignor Prestwick came forward to look at the computerized song list. He stepped up to the mic and began to sing *Hello Muddah, Hello Faddah* and the adults guffawed, but the youngsters wondered what was so funny. As the ditty went on they began to laugh, too. There, on the stage in front of all the wedding guests, a Catholic priest was singing the silly lyrics of the Allen Sherman spoof. By the time he finished the crowd was roaring.

Agnes and Gail arrived a few minutes later, letting everyone know that the bride and groom were on their way.

Matthew and Erianna were met with a round of applause as they walked into the grotto and up to the microphone.

"Thank you all for coming today," Matthew said as he held his wife at his side. "We are grateful that our friends and family could join us for this special Mother's Day celebration. And thank you to my brother for doing us the great honor of performing our wedding ceremony.

"I've waited a long time for this, and today I am happy to say that I am, at last, a husband and a father. Grace, Nathan, I love you both." He turned to his wife. "Erianna, you have made all my dreams come true."

They stepped down and Matthew took Erianna in his arms as the DJ spun the classic hit by George Strait, *I Cross My Heart*. They began a country waltz and Matthew, who was by now an old hand at country-western dancing, guided her with ease. After their second circuit he pulled his bride closer and brought her right hand to his chest, covering it with his own. He switched to a basic box step, and as they danced Erianna brought her cheek to his and closed her eyes.

When the song ended Tim called out, "Traitor."

Tim and Faith were getting ready to leave. Matthew let Erianna know and she quickly searched for and found Doro.

"We need to set up for the group picture."

Doro nodded and Erianna went to waylay the couple for a few minutes more.

"Please don't leave just yet. I know your daughters are probably waiting to celebrate with you at home, but if you don't mind I'd like to get one group picture before you go."

Doro and the photographer corralled the guests around the grotto of St. Mary. Several folding chairs were brought over and Doro directed the guests into position. The front row included Lucinda, Helen, Monsignor John, Pap and Ginny. Erianna and Matthew stood in the center of the frame behind those in the chairs.

Erianna moved to Matthew's right so that when the shots were taken she could turn slightly toward her husband and hide her injured cheek. Their children stood on each side of the newly married couple, and the others filled in the spaces around them.

There was a short fieldstone wall that stepped up to the statue of St. Mary in her grotto, and several of the guests took their spots there. The remaining attendees were positioned so that the back center would be the highest point in the shots and decrease on each side. The resulting photographs would show a modified semi-circle of guests, with the newlyweds standing front and center.

Doro and Ginny slipped out of position and grabbed bags of flower petals. Each bag was quickly dispersed to random people in the group.

"Okay everybody," the photographer began, "here's what I'd like you to do. When I give you the signal I want y'all to reach into the bag nearest to you and scoop up a handful of rose petals in your cupped hands so they don't get crushed." He demonstrated. "Like so. Those of you holdin' the bags, when they're empty you need to toss them aside, out of the range of my shot. And when I say 'go' I want you to toss your petals up in the air."

Once again he demonstrated, making the motion of bringing both cupped hands up and out as the petals were released.

"Is everybody ready?" At their nods he moved behind his camera on its tripod. "Okay, reach in now and scoop out your handful of petals."

They followed his direction and the empty bags were tossed aside as they all made ready. Matthew and Erianna were the only ones not holding any of the wide variety of colored rose petals, from deep red to pure white and every shade of pink in between.

"Look at me, Matt," Erianna murmured. "And just let the petals fall around us."

"Okay," he smiled sweetly as he took her hands in his.

"I'll count us down. Three, two, one, go."

Everyone, including those in the front row, raised their arms and sent petals flying into the air. At just that moment the DJ, who had been schooled by Doro and Ginny, pulled a cord from behind the grotto and a canvas sheet was drawn away from a shallow, expansive overhead shadow box with extra wide screening at the bottom which had been suspended from the overhanging limb of a large sugar maple tree.

Colorful petals began to drift down through the holes in the screen. As the DJ pulled a second cord, more and more petals were released when the shadow box moved back and forth. The effect was not unlike that used on old movie sets where

Styrofoam was used to mimic snow falling when shooting on an indoor set.

"Everyone look here and smile."

They all did, with the exception of the newlyweds, who had eyes only for each other.

"Now everybody look up. That's great, now try to reach up and catch the petals. Wonderful. Toss some back up into the air."

Everyone caught on. Some people were playing with the petals while others mugged for the camera. The photographer continued to direct the group as petals floated down and were tossed back into the air, all the while snapping away with his digital camera. The effect was breathtaking.

Bright smiles and laughter permeated the air as more and more petals fell, from the feet of those sitting in the front row to those standing on the stone wall in the back. Matthew brushed the back of his fingers across Erianna's injured cheek and then bent his head and kissed his bride. Petals floated all around them.

Erianna threw her head back and laughed. They looked to the sky as the colorful shower rained down. Then Erianna brought her injured cheek to his and they turned to the camera and smiled.

She would always remember this fantastical moment.

The reception was winding down. Matthew and Erianna walked the McGraw's to the pathway and said their goodbyes.

"Thank you, Faith, for pinch hitting," Erianna said. "I'm so happy you came today."

"I had a wonderful time." Faith leaned down and in a stage whisper said, "I'm stealing that rose petal idea."

She offered her well-wishes to Matthew as Tim came over to Erianna.

"You know, the first time I met you I thought you were a meek, unassuming woman. But I see now that you've got a strong backbone and a heart of gold. It took a lot of guts to defy your father. You're a very brave woman."

"I couldn't have done it without your words of encouragement."

Erianna gave him a peck on his cheek. Bringing her lips to his ear she whispered, "Turns out he's not my biological father. You and I have more in common than we knew."

She stepped back and brought her index finger to her lips. The twinkle in his eyes let Erianna know that her secret was safe with him.

After they left the Keegans approached the newlyweds with Grace and Ned at their sides.

"Mom, Matt," Ned began, "Phil and Laurie are going to hit the road. They have a long drive and it's getting kind of late."

Phil stepped forward to shake Matthew's hand. "I'm glad we decided to come today. I wasn't sure how I would feel about Erin marrying again, but after seeing all of you together I realize that it's the best thing that could have happened for Grace and Nathan. I can see that you love them and will keep them safe. That's all I've ever wanted for them."

Phil bent down and addressed his son. "You know, Ned, Matt is going to be your father now. You should probably start calling him 'Dad', don't you think?"

The boy thought about that for a moment and then reached out to give Phil a hug goodbye. Grace followed suit. "Bye, Phil, bye Laurie," they waved in unison as the couple walked up the path and out of sight.

Matthew and Erianna stood at the bottom of the walkway to say goodbye as their guests left. Brock, Agnes and her family headed out next.

"Thank you, Aunt Aggie," Matthew said, "for what you did today."

"I hope it brings her some peace," she replied.

"I'm going to hitch a ride with my sister," Brock informed them. "I think Lucinda and Helen are going to stay for a while longer and have Bob drive them home later."

Chip and his family said their goodbyes. Then Ryan came over to let Erianna know that he would be driving Pap, his brothers and his grandma Helen home in Pap's large, eight passenger van.

"Grace and Ned are coming with me, too," he told his Uncle Matt. "I think Grandma Lucinda is planning on riding back to the farm with you guys."

As Doro, Ginny and Bob broke down the venue the others headed back to Berrington Farm. Lucinda, Helen and Pap gathered in the living room with Erianna, Matthew and their children. Lucinda settled in on the couch beside Helen and Pap sat in his wheelchair on the far side of the room.

The children sat at Erianna's feet and Matthew pulled the piano bench over to sit next to his bride. When the door between the units was closed and everyone had settled Erianna spoke to her children.

"I'm sorry you had to witness that today," she began. "But knowledge is power and now you both know the reality of physical abuse. It isn't pretty, and it's all too common these days."

"So this isn't the first time he hit you, right?" Ned asked.

"Yes, that's right." At his look of dismay Erianna continued. "But he never broke my spirit. It only made me stronger."

"Why does he hate the Prestwicks so much?" Grace asked.

"I really don't have an answer for that. I can only guess that he resents their power and wealth, and the Prestwick family is *very* powerful. They own most of the town of Prestwick, as well as several successful manufacturing plants.

"There's something else you need to know, and I want you both to listen and not interrupt until I've finished."

At their nods, Erianna began. "When I was growing up I had a terrible crush on Matt, but he never knew about it because I kept it a secret. On the evening before high school graduation Chip convinced me to get up on stage and sing at a party.

"I used to sing all the time when I was little, but only when no one else was around because my father disapproved. I would go down the street behind Dr. and Mrs. Neading's home and sing. They had a huge back yard and it fell off into a gully where the acoustics were really good. It was my favorite place to hang out and be alone.

"When I sang in public the night before graduation Matthew noticed me for the first time—really noticed me. We started dating, but we didn't tell anyone, and over that summer we fell in love. Somehow my father found out, and on the morning of my eighteenth birthday he beat me. The beating was so severe that he damaged my vocal cords and ruptured my uterus."

She looked at Ned. "Do you know what a uterus is?"

"Of course I do, I'm not stupid. A uterus is the female organ where a baby grows."

"That's right. Well, he ruptured my uterus and I hemorrhaged. The injury was so extensive that the doctors couldn't stop the bleeding and they had to perform an emergency hysterectomy." Once again she looked at Ned.

"They took it out?" he asked.

"That's right. But it was really a blessing in disguise, because I now have both of you, the most wonderful children a woman could ever hope for. I love you so much. Even though you didn't grow under my heart, you certainly grew in it."

"Oh, Mom, that's terrible," Grace murmured. "If a father loves his child, how can he do that to her?"

"I'm glad you asked me that. I just found out today that Clyde Pruitt is *not* my biological father."

She waited for that statement to be digested.

"My biological father died before I was born and Clyde married my mother knowing that her baby wasn't his. I suppose some people cannot love a child that's not their own flesh and blood, but I have no problem doing so. I can't imagine not loving you two. You are my life."

When Erianna sat back, there was a silent pause.

"There's more to this story, isn't there," Grace probed. "Why didn't you and Matt get married? You guys *were* in love, right?"

Grace turned to Matthew. "Was it because she couldn't

have your children, like Lucinda said? Because she couldn't give you heirs?"

"No, Grace," Erianna spoke up before Matthew could respond. "It was because when I regained consciousness in the hospital I couldn't remember anything about what happened. I had what the doctor's diagnosed as post-traumatic amnesia. I had lost my memory of my entire senior year.

"Apparently, after I was finally released from the hospital I met and fell in love with your father. To be honest with you, to this day I have no recollection of the time period immediately following the assault. But I suspect that my parents wouldn't let me come home to Prestwick, so Matt and I never had a chance to reconnect."

Erianna looked over at Helen.

"That's true," she confirmed. "After you were released we arranged for you to go live with your aunt in Florida. We were able to keep the story out of the newspaper, and Matt left for college not knowing what had happened to you."

"My first clear memory after that time is being married and living in Hudson, and adopting you, Grace. I'm not sure if I will ever recover those months in between, and maybe it's all for the best. I must have been in a lot of pain and I'd just as soon let that go."

"Do you remember your senior year now?" Ned asked.

"Yes, I do. Last fall, when Chip Neading and his family came for the trail ride, he made some offhand remark that brought it all flooding back. Once I remembered how much I loved Matt and he loved me, he asked me to marry him and I accepted."

"Did Grandpa beat you up a lot?" the boy wanted to know.

"'A lot' is a relative term, Ned. He didn't hit me every day, and today was the first time he did so in public."

"I hate him!" Grace hissed. "He's evil!"

"Clyde Pruitt is a despot and a narcissist," Lucinda spat.

Both children turned to look at her.

"Despot?" Grace asked.

"Narcissist?" Ned followed.

"A despot is—"

"Grandma, stop," Matthew interrupted, raising one hand.

Lucinda looked at her grandson. He frowned slightly and shook his head a little. Erianna sat back and waited, saying nothing.

Grace looked at her brother, and Ned shot up and ran from the room. He hurried back from the family room with a large dictionary in his arms. Sitting on the floor with his legs crossed and the dictionary in his lap, he flipped through the pages as Grace spelled out the word 'despot'. She scanned the column and when her finger stopped she read the definition out loud.

"Despot—a noun meaning a ruler with absolute power. A person who wields power oppressively; a tyrant."

The children looked at each other and nodded. Then Ned began to turn the pages again.

"N-a-r—" he looked at Grace. "Do you know the derivation?"

"I'm pretty sure it's from the Greek. There was a man named Narcissus in Greek mythology," she told him, already understanding the meaning of the word.

"Okay, I'll try C. N-a-r-c-i—" he turned the pages and ran his fingers down the columns. "Here it is. Narcissist. N-a-r-c-i-s-s-i-s-t. It is Greek. Noun, a person who has an excessive interest in or admiration of themselves. An extremely self-centered person who has an exaggerated sense of self-importance."

Ned closed the dictionary and set it aside.

During the delay in the conversation Lucinda turned to look at Helen. Lucinda's initial annoyance at being cut off became admiration of Erianna's teaching style, and the young lady grew several notches in her estimation.

"So he's a despot and a narcissist. And I still hate him," Grace told her mother.

"Hatred is a very destructive emotion, Grace."

"I don't care. I'll hate him until the day I die. Don't you hate him for what he did to you, for what he took from you?"

"Honestly? There were times when I hated Clyde. But all that did was make *me* miserable and unhappy. And besides, driving me to hate was his goal. He wanted me to feel hatred. He wanted to break my spirit so that I would be as miserable as he."

"I don't understand that, Mom. Are you telling us that you loved him? How could you?"

"Well, I never said that I loved him. But, I chose not to hate. Holding onto hatred and resentment made me feel sick, deep in my belly and up here." She tapped her head. "I'd much rather lead a happy life than an angry and resentful one."

"And so you decided to let go of all the bad stuff and look on the bright side?" Ned asked his mother.

"Exactly. I didn't want to walk around like Charlie Brown with a dark cloud over my head all day long. I like having blue skies above and the sun shining down on me."

"It's not that easy, Mom."

Erianna shrugged. "Well, I can't tell you how to feel, Grace. Try to think of it this way. Feeling hatred takes a lot of hard work. You have to wake up every morning and recall all those bad thoughts and memories. And you have to keep hanging onto those negative feelings all day long, every single day. But, you only have to let go once. And while I certainly will never forget, I refuse to let hatred rule my life."

"Look at Grandpa," Ned said to his sister. "He's a very angry man and I'll bet he doesn't even know what happiness feels like." He turned to his mother. "I'm going to listen to your advice, Mom, and wake up every day and try to be a happy person."

"You already are, Ned. You already are," his mother cooed. "And you are too, Grace. Just take some time and think about it."

When Ginny, Bob and Doro got home, they helped Pap get settled in his bed. Lucinda and Helen went next door and Grace headed upstairs to change her clothes.

"I'll see you on Friday, Mom."

"I'm coming home tomorrow."

Grace stopped on the lower landing. "You're not going on your honeymoon?"

"No. Plans have changed."

This was the first time Matthew had heard about it, but he accepted Erianna's decision. He understood that she needed to be with her children after everything that had happened.

"Mom—" Grace put her hands on her hips. "You don't have to worry about us."

Erianna smiled. "I'm not. It's just that my face is pretty messed up and it's going to get a lot worse before it gets better. And if the Hilton Head police spot me walking around sporting a black eye they'll naturally assume that Matt gave it to me. The last thing we need right now is to have him arrested for battery on his honeymoon."

Matthew chuckled. "You're right, I hadn't thought of that. I certainly don't want to spend my honeymoon in jail."

The newlyweds climbed into the backseat of Matthew's Buick LaCrosse. Henry moved the passenger seat all the way forward for added legroom, and Erianna snuggled up against her husband and nodded off as they rode to his condo.

"Hey, my honeybee, it's time to wake up now. We're here."

Erianna sat up and looked around. "Sorry," she yawned. "I fell asleep."

Matthew hadn't minded one bit that she had slept in his arms. He'd waited a lifetime for this day and if, after the emotional highs and lows of the day she needed to shut down for a while, who was he to judge.

Henry pulled her suitcase from the trunk and Erianna giggled. "Looks like I over packed."

He smiled and signed that the piece wasn't all that big.

"I've never been here in the daytime," she commented as the elevator doors opened and they walked into Matthew's place.

She wanted to take in the spectacular view so she stepped out onto the balcony overlooking the Ohio River. Matthew brought her a tumbler of bourbon and they stood side by side as the light slowly faded.

Erianna excused herself and went to the bedroom to freshen up. When she returned a short time later she was still wearing her wedding dress, minus the bolero jacket, and Matthew was surprised. He assumed that she had gone in to change.

"Are you hungry?" he asked.

"No, but I wouldn't mind if you freshened my drink."

Matthew wanted nothing more than to carry her to his bed and make love to her, but they went inside and he dutifully poured another shot of Jim Beam and added a little ice for her. The sun had set and the apartment was cast in deep shadow as the last of the light faded.

He stood at the softly-lit bar, filled his glass and downed its contents. Erianna's lips twitched. It seemed that her husband was nervous and in need of a little liquid courage. Taking one last sip of her bourbon, she set the drink aside.

"Come with me," she murmured.

Taking his hand, she led him down the hall and through the bedroom door, locking it behind them. Matthew seemed unsure so Erianna took the lead.

"It seems, Dr. Prestwick, as though you're a bit overdressed." She eased him out of his suit jacket and backed him against the door. "Have I told you how handsome you look today?"

She brushed her hands along his chest and reached up to loosen his tie. His Adam's apple bobbed as he swallowed.

She pulled the tie from his shirt collar ever so slowly, ever so sexily. Her fingers worked the buttons of his shirt, exposing his skin as she freed the tails from his trousers and pulled it off, casting it aside.

She watched his expression as she slowly finished undressing him. She did not stop until he was completely naked, and then she took his hands in hers, stepped back and guided him to an armless padded chair that she had moved to the foot of the bed, directly across from the mirrored make-up table.

He was naked, and hard, and throbbing, but she was still fully clothed. So he reached for her, but she stepped back.

"You are such a handsome man." She took another step back. "I'm a very lucky woman."

"Erianna—"

"Do you like my shoes?"

He looked down and his eyes widened as his Adam's apple bobbed again. She had changed into the red stilettos that she had worn on Valentine's Day. Matthew's mouth watered. He was a slave to her ministrations.

Erianna moved to the make-up table and took a seat on the swivel stool. With her back to him she began to pull the pins from her hair.

He was in agony, but he remained seated and let his bride continue the foreplay. She picked up a brush and ran it through her hair as he watched. Then she turned toward him, rose, and bent over, running the brush from the base of her neck to the end of her golden tresses.

Suddenly, with an arch in her back, she straightened and flipped her hair back. The move rivaled that of Rita Hayworth in the classic movie *Gilda.* Matthew gasped and his swollen manhood jerked.

Dropping the hairbrush onto the table, she reached up and released the top button from its loop at the back of her dress. The center back seam of the silk crepe was not joined. Instead, a long keyhole opening had been left in the upper section of the dress.

Erianna let the pale orchid top slip from her arms, exposing her strapless flesh-colored bustier. The upper half of the long-line bra was lace and it exposed most of the upper swell of her breasts.

"Do you like what you see?" She brushed her fingertips across her exposed skin.

"Yes," he rasped.

"Would you like to see more?" she teased.

He nodded. Matthew was in her thrall, powerless to stop the torture of her sensual game.

Erianna reached behind her and slowly freed the covered buttons from the loops running down the silk Carmeuse cummerbund. With that task completed she turned her back to him and slowly slid the zipper of the skirt down. The garment fell to the floor, puddling at her feet.

"Oh my god," he groaned.

Erianna was left wearing only her sexy undergarments, what little there were of them. When she had excused herself earlier and gone to freshen up, she changed into a pair of silk stockings that ended at mid-thigh and a G-string panty that had so little material that she needn't have bothered. Her backside was bare and bits of string on each hip were tied in a bow, holding the tiny panty in place.

Stepping out of the dress, she bent down and picked it up, laying it across the table. Then she raised her hands and ran her fingers through her golden locks as she arched her back. Turning to the side, she lifted one red shoe onto the swivel chair and ran her fingers up her leg, from her shoe to the top elastic band of the silk stocking.

Never in his wildest dreams had Matthew imagined such a scenario.

Erianna moved toward him at last, spread her legs and straddled him.

"I've waited so long for this," she murmured. "So very long."

She bent her head and kissed him as he ran his hands up and down her torso, marveling at the narrowness of her waist and the softness of her creamy skin. He reached around and cupped her backside, rubbing and squeezing her cheeks as she moved against his steely length.

"Oh, Matthew, I love you so."

With a low, deep groan he brushed his lips along her jawline to the sensitive pulse point just below her ear. He traced the line of her neck, moving ever lower as she arched her back in invitation. When he reached the bit of lace covering the upper swell of her bosom he tugged it down to where the underwire met the material at her ribs.

Their movements became feverish as he suckled her swollen peaks. She wriggled against him and he pulled her tighter in his arms. When Erianna reached down and grasped the velvety length of his manhood he stopped her.

"Don't do that, darling, or this will be over before we get any further." He reached up to pull her lips to his, thrusting his tongue into the sweet recesses of her mouth.

He'd had enough of the swatch of cloth blocking his entry, so he untied the strings at her hips. Erianna lifted herself so that he could pull the G-string away. He kissed and fondled her breasts as she lowered herself onto his shaft, sliding ever downward, drawing him deep inside her.

"Mmmm," she purred.

He placed his hands on her hips to help guide her as she began a slow, steady rhythm. She plunged down and rose up, time and again as their tempo increased. When she kissed him her hair fell around his face, enveloping him in a curtain of silk. And when she arched and threw her head back he brushed his lips over her sensitive skin.

The friction of their coupling heated their flesh, intensifying their pleasure as they climbed. Matthew called upon every ounce of self-control to prolong their lovemaking. When the spasms of her orgasm began he clenched his jaw and hung on for a few more seconds before his seed filled her.

Chapter 22

Matthew rolled over and found himself alone in the bed. He looked at the clock. It was four-thirty. He switched on a light and looked around. The bathroom door was open but the light was off. Then he noticed that Erianna's clothes were gone and her suitcase was no longer resting on the luggage rack by the closet door.

He got up and slipped into a pair of sweats and a tee shirt. Opening the bedroom door, he padded down the hall and found Erianna standing in the living room staring out into the darkness. She was dressed in jeans and a pullover sweater, and her hair was pulled back from her temples into her standard ponytail. With her arms folded across her chest she seemed to be lost in thought, unaware that he was in the room.

Matthew moved toward her slowly. "Erin?"

She didn't respond.

"Erianna?"

She sighed. "It's early, go back to bed."

"Can't you sleep?"

"No. I didn't want to wake you so I came out here."

With her back to him Matthew couldn't see her face. "What's going on? Is your cheek bothering you?"

She shrugged. "I just couldn't sleep."

He closed the distance between them and wrapped his arms around her. "Talk to me honey. What's bothering you?"

It took a long time for her to answer. Finally she lowered her head and said, "Maybe what my father says about me is true. Maybe I am a slut."

"Stop!"

She stiffened and he forced her to turn and look at him. "I have no idea what's going through that pretty little head of yours, but whatever it is, just stop."

"Okay," she answered tremulously.

He knew by her tone that she was only mollifying him. "Dammit—" he growled in frustration. "Why is it that every time we make love you let that bastard get into your head?"

"I—" she didn't know what to say.

He enveloped her in the safety of his embrace, but she flinched when her left cheek brushed against his chest. Without another word he lifted her into his arms and carried her back to the bedroom. Crossing to the master bath, he set her down and switched on the light.

Erianna shrank from the glare of the bright light.

"Jesus," he swore. "That eye is swollen shut and your cheekbone is badly bruised."

"I'm alright," she assured him. "It doesn't hurt."

"Bullshit. You know I don't believe you. You're the world's worst liar."

She turned her face away. "I feel like crying, but that will only make things worse."

She made a small sound of distress. "Oh, Matthew, why do I always feel so—" she searched, but unable to find an appropriate adjective she said, "dirty after we, you know, after we have intercourse."

His stomach lurched and his heart ached for her. "You won't always feel this way. Over time you'll see that making love isn't an immoral act." He paused and ran his fingers through his hair. "I thought we settled this last fall. There's nothing wrong with enjoying sexual relations with your husband."

"I know. It's just that I behaved like a wanton and a tease last night, just like Clyde said I was. I don't know what came over me, acting that way. And on my *wedding night*. It was shameful."

His lips curled slightly. "I swear, Erianna, I don't know where you come up with these antiquated words. Nobody, and I mean nobody, uses the word 'wanton' anymore."

Her spine stiffened. "It's a perfectly good word, Matthew, and it accurately describes my behavior. Maybe *you* should expand your vocabulary. And stop cussing," she finished with a huff.

Matthew realized that no amount of talking would knock any sense into her. Only many more nights of lovemaking would dispel Clyde's denunciations from her thoughts.

"Okay, no more cussing. Let me get a quick shower and we'll head home. Meanwhile, why don't you go to the kitchen and put a frozen bag of peas on your eye. I won't be long."

Matthew's personal items were finally moved from the basement to the master bedroom. When he came to bed that night he found his wife asleep in the old beat-up recliner in the sitting room.

He knelt before her. "Sweetheart, it's time for bed." He had intended to lift her from the chair, but Erianna objected.

"I can't. When I lay flat my face throbs. I'll just sleep here."

Matthew thought for a minute. Then he went into the bedroom and turned down the covers. She only had two pillows on the bed, not nearly enough, so he trudged down to the basement and grabbed the pillows he had been using when he slept over.

The door between Erianna's house and the duplex suite was closed, so Matthew used the intercom to call Pap. Finding him still awake, he went next door and asked for spare pillows, then went back upstairs, spread them on the bed and stepped back. *Not enough.* He walked down the hall and took the two pillows from Ned's lower double bunk.

When he was satisfied that Erianna would be comfortable sleeping propped up in the bed he went back to the sitting room to collect his wife. He lowered her into the cocoon of pillows and lay down next to her.

The following night he came into the bathroom while she was brushing her teeth and made love to her, entering her from behind as she stood at the sink.

Erianna avoided going to the stables all week so that boarders would not see her bruised and battered face. By the end of the week most of the swelling had disappeared, but her skin was still black and blue. She stayed home from mass that Sunday, and the bruising slowly faded to a greenish puce.

It took more than two weeks for her face to heal completely, and not a moment too soon. The school year was ending and Berrington Farm's busiest season was upon them.

One Saturday afternoon, when Erianna was cleaning up the mid-day dinner dishes the phone rang. She dried her hands and picked up the cordless receiver.

"Berrington Farm."

"Hello, Erianna."

She suppressed a long-suffering sigh. "Hello, Mom."

"How are you?"

"I'm very busy."

"Oh, well I hoped you'd have a few minutes to talk."

"No. I don't. And there's nothing to talk about."

"I don't like your tone, young lady."

"I don't care, *Mother*."

Matthew walked into the family room just then and Erianna placed her index finger to her lips. She turned on the speaker so that he could listen in.

There was a pregnant pause before she said, "I have work to do. Goodbye, Mom."

"Wait. Don't hang up. We really need to talk."

Erianna sighed audibly. "About what?"

"Well, I was wondering if you could talk to Lucinda Prestwick for me."

"Talk to her about what?"

There was another long pause. "I was hoping that you could get her to back off."

She rolled her eyes at Matthew. "No."

"But—no one will let us shop at their stores. Even the grocery store declined our debit card. How did she manage that? All my groceries were scanned and packed, but my card was rejected. It was so humiliating."

"That's not my problem. Drive to New Richmond and do your shopping there."

That suggestion was met with silence.

"Won't you just call her and ask her to—"

"No."

"Well, then I need you to transfer some money into our account."

Erianna looked at her husband and blushed. She had hoped that he wouldn't find out that she had been supporting her parents financially. His lips thinned, but he said nothing.

"No."

"What do you mean no? I need five thousand dollars transferred as soon as possible."

"I said no."

"Really, Erianna, what's gotten into you? You're a rich woman now. Your father and I—"

"He's not my father."

"What?"

"You heard me. Clyde Pruitt is *not* my biological father."

"Of course he—"

"No. He's not. Aaron Meecham is my father, not your husband. I know everything, Mom. Agnes and Gail told me the truth."

Clyde's voice came over the speaker. Erianna knew that he had probably been listening in. He usually did.

"You little bitch. You transfer that money right now."

"Contrary to what you believe, *I* am not wealthy. I'm a hard-working woman and I don't have any more money to spare for you."

"Then get it from that bastard husband of yours," Clyde demanded. "He has more money than God."

"No."

"You are the spawn of the devil!" Clyde screamed.

"And you are both sadists," Erianna answered in a calm voice.

Colleen gasped. "How can you say that to me? I never laid a hand on you."

"That's true, you didn't. You left that particular perversion to your husband. You stood back and took your pleasure in watching him beat your firstborn daughter."

"You ruined my life!" Colleen cried.

"No, Mother, you did that all on your own when you set out to trap Aaron Meecham. You made your bed, now lie in it."

"You fucking whore," Clyde roared. "You transfer those funds or I'll come down there and burn your house to the ground. And I'll make sure that you go up in flames with it."

Erianna hung up. "Well, that was—" she looked at Matthew. "Uncomfortable."

He went to her. "I'm proud of you," he said as he took her in his arms. "Does he always threaten you?"

"Yeah, but he usually says he's going to beat me. He's never threatened to set fire to the house before." She paused. "Do you think I should be worried?"

The phone rang again. "Don't answer it," he said. "Let it go to the machine."

It stopped after three rings. "Uh oh."

"Mom?" Grace's voice came over the intercom. "Grandma Pruitt's on the phone for you."

Erianna had no choice. She picked up the phone.

Colleen did not mince words. "We need the money, Erianna. You always say no, but then you give it to us. I don't know why we have to play these games, just transfer the money like you always do."

"I said no and I mean it. Don't call here again, Mother. I want nothing more to do with you. Goodbye."

Grace came bounding down the stairs just as her mother hung up.

"Do you think there's a way to block that number?" she asked her daughter.

"I don't think so. That's a really old phone. It doesn't even have caller I.D. All it can do is forward calls to and from the stable office."

Matthew turned to Grace. "We need to go buy a new phone."

Grace nodded.

It rang again. Erianna was getting a headache and she pinched the bridge of her nose with her fingers. They let the call go to the machine and Clyde ranted and into the recorder.

They stood listening as he made foul accusations about Erianna's mental acuity and once again threatened to set fire to the house as well as the stables. This time he demanded ten thousand dollars, giving Erianna a forty-eight hour deadline to transfer the funds.

He also made threats about Lucinda, shouting that Erianna better put a stop to the dowager's efforts to blackball them in town, *or else*. His intent was clear.

"He doubled the amount," Matthew said after the man hung up.

Erianna waved a hand. "He does that. I'll just transfer the five thousand and he'll back off."

"You can't give in to their blackmail anymore, Mom," Grace interjected. "If you do it'll never end."

Grace looked at Matthew. "What do you think?"

"Well—" he was hesitant, unsure how Erianna would feel if he spoke up.

"You're family now, *Dad*. You're allowed to voice your opinion."

Erianna nodded in agreement.

"Well, how long have you been giving them money?"

"Since we moved here," Grace supplied when her mother didn't immediately answer. "She's been forced to send them thousands, if not hundreds of thousand dollars. They're living high off the hog while Mom scrimps for every penny."

Matthew, in fact, had known that Erianna sent her parents money since the day he'd snooped on her computer in the stable office.

"You do know that Clyde was given a large cash settlement after his accident, as well as a generous monthly pension, right? And he also receives social security disability payments."

Erianna's eyes rounded. "No, I didn't."

"They should be able to live quite comfortably without your assistance."

"But, they told me they couldn't make ends meet and that they have no money for my sisters' college tuitions."

"That's just not true, Erin. I negotiated their settlement myself. They have more than enough money, and besides, why should you be obligated to pay for Julia and Joanna's educations?"

She had no answer for that.

Up-to-date phone systems were installed in Erianna's house and at the stables, and those affected by the threats were made aware of the situation, including the Village of Berrington Police Department. The forty-eight hour deadline passed and Erianna worried about her home and family.

Colleen called twice more, but Erianna stuck to her guns and refused to transfer the requested funds. She kept her conversations with her mother short and hung up the moment she heard Clyde begin to speak. Every call was recorded. Erianna finally made the difficult decision to block her parents' number and Pap began to closely monitor all traffic onto the property. Weeks went by, but Clyde did not make good on his threats.

In the evenings Erianna and Matthew would settle in their room, and with his urging she talked about her dreams for making improvements to Berrington Farm. She told him about her idea to refurbish the old farmhouse and turn it into a bed and breakfast, which she thought would bring in much needed revenue.

One evening he asked to see her drafts for the dressage and show jumping rings she had once considered building on the southern acreage when the leases expired. Erianna's idea was to attract horse shows and junior class three-day eventers to the Farm. Matthew also found schematics for an indoor riding facility among the paperwork.

All those dreams had been put on hold when her parents started draining her accounts, and Matthew asked Erianna if she might take it up again if she received a large infusion of cash. But she was adamant that she would not accept his largess. When he pointed out that he only wanted to replenish the funds that her parents had absconded, she shut him down and refused to have any further discussions about it.

Matthew talked about his desire to have more children and even suggested that he officially adopt Grace and Nathan. He told her how much he loved being a father, but that he had missed out on their infancies and that longed to hold a baby in his arms.

The busy summer season was ending and the kids had started back to school when, on a Thursday afternoon a car pulled onto Donovan Lane with Ohio license plates. Erianna was working a horse on the cross-country course when Pap sent out an alert.

Gus ran to his old, beat-up pickup and tore up the lane. He intercepted the vehicle and blocked it with his truck just before the Camry reached Bob and Doro's house.

Shotgun in hand, he approached the driver's door. "What's your business here?"

The driver lowered her window. "I'm Erin's sister, Julia. My mother and I have come for a visit."

"You're not welcome here," Gus growled. "Turn your car around and go back where you came from," he ordered.

"But she's expecting us."

Erianna saw Gus run for his truck and speed up the lane. She turned her gelding and galloped after him. By the time she reached the scene Gus was shouting at the driver. Recognizing her parents' Toyota she dismounted, tied the horse to the fence rail and ran to the car.

Colleen lowered her passenger side window. "Erianna, tell this man who we are."

She bent down and looked across at the driver. "Julia? What are you doing here?"

"Mom said you invited her for a visit. She asked me if I wanted to come along, and since I've never seen your place I decided to drive her."

"I didn't invite her. I haven't talked to her since—"

"What's that walker doing in the back seat," Gus hollered. He raised the shotgun. "Open the trunk. Now!"

Just then Bob pulled up and parked in the grass next to the silver Camry. "What's going on here?"

With the rifle pointed at her, Julia was frozen in fear. Still standing on the passenger side, Erianna told Gus to lower the shotgun, which he did.

"Julia, is Clyde in the trunk?"

"Yes," she finally admitted. "He said he wanted to surprise you."

Erianna gave her sister a reassuring nod. "Open the trunk for me."

Gus and Bob moved to the back of the car and Gus pointed the shotgun at the trunk as Julia released the latch from her key fob. The siren of a police car was heard approaching as the lid popped up.

"Get out of there!" Gus shouted.

Bob helped the old man climb out of the trunk and Erianna opened the back door to retrieve his walker.

"Don't hurt him," Colleen pleaded.

"Stay in the car, Mom."

Clyde began to curse. "Get that thing out of my face, you fucking hick."

Gus pulled back the slide of his pump-action shotgun. "Just give me an excuse, you asshole. C'mon, make your move. I'll blow you straight to hell."

When Erianna stepped between them Gus immediately lowered his weapon. She handed Clyde his walker.

"There's a full gas can in here," Bob told them.

The police cruiser pulled up behind the group just then and Gus went to store his firearm on the gun rack in the cab of his truck.

Clyde was frisked and a butane grill lighter was found in his pocket. He was cuffed, read his rights and placed under arrest. The gas can and lighter were collected as evidence, and when a second unit arrived the women were also cuffed and detained at the police department for questioning.

The Camry was impounded, and by the time the kids got home from school that afternoon the scene had been cleared.

Clyde Pruitt was charged with attempted arson, a Class A-1 felony. Colleen was charged as an accessory. Julia was released after it was determined that she played no part in the scheme and was unaware of her parents' intent.

An attorney was hired and a plea negotiated. In exchange for Colleen's charges being dropped to misdemeanor criminal mischief, Clyde pled guilty to attempted arson in the third degree. He was sentenced to time served and five-years probation, ordered to complete two hundred hours of community service and pay a substantial fine. In addition, both agreed never to set foot in Harrison County again.

When all was said and done the Pruitt's were truly destitute. Attorney fees and fines had drained their hidden assets.

Having earned her nursing degree in May, Julia Pruitt moved back in with her parents and supported them from her salary at the local hospital while her sister, Joanna, continued her coursework at the Ohio State University.

Neither Matthew nor Erianna attended the sentencing hearing for her parents. When she learned of the outcome she breathed a sigh of relief, believing that, at long last, she'd been freed from the yoke of her parents' stranglehold on her.

Matthew sat across the dining room table from a silent, but fuming Clyde Pruitt at their home on Crestwood Drive. Colleen and Julia were also present as Matthew began his proposal.

"You and your wife will sign over the deed to this property to your daughter, Julia. You will move out of this house by the end of next week. I have located and purchased a condo in a fifty and over living community in Gainesville, Florida, not far from your sister, Wanda," he said to Colleen as he passed them each a brochure of the facility.

"I will pay off the rest of your fines and provide you with a reasonable monthly allowance," he told them.

After their arrests the Prestwick Foundation had rescinded their quarterly payments.

"With that and your social security income you should be able to live quite comfortably."

Clyde snorted. He had sold their car just the week before in order to make the next payment on his fines.

"We have no money to hire movers, you god-dammed bastard, or to even get there. You reneged on my pension."

Matthew was unsympathetic. "What did you think would happen when you threatened Lucinda? Where did you think those funds were coming from, the cabbage patch? You shouldn't have bitten the hand that fed you."

Colleen looked as though she had aged ten years in the last few months. She'd been ostracized by the people of Prestwick and had lost everything.

"What about my youngest daughter?" she asked. "She's still going to Ohio State and we don't have the money for her tuition."

"I'm sorely tempted to tell her to take out student loans, but I will personally proffer her tuition payments so she can complete her degree in education. But she'll have to figure out on her own how to pay for her room and board. Erianna will not foot the bill for Joanna's tuition and living expenses like she did for Julia."

Julia gasped and Matthew turned to her. "That's right. Your parents absconded with over a hundred and thirty thousand dollars of my wife's money, all so that the lot of you could live like royalty while she struggled."

"Is this true?" she asked her mother.

The ashen skin of Colleen's chin began to quiver and she lowered her head in shame.

"You will agree never to set foot in either Harrison County, Kentucky or in the town of Prestwick. Not ever again. Do you understand?"

Clyde's face turned red and he glared at his archenemy.

"I probably shouldn't have done this, but I bought your car back from the dealer where you sold it. It's parked out front. I'll sign the title over to you on the condition that you register it in the State of Florida.

"You will pack only your personal belongings. The condo is fully furnished so all of this furniture is to remain here. But you can take your pictures and other mementos with you if you like. That's up to Julia."

He passed out folders containing the documents that would need to be signed by each of them. "Review these tonight and bring them with you to my office tomorrow morning at ten. A Notary will witness your signatures."

"I'm not handing my house over to anyone for nothing. I own it free and clear. I'll put it on the market and sell it before I give it away."

Matthew looked directly at Clyde. "If you don't consent to my terms and conditions charges will be filed against you for attempted murder, assault and battery by the end of the week."

He hoped that Clyde didn't know that there was a statute of limitation for attempted murder that had long since passed.

"Attempted murder? What the fuck are you talking about?"

"I'm talking about the attempted murder of your oldest daughter, here in this very house."

At Clyde's apoplectic look, Matthew continued. "Did you think you were in the clear? Did you think she'd never remember how you pinned her to the wall and beat her? Well, I've got news for you. She remembers everything, including how you took your screwdriver and drove it inside her, rupturing her uterus. And she remembers you strangling her into unconsciousness."

"The bitch lies! You can't believe a word that comes out of that whore's mouth. Did she tell you those dammed lies so that you'd come here and steal my house?"

"Dad," Julia pleaded. "Don't."

"Erianna knows nothing about my being here. And none of you are to tell her anything about this. Come to think of it, there will be an additional document for all of you to sign tomorrow. A non-disclosure agreement stating that if you ever try to contact her or inform her of our arrangement then you will lose your housing and allowance."

"Including me?" Julia asked.

Matthew studied her. "We can discuss that privately another time. But for now, you will *not* try to contact your sister. Do you understand?"

Julia nodded. "But, what if I decide not to stay in Prestwick?"

"Well, that's up to you. Give the place to your sister or sell it and give the money to your parents, I really don't care. They're quite accustomed to taking from their children. But if you do that, there will be no monthly stipend. And I'll tell you this, it won't take them long to blow through all that money, and then they'll start bleeding you dry just like they did to Erianna. I assume, since you're living here now, that you're paying all their bills."

Julia nodded.

"Word around town is that you're dating a doctor from Prestwick Mercy Hospital and that you two are getting serious. That's why I decided to have your parents sign the property over to you. As for the rest, that's not my concern."

"But why do we have to leave our home? I've lived here all my life," Colleen told him.

"I consider it just punishment for what you put Erianna through. If you choose to stay, charges *will* be brought and the whole town will know what Clyde did to her. I'll make sure of that."

He turned to Clyde. "Actions have consequences, or haven't you learned that by now?"

"You wouldn't send Clyde to jail. You wouldn't do that to us, would you?" Colleen cried. "Why can't you let us stay here? Please—be reasonable. Just leave us alone."

Matthew sat back. With an air of nonchalance he said, "This

town is dead to you. I'm offering you a way out." Then he leaned forward and looked directly at Colleen. "And I promise you this. If you decide to stay here the Prestwick family will use all of our considerable power and influence to see that Clyde is locked up for the rest of his life."

"Take the offer, Mom," Julia implored. "He's right. This town *is* dead to you. You told me yourself that no one will talk to you and you can't even shop here. He's offering you a fresh start, and it's a very generous offer. Please, Mom, *please*. Take his offer."

Matthew got home late that night. He changed his clothes and sat down on the couch to relax. He and Erianna talked about this and that, but he did not mention his meeting with her parents. He watched his wife as she sat in the recliner, studying her graceful movements as she worked a small crochet hook through the yarn of a sweater to attach a sleeve to the body of the piece. He was fascinated by her skills.

"Are your fingers ever idle?"

"They can be." She set the sweater aside and rested her hands quietly in her lap. "What's wrong?"

"Nothing. I had a long meeting with a difficult client and I'm not sure about the outcome. It was probably just a waste of time." He shrugged.

He got up from the couch and went over to hunker down at her feet. Taking her hands in his, he brought one to his lips and brushed featherlight kisses across her knuckles, then kissed the pulse point at her wrist.

Erianna cupped his cheek with her palm and he closed his eyes as she caressed him. Bringing her other hand to his face, she drew him to her and kissed him as he covered her hands with his own.

"Erianna," he moaned in sweet surrender.

She ran her fingers through his hair and traced his ear with her fingertips. He loved her hands and was soothed and comforted by her touch. Unbuttoning her blouse, he freed the clasp of her bra.

Erianna leaned forward and guided his lips to her breasts, arching her back as he suckled her now turgid peaks. With her hands still framing his face, she guided his lips from one breast to the other.

"Mmm."

He slid her top down her arms. She shrugged free and then slid off the recliner, kneeling before him. Taking off his sweatshirt, he pulled her against the solid wall of his chest. Reaching around her, he cupped her backside in his hands, and as they kissed he gently ran his hands across her perfectly rounded cheeks.

She wriggled against him and moaned softly. "Ohhh."

Matthew knew that he was taking a risk making love to her here in the family room. But she was so sexy and her hands so magical on his skin that he was unwilling to interrupt their foreplay long enough to take her upstairs.

Her hands moved down his chest, across his well-toned abs and moved to the waistline of his jeans. He helped her to unsnap and draw down his zipper. Their kisses became more passionate as they slowly undressed each other.

When her legs were freed from her jeans she followed his lead as he guided her to the end of the oval coffee table and placed her hands on the edges.

When he moved behind her she ran her hands further down the length of the table and bent forward. Lowering his chest over her back, he breathed in the sweet scent of her silky hair, inhaling deeply as she began to wriggle her backside against him.

"Mmm," she purred.

He ran his hands down her arms, clasping them over her fingers as she clung to the edges of the table. Her skin quivered at his touch, and when he positioned himself against her she was ready for him. He kept her arms extended as he entered her, pushing ever deeper into her fiery depths.

"Ahh," she whispered.

He began to ride her, thrusting and withdrawing as he held her hands in place. He did not increase his tempo, but kept his movements steady as he made love to her. She urged him to a faster pace, but he held her pinned as he slowly rode her.

She threw her head back and arched against him in a silent plea for more, but he resisted, and his controlled rhythm continued. Erianna began to move against him, urging him for more, but he remained unyielding, and her breathing became labored as the delicious torture continued.

"Matthew—*please*." Her voice rose a little, and still his tempo did not change.

She'd never known such sweet agony. On and on he slowly rode her until she could take no more. As she toppled over the edge he quickly moved his hands to her hips and his powerful thrusts rapidly increased. She shuddered uncontrollably as her orgasm intensified. When his seed spilled deep inside her she cried out and Matthew clamped a hand over her mouth to muffle the sound.

Once they returned to earth he picked her up and carried her, naked, to bed and made sweet love to her again.

Chapter 23

By Thanksgiving Matthew convinced Erianna to have a child with him. Grace and Ned had also taken up the mantle, assuring their mother that they wouldn't feel displaced by a new baby.

"We know how much you love us, Mom," Grace said. "We're not worried that you'll love us any less if you and Dad have a baby that's yours biologically. After all, you always say that there are many ways for people to come together as a family."

"Yeah," Ned agreed. "After you and Matt got married Ryan, James and Theo became our cousins. Doro and Bob told us to start calling them Aunt Doro and Uncle Bob, and the boys call you Aunt Erin now. We're all family, and a new baby will have lots of people to love it unconditionally, just like we all love each other."

Finally relenting, Erianna began taking medication that shut down her normal ovulation cycle. Matthew gave her a daily shot to stimulate the production of eggs and every few days she was examined by a doctor in Cincinnati who, through blood tests and ultrasounds, monitored her follicle growth.

Though not an easy process, she tried her best to maintain her normal easygoing disposition as her hormones raged. Every time she felt overwhelmed and ready to snap she would picture her husband's blissful expression when, after umpteen conversations at the supper table, she finally agreed to have a baby with him. He could not have been happier.

When the doctor determined that the follicles were ready, Erianna received an injection to mature the eggs. Several hours later the retrieval procedure was performed. She was put under IV sedation, and after the ultrasound-guided needle had successfully collected half a dozen eggs Matthew took her to the condo and put her to bed so that she could rest and recuperate.

"What happens now?" she asked him as she sat propped up against the pillows while he waited on her hand and foot.

"Now we hire a surrogate to carry our fertilized embryos and we have a baby soon."

"Isn't it going to be a difficult process to find someone willing to give birth to another woman's baby?"

"It can be. But I've already found a lady in Columbus who is willing to carry our child. She's married and has two kids of her own, and she had very easy pregnancies with no complications. The couple planned on having more children, but her husband, who was in the military, was severely injured in Afghanistan and he's a paraplegic now."

"But, if they wanted more children won't she have trouble giving the baby away after it's born?"

"No, I don't think so. They've undergone extensive therapy with a psychologist and I've met and spoken with them as well. She told me that she loves the feeling of being pregnant, and that she and her husband both believe it would be a selfless act, helping another couple to have a child. They're very nice people and they're committed to doing this, if not for us then for someone else. And they really need the money this will bring in."

Although she had misgivings, Erianna did not voice them, opting to trust her husband and hope for the best. He assured her that he would handle everything from here on out and that she needn't be directly involved in the rest of the process. She didn't ask, but she knew that a hefty fee would be laid out for the service performed.

For the first time since the children were little Erianna did not take them to Prestwick on Christmas Eve to drop off presents for her parents and sisters. She held true to the edict that Grace and Ned would never have to see their grandparents again. She had not seen or heard from Clyde or her mother since the incident on Donovan Lane.

The holidays were happy ones and the new year brought hope for a happy and prosperous future. Matthew replaced the funds that her parents had appropriated from her, but Erianna did not notice the windfall until mid-January.

"I'm not taking your money," she told him when she realized that her coffers had been replenished.

"Yes, you are. You had so many dreams, most of which were stolen from you in one way or another. There's no earthly reason why you shouldn't be able to make those dreams come true, just like you would have before your assets were drained."

"No, Matthew, it's not your responsibility to fix the ills of the world and I'm not taking your money. There'll be no ifs ands or buts, *I won't do it*."

Daily squabbles ensued, and after about a week of the back and forth Grace came home one afternoon to find them arguing yet again. Grace, being Grace, added her two cents to the discussion.

"You know, Mom, he does live here rent free, so to speak." She winked at her father. "Why shouldn't he be allowed to invest some of his capital to make improvements to the property? If you offer him a share of any profits then over time you will, in essence, be paying him back for his initial investment."

But her mother would not listen to the logic of that argument. "I'll find a way on my own, Grace. I won't be beholden to anyone—"

"He's not just *anyone*, Mom. He's your husband."

That evening when they went to bed Erianna was still adamant that the funds would be returned to his account.

"Do you remember the day you came to my office to go over the Prenup?" Matthew asked her.

"Yes."

"Do you remember what you said to me at the restaurant that night?"

"I said a lot of things, Matt. Where are you going with this?"

"You asked me if I noticed that you argue with me a lot. Do

you remember that? You said that it was something you needed to rein in. I believe those were your exact words."

"What's your point?"

"My point is that you need to stop arguing about this. I'm not going to change my mind, no matter how long you go on about it, so you need to *rein it in* and just accept the fact that your husband has, as Grace put it, decided to make a capital investment—in you."

"That's really underhanded, Matthew."

Yes. It was. But it worked.

Matthew continued to travel and Henry took up semi-residence in the basement, sleeping in the Murphy bed where Matthew had spent many a night before they were married. Erianna and the children took sign language lessons from a church member whose son was born profoundly deaf, and he seemed pleased by their willingness to learn.

The blueprints for the old farmhouse were retrieved from the dead files in her attic and Erianna began, once again, to make plans for the conversion of the house to a bed and breakfast. Surprisingly, Henry and Ned took great interest in the project.

An architect from Georgetown was employed to draw up the plans, which called for a large, multi-story addition to the South side of the old house. There would be a total of four bedrooms and two baths on the second floor, which required the addition of one bedroom and a bath. The third floor, which currently housed only two bedrooms and no bath, would be reconstructed to include two additional bedrooms and two added bathrooms. And the first floor construction would expand and update the kitchen into the new space and add a dining room where guests would be served their breakfast.

Subs were hired and two Pods were brought onto the property to store the ranch house furnishings while the work was completed. With Henry's oversight the project moved forward, and Erianna prayed that the job would be finished before the busy season started. Ned, ever at Henry's heels, watched the renovations with a critical eye and asked many questions while Henry guided Erianna through the restoration process.

"Who are you going to get to run the place?" Matthew asked one evening at supper.

"Well, I've been thinking—" She stopped short and looked at her husband. "Sorry."

Matthew smiled brightly. "Don't be. I love hearing those words."

The kids looked askance. They were in the dark, not understanding what that exchange was all about, but neither of their parents was forthcoming.

Erianna continued. "I have a very good friend from Hudson, Sue Lofgren. She has one daughter, Alexis, who is Ryan's age. Sue was married to a man who battered her, and one night he got into a drunken fistfight at a bar. When the police were called her husband attacked one of the cops who tried to break up the brawl, which had spilled out into the street. He stabbed the officer with a knife. Long story short, he's in prison now and she divorced him."

"Do you think Aunt Sue would want to come down here and run the bed and breakfast for you?" Ned asked.

"She might." Erianna looked at her husband. "She makes her living waiting tables and she's a wonderful cook. She has a gregarious personality and more energy than anyone I know. She has this way with people, I don't know what it is, but she just loves everybody and I don't know of anyone who doesn't like her. She considers everyone she meets as her friend."

"But Mom," Grace protested. "Sue can run the day to day, she'd be great at that. But she'll never be able to manage the business end of the operation. And neither will you, for that matter."

When her mother frowned Grace added, "No offense. But neither of you has any business savvy. Who's going to do the advertising, and the purchasing, and the billing? You need to get a website up and running and put packages together that include horseback riding excursions and the like. And you need to print brochures and send them out to travel agents and horse clubs. Plus you need to start booking show competitions to attract more people to the farm. Who's going to handle all of that?"

"Umm."

Henry began to sign. "I could take care of it for you."

"No. Thanks for offering, Henry, but you're already doing enough for me. Besides, you work for Matt, and I'm sure he wouldn't want you to be distracted by dealing with my business."

Henry quickly typed. "After it's up and running, there really won't be that much time involved. I've done this before. I have a degree in hotel management and hospitality."

"But you've already missed a couple of business trips with Matt because you've been acting as my project manager. I really feel guilty that you missed those trips and I just can't ask you to take this on. You have enough to do as it is."

"If you feel that guilty about it, why don't you offer him a salary for his work?" Ned suggested.

Erianna looked to Matthew for advice.

"Henry is his own man," he said. "He makes his own decisions. And if he's willing, I'm certainly not going to object."

She took some time to think about his proposal. When their meal was finished and the dishes done she sat back down with Henry, Grace and Ned while Matthew went down to the stables to take care of the chores.

"If you're serious about doing the job, then I *should* pay you a salary. Ned's right. You should be paid for your work."

Henry shook his head. "I don't need a salary," he typed. "Matt is more than generous and I have more money than I'll ever be able to spend."

"Well, then you should at least have a title," Grace said. "You should be named the Operations Manager for the bed and breakfast."

"That's a good idea, but he needs more than just a title, Grace," her mother said. "He should at least be given an hourly stipend for his work."

"Stipend?" Ned asked. He went to the dictionary on the shelf by the back sliding door to look it up.

"That's not necessary," Henry signed.

"Then I have a counterproposal for you. In exchange for your work you can move into one of the rooms at the farmhouse. You'll have your own private quarters, like you do at the condo, and you won't have to sleep in the basement anymore."

Henry thought about that idea for a time. Then he typed a long message. "Your original plans included an apartment in the basement for whoever would be hired to run the bed and breakfast. But those plans were rejected when you decided that a first-floor suite would be a better idea for the proprietor. Why don't I go ahead and build myself the apartment downstairs? I'll pay the additional cost, and that way you won't lose the revenue from renting out the room you're offering me."

"That's a really good idea, Mom," Ned agreed. "I saw those blueprints, and it would be a perfect apartment for him."

"That's an excellent solution," she agreed. "But isn't it too late to make the changes and have the work completed? Aren't we too far along in the renovation?"

"No, it's not too late, not if we make the changes immediately," Henry typed.

"Okay. Then it's all settled. But you are *not* going to pay for the additional work. I have enough to cover the cost."

When Henry shook his head, Erianna stopped him with an upraised hand. "I insist. If you won't agree to that then the deal is off, Mr. Operations Manager."

Matthew took his wife out of town for a long weekend to celebrate their first wedding anniversary. They went to a Bed and Breakfast in the Blue Ridge Mountains of northwestern Virginia. He chose the quaint, eighteen-room inn, which boasted two hundred acres of trails for horseback riding, so that Erianna could get an idea of how similar operations were run.

After carefully studying the interior design of the inn, she was relieved to know that she had made wise decisions in her style choices. She had reused the majority of the original bedroom furniture from the old farmhouse, which included hardwood headboards and dressers that had been sent out to be stripped and refinished.

There was also a beautiful queen-size brass bedframe that she paired with soft, moss-green and lilac floral draperies and a matching comforter, both of which she had sewn herself. It gave the bedroom a Victorian vibe, and she filled the space with dresser and side table doilies and Victorian era knick knacks such as a water basin and pitcher to enhance that feeling.

With eight bedrooms in the newly refurbished farmhouse, Erianna had used her ingenuity to furnish the additional bedrooms. She made upholstered headboards, giving some rooms a country flair with whitewashed dressers she found at flea markets and bedding purchased from local quilters in shades of either blues and yellows or pinks and greens.

One headboard was upholstered in leather and she gave that room a Wild West theme, with wrought iron nightstands and distressed wood dressers and side chairs. Some rooms were painted, while others were wallpapered. No two rooms were alike, and after her visit to the bed and breakfast in Virginia, Erianna was relieved to know that she was right on track with her choices.

All in all, it was a wonderful weekend, even though the weather did not cooperate and they didn't have a chance to ride the trails.

The following Monday was Matthew and Erianna's official anniversary date and the weather was still overcast and raw. The families gathered for supper at the duplex to celebrate the occasion. As usual, everyone scattered to eat their meals.

Matthew came home halfway through supper. "Sorry, there was a late meeting and I couldn't get out any earlier." He gave his wife a peck on her cheek and offered her a warm smile. "How was your day?"

Erianna smiled. "It was fine." She loved her husband. He never seemed to need down time to transition from work to home life, and he rarely came home after a long day at the office in a bad mood.

The kids seemed more animated than usual, and as Ginny served cake and ice cream Doro became impatient with them.

"You guys are raising such a ruckus you're driving me nuts. Go next door," she ordered in a clipped tone, and she shut the door behind them.

When she sat back down at the bar, Doro sighed heavily. "Well, I have some news." Bob came over and stood at her side. "Hold onto your hats—" she paused and took in a deep breath. "I'm pregnant."

"You are?" Ginny's face lit up. "Another grandchild? I can't believe it!"

"*I'm* not so happy," she admitted. "This was obviously a mistake." She looked at her husband. "Someone shouldn't have such strong swimmers."

"It's not my fault," Bob said. "You know very well you forgot to use your diaphragm."

"Well at my age this sort of thing shouldn't happen, diaphragm or no."

The women gushed as the men rolled their eyes, and Doro talked about the difficulties she was about to face, having a baby when she was nearing forty. She told them that she was due somewhere around Christmas, and that she hoped that it was a girl so that she could name her Christine.

After a while Matthew interrupted the gaggle when he approached Erianna and sat down on the stool next to her. He took her hands in his and said, "I have some news, too. We're also pregnant."

"We are?"

He nodded. "We're well past the first trimester and we're due in early October."

Erianna sat unmoving and no one spoke.

"I'm so happy," Matthew told her as he gave her hands a gentle, reassuring squeeze. "I hope you're happy, too."

"We're going to have a baby?" she repeated at last, as if she was unable to take in what he just told her.

"Yes, my little honeybee. We're having a baby. Our baby. Yours and mine."

"Do—do you—" she was having trouble collecting her thoughts. "Do you know what it is? A girl or a boy?"

"Not yet. The doctor knows, but I wanted to wait and talk to you first before I found out."

"A baby," she breathed in astonishment. "Is everything okay with the mother?"

Matthew frowned. "You're the mother, Erin. But to answer your question, the surrogate is in perfect health. She breezed through the first trimester without any problems whatsoever."

"Oh, good," she sighed in relief.

Pap finally spoke up. "Well, we're going to be hearing the pitter-patter of little feet in both houses before long. Congratulations to you both."

"There's more," Matthew said.

"More?"

He nodded. Using his sister's phraseology he said, "Hold onto your hats—it's twins."

"What!" Doro exclaimed. "Twins?"

Matthew puffed up like a peacock and his smile was as broad as the Cheshire Cat's. "That's right. We're going to have two babies."

"Oh my God." Erianna nearly fell off her stool. "Are you sure?"

"Sure as we're sitting here right now. This farm is about to be blessed with three babies, not two."

Erianna launched herself into her husband's arms. "Oh, Matthew. Matthew—" She began to laugh. "First Doro, and now us. I can't believe it."

Neither could anyone else.

* * *

Matthew cuddled his wife against him as she slowly regained her senses after they made love that night.

"One year today," he murmured.

"Mmm."

Limbs intertwined, he played with a thick lock of her hair. "Do you want to know if the babies are girls or boys?"

"Mmm."

He grinned. His beautiful wife was still incapable of cohesive thought. He held her in his warm embrace until, as he was nodding off she finally spoke.

"I wonder where we're going to put two babies."

"We'll figure it out," he yawned.

The following weekend the Donovan boys, Grace and Ned were rounded up and given the happy news that by the end of the year there would be three new babies joining their families. Although initially shocked, they all seemed to take the news well and there were no angry outbursts or voiced objections.

Doro stopped accepting new catering jobs and the women began driving to flea markets and secondhand shops for cribs, strollers and the like. After talking the matter out with Matthew, they decided to convert the master sitting room/sewing area into a nursery. And Erianna accepted the fact that as they got older, the upstairs library, which was open to the stairway with just a wrought iron railing along the shared wall would have to be closed in and drywalled to add an additional bedroom to the second floor of the house.

By early summer, Sue Lofgren and her daughter took up residence in the Village of Berrington. Henry was happy in his new basement apartment and the old farmhouse was christened the Berrington Farm Bed and Breakfast.

Erianna had worried that Alexis would resent being uprooted from her home and friends, but with Ryan and Grace's support she was immediately welcomed in the Village. When the high school softball coach found out what a talented player Alexis was he immediately recruited her to play on the varsity team.

Matthew saw to it that scouts from the University of Kentucky and Eastern Kentucky University came to watch her play, and she would ultimately be offered partial scholarships to both colleges. Alexis, who would never have been able to afford college tuition on her own, was thrilled to know that she would be attending a university after her senior year at Boone High School.

Ironically, but not especially surprising to Erianna, Gus took an immediate liking to Sue. A tall, statuesque woman with lively, sparkling brown eyes and frizzy brown hair, they were an odd couple. Short and wiry, Gus was the opposite of Sue, who was an imposing, solidly-built woman. Nonetheless, before long they became the best of friends.

He started going over to the farmhouse for breakfast every morning and, at her insistence, Gus began to take her to the Hoot 'n Holler with him. It didn't take her long to learn country-western dancing. She loved every minute of it and the regulars quickly became acquainted with her.

It was a busy, hectic time on Berrington Farm. Matthew received regular updates about the progress of the pregnancy from the surrogate's doctor in Columbus and he passed the news on to his wife. Both had decided that they did not want to know the sex of the babies until they were born.

Lucinda and Helen threw a surprise shower for both expecting women. It was there that Erianna learned that her parents had moved to Florida. Her sisters were among the guests, but Julia did not reveal the true details of their parents' relocation. As per her agreement with Matthew she told no one, including her younger sister, saying only that they had decided to retire to a warmer climate.

As their due date drew closer Matthew stopped traveling, keeping the jet grounded so that they would be able to fly to

Columbus for the birth of their babies. And on the last day in September, after Sunday mass they received the call that the surrogate, Paula, had gone into labor.

Matthew and Erianna flew to Columbus and arrived at the hospital by mid-afternoon. Matthew had pre-arranged to have two adjoining rooms for the delivery. He settled his wife in the room next to the surrogate's as the woman labored. He moved between the rooms, checking on Paula's progress as Erianna sat waiting next door. And at eleven-thirty that night she was told that the woman had transitioned and was ready to start pushing.

Just after midnight Matthew carried his newborn daughter in to meet her mother, who was sitting in a rocking chair wearing a disposable hospital gown.

"She's a girl," he whispered as he bent down and placed the infant in Erianna's arms. "She was born a few minutes before midnight."

Erianna looked down at her daughter, who had her father's brown eyes and a spattering of fine, dark hair. "You're so beautiful," she cooed to her daughter. "You're going to grow up to look just like your father."

Erianna held her daughter and began to rock her as Matthew went back to the delivery room. While he was gone a nurse came in to check on Erianna and the baby, who slept soundly in her mother's arms.

Nearly a half hour later Matthew returned with another baby in his arms. He knelt in front of his wife. "This little guy didn't want to come into the world head first, but the doctor managed to turn him and he was born at twenty minutes after midnight."

"A boy," Erianna smiled brightly. "We have a girl and a boy."

Matthew nodded. "And they're both healthy."

The newborn boy was fussy. "Give him to me. Maybe he'll settle down once he's next to his older sister," she suggested.

Erianna readjusted her daughter in her arm so that the boy could rest alongside her. Matthew looked on as the twins were gently rocked in the arms of their mother.

"You don't have a hair on your head, do you little guy?" she spoke to him in a soft, quiet tone. "But you're just as beautiful as your sister."

The boy began to settle down and looked up at his mother.

"I think he's going to have your eyes," Matthew whispered.

"It's too early to tell," Erianna murmured as she studied her son. "But our daughter definitely favors you."

"You know, we never talked about names."

Erianna watched as her children slept. "Do you realize that our twins were born, not only on different days, but in different months?"

"That's true, I didn't think about that until you pointed it out."

Erianna looked off saying, "Did you know that Grace was given her name because she was born on a Tuesday?" She paused, calling to mind the old nursery rhyme. "Tuesday's child is full of Grace."

"Really? That's a unique way to name a baby. What is Sunday's child?"

"The child that is born on the Sabbath Day is bonnie and blithe, and good and gay."

Matthew reached out and touched his daughter's head. "How would you feel about calling her Bonnie?"

"Bonnie Prestwick." Erianna rolled the name over on her tongue. "Bonnie Joan."

The newborn pursed her lips and opened her eyes to look at her mother, as if in response to her name being said. Matthew chuckled softly. "I think she likes it."

"Okay," Erianna agreed. "Bonnie it is. Now as for our son, his birthday is Monday, October first." She paused and shook her head. "I just can't get over it. Our twins have been born in different months."

"What is a Monday's child?"

"Monday's child is fair of face."

"Well that fits. I think he's going to favor you, and you're more beautiful than the sun and the stars, my golden goddess."

Erianna blushed prettily. "You're just prejudiced."

Matthew wanted to kiss his wife, but was afraid he would disturb the sleeping newborns. "Do you have a name in mind that fits a Monday's child?"

She shook her head. "No. I don't. But in Gaelic, fair, or blonde as it were, is translated as Kenyon."

"How do you know these things?"

"I'm a fount of useless information," she winked. "But we really don't know yet if he will be fair, like me, or have dark hair like his sister." She studied her son. "Would you like to name him Kenyon or maybe Kenneth Prestwick?"

Matthew thought about the name, but rejected it. "No. Bonnie and Ken—that's a little too close to 'Barbie and Ken.'"

"Mmm. That's true. Did you ever think about what you would name your son if you ever had one?"

"Well, I was always partial to Benjamin. Ben—it's a strong, solid name. Benjamin Prestwick. What do you think?"

Erianna frowned a little. "I can see how you would like that name. It translates from the Hebrew as 'son of my right hand', a fitting name for the heir to the Prestwick holdings. But if we decide on Ben, I think we should rethink the name Bonnie for our daughter."

"Why?"

"Because Bonnie and Ben is a little too kitschy, don't you think?"

"No. I really don't care that people use the same first letters when they have twins. Their names suit who they are. Grace, Ned, Bonnie and Ben. The names flow well when you say them all together and each one is a good fit for each individual."

Erianna nodded. "Alright, I agree. Bonnie Joan and Benjamin—Francis?" she suggested. "That would please Lucinda, I'm sure."

Matthew nodded in agreement. "Bonnie and Ben, welcome to the world."

Erianna was sitting in the duplex with Ginny giving the twins their two o'clock feeding when Matthew came home.

"You're home early," Pap noted.

"Yeah," he said as he walked over to his wife, who was sitting on the couch. "We need to talk."

Matthew took Bonnie from her arms and carried her over to Pap. "Would you mind giving her the rest of her bottle? I need to talk to Erin."

"What's wrong?" she asked, but her husband did not respond. Instead, he took her by the hand and led her through the door, shutting it behind them and leading her to the couch in the family room where they sat, side by side.

Erianna grew concerned. "What is it, Matt? Did something happen?"

"No. Nothing's wrong. But we need to have a serious discussion and time is of the essence."

"Okay—" she sat on the edge of the sofa, waiting for him to explain.

"I got a call from the fertility doctor this morning. He wanted to know what we wanted to do with the three embryos we have left."

"Three embryos?" Erianna frowned.

Matthew ran his fingers through his dark, wavy hair, unsure how to proceed. He looked at his wife and took a deep breath, expelling it slowly as he gathered his thoughts.

"The doctor wanted to know if we intended to implant the remaining embryos someday, or if we were going to continue to store them, or destroy them.

"You see, there is a woman from Indiana who is ready to become a gestational carrier, and Dr. Johnston had planned to implant embryos from another couple into the woman—today. But none of the fertilized eggs from the couple who hired the woman are viable, so it's pointless to implant them. The doctor called me to ask if we wanted to have our embryos implanted.

"Apparently, he called two other couples before us, but neither was ready to move forward at this time. The surrogate has gone through the pre-implantation process and is ready now, and I need to know if you would like to take advantage of this opportunity to implant the rest of our embryos."

Erianna was startled and confused. "The rest of our embryos—" she repeated.

"I know it's sudden and we haven't talked about what would happen to our remaining fertilized eggs. But when he called me, I got to thinking about what we should do with them. And the more I thought about it the more I realized that I didn't want to discard them or leave them frozen in perpetuity. I just can't bring myself to do that."

Erianna got up and began to pace. Matthew turned and watched as she moved back and forth along the traffic area between the kitchen and the dinette table.

"I never realized we had embryos in storage," she admitted when she came back to the couch and looked at her husband. "I didn't know that all six eggs had been fertilized. I thought that they only fertilized the two that were implanted and the rest of the eggs were discarded. And now I'm not sure—I don't know what to think."

"I'm sorry. I guess that's my fault. I should have explained things better when we went through the process the last time."

"I don't know what to do. Three more babies—I" she paused, shaking her head.

He reached for her hand. "Come and sit down and I'll try to clarify."

Erianna hesitated, but finally sat down again.

"Six eggs were harvested in total. And they were *all* fertilized with my sperm at the time they were collected. The doctor chose three strong candidates for implantation the last time, but only two survived. That's very common in these procedures.

"There are three remaining fertilized eggs in cryogenic storage, but of those three one is definitely not viable. Between the other two, only one is likely to grow. The other has some possibility, but the odds aren't good. Honestly, Erianna, there's no guarantee that any of them will result in pregnancy, but I just can't stand the idea of destroying them.

"If we decide to move forward, it has to be right away. We have to make the decision today. The doctor is waiting for a call back. The woman is ready now and the procedure will be performed tomorrow. I'm sorry for springing this on you out of the blue and giving you no time to think about it, but I really need to know what you want to do. As for me, I believe that life begins at inception and I would like to at least give them a chance at life."

Erianna sat back and closed her eyes. She was not very good at snap decisions, but in this instance she had no choice. After calming herself and praying for guidance she realized that the decision was an easy one.

"I agree with you, Matt. We should at least try."

"Are you sure?"

She smiled. "I'm sure."

Matthew stood up and pulled her into his arms. He tried to kiss her, but she pulled away. "Don't you have a phone call to make?"

He chuckled. "You're right. If I kiss you now it'll be hours before I realize I haven't returned his call." With a leering grin he pulled out his cell and made the call to Dr. Johnston.

Chapter 24

Doro went into labor in the early morning hours on December nineteenth. Bob drove her to the UK Healthcare Center in Lexington. They had chosen to find out the sex of the baby ahead of time and knew that they were expecting another boy. She labored all day and into the night. Finally, at two in the morning on December twentieth she gave birth to a healthy, eight pound boy whom they named Christopher.

Both the Donovans and the Prestwicks stayed home for Christmas. Lucinda and Helen came to the Village of Berrington to celebrate the holiday, and Erianna sang in church during midnight mass. Helen stayed overnight with Doro and Lucinda was offered the guest bedroom in Pap and Ginny's suite so that she would not have to go up and down the stairs.

Just a week before Grace's birthday on February twenty-first Matthew was informed that the surrogate was, indeed, pregnant. Although he had not met her before the implantation procedure, when he learned that he and Erianna were expecting again he traveled to Lawrenceburg, Indiana to meet the woman.

As Matthew had suspected, only one embryo survived the implantation. The baby was due the week after Labor Day, and when the surrogate was past her first trimester Matthew told Erianna that they were expecting another child. She was both relieved and a little bit saddened to learn that only one embryo had taken, and once again they decided not to learn the sex of the baby until it was born.

It was a happy time on Berrington Farm and, as usual, a very busy time. Gus and Erianna spent months marking and clearing additional riding trails, bypassing the short, steep hill that had been so treacherous for both horses and riders.

The horse shows from the previous summer had run in the red, but they did attract more business to Berrington Farm. Her stables were now at near capacity as nearly a dozen horse owners had signed boarding contracts after the competitions, and additional sponsored events were scheduled for the upcoming summer.

With the twins' arrival Ryan and Alexis, who had quickly learned the ropes at the stables, each pitched in to help with the pre-dawn chores. Ryan got up early on Monday, Wednesday and Friday to help Gus, while Alexis took the baton on Tuesday and Thursday mornings. Erianna paid them for their work and was effusive in her thanks for the willingness.

True to form, Erianna put the babies on a strict schedule and as they grew and began sleeping through the night they became happy, healthy, settled babies. Both received lots of love and attention from their large, extended family and they regularly spent part of their days with Christopher, who was just two and a half months younger than them.

Doro went back to her catering business part-time in the spring and Ryan was accepted at the University of Kentucky in Lexington. He confessed to his Uncle Matt that his dream was to manage the Berrington Country Club, with the ultimate goal of one day owning it. Ryan was a homebody, but he also admitted that he would follow Grace to the ends of the earth if need be, and she had big dreams.

Alexis accepted a partial scholarship at Eastern Kentucky University and Matthew offered her grant money for the remainder of her tuition and boarding fees. In the fall she would begin studying for her bachelor's degree in Sports Psychology and play on the EKU softball team. Sue was relieved that her daughter would be just a little over an hour's drive south in Richmond so that she could go down to watch her daughter's home games while Erianna, Henry and Doro held down the fort at the bed and breakfast.

When the school year ended and Ryan and Alexis graduated a huge party was thrown on the farm. Bob, Matthew and Gus erected a stage in the far southwest pasture and a local band was hired to play. The entire graduating class and their parents were all invited.

Matthew insisted that a karaoke system also be set up so that graduates could get up and sing during breaks, and everyone seemed to love it. Students and parents alike took to the mic, including Ryan and his father, who got up and sang an off-key rendition of "We are the Champions."

Erianna took a turn, singing the Faith Hill song "This Kiss" that Tim suggested was one of her husband's favorites. Matthew tried his hand at 'Check Yes or No" and his wife laughed at his antics. It was a wonderful party.

Matthew began taking Grace on college exploratory trips over the summer after she received nearly perfect scores on both her SAT and her ACT tests. Since Erianna never attended college she had no idea how to navigate these waters and little time to research the procedure. So she was relieved when Matthew took on the responsibility. The mail was filled with packets from a wide array of colleges, and Grace received offers of full academic scholarships from several prestigious universities, including Notre Dame, Vanderbilt and Auburn.

The bed and breakfast began showing monthly profits and Erianna's stables were abuzz with daily activity. A Level-3 Certified Riding Instructor came several days a week to teach classes in conformation for those interested in showing their horses.

At long last Erianna's business was taking off and she was running in the black.

At the end of the growing season the leases on her land at the south end of the property would expire and she had future plans to build dressage and show jumping rings with viewing stands on that land.

* * *

As the babies grew Erianna renovated the horse stall next to her office into a mini daycare room. The stall was sanitized, painted, heated, and carpeted, and a doorway was cut between her office and the new playroom. The stall door was replaced with permanently affixed, floor-to-ceiling bars so that the children could watch the comings and goings of the horses and riders.

Gus wisely pointed out that the babies, who were both pulling themselves up and beginning to toddle around, could reach out through the bars, and he worried that a horse might try to nip at them as it walked past. So Erianna added screening to keep little fingers safely inside the room. There were sleeping mats on the floor and both Bonnie and Ben became accustomed to taking their naps in the playroom.

Things were beginning to wind down at the end of the summer season and the kids were scheduled to start back to school on August nineteenth. Erianna was all set for the arrival of the new baby in early September. But, on the Friday morning of August sixteenth she received an urgent call from Matthew.

"You need to get up here now." He did not mince words. "The baby is coming. The surrogate's water broke this morning and she just checked in at the hospital here in Cincinnati."

"But, Matthew, the baby isn't due for another three weeks."

"I know. I'm on my way to Good Samaritan Hospital now. Drop everything and get here as soon as you can."

Erianna grabbed up the twins and ran for home. With no time to waste she cleaned up in the basement and ran upstairs.

"Pap, where's Grace?"

"She went to the Club for her lifeguarding shift. Why?"

"Call over there and tell her to come home right away," she ordered. "The baby is coming early and I have to get to Cincinnati as quickly as I can."

"I don't think she'll be able to come home now. She's probably the only guard on duty this early in the morning."

"Is Doro home? Where's Ginny?"

Erianna's clipped tone was unusual and he knew that she was stressed. He called over to see if Doro was there.

"Ginny went to the grocery," he told her as he made the call. "Doro? Erin has to leave for the hospital. The baby is coming early and she needs to leave right away."

"Does she need me to take the kids?"

"Could you?" Erianna called out.

"I was going to take the boys shopping for school supplies in a bit, but we don't have to do that today. I'll be right over."

Erianna ran upstairs to change and pack her overnight bag. She put the twins in their cribs, but they didn't want to be restricted and both began to fuss. She ignored them, gathering up the items she had already pre-packed for the newborn and, leaving Bonnie and Ben in their beds, she ran downstairs to put her things in the Subaru.

When she came back in Doro was there with Christopher in tow. She quickly brought her sister-in-law up to speed. "Grace is lifeguarding and Ned is with Jamie and Theo. They took out a trail riding group, and they should be done in a couple of hours."

The babies could be heard crying upstairs.

With Christopher on her hip, Doro went to Erianna. "Don't worry about us," she said as she offered her sister-in-law a quick hug. "Just make sure you get there in one piece. No speeding!"

"Call us and let us know how things go," Pap said, adding, "whenever you get a chance."

"Tell Gus where I've gone," she called out as she ran for her car.

Erianna was too late. The baby was born about twenty minutes before she arrived at the hospital. She pulled into the front circular drive where Henry was waiting to take her SUV and move it to the parking garage. She ran through the front doors, and Matthew met her as she got off the elevator.

"It's a boy. He's small, but he seems to be fine. The doctors are monitoring him in the NICU to make sure that he's breathing well."

He took her hand and tucked it in the crook of his arm as he guided her through the halls toward the NICU unit.

"Did you get to hold him?"

"No. Not yet."

"How is Caroline? Is she okay?" Erianna asked, worried that the surrogate might be in danger as well.

"She's fine. We don't know why her water broke so early, but her labor went quickly and she suffered no complications from the birth."

The premature boy weighed a little under six pounds. Matthew and Erianna suited up and were permitted to hold their tiny son. He suggested that they name the boy Aaron, but Erianna rejected that name, not liking the idea of the homophone.

In the end, they both agreed to name their youngest son Leo David, for he was born under the sign of Leo, the Lion and because his maternal grandfather was named Leo Meecham. His middle name was chosen to honor Matthew's father.

The condo was quickly made ready for the arrival of little Leo. The twins were brought to Cincinnati to stay while their parents took turns at the hospital with the newborn, who spent several days in the NICU to make sure that he was breathing and eating well before he was released.

Both parents agreed that Leo was too small for the long car ride to the Farm. And so they all spent a couple of weeks in the Queen City, caring for the newborn and monitoring him closely to ensure that there were no complications from his early entry into the world.

And three weeks later, Leo finally came home to Berrington to meet the rest of his siblings on his original due date of September sixth.

Erianna was sitting on the floor of the nursery with all four babies. It was late afternoon on the Tuesday before Thanksgiving. Doro was catering the soccer banquet at the Berrington Country Club and Bob had gone to pick up Ryan from UK, so Erianna had her hands full.

As Leo slept soundly against her chest in the homemade baby sling that she had sewn, Christopher sat beside her while she read a book to him. Ben was playing in the hallway with building blocks, trying to stack them as high as he could with his chubby little fingers. Bonnie had wandered off while Erianna was reading.

Outside the converted sitting room doorway, the upper hallway railing ran straight for about seven feet before it curved downward at the top step. Opposite the railing was the interior wall of a large, cedar-lined hallway linen closet.

In order to keep the kids corralled, but in an effort to give them as much play space as possible in the cramped makeshift nursery, which now housed three cribs, Matthew and Erianna had installed a wide baby gate between the closet wall and the curve of the railing where the steps began. Fine mesh netting ran from the top of the railing to the ceiling in order to prevent the children from toppling over the edge and falling down the stairs.

Bonnie was tired and hungry, and very fussy. As she wandered away from her mother, who was sitting on the floor just inside the doorway, she toddled over to where Ben was playing and knocked over his building blocks. When the boy objected she picked up a small block and tried to throw it at him.

"Play nice, young lady," Erianna admonished her daughter, but Bonnie was in no mood to listen. Instead, she squatted down and scattered the blocks every which way with her hands. One of the blocks fell through the rails and down to the lower landing. Ben whined and his lower lip curled as he pouted.

Erianna set the book aside, got up, scooped Bonnie into her arms and deposited her errant daughter into her crib. Without a word she handed the girl her blankie. As she sat down again and crossed her legs Bonnie began to cry. Erianna picked up the book she had been reading to Christopher as Ben came in and snuggled up to her.

She looked at Bonnie and shook her head. "You stop that now and lie down. Little girls who don't play nice have to lie down."

Bonnie threw herself onto her mattress and curled her fingers around the silky edge of her blanket as Erianna began to read again.

Matthew stood at the bottom landing holding the block that had fallen at his feet. He couldn't help but smile. His wife had the patience of a saint. He waited until she finished the book before he went upstairs.

When Ben saw him he got up and ran to his father. "Dee-add!"

Matthew picked up the boy as he stepped over the gate, hugging him and giving him a loud, long kiss on his plump little cheek.

"Ginny says five minutes until dinner."

Erianna nodded.

"With Ben still in his arms, Matthew bent down. "Hey there, Christopher. Are you gonna eat with your cousins tonight?"

Chris waved his hands up and down in excitement. All the children were hungry and they understood the word 'eat'.

"What's with her?" Matthew asked as Bonnie stood up and began to pull and tug the side rail of her crib, raising a ruckus in order to get her father's attention.

"That one needs supper, a bath and bed, in that order. She decided not to take her nap this afternoon." She turned to Bonnie. "Stop that."

Erianna looked at her husband and rolled her eyes.

"It's time to put our toys away. Are you going to help us, young lady?"

"No." Bonnie flopped down on her bed again.

Matthew set Ben on his feet. "I'll take care of her." He scooped his errant daughter up and carried her with him to the master bedroom while he changed his clothes.

"Okay guys, let's pick up our toys."

Erianna began to sing as they picked up the blocks and put them in a bin. *Put your toys away, don't delay. Help your mother have a happy day.* She repeated the verse again, and with their task completed she scooped Christopher onto her hip and opened the gate. She started down the stairs, stopping on the third step to wait for Ben, who had been trained to sit down and turn around before sliding down the stairs backwards.

By the time she and Ginny had Ben and Chris in their high-chairs Matthew came in with Bonnie. Ginny had their scrambled eggs, baby peas and carrots, and homemade applesauce in their divided serving bowls, which had suction cups on the bottom to secure them to the highchair trays.

The adults were helping the babies as they ate and drank their milk from Sippy cups when the doorbell rang.

"I'll get it," Erianna said. "That's probably Katie. She and Grace are supposed to work on their economics reports tonight."

She went to the door and turned on the porch light. But it wasn't Grace's friend standing on her front stoop. It was Colleen.

Erianna stepped out onto the porch and closed the door, making sure that she turned the lock on the handle so that her mother couldn't get inside. Clyde was shuffling up the walkway from the driveway.

"Mom? What are you doing here?"

"We're on our way to Joanna's place in Columbus for Thanks-giving and we decided to stop by to see our grandchildren. Is that Leo?"

Erianna moved off the porch and into the grass, covering her slumbering infant more securely so that her mother could not see him. "You're not supposed to be here, Mom. You need to leave right now before someone sees you."

"You mother has the right to see her grandchildren," Clyde snapped.

"No. She doesn't. If you leave right now I won't call the police."

"I have three new grandchildren and I've never even seen them, Erianna. We won't stay long. Just let me take a look at him." Colleen took a step toward her daughter.

"No!" Erianna retreated.

"You goddamned snob, thinking you're better than us. Let her see the little bastard."

Bob's truck was just pulling in next door, and his headlights illuminated Erianna's front yard for a moment as he turned into his driveway.

"Get back in your car and leave my land—now," Erianna demanded.

"You fucking bitch," Clyde hissed. "Who do you think you are, ordering me around!" He reached down and grabbed one of the hand-sized river rocks that Erianna had used to line the evergreen bed along the edge of the front walkway.

She turned to run, clutching her baby with both arms to try and protect him from what she knew was coming. "Bob!" she screamed.

The rock struck the back of her head, and as the pain exploded her vision blurred. She staggered a little, but managed to stay on her feet.

"Help!" She cried as she tried to keep her legs moving, unsure now which direction she was going. "Help me!"

Raising her left hand to the back of her head, she realized that she was bleeding. Just then a second rock struck her ribs just under her upraised left arm.

The blow sent the air from her lungs and she fell to her knees. Her only thought was to protect her crying baby, so she rounded her shoulders and clutched Leo to her chest, wrapping her arms around him in a cocoon as she waited for the next blow.

Bob and Ryan were just getting out of the truck when they heard Erianna scream. They took off at a run to help her, not realizing at first that her parents were standing on the walkway. Ryan was nearing Erianna when she was struck by the second rock, and he reached her just as she collapsed to the ground.

Bob charged past his son and, as Clyde grabbed another paver he hollered, "Drop it!"

"Fuck you!" He pivoted and heaved the large rock through the front plate-glass window.

Bonnie fussed all through supper. Matthew tried everything he could think of to get the girl to eat, but she was overtired and didn't want to cooperate. He was so busy trying to get at least a few bites into her that he didn't notice how long Erianna had been gone, and the baby's protestations were drowning out the commotion happening outside.

When the front window shattered Matthew jumped up in shock. It took him a second or two before he turned to run for the front door.

"Stay with the babies," he ordered Ginny. Racing past the center hallway he shouted to Pap, "Call the cops!"

When he got to the front door and tried to open it Matthew realized that it had been locked. Turning the latch on the handle, he wrenched it open and ran outside. Bob was wrestling with Clyde Pruitt as Colleen looked on, and Ryan was crouched beside Erianna, who was sitting on her heels in the grass.

He ran to his wife. "What happened?"

"That guy hit Aunt Erin with a couple of rocks. Her head is bleeding," Ryan answered as he picked up one of the bloodied missiles and showed it to Matthew.

"Are you okay?" he asked her.

"Can't—can't breathe," she coughed.

Ned ran out the front door just then.

"Nathan, go tell Pap to call an ambulance and bring me a clean cloth and an ice pack.

"And tell Gus to get up here," Bob added. "Tell him to bring his gun."

The boy nodded and took off at full speed.

As Matthew examined the back of her head, trying to determine the extent of Erianna's injury in the gloom he said to Ryan, "See if you can help your dad."

He glanced over at Clyde. "Get those two out of here," he said in a raised voice so that Bob could hear him. "Lock them in the back of their car until the cops get here. And make sure they don't have the car keys on them."

"Take the old bat's purse," Bob told his son as Ryan went to escort Erianna's mother to the Camry.

"You better frisk him, Dad. The last time he had a butane lighter on him, remember?"

"Right."

Matthew turned back to his wife, who was gasping for breath and coughing.

"My baby," she moaned. "*My baby*."

Did one of the rocks hit Leo?" he asked.

Grace appeared just then. "The cops are on the way and Sue is coming over to help Ginny and me with the babies."

"Okay."

"Leo—" Erianna murmured.

Grace hunkered down in front of her mother. "Is Leo hurt?"

"My baby," Erianna gasped. But when Matthew tried to pry her arms away, Erianna refused to cooperate, clutching him tightly against her chest.

Grace tried to reason with her mother. "Let me take Leo for you, Mom. You're bleeding. Give him to me so that he doesn't get any blood on him."

Erianna looked up at her daughter. "He tried to—hurt my baby," she wheezed.

Grace nodded. "Dad and I are here now. We're here. He's safe now. We'll take good care of Leo for you."

But her mother refused to let go of her son.

"He's crying, Mom. Do you hear him crying? Let me take him inside where it's warm. Please, Mom. *Please*."

Erianna finally loosened her hold and Matthew slipped the baby sling from around her neck. It was soaked in blood. Grace managed to free Leo from the cloth and she shuffled around on her knees to let her father examine the infant.

When Matthew determined that the screaming baby wasn't hurt he gave Leo back to Grace, who quickly carried him inside.

Ned came back with the cloth and an ice pack just as Gus arrived with his shotgun. Bob left the Pruitts in Ryan and Gus's custody and came over to help Matthew.

"She was hit by at least two rocks that I saw. Her head is

bleeding, but where did the second rock hit?"

"I don't know," Matthew admitted. He tried to lean her back against his chest, but she gasped for air. "Will you get my medical bag from the trunk of my car? The keys are—"

"I'll get it," Ned volunteered as he took off once again to complete the task.

The sound of sirens was getting louder. By the time Ned came back with his father's medical bag Grace appeared at the front door saying, "The cops just turned onto the lane."

"Pull out my stethoscope, will you, Bob? I don't like her shallow respirations."

Matthew listened to her breath sounds. "Jesus," he swore. "I think she has a pneumothorax."

Erianna was transported to the hospital and, just as Matthew suspected, she had two cracked ribs on her left side where the second rock had struck her, causing her lung to collapse. A chest tube was inserted to remove the trapped air and re-inflate the lung. She required several stitches for the cut on her head and was closely monitored for the next twenty-four hours for signs of a concussion.

Erianna spent the next week at the Harrison County Memorial Hospital, a Level IV Trauma Center in Cynthiana.

It took a total of eight weeks for her to fully recover, and during much of that time she was restricted from lifting her babies. Matthew hired a church member to assist his wife in the care of the children while she recuperated.

Clyde and Colleen were taken into custody for the second time in Harrison County. Clyde was charged with first degree Felony Assault, a Class B felony. Because of his prior plea deal and his probation violation the County Prosecutor threw the book at him.

Colleen was also charged with a probation violation and as an accomplice in the commission of her husband's crimes.

Matthew immediately evicted them from their condo in Gainesville and cut off all support payments. Neither Julia nor Joanna would agree to house and support their parents, and for the first time in her life Colleen found herself homeless and penniless.

"Your Honor, thank you for giving me the opportunity to read my victim impact statement before you sentence Clyde Pruitt today. I'm not here to condemn Clyde and my mother for their actions. That is not my intent, for I don't consider myself a victim.

"I hope that you will not consider my statement when you hand down your sentence. You shouldn't. There can be no emotion involved in your decision. The legal system only works when it is applied without regard to emotion."

Erianna turned to address Clyde as her mother sat solemnly in the gallery behind him.

"I've heard many people comment that I must have had a miserable childhood. They've told me that they hate you for what you did to me. But I don't agree. If I hate, then you have won, and that is exactly what you want. You want me to hate, as you have hated all your life.

"I know nothing of your childhood, I only know my own, and the lessons I learned were invaluable. I learned to stand on my own two feet and face whatever adversities came my way with a positive attitude. I learned the value of a hard day's work and the satisfaction of a job well done. And I learned how to forgive and how to ask for forgiveness.

"When you attacked me on my eighteenth, birthday I believe in my heart that your goal was to take my life. I've often wondered why. Maybe you thought that my death would in some way lessen the rage that consumes you. But, I can never know for sure.

"There is a phenomenon called cutting. The compulsion to cut apparently releases endogenous opiates into the circulatory system. It gives the cutter a rush, a high that they cannot achieve any other way. Maybe the abuse you meted out gave *you* the rush that you so desperately craved. But, I'm not a psychiatrist and I don't know about these things.

"What I do know is that you took great pleasure in your physical abuse of me. I could see it in your expression each time you struck me. And up until my eighteenth birthday I was your only casualty.

"But your attack that day was meant to harm not only me, but others as well. On that day your clear intention was to take my life so that I would never be with Matthew. And although your attempt to kill me did not come to fruition, you did accomplish your goal. You stole our future together and our ability to have a family. You must have felt more pleasure during that assault than you ever had, before or since."

Erianna paused and glanced at her husband in the gallery before continuing.

"So, here we are today, with you facing the judge, no doubt hoping for a lenient sentence. I hope he is lenient, for your prison has always been your own hatred. And despite your best intentions I am happily married to the love of my life with children, both adopted *and* biological, whom I love more than I thought was possible."

She turned back to the judge. "Your Honor, Clyde Pruitt has never been a danger to anyone but me. Since I moved to Kentucky he has extorted money from me, attempted to burn my property to the ground and physically assaulted me.

"But his only *victim*, as it were, is himself. Although I hold no love for the man, neither do I hate him. I believe he is living in a hell of his own making, and for that I pity him."

Clyde shot out of his chair. "You fucking bitch!" he screamed. "Don't you fucking pity me, you—"

The judge slammed his gavel on its block several times as court officers moved in to subdue the convicted man. "Sit down, Mr. Pruitt," the judge ordered. "Sit down this minute. There will be no more outbursts in my courtroom."

With that, Erianna left. She did not wait for the sentence to be handed down and she did not look at her mother as she left the courtroom.

Clyde Pruitt was ordered to serve a term of ten to twenty years in the State Penitentiary in Eddyville, Kentucky. After his sentencing, Colleen's plea deal was accepted. She was given one year in jail. As she had already spent over a hundred days locked up because she could not make bail while her plea was negotiated, she was ordered to serve the remainder of her sentence in a halfway house. Her driver's license was permanently revoked and a hefty fine imposed.

And, for the first time in her life, Colleen Pruitt was required to obtain employment.

"Are you okay?" Matthew asked his wife as he drove her home that day.

With a bright, beautiful smile she responded, "I've never been better."

When she went to bed that night, Erianna found a note on her pillow.

Sweet Erianna,

You are my one and only love,
Without you I am lost.
You are my sun, my moon and stars,
I see the light in you.
You are my song, my poetry,
With you my dreams come true.
You are my joy, my breath, my all,
With you I am fulfilled.
You are my wife, my heart, my soul.
Now and forever, I will always love you.

Matt

Made in the USA
Monee, IL
28 December 2022

19501583R00246